MARATHON MAN

As Thorpe bounded across the lunar wasteland, his muscles began to ache and his breathing came in deep-throated gasps. His heartbeat pounded in his temples with the sound of thunder. The temperature inside his suit began to rise.

Then he saw the monorail train rushing silently down the opposite slope of the depression. He redoubled his efforts, bounding in giant leaps across the rocky landscape.

Finally, Thorpe reached the top of a small mogul and found himself a hundred meters from the train. A number of vacuum-suited figures were milling about outside it. He shouted once, then felt his legs give way.

By Michael McCollum
Published by Ballantine Books:

ANTARES DAWN

ANTARES PASSAGE

A GREATER INFINITY

LIFE PROBE

PROCYON'S PROMISE

THUNDER STRIKE!

THUNDER STRIKE!

MICHAEL McCOLLUM

A Del Rey Book
BALLANTINE BOOKS • NEW YORK

To Catherine,
Always!

A Del Rey Book
Published by Ballantine Books

Copyright © 1989 by Michael McCollum

All rights reserved under International and Pan-American Copyright Conventions. Published in the United States of America by Ballantine Books, a division of Random House, Inc., New York, and simultaneously in Canada by Random House of Canada Limited, Toronto.

Library of Congress Catalog Card Number: 88-92824

ISBN 0-345-35352-8

Manufactured in the United States of America

First Edition: June 1989

Cover Art by Barclay Shaw

PART I

VISITOR FROM THE DEEP BLACK

CHAPTER I

For millions of years the Sun had merely been the brightest point of light in the sky, a cold beacon little different from the thousands of others visible in the ebon firmament. Now it was growing perceptibly larger month by month, year by year. The change was not without precedent. A billion years earlier the planetoid had collided with a bit of orbiting debris out beyond Pluto. The force of the impact had altered its orbit forever. One hundred eleven times the planetoid had plunged deep into the fires of the inner Solar system, whirled quickly around the Sun, and then retreated once more into the cold black. The ordeal had been presaged each time by a brightening of the distant yellow star.

About the time the Sun began to show a visible disk, the ice plains and cliffs began to stir with ethereal winds as hydrogen and oxygen frost turned slowly to vapor. Initially the winds were as insubstantial as wraiths, little more than individual molecules escaping the planetoid's weak gravitation. Later, when the Sun had grown still larger in the sky, the snowy surface began to emit gentle puffs of gas, dust, and vapor. Weak though it was, the planetoid's gravity was sufficient to wrap it with a wisp of vacuum-thin fog. By the time the flying mountain crossed the orbit of Uranus, the fog had grown thick enough to obscure it from anyone who might pick it out among the background stars.

Amber Hastings sat at her desk and wistfully watched Farside Observatory's big hundred-meter-effective compound telescope swing ponderously into position. Her vantage point was almost directly up-sun from the giant instrument. As she watched, lengthening black shadows stretched across the floor of Mendeleev Crater. The view was from one of the pylon cameras situated to provide a panoramic view of the Solar system's largest astronomical instrument. In the background the gray-brown wall of the crater's western rim thrust above the curved horizon in stark relief unsoftened by atmosphere.

The telescope appeared to be a species of giant metal flower springing forth from Luna's airless, sterile soil. The flower's hexagonal leaves reflected their surroundings with the distortion of parabolic mirrors. At three places around the instrument's periphery, flat mirrors were lifted skyward on cherry-picker booms in semblance of weirdly jointed stamens. The likeness to an alien plant was heightened by the telescope's dust dome, whose eight sections lay folded back like the petals of a rose.

Amber watched as the giant instrument finished pivoting toward a section of sky near Galactic-South. Starlight was reflected from the telescope's five-meter-diameter mirrors into the Number Three concentrator, which sent the highly focused image to the beam director. From there the photons were directed into the observatory's instrument room fifty meters below the crater floor. There the light was sampled by an array of sophisticated devices in the hope that it could be made to yield its secrets.

Amber Elizabeth Hastings was a typical Lunarian, tall by Earth standards—180 centimeters—and tending toward lankiness. The shorts, singlet, and slippers that were normal attire for Luna's air-conditioned cities did little to hide a full, if large-boned figure. She was a Nordic blonde with blue eyes. In contravention of the short hairstyles preferred by most Lunarian women, she wore her hair at shoulder length.

Amber had been born twenty-five years earlier in the small community of Miner's Luck, located near Darwin Crater in the Nearside highlands. At age eighteen she had entered the University of Luna with the intention of becoming an environmental engineer. She had quickly decided that a life spent in the bowels of Luna's cities held no attraction for her and had begun to search for a new profession.

Attending a university was supposed to prepare one for later life. In Amber's case, it had only emphasized her antipathy to the usual courses of study. The only class she enjoyed during her freshman year was Introduction to Astronomy.

Like most Lunarians, Amber had never paid much attention to the sky. Luna's underground cities gave few opportunities to stargaze. And since Amber had been raised on Nearside, whenever she did have occasion to study the sky, the view overhead had always been dominated by the Earth. Compared to the Mother of Men, the tiny pinpricks of light that were the stars seemed pale and insignificant.

Introduction to Astronomy had opened her eyes to the universe beyond Luna. She had marveled at the spiral sweep of the Andromeda Galaxy, been awed by the blazing blue-white glory of the Pleiades and had sighed over the muted multispectral beauty of the Horsehead Nebula. Each new revelation had caused her to want to learn more. So, at the end of her first year, Amber had switched her major to astronomy, intending the change to be a stopgap until she could find something permanent.

Three years later, and somewhat to her own surprise, Amber had found herself the recipient of a Bachelor of Astronomical Science degree. With it had come an offer for a job on the staff of Farside Observatory. She had accepted happily amid visions of quickly making a brilliant discovery. Reality had turned out to be less glamorous.

As in so many other fields, the computer revolution had changed astronomy forever. Gone were the days when a lone scientist bundled up against the cold air and spent the night in the observation cage of a giant telescope. Gone, too, were the weeks and months spent poring over photographic plates with magnifiers, or in tediously plotting the absorption lines of stellar spectrums.

A modern astronomer could sit in his easy chair anywhere in the Solar system, work out an observation program, and transmit his request and charge number to his observatory of choice. In due course he would receive multispectral views and numerical data, all neatly annotated. In between request and result, the process was virtually untouched by human hands.

In the last quarter of the twenty-first century it was an observatory's computers that pointed its telescopes and directed them to track the stars through the sky. The computers controlled viewing times and exposures, recorded the data and produced the reports. Sometimes while analyzing data, the computers chanced upon discoveries unrelated to the objects under study. When that happened, they sought the attention of the human staff.

Thus it was that Amber Hastings was monitoring the big telescope when the observatory's computer signaled for her attention.

"What is it?" she asked, stifling a yawn.

"I have an asteroid/comet discovery report," the machine said in its too perfect baritone. "Do you wish to review it now?"

"Might as well," she replied. "I don't get off duty for four more hours."

As the most junior of Farside Observatory's staffers, Amber had been assigned as Intra-System Specialist, which meant that she was in charge of confirming and recording new sightings of comets and asteroids. In her three years with the observatory, she had checked out half-a-thousand sightings. The excitement had long since worn off.

The screen in front of her lit to show a starfield. She recognized Open Cluster NGC 2301, which had been the subject of a long observation program two weeks earlier. Surrounding the cluster was a thicket of stars. Amber let her gaze sweep quickly across the screen. At first she saw nothing out of the ordinary. Then her eyes were drawn to the screen's lower right-hand corner. There she found a dim smudge of light.

"That it?" she asked as she reached out to touch the image with her finger.

"Affirmative," the computer responded. "This frame was taken ten days ago at 13:12:15 U.T."

Amber read off the object's position data, noting that it was nearly in the plane of the ecliptic and off in the direction of Monoceros. "What makes you think it's a comet? That area is near the Rosette Nebula and that big patch in Orion."

"The spectrum is that of a typical comet coma shining by reflected sunlight."

"Dopplered?"

"Yes."

"How far?"

"Sufficient to indicate a velocity of ten kilometers per second inbound along the observation vector."

"Interesting," Amber mused. "Size estimate?"

"None."

"Distance estimate?"

"None. This is the sole view of the object."

Amber nodded. One of the great frustrations of astronomers was the lack of a method for determining distance from a single photograph. To triangulate an object's position, it was necessary to obtain two views from widely separated points, or three views taken at different times from a single vantage point.

Amber noted the details of the original sighting, including the fact that only one-quarter of *The Big Eye*'s 400 mirrors had been active. It was not unusual for the telescope to be split into three independent clusters, each of which would then study a different section of sky. Indeed, it was the ability to pursue multiple observations that enabled Farside Observatory to keep up with demand. Even so, the waiting list for the big telescope was a long one.

"When will *The Big Eye* be able to recheck this sighting?" Amber asked.

"Eight months, barring cancellations or unscheduled maintenance," the computer responded.

Amber sighed. "Swing the sixty centimeter into position and get me a second view."

"I am unable to execute your command. That section of sky is no longer visible. It set behind the western rim three days ago."

"How long before it rises again?"

"Two weeks."

"Very well," Amber replied. "Schedule a sixty-centimeter observation as soon as possible following its reappearance. If you don't find the object at its previous position, run a standard survey for three fields-of-view around that point. Notify me when you have completed your task. Repeat."

The computer repeated Amber's orders, then returned the screen to its picture of *The Big Eye*. Amber returned to her other work and forgot about whatever it was that the computer had discovered.

Thomas Bronson Thorpe bounded into the black sky in a jump no Olympic athlete had ever dreamed of. The sound of his own breathing was loud in his ears as he rose a dozen meters above the pockmarked plain. The Sun was below the horizon, but the crescent Earth, with a slightly fuller Luna beyond it, was high in the sky. The blue-white radiance of Earthshine cast a twilight glow over *The Rock*'s barren landscape. As he reached the top of his arc, Thorpe let his practiced gaze sweep across the small world. Everywhere around him lay the clutter of heavy industry. To most it would have seemed a horizon-to-horizon junkyard. To Tom Thorpe every empty gas cylinder and bit of used cable was a testament to humanity's triumph over an uncaring universe.

Contrary to its name, *The Rock* contained very little stony matter. In fact, it was nearly pure nickel-iron. For billions of years the asteroid had followed its elliptical path around the Sun, occasionally passing close to the beautiful blue-white world that was Earth. Because of the asteroid's small diameter—four kilometers—and the ten-degree inclination of its orbit, *The Rock* had evaded notice for much of history. Its anonymity had come to an end in 2037. In that year it had approached to within two million kilometers of Luna, *The Rock*'s closest passage in more than a century.

The asteroid might have escaped notice even then had its discovery been left to the optical astronomers. They had their instruments focused far beyond cislunar space; indeed, outside the Solar system altogether. Their interest lay in exploding galaxies and distant quasars. They left the mundane business of adding yet another minor planet to the list of known Earth-approaching asteroids to others.

Luckily, the volume of space between Earth and Moon had long been saturated with traffic-control radars. As *The Rock* made its approach, one such radar suffered a breakdown in its ranging circuits. Rather than report only those signals it had been designed to see, the radar began registering everything in sight. When it announced a swiftly moving object two million kilometers beyond Luna, the traffic-control center at Luna City quickly took notice. The center tracked the rogue asteroid for more than an hour before it drifted below their local horizon. The traffic controllers computed the mystery object's path. They reported the information to the System Astronomical Union, where it languished for two decades.

There had been schemes to mine the mineral wealth of the asteroids as far back as the mid–twentieth century, and actual attempts early in the twenty-first. All had failed. The time and distance involved in travel to and from the Asteroid Belt had made the mines too expensive to operate.

In the year 2060 a graduate student by the name of Halver Smith chose asteroid mining for his doctoral thesis in Business Economics. Smith concluded that there was nothing inherently uneconomical about such operations. Indeed, a cubic kilometer of asteroidal metal delivered to Earth was worth more than the combined gross national products of the three largest nations. The problem remained the delay inherent in shipping supplies to the Asteroid Belt and returning product to Earth.

Smith suggested a solution to the problem. Instead of traveling to the Asteroid Belt, he reasoned, why not move an asteroid into orbit about the Earth. He dubbed his idea the "Mountain to Mohammed Method." Such a plan would require the discovery of the proper asteroid in the proper orbit. To buttress his arguments, Smith searched the Astronomical Union's data banks for likely candidates. It was during his search that he came across the report of the close approach of 2037.

Halver Smith was rewarded a Ph.D. in Business Economics. His proposal had not, however, been thought very practical. After graduation he used a small inheritance to invest in a new process for extracting rare earths from low-grade ore. It had proven a once-in-a-lifetime investment. Halver Smith had quickly earned a fortune. As his wealth grew, he began to seriously consider putting his thesis into practice.

Tom Thorpe was a newly minted graduate of the Colorado School of Mines when he answered Halver Smith's advertisement for vacuum-qualified mining engineers. The job, he soon learned, was the exploration of an Earth-approaching asteroid. He and a dozen other young vacuum monkeys had clustered around the viewports of the prospecting ship *Sierra Madre* as it made its final approach. At first sight of their destination, Perry Allen, the most vocal of the group, exclaimed, "It's nothing but a goddamned rock!" The name might as well have been applied with quick-drying adhesive.

They spent the next month swarming all over the asteroid. They drilled deeply into its surface and assayed the purity of their samples. They probed even deeper with powerful sonic beams. Their analyses confirmed that *The Rock* was a treasure trove, a nearly pure chunk of nickel-iron seamed with copper, silver, and gold. Ten months later Thorpe had found himself back on *The Rock*, in the company of a full crew of mining specialists and a shipload of heavy equipment.

"Better be careful with that jumping!" a woman's voice said in his earphones. "I'd hate to see you break anything."

Thorpe gazed down at the figure standing on the plain some thirty meters below him. The red-orange vacuum suit effectively hid the identity of its wearer; only in his mind's eye could Thorpe see the short, slightly plump figure of Nina Pavolev. Two years his junior, Nina was his executive assistant and his sometimes lover.

"I've been doing this for ten years now," he said over the

general communications band, "and haven't broken my neck yet!"

"That's what they all say just before they do!"

Thorpe settled slowly back toward the surface, grounding a full three minutes after the gentle push that had sent him skyward. He took the impact with flexed knees, absorbing just enough energy to keep from rebounding into the sky.

"When I was a boy back on Earth, I always dreamed of flying like an eagle. Now I can. It's exhilarating. You ought to try it."

"No, thank you. Life is too short to take needless risks."

"You don't know what you're missing," he persisted.

"I'll take your word for it. Shall we begin the tour, boss?"

"Anytime you're ready, O conscience mine!"

Tom Thorpe had not remained a vacuum monkey. In the three years following his return to *The Rock*, he had moved up to gang boss, then shift leader. Those had been the years they had spent turning *The Rock* into the Solar system's largest spaceship. The modifications had begun by blasting a thrust chamber out of the heavy end of the asteroid, the end they had dubbed the "Acorn's Cap." While Thorpe's crew worked at excavating the chamber and its connecting tunnels, other crews installed giant clusters of attitude-control jets, which had initiated the long process of lengthening the asteroid's eight-hour day. Shortly after the de-spinning process began, Perry Allen was killed in a freak accident. Tom Thorpe found himself thrust suddenly into the position of Second Assistant Power Engineer.

One of his new duties had involved overseeing the operation of *The Rock*'s propulsion system. Like most large spacecraft, the asteroid was powered by antimatter. Thousands of power packs had been shipped from the big power satellites. The packs were simple toroidal pipes filled with hard vacuum and surrounded by self-sustaining magnetic fields. Each contained enough antimatter to power a normal spacecraft for a hundred round trips to the Moon. Yet each fed *The Rock*'s massive ion engines for less than a day before exhaustion.

It had taken four years of powered flight to move *The Rock* into an orbit that ranged from 800,000 to 1.2 million kilometers above the Earth. With the end of powered flight had come reassignment for all personnel. Thorpe was promoted to the position of Supervisor, Surface Operations. Later he was advanced to assistant Manager of Operations, and finally to Manager of Operations. Despite his rise to the asteroid's top job, he still made it a point to inspect *The Rock*'s various facilities once each week.

Thorpe and Nina Pavolev hooked up to one of the many guide cables that ran across the asteroid's surface. Soon they were making their way toward the horizon in a series of giant bounds. After a few hundred meters the large Mylar-covered panels of the solar furnace began to rise above the horizon. Thorpe shouted a warning to Nina to adjust her faceplate glare shields and then did the same just as the Sun rose above the horizon. The two paused long enough to let their eyes adjust before moving on.

Off to their left Thorpe could see the warning beacons that stretched in a line around the Acorn's Cap. That end of the asteroid was still "hot" from the nuclear caldron that had operated there. The annihilation reaction had boiled a billion tons of *The Rock*'s substance into space. It would be more than a century before the area around the thrust chamber would be cool enough for mining. Even then it was doubtful that the metal would be needed.

Thorpe leaned back and gazed up at three large conical shapes that were taking shape overhead. They were the ore bodies comprising *The Rock*'s delivery system for refined metal. Constructed of vacuum-foamed iron, each O.B. had a specific gravity less than one. When dropped into the Earth's atmosphere, they quickly slowed to a few hundred kilometers per hour. At the end of their long dive they splashed down into an ocean and then bobbed to the surface.

"The schedule says they'll be hoisting a billet in a few minutes." Nina's voice echoed in Thorpe's earphones. "Care to watch?"

"Sure. We'll see how that new lift supervisor handles his crew."

Thorpe led Nina along the guide cable for another quarter kilometer. As they bounded along, a series of three towers slowly rose above the horizon. They had the appearance of old-style launch gantries. As they approached more closely, they could see a thick plate of gray metal lying on the ground at the center of the triangle formed by the towers.

The towers were *The Rock*'s elevator cum launch pad. Cables ran up the outside of each gantry, looped over the top, then back down to where they were attached to the corners of a hexagonal metal billet. During launch the cables were reeled in by electric winches, causing the plate to accelerate skyward as it rose up the towers. When it reached the top, the winches would be declutched. The plate would continue upward at a speed well above local escape velocity. The billet would rise until it approached the hovering reentry vehicles. Brakes would then be applied to slow the unreeling cables. If properly done, the nickel-iron billet would come to a halt just as it reached the working level two kilometers overhead.

As the two observers watched, the heavy nickel-iron plate began to levitate. It rapidly gained velocity. In a matter of seconds it was floating skyward, unimpeded by the trailing cables. Thorpe watched until it had dwindled almost to invisibility. He was about to turn away when something happened. The plate, which had maintained absolute stability during its long climb, suddenly began to tumble.

"What's the matter?" Nina asked, her fear clearly evident in her voice.

"One of the cables has snapped!" Thorpe yelled as he craned his neck to look skyward. He caught a glimpse of a descending snakelike shape, shouted a warning, and turned to run. The next thing he felt was a searing pain in his right leg. His scream dwindled to inaudibility in less than a second as his suit was enveloped in a cloud of red fog.

CHAPTER 2

Amber Hastings sat in the Farside Observatory staff lounge and enjoyed a breakfast of waffles smothered in strawberry syrup, hot buttered toast, and tea laced with levosugar. She watched the lounge viewscreen as she ate. Normally it would have been tuned to the newscast from Luna City. Instead, someone had patched into a view from one of the surface cameras. It showed a large-wheeled, articulated vehicle making its way along the rough track leading from Hadley's Crossroads. The undulating crater floor made the transport's headlamps dance across the screen, leaving phantom trails of activated phosphors in their wake.

The transport was a Translunar Greyhound Lines rolligon. It made the 120-kilometer run twice each month—once at the start of the long lunar night and again just before dawn. Hadley's Crossroads was the closest stop on the circumlunar Monorail Line and the point through which all of the observatory's supplies were shipped.

As she savored her breakfast, Amber considered the paradox of siting one of humanity's most advanced scientific instruments in the wilderness. It was a paradox familiar to astronomers of all eras. Astronomers on Earth had long fought a losing battle against the encroachment of civilization. No matter how remote a mountain they chose for their instruments, sooner or later the sky would begin to reflect the lights of a nearby city.

Light pollution was no problem for Farside Observatory, but oxygen pollution was. In the airless environment of Luna, spacecraft exhausts sprayed monatomic oxygen over hundreds of square kilometers. Monatomic oxygen poisoned the special optical coatings on *The Big Eye*'s mirrors, and any appreciable amount of it would seriously degrade the telescope's performance. To protect against such damage, the observatory's director had banned all spacecraft within seventy-five kilometers. Thus, the only way in or out was overland. Amber would be due for leave in another couple of months. She was looking forward to going home, but not the four-hour rolligon ride to reach the monorail.

"So there you are!" someone said from behind her.

Amber turned around to discover Niels Grayson standing over her. Grayson was one of the senior astronomers and Amber's mentor. Rumor had it that he would be the next director of the Observatory if old Dr. Meinz ever decided to retire. She hoped the rumor was correct. The other candidate for the job was Professor Dornier, who topped Amber's list of the people she would rather not work for.

"Hello, Niels," she said. "Looking for me?"

"That I am, my most beautiful assistant."

"I'm your *only* assistant."

"Which only proves my point. Mind if I sit down?"

"Be my guest."

Grayson sat on the aluminum bench across from Amber. He cradled a low-gravity cup in his hands and sipped coffee from it. He gestured toward the screen. "I notice the rolligon's coming in."

"Right on time. I wonder if Supply remembered to send that new interferometer this time."

"They said they would. Still, with them that doesn't always mean much."

"If they've messed up this time, I'm going to ask permission to go to Luna City and rearrange some skulls."

"You'll have to stand in line. Doing anything tonight?"

There was something in Grayson's tone that caused Amber to regard her supervisor with suspicion. The question had been almost too casual. "Not a thing. Why?"

"I thought you might want to come over to the apartment for dinner. Margaret was saying just the other day that she hasn't seen you in weeks."

"We saw each other in the gym not two days ago."

"That must have been after she made the comment."

"Come on, Niels, I know you. You've got an ulterior motive. Who else is going to be there?"

"We do have a V.I.P. coming in on the rolligon," he said, gesturing at the screen. "I thought I'd have him over as well."

"Who is he? University brass?"

"Worse."

"Government!"

He nodded. "Auditor from the Office of Scientific Appropriations. He's here to see that we aren't wasting the Republic's money."

"Surely they aren't talking about cutting our budget again!"

"Could be."

"But they can't! We're operating shorthanded as it is. Next thing you know, we'll have to go on double shifts."

"I don't think it will go *that* far," Grayson replied. "Still, the director has asked me to entertain our guest. Maybe it will soften his report if we treat him nice. How about being a fourth for a few games of bridge?"

"I don't know, Niels. The last time I played hostess for you, that astronomer from Australasia kept trying to paw me all evening."

"This won't be like that. It's just a quiet dinner party with a

few hands of bridge afterward. Director Meinz has it straight
from the chancellor that our visitor is a fanatic for the game.
You're the best player on the staff, and we can't very well play
three-handed."

"All right. What time do you want me there?"

"My apartment, 2000 hours. Dress casual. Margaret will have
drinks waiting."

Amber sat at her desk in the lower levels of the administrative
section and powered up her terminal. The screen instantly lit to
display her daylist. She let her eyes scan down the list with practiced efficiency. There were the usual reports and summaries to
get out, data to correlate, and at the bottom, a private message
from Director Meinz. She keyed for acceptance. It was an official
invitation from the director requesting her attendance at Niels
Grayson's apartment that evening. The message was dated late
the previous day. Its tone betrayed far more anxiety than had
Niels's invitation at breakfast. Amber dictated a reply and wondered just how serious the observatory's fiscal problems really
were.

As soon as the computer beeped its acceptance, she returned
to her review of the day's activities. She noted an item three
levels up from the director's message, frowned, and keyed to
engage the computer's voice circuits.

"Yes, Miss Hastings?" the machine answered promptly.

"What's this Item Nine on my daylist?"

"That is the reference number for the observation you requested fifteen days ago."

"Refresh my memory."

"The matter of a comet sighting in Monoceros. You asked that
an observation be made by the sixty-centimeter instrument as
soon as that portion of sky was once again visible."

"Oh, yes. Put it up on the screen!"

Her workscreen changed to reveal a starfield. It was the same
field that she had seen two weeks earlier while working the
graveyard shift. She glanced at the region where the comet had
been. It was still there.

"Overlay the two images," she ordered.

The screen seemed to blur for a moment, then refocused as the
computer synchronized the two views. The fixed stars were di-

mensionless points, but the target object showed as a pair of tiny diffuse clouds.

"Engage blink comparator mode!"

For a moment nothing happened. Then one image disappeared. It reappeared a second later just as its twin vanished. Amber sat looking at the screen as the fuzzy dot jumped back and forth at the rate of one jump each second.

"Is that enough to get an orbital fix?" she asked.

"It is," the computer responded. "The object is some 1.2 billion kilometers from the sun. Its orbit is a very long cometary with perihelion somewhere beyond Mars."

"How long a cometary?" Amber asked.

"On the order of nine million years."

Amber whistled softly under her breath. One of Sol's errant children was making an infrequent visit to the inner system. If the computer's estimate of the orbital period was correct, this was only the five hundredth time that particular object had approached the Sun since the birth of the Solar system.

"Size estimate?"

"Not possible. The comet nucleus is obscured by the coma. Perhaps it would be visible in a larger instrument."

"That damned sixty!" Amber muttered. The telescope she was being forced to use was one of the observatory's lesser instruments. It was equipped solely for visible light work and had a photo-array system dating back twenty years. It was, in the words of more than one junior staffer, a piece of junk.

"Show me the orbital tolerance," Amber ordered.

Again her screen changed—it displayed a three-dimensional chart of the Solar system. A series of ellipses appeared on top of the concentric circles that represented the orbits of the planets. The ellipses ranged from red to violet, with green representing the nominal orbital path. The red and violet were the two possible extremes when all sources of observational error were taken into account. The rainbow of colors intersected between Saturn and Jupiter, then diverged in both directions. The point where all lines came together was the object's current estimated position.

Amber let her gaze follow the object's inbound path to where it crossed Jupiter's orbit. "Show me a speed-up of the orbital motion along the nominal path."

"Working."

As she watched, the family of ellipses disappeared, leaving

only the emerald-green line on the screen. A golden comet symbol swept inward, picking up speed as it went. As it approached Jupiter, the golden comet merged with the big planet's white banded sphere.

"Stop! Center on Jupiter and enlarge ten times. Begin again at the point where the comet comes on screen."

The screen changed scale, and the scene repeated. The golden comet slid down the green arc while the Jupiter symbol curved sedately toward the comet. This time the two icons passed within a few millimeters of each other, then separated.

"I note a close approach situation here," Amber said, more talking to herself than to the computer. "What is the minimum separation distance?"

"On the nominal orbit, the comet will pass within 100,000 kilometers of Jupiter."

"That's practically a collision!"

"That is true."

"Have you considered the effect of Jupiter on the comet's orbit?"

"Insufficient data," the computer replied with matter-of-factness that Amber found irritating. "The possible range of approach orbits makes such a calculation meaningless."

"Compute it anyway. Show me the departure orbits for red, yellow, green, blue, and violet orbits."

"Executing."

Amber mused about the situation as the new lines slowly appeared on the screen. Jupiter was the hundred-kilogram bully of the Solar system. With a mass two and a half times that of all the other planets combined, the King of Worlds tugged at its neighbors across vast distances. It had been Jupiter's influence that had prevented a planet forming where the Asteroid Belt orbited.

As the computer had predicted, the uncertainty about how close the comet would approach Jupiter had a dramatic effect on the postencounter orbit. One orbital path showed it being flung completely out of the Solar system. Another showed the comet plunging into the Sun. A third showed it going retrograde after a hairpin turn around the giant world.

It was clear that an encounter with the King of Worlds was in the making and that almost anything could happen.

* * *

"I'm so glad that you could come, Amber."

"My pleasure, Margaret," Amber replied as Niels Grayson's wife ushered her through the door of the senior astronomer's apartment. Margaret Grayson was a tall redhead whose face and figure belied her fifty years. Over the years she had assumed the role of supreme arbiter of matters social in observatory society. She was also a first-rate photo interpreter. Amber had found reason to be impressed with her abilities each time the two had worked together.

"What a beautiful jumpsuit," Margaret commented. "Is it new?"

Amber felt an inner glow from the compliment. She was clad in a stylish gray garment, with matching black pearl earrings and necklace, and high-topped formal boots. The jumpsuit had cost her a week's wages the last time she had been home. One of the reasons she had accepted Niels Grayson's invitation was the opportunity to show off a bit. "Not really. I've had it for a while."

"Well, it's lovely."

"Thank you. Is Niels here?"

"He and our guest are in the study. Come along and I'll introduce you."

Amber followed Margaret through the spacious underground apartment to Professor Grayson's study. The room was furnished with the metal furniture common to lunar dwellings, and the walls were cluttered with astronomical photographs.

"Ah, here is our other guest!" Grayson exclaimed as the two women entered the room. "John, may I introduce my assistant, Amber Hastings? Amber, this is John Malvan of the Office of Scientific Appropriations."

"Mr. Malvan," Amber said, holding out her hand to the government man. Malvan was about fifty, with white hair and the lined face of someone who carried his work home from the office. It took her a moment to realize that he was also missing his right arm.

"A privilege to meet you, Miss Hastings," Malvan replied, gripping Amber's right hand firmly with his left.

"We aren't very formal here at the observatory, Mr. Malvan. Please call me Amber."

"Very well, Amber. My name is John."

"Hello, John."

"Now that the introductions are over," Margaret Grayson interjected, "I'll go check on dinner. Amber, would you care for a drink?"

"I can help myself, Margaret."

"Very well. I'll leave you professionals to talk shop. See you in a few minutes."

"Hmmm, I've got to step out for a moment too," Niels said to Malvan. "I'll get those papers we discussed earlier."

With their host and hostess gone, Amber and Malvan stood in awkward silence for a few moments. "Professor Grayson has been telling me about his work on supernovas," Malvan said finally.

Amber nodded. "Niels is the reigning expert on Supernova 1987A. That's it over there on the wall, third photograph from the left. If you want to know anything about its origin, development, or ultimate fate, you only have to ask him."

"Ah, yes. He mentioned that earlier today. I would think you astronomers would have something more recent to study."

Amber laughed. "I wish we did! Really good supernovas don't come along very often. There are only one or two per century in the galaxy, and most of those are hidden from us by interstellar dust. In fact, only nine major supernovas have been observed over the last two thousand years. The brightest was Kepler's Star in October, 1604. That was followed by a four-century drought which ended in 1987."

"So S-1987A is really the only supernova observed since the invention of the telescope!" Malvan replied.

"The only close-in supernova," Amber agreed. "Of course, there are the supernovas we see in other galaxies, but they are too far away to get any real information from."

"Fascinating!" he said, in a way that made Amber think he really meant it.

They continued discussing supernovas in general until Amber sensed that Malvan was losing interest. She changed the subject. "How long do you plan to be here, John?"

He shrugged. "This is just a get-acquainted trip. I'll be reviewing your accounting system and records structure for the next ten days, then head back for Luna City. After that, we'll be running a wall-to-wall inventory on you. That will take a month or so to arrange, and another month to accomplish. We'll be calling on the observatory staff to help out on that."

"What have we done to deserve this?" Amber asked, trying to

make it a joke. Somehow it did not come out that way.

"Just routine," he assured her. "Parliament is facing a tight budget this year, and they want to make sure that they get value for appropriated funds."

"Are you saying that they are likely to cut our budget again?"

"I really couldn't say, Amber. That isn't my department. I just do the audits."

At that moment Niels Grayson rejoined them. He had a large sealed file folder in his hand. "Sorry it took so long. Couldn't find my damned briefcase. How are you two doing?"

"Excellent," Malvan replied. "Amber has just been explaining the significance of supernovas to me, and I, in turn, am educating her on government appropriations."

"I hope she put in a good word for *our* appropriation," Grayson said.

"Believe me, she has been a most effective advocate!"

"Margaret has dinner ready. Shall we adjourn to the dining room? Afterward, we'll set up the game."

At dinner Niels asked Malvan how long he had been a government auditor. To everyone's surprise, he told them that he had been employed by the Republic of Luna only three years. "Before that," he said, "I was an ice miner. I had to give it up when I lost the arm."

"Mining accident?" Margaret Grayson asked.

He nodded. "Got it caught between a chunk of ice and a rock wall. Crushed it beyond repair."

"Sorry to hear that."

Malvan shrugged. "I was lucky. It could have punctured my suit, too. Anyway, I'd always had a head for figures, so I got this job after going through retraining."

"Do you miss being a miner?" Margaret asked.

Malvan laughed. "Mrs. Grayson, *anything* beats ice mining. Problem is, most things don't pay as well. Enough about me. What does this charming young lady do here at the observatory?"

"I'm Intrasystem Specialist," Amber answered.

"And what does an Intrasystem Specialist do?"

Amber explained her task.

"It sounds exciting," Malvan said.

"It isn't."

"You're being too modest, dear," Margaret said. "Why, I

heard you sent a sighting report off to the Astronomical Union just this afternoon."

"What's this about a sighting report?" Niels demanded.

"I sent you a copy," Amber replied. "You'll find it on your dayfile."

"To Andromeda with that, young lady! You know I'm always behind reading my mail. What's happened that's important enough to alert the union?"

Amber explained about the comet sighting and the close encounter with Jupiter. "Of course, I can't really tell much with only three weeks of separation data to work from. Still, I thought it best to alert the union as soon as possible."

"How long to closest approach?" Grayson asked.

"Fifteen months, give or take a few weeks."

"Any idea of the size of this body?"

Amber repeated what the computer had told her. "Coming out of the Oort Cloud, it could be a relatively large nucleus," she added.

"Oort Cloud?" Malvan asked.

"That's where comets come from. It extends from Pluto halfway to the nearest star. Mostly it's just the odds and ends left over when the Solar system coalesced. With a nine-million-year orbital period, the comet penetrates deeply into the cloud."

"Are you saying this comet comes from a point halfway to the nearest star?"

"Not that far. A couple of thousand astronomical units," Grayson replied before turning to Amber. "What are you observing with?"

"The sixty-centimeter, and it isn't up to the job. Think I can get access to *The Big Eye*?"

"Well, we can certainly see what we'll be disrupting."

John Malvan hoisted hs glass. "This would seem to call for a toast! After all, it isn't every day that a new comet is discovered. To our young Galileo here!"

As glasses clinked around her, Amber squirmed uncomfortably in her seat. To be toasted for something as inconsequential as a comet sighting was embarrassing. She hoped that Niels Grayson would not repeat the story to anyone. The other young staffers would kid her unmercifully about it.

* * *

"Get back in that bed!"

Tom Thorpe glanced around at the sound of the nurse's voice. She had caught him leaning on his crutches, rummaging through the closet of his hospital room. His frown deepened as he turned his back on the guardian in white and continued his search. Finally he said, "I know they delivered street clothing for me while I was down in therapy, Nurse Schumacher. What have you done with the packages?"

"If you must know, Herr Thorpe, the delivery robot left them at the nurse's station. That is hospital policy. Now get back into that bed until Dr. Hoffman releases you. Or shall I call an orderly to have you forcibly restrained?"

"No thanks," Thorpe replied. "I can be a good boy for another few hours."

Thorpe slowly climbed back into the narrow hospital bed that had been his home for the past month. Despite his argument with the nurse, he was glad for the rest. He had forgotten how heavy Earth gravity was. The fact that he was on Earth at all indicated how close to death he had been after the accident. Normal procedure called for a strict regimen of diet and exercise before returning to standard gravity. To do otherwise risked heart failure. His presence in a hospital bed in the Swiss Alps was evidence that heart failure had been the least concern of his rescuers.

Thorpe remembered very little of the accident, although a month in bed had given him plenty of time to read the report. The lift operation had gone perfectly, to the point where the cable operators had begun slowing the load. Then one of the cable brakes had seized, causing the Number Two cable to jerk to a halt. The sudden stop had placed too much strain on the cable, causing it to snap somewhere between tower and load. Relieved of its tension, the broken cable had rebounded like a cracked whip.

In one way Thorpe had been lucky. If the ten-centimeter-thick cable had landed on him, there would not have been enough left to identify. As it was, the broken end crashed down a hundred meters from where he and Nina had been standing. The impact shattered the cable's strands and sent a cloud of shrapnel in their direction. One piece hit Thorpe just below his right knee, punched a hole through his vacuum suit, and shattered his leg. His suit had depressurized immediately and unconsciousness quickly followed.

Stabbing pains in his eyes and ears were usually the last thing a victim of rapid decompression ever felt. Thorpe remembered thinking that as he blacked out. As soon as Nina saw the cloud of red vapor explode from Thorpe's leg, she began calling for help. She had then stripped the slip-ring harness from her suit and used it to tie a crude tourniquet around Thorpe's thigh. The tourniquet had sealed well enough that she was able to repressurize Thorpe's stricken suit. The emergency response team had arrived three minutes later. They had stuffed Thorpe into an emergency bag and inflated it on the spot. After that, it had been a race to see how quickly he could be gotten to an Earthside hospital.

"Doctor will see you now, Mr. Thorpe."

Tom started at the touch of a hand on his arm and the sudden voice close by his ear. He opened his eyes to see a different nurse leaning over him. He glanced at the window. From the angle of sunlight, it was obvious that time had passed. His exertions had tired him enough that he had fallen asleep.

Thorpe managed to pull himself to a sitting position in time to see the familiar balding figure of Dr. Eric Hoffman stride through the door, with the ever-present unlit cigar clamped between his teeth.

"Good morning, Herr Thorpe. How is your leg?"

"It hurts."

"Sehr gut!"

"You wouldn't say that if you were on my side of it."

"I would say that were I in agony! Remember, we were not sure that we would be able to save the leg when you first arrived. It is the reason you were sent here to Bern. Believe me, a dull ache is a very healthy sign."

"It still hurts."

The doctor subjected Thorpe to a twenty-minute physical which included the usual prodding and poking. He finally signaled the end by saying, "All right, you may replace your gown."

"Well, Doctor, am I fit enough to get out of here?"

The doctor nodded. "You seem to be well on your way to recovery. Your eyes have lost that bloodshot look, and your eardrum has healed nicely. I have looked at your test results, and you seem not to have been permanently affected by the anoxia. Finally, despite the pain, the pins in your leg are grafting onto the bone as expected. Where do you plan to go when you leave here?"

"The company has checked me into a convalescent home on Oahu."

"Ah, Hawaii! A lovely place. Frau Hoffman and I vacationed there five years ago. Well, soak up a great deal of sun and keep off that leg, at least until after the cast is removed. That should be in about two weeks."

"Thank you, Doctor. Uh, I'm sorry if I haven't been the best patient at times."

The doctor shrugged. "I have had worse. I understand you were looking for your clothes this morning. I will have Nurse Schumacher bring them to you now. And I will order the pharmacy to send up something to ease the pain. Enjoy yourself in Hawaii, Herr Thorpe. Perhaps when you are healed, you will come back to *Schweiz* for the local skiing, *ja*?"

"Perhaps, Herr Doktor!"

"*Gut!* Now, I must attend to my other patients. Good-bye, and good luck!"

CHAPTER 3

Halver Smith watched the holoscreen that dominated one wall of his office. The view was from an aircraft circling 4000 meters above the Pacific Ocean at a point 300 miles southeast of Honshu, Japan. The picture was being relayed to Sierra Corporation headquarters via one of Smith's private satellite channels. As the aircraft circled, its camera operator tested his equipment by panning the ocean below.

The steel-blue water was studded with whitecaps kicked up by a cold north wind. When Smith had checked the weather for the area, he had shivered and muttered thanks that he was not there in person. He let his gaze scan the screen, searching for one of the tiny black shapes bobbing on the surface of the sea. Three large ocean-going tugs had been arrayed around a five-kilometer circle from which all surface traffic had been cleared. They were waiting for a delivery.

As Smith watched, the scene shifted. The steel-blue of the sea was replaced by the pale blue of the sky. The screen readouts showed that the camera was looking upward and to the west. Suddenly there was a black dot at the center of the screen. The dot quickly expanded into a disk, then turned into a blunt cone as the camera tracked the incandescent target. Despite its small size on the screen, Smith knew the cone to be quite large—some 250 meters in diameter. As it plunged through the atmosphere, the cone trailed a long streamer of superheated air.

There was a moment of disorientation as the ore body flashed past the high-flying camera plane. For an instant Smith found himself looking at the cone's upper surface with its forest of internal bracing. Then the view switched to a camera mounted on one of the waiting tugs. The surface camera followed the ore body through its last few seconds of flight.

The cone impacted less than a kilometer from the waiting ship, sending a vast geyser of steam and spray skyward. A few seconds later the camera ship was rocked by a loud thunderclap. The sound was relayed to the speaker in Halver Smith's office. The thunder was followed by a meter-high wave that raced away from the point of impact. Nothing was visible for long seconds save the rapidly boiling sea. Then a rust-colored mass rose slowly into view from the depths. The water around it continued to boil vigorously as the ore body bobbed peacefully on the surface of the sea.

There was a sudden tilt to the scene as the tugboat changed course and headed directly for the impact point. Halver Smith did not wait to see the rest. It would be hours yet before the three tugs had the million-ton mass under tow, and a week or more before the rusting construct could be dragged ashore at the Kyushu smelter. Neither operation was Smith's concern, however. Sierra Corporation had fulfilled its obligation to Nippon Steel the moment the ore body had bobbed to the surface. From then on it was the Japanese corporation's headache. That was just as well. Smith had troubles of his own.

There were those who counted Halver Smith among the richest men in the world. They were right as far as they went. The problem was that they never went far enough. They saw his estate overlooking San Francisco and his holdings in Mexico, the

South Pacific, United Europe, and Australasia, and they counted him rich. They noted his twenty-eight-percent ownership of Sierra Corporation, his portfolios overflowing with gilt-edge stocks, his paintings and sculptures, and they envied him. They noted his luxury ground cars and aircraft, his personal yacht, the *Sierra Seas*, and they declared him a mega-mogul—one of those monied individuals whose lives were luridly chronicled by the least responsible segment of the mass media. What they did not see was that great wealth brought with it great responsibility, and that paper worth does not always translate into liquidity.

Halver Smith was something of a gambler. Just out of college he had gambled 100,000 credits on an unproven process for extracting samarium, yttrium, and praseodymium from low-grade ore. He had won big. Later he had gambled everything that he could capture an asteroid. That gamble would pay off handsomely in the future. The splashdown he had just witnessed was proof of that. At the moment, however, the project had left him deep in debt. His load of fiscal obligations was straining Sierra Corporation to the limit. Halver Smith was walking a tightrope. One slip and his hard-won empire would collapse around him.

Unlike many in his class, Smith actually worked for a living. He was often the first executive at his desk in the morning and the last to leave at night. He had always been something of a workaholic, and his affliction had grown worse since the death of his wife in a boating accident five years earlier. He never allowed himself to forget that there were people counting on him.

Having watched another successful delivery, he turned back to the day's work. He had slightly more than half an hour before his afternoon appointment. In that time he might well dispose of the stack of papers in front of him.

The first report came under the heading of "Imitation is the Sincerest Form of Flattery." With the arrival of *The Rock* in high Earth orbit five years before, Sierra Corporation had largely cornered the market in refined metals. Despite horrendous start-up costs, Smith could still deliver a ton of iron to the smelters for less money than most surface mines. Where his competitors were forced to sift through one hundred tons of ore for each ton of refined iron, Smith's ratio was closer to two to one. Even his "slag" was valuable, containing nickel, iridium, gold, silver, and a host of other valuable metals.

It had not taken long for the smart money to realize that what Sierra Corporation could do, others could copy. Even while *The Rock* was in transit, several other asteroid capture attempts had been organized. Of those, only System Resources, S.A. had reached the orbital operations stage.

Their asteroid was named Avalon. It had originally circled the sun just beyond Venus, and was one of the Alten class of minor planets—so named because Alten was the first known asteroid whose orbit lay entirely inside that of Earth. Avalon was one of the asteroids Halver Smith had considered in his doctoral thesis. He had rejected it because of its size. Avalon measured nine by ten by twelve kilometers and was shaped like a lopsided potato. It was several times more massive than *The Rock*, and correspondingly more difficult to move.

Smith had followed the progress of the Avalon Project with considerable interest. System Resources had been nudging the asteroid into an expanded orbit for the past four years. At the moment, Avalon was midway between Earth and Venus. Current estimates called for it to arrive in five years.

The report Smith held in his hand was SierraCorp's monthly projection of Avalon's effect on the iron market. Estimates called for refined ore to drop twenty percent in price immediately, then gradually slip another ten points as both operations went to full production. As Smith read the monthly projection, he found a reason to frown. The analysts pointed to recent pronouncements by Carlos Sandoval, System Resources' CEO, that they would begin mining operations while Avalon was en route. The first ore bodies were expected to reach the home planet within the year.

Despite his intention to get through his paperwork, Smith was still pondering the problem when 1600 hours rolled around.

"Mr. Thorpe is here for his four o'clock," Smith's secretary said over his office intercom.

"Send him in, Marla. Then ring down to the commissary. Have them send up a plate of rolls, a pot of coffee and one of tea. Also, if they have any of those eclairs left over from lunch, have them send two of them, as well. It's too nice a day to diet!" Smith had a weight problem, which he fought sporadically. His staff had noted with amusement that the iron-willed mover of worlds had no willpower when it came to chocolate.

Halver Smith met Tom Thorpe at his office door. Smith had not seen Thorpe except via phone screen for more than a year. The first thing he noticed was the gaunt look of a man recovering from a serious injury. Otherwise, Thorpe had changed little. The mining engineer's 195-centimeter height, muscled body, and rugged features still gave him the look of a professional athlete. Smith knew from Thorpe's file that he was thirty-five. He could easily have passed for five years younger. The only indication of his age and responsibility was a sprinkling of gray amid his dark brown locks.

"Hello, Thomas," Smith said warmly as he held out his hand. "Good to see you looking so well!"

"Thank you, sir. You are looking fit yourself!"

Smith patted his waistline. "If only it were true. Come sit down. How's the leg?"

"It still gives me a twinge now and then. The doctors say that's normal."

Smith nodded. "I broke my arm once. Between the itching and the aches, it almost drove me crazy. Still, it healed eventually. Come, let's get you seated!" When the two of them had settled into powered chairs, Smith asked, "How was Hawaii?"

"Great, sir. I've done nothing but lie on the beach, fish, and chase women for the past month."

"Catch any fish?"

"Yes, sir. Both times I went out."

"And the women?"

"Uh, the fishing was good in that department too."

"Good! We like our employees happy." Smith leaned back in his chair and felt the cushions reconfigure themselves. He rested his elbows and stared at Thorpe through steepled fingers. "You know you scared me half to death! What the hell were you doing out on the surface, anyway?"

"Making my weekly rounds, sir."

"The reports I received say that you were damned lucky Nina Pavolev was there."

"Yes, sir. I've been trying to decide how best to thank her."

"What she did calls for a Paris original, at least."

"Yes, sir. Know of any good dress shops in town?"

Smith laughed. "Check with my secretary. I swear, that

woman must spend two hundred percent of what I pay her on clothes."

"Thank you, sir. I will."

Smith's mood changed. He stared at his subordinate for nearly a minute before speaking again. "You know, of course, that I've been receiving progress reports on your recovery."

"I didn't, but it doesn't surprise me."

"The doctors all agree that your body is mending nicely. They aren't nearly as confident about your mental state. I understand that you've been having nightmares."

Thorpe hesitated, then nodded slowly. "Every night at first, not nearly so often lately."

"Care to tell me about them?"

"Not much to tell. I dream that I'm underwater. I struggle toward the surface, but never quite make it. About the time I think I'm going to drown, I wake up gasping for air. My heart is pounding, and my body's covered with cold sweat."

Smith nodded. "Understandable for a man who has survived explosive decompression. Still, I wonder if it's wise to put you back in harness so quickly."

"Sir, I'm ready! Hell, the nightmares aren't caused by the accident. I haven't been able to sleep comfortably on Earth since I first went to space. It's the gravity that's suffocating me!"

"I can do something about that. I've had a special project in mind for about month. I'd like you to take it over for me."

"You aren't sending me back to *The Rock*?"

Smith shook his head. "Not right away. Eric Lundgren's doing a good job filling in for you at the moment. He can handle things until you're ready."

"I'm ready now!"

Smith sighed. "You're a good man, Tom, and I appreciate your desire to get back to your job. Still, I can't overlook the doctors' opinion. They say you could suffer burnout if we rush things."

"They're wrong, sir. I feel fine."

"Good. That means there will be no problem if I send you to Luna."

"To the Moon, sir? Why, for God's sake?"

Smith got up from his chair, crossed the room, and retrieved several reports from his desk. One was the Avalon report. "Read that. When you're finished, we'll discuss it."

Smith's secretary arrived with the refreshments while Thorpe leafed through the report. She poured Smith a cup of coffee and Thorpe one of tea with lemon. She then arrayed a plate of cookies between the two men.

"Where's my eclair?" Smith demanded.

"Dr. Reynolds confiscated it in the elevator. He said that if he caught you eating any chocolate, he would personally administer your shots this week. He claims to have a dull needle he's been saving."

"You can tell Dr. Reynolds that I will get him for this."

"Yes, sir."

Smith turned to Thorpe, who had put down the report to watch his secretary leave the room. "What do you think? Are they really going to begin mining operations before they get Avalon into parking orbit?"

"No reason not to. The only thing that stopped us was the need to get permission from the various international commissions. We still managed to do a lot of preparatory work. Avalon's crew has more free time than we did, and all of their certificates are in order. Why not get some of their investment back early?"

"That's what I thought," Smith said. He handed Thorpe a second report. "What do you make of that?"

Once again Thorpe scanned the document. "It's an announcement by the Astronomical Union concerning a new comet."

"See anything unusual about it?"

Thorpe shrugged. "Only that it's going to pass close to Jupiter. Otherwise, it appears to be a fairly typical piece of sky junk."

"Take a look at the last page. There's an approximation of the new orbit there."

Thorpe turned to the page indicated and studied the columns of figures. "I can see why the astronomers are excited. This baby's seen the Oort Cloud for the last time. From now on it will be circling between Venus and Saturn."

"It strikes me that some people might find such an orbit to be commercially attractive."

Thorpe frowned. "Why? Every stone in the Asteroid Belt has a smaller velocity gradient with respect to Earth. No serious developer would give this eccentric an orbit a second look."

"That was my own first thought," Smith agreed. "It's a bad deal when you consider the physics of the situation. Still, I wonder how the media will react to this close encounter with Jupiter?"

Thorpe shrugged. "They'll give it a big play, I imagine."

"And what if some smart operator announces that he is going to capture this very famous comet? Will the average investor be smart enough to recognize it as a gimmick?"

"Not much chance of anyone doing that, is there?"

"Perhaps one in ten," Smith replied. "Enough to justify action on our part."

"Action, Mr. Smith? Why? So long as we don't fund such a harebrained scheme, what do we care?"

"We care, Thomas. The last time there were rumors of a capture being organized, our stock dropped seventeen points in three days. I will be spending much of the next year in delicate negotiations to refinance our debt. Any such ripple in our stock price would seriously erode my negotiating position."

"If someone does try to organize a capture, we'll merely put out the truth. That will stop them cold."

Smith shook his head. "Any such statement would only call attention to the capture program. Investors would think we were afraid of the competition. We might confer legitimacy on the charlatans and begin a feeding frenzy on the exchange."

"Then how do we parry?" Thorpe asked, confused.

"We block the attempt before there is one."

"How?"

"We obtain the comet's exploitation rights ourselves. If we own the rights, no one else will be able to move."

"Damn it, Mr. Smith, we need another asteroid like we need a tax audit! It isn't even metal. If I remember right, most comet nuclei are conglomerations of mush."

"I didn't say that we would *exercise* our claim. I merely suggest that we assert it."

"But the only way to lay claim to an astronomical body is to establish a permanent presence. Mounting an expedition to settle this comet nucleus will cost a fortune."

"That is the normal method of laying claim," Smith agreed. "It is not, however, the *only* method. There is a special clause in the law." Smith handed Thorpe a computer printout. "Read the last section of the statute, the one entitled, 'Rights-of-Discovery.'"

Thorpe did as directed. His frown turned gradually into a look of understanding. "It says here that all rights belong to the discovering individual/organization for ten years after the initial report to the Astronomical Union. After that, the 'permanent presence' clause takes over."

"So you see, Thomas, it won't be necessary to occupy the comet nucleus in order to claim it. We merely have to purchase the exploitation rights from the discoverers. In this case, that is Farside Observatory, Luna."

Thorpe glanced down at the hard copy of the old statute. "It says 'individual/organization.' Doesn't that mean that the rights belong to this A. Hastings?"

"I wish it did," Smith replied. "It would be cheaper to deal with an individual than with an observatory. However, the legal department points out that the astronomer works for the observatory—is on the staff, in fact—and that he was using observatory equipment at the time of the discovery. Both points give the observatory a strong claim to being discoverer-of-record. I want you to proceed to Luna and negotiate an option on those rights."

"Wouldn't it be better to send someone from Legal?"

"They could negotiate a contract well enough," Smith agreed. "Remember our goal, however. If we are to protect our stock, no one must suspect that this is a ruse. If I were truly interested, I'd send one of my best technical experts. Therefore, I have to send that same person now. Your presence on the Moon will be the factor that makes this whole thing believable."

"How much should I offer?"

"We're still calculating that. You'll have a number before you leave. It will be sufficiently generous that no one will question our sincerity . . . I hope."

Amber Hastings sat in her office and reviewed the data she had collected on Comet P/2085 (G). The catalog number was new, having been assigned the previous week by the Astronomical Union's Department for Classification and Nomenclature. Amber still found it strange to refer to the inbound body by its official number. Prior to it being registered, she had merely called it "the comet," or simply "it." Other staffers had taken to calling it "Amber's Accident" and "Hastings's Horror." The latter name had been adopted by an irate deep-space astronomer after Amber suggested diverting *The Big Eye* to look at her discovery.

Normally, a classification number was all that distinguished a comet from its brethren. The particular comet in question, however, was destined to become famous. Already the observatory had received inquiries from news organizations throughout the system. There had even been a cable from the editor of *The Callisto Scientific Station Online Gazette*. All had asked for more details on the close encounter and the postencounter orbit. The interest from the press had convinced the Astronomical Union that the comet deserved a name. So, in accordance with long tradition, they asked its discoverer to suggest one.

"They want me to name it?" Amber had asked Niels Grayson when he told her about the A.U.'s request.

"That's your right as discoverer. If you don't suggest something, they'll probably just tack your name on to the designation."

"You mean *they'd name it after me*?"

"It's traditional, you know."

"They can't do that!"

"Why not?"

"Because."

"Good answer," Grayson had said with a chuckle. "But unless you come up with a better suggestion, they'll do it."

The idea of having a Comet P/Hastings in the annals of astronomy did not sit well with Amber. She had read horror stories about what happened to young astronomers who made important discoveries. Better by far, she decided, to suggest a name of her own and save herself a future fraught with professional jealousies.

Naming a comet, she quickly discovered, was not something one did in a vacuum. Nearly everyone at the observatory had a favorite name. It was a situation guaranteed to make enemies, as she learned when Director Meinz called her to his office.

"You wanted to see me, sir?"

"Ah, there you are, Amber!" Meinz said. "Come in and sit down. I want to congratulate you on your discovery."

"It was more the computer's discovery than mine."

"Yes, there is that, isn't there? Have you considered what you are going to name it?"

"I haven't really given it much thought, sir. Too excited, I guess."

"Be careful with your selection," Meinz warned. "After all, this is one of the greatest honors our profession can bestow. You wouldn't want the Committee on Names to reject your choice."

"Do you think they would, sir?"

He nodded. "If they thought you were being frivolous, or had made an inappropriate choice. I wouldn't call it 'Buttercup,' or anything silly like that. No, to clear the committee requires a name with special significance to the community of astronomers. Tradition limits your choices to two categories. You can name it after a figure from mythology, although that is seldom done in the case of comets. Or else, you can choose to honor an individual who has made a significant contribution to the field. You might, for instance, name it after someone here at the observatory."

"You're the only one at Farside Observatory worthy of such an honor, sir."

The director had beamed at what Amber had not intended to be a serious suggestion. "Comet P/Meinz, eh? It does have a certain ring to it. But, of course, I don't want to sway you. You are discoverer-of-record. That makes the name your responsibility. Just remember what I said about the committee. And, should you choose to honor a prominent astronomer—say someone such as myself—it can only enhance your career."

Following her interview with the director, Amber became a lot more cautious about whom she discussed the matter with. Her caution did not stop the suggestions. By the end of the week she had collected twenty-eight suggested names.

She did not like any of them.

CHAPTER 4

Tom Thorpe lay in his acceleration couch and watched Luna grow large as the landing craft fell toward the plain known as Oceanus Procellarum, the Ocean of Storms. The screen at the front of the ferry's cabin showed a magnified view of that region, including Copernicus and Kepler craters. Thorpe searched midway between the two until he found the scattering of lights, silhouetted against the dark surface, that marked the location of both the Moon's capital city and its busiest spaceport. He fancied that he could see the fifty-kilometer spur of the Luna City mass driver, but realized that was probably too much to ask. As the ferry fell, a countdown clock reeled off the seconds to engine ignition.

"Impressive, isn't it?" his seat mate asked.

Thorpe turned to the man who had boarded the craft at Luna Equatorial Station, then dozed off immediately after strapping in. His attention had been so absorbed by the landing that he had not noticed that his companion was awake.

"Quite impressive," he agreed.

The man, who was in his mid-fifties, gestured at the viewscreen. "This is my favorite part. Not many people appreciate Luna's beauty, but I'll match the vista of a lunar highland against any sunset Earth ever produced."

"It has a certain raw majesty," Thorpe admitted.

"Damned right it does! Who says scenery has to be blue, white, or green? By the way, my name's Hobart. John Mahew Hobart."

"*The* John Mahew Hobart?"

"Guilty as charged. I take it you've heard of me."

Thorpe nodded. John Hobart was the leader of the Nationalists in the Luna parliament. He was a firebrand orator who was tireless in his defense of the Republic of Luna and its ten million citizens. "My company lobbied parliament when you first proposed your tax on exporting ice."

"Lobbied on which side?"

"Not yours, I can assure you. My name is Tom Thorpe. I work for Sierra Corporation."

Hobart frowned for long seconds, then smiled as recognition hit him. "Thorpe! Of course, you're Operations Manager aboard *The Rock*! I thought the name sounded familiar. My assistant talked to you just before the vote. He was quite impressed with your grasp of the issues."

"Apparently not enough to sway your opinion."

Hobart laughed. "That would have taken an act of God. Still, you gave us a run for our money, and I always respect a worthy adversary."

"Likewise."

The Nationalists had sponsored a tax on exported ice, arguing that those who depleted Luna's natural resources should be made to pay for the privilege. The argument had struck a responsive chord with Lunarians. Compared to the surface of the Moon, the Sahara Desert had a flooding problem. Little wonder that the inhabitants of Luna had strong feelings about water. It did not help that they could see an unlimited supply of the stuff hanging directly overhead. And even though Earth's stock was vastly greater than Luna's, its deep gravity well made tanking water to orbit impractical. Luna's weak gravity had thus made it the largest exporter of ice in the Solar system.

Luna's tax had come as a shock to those living in the space habitats. Besides its obvious uses, water was the raw material from which oxygen and hydrogen were electrolyzed. The Luna tax had doubled *The Rock*'s yearly cost for consumables. Despite that, Thorpe could not really blame the Lunarians. For unlike the people of Earth, those who lived beyond the atmosphere knew the value of a kilo of ice.

The countdown clock slowly worked its way down toward zero. As it did so, Hobart cautioned Thorpe to make sure he was strapped in securely. His announcement preceded the pilot's by a few seconds. There followed a brief period of anticipation as the lunar surface grew rapidly larger.

As the clock reached zero, magnetic fields were rearranged and a few nanograms of antimatter injected into the ship's thrust chamber. There they encountered a powerful jet of water. Antimatter encountered normal matter and combined in a burst of raw energy. The resulting temperature rise turned the water directly into plasma. Within milliseconds an incandescent plume leapt downward from between the landing craft's huge splayed feet, and its descent began to slow.

"Mr. Thorpe?"

"Yes."

"I'm Grandstaff, SierraCorp representative here in Luna City."

"Hello," Thorpe replied to the small, balding man who met him outside of Luna customs. Tom could not help thinking that someone with Grandstaff's knobby knees would do well not to wear shorts. "I take it that you received Mr. Smith's instructions."

"Yes, sir. I've arranged a preliminary meeting with the Chancellor of the University. He'll see you at 1400 tomorrow."

"And when do I leave for the observatory?"

"I've booked passage for you on the Circumlunar Monorail four days from now."

"Why so long?"

"The last leg of the journey will be overland. The next scheduled run to the observatory leaves the first of next week."

"Perhaps I could charter a ship."

"Oh, no!" Grandstaff explained the observatory's pollution problem and the extremes to which the astronomers went to protect their telescopes.

Thorpe sighed. "Then I guess I wait. Care to recommend some of the local sights? This is my first trip to the Moon, you know."

"Well, sir," Grandstaff replied, "there's the day excursion to the Tranquility Monument. That is very popular. Then, of course, there are the nightclubs on the Grand Concourse. Or, if you're a history buff, you might tour the sites of the revolution—"

"You could do worse," a voice said.

Thorpe and Grandstaff turned to see John Hobart standing behind them. The M.P. had cleared customs in a matter of seconds, and Thorpe had thought him long gone.

"Good afternoon, Citizen Hobart!" Grandstaff effused. His manner made Thorpe wonder if he were about to genuflect. "May I introduce Thomas Thorpe . . ."

"We've met, Willy," Hobart replied. "I'm afraid I forced Mr. Thorpe to listen to my snoring during much of the approach."

"You hardly snored at all."

"That's not what my wife generally tells me. What brings you to Luna, Mr. Thorpe? Business or pleasure?"

"A little of both. Mostly I'm recuperating. The doctors thought it would do me good to get off Earth. The gravity, you know."

"Oh, have you been sick?"

Before Tom could reply, Grandstaff told Hobart about the winch accident.

"You're damned lucky to be alive!" Hobart exclaimed when Grandstaff finished. "Coming that close to the grim reaper must change a person's outlook."

"Well, I don't complain about getting up in the morning as much as I used to."

That brought a laugh. "I'll bet you don't! How long will you be staying in Luna City?"

Thorpe gestured toward Grandstaff. "My guide tells me that I've got four days to kill."

"I'm having a small gathering of friends at my home tomorrow evening. I would be honored to have you as my guest. You're invited, too, Willy."

"Thank you, but my wife has made other plans," Grandstaff said.

"May we count on you, Mr. Thorpe?"

"I don't want to put you out."

"Nonsense! We Lunarians are too damned clannish. You can't blame us. We're ten million people to Earth's eight billion! It's enough to give anyone an inferiority complex. Still, we need to occasionally meet strangers to remind ourselves that there are other people in the universe. Besides, moving *The Rock* was a major accomplishment. I'm sure my guests will be fascinated to hear how it was done."

"Very well. I'll come."

"Excellent! I'm in Pressure Four, Third Sublevel, Kepler Corridor. If you can get that close, just ask anyone where my apartment is. Dinner will be served at 2000 hours. You might want to get there a few minutes early for drinks."

"Thank you."

"My pleasure."

When the legislator had moved off, Grandstaff turned to Thorpe. "Amazing!"

"What is?"

"You sit next to the man for a few hours, and he invites you home. I know people who have been trying to wangle an invitation to Hobart's for years!"

Thorpe shrugged. "We crossed swords on the ice tax. Maybe he wants to rub my nose in the fact that we lost. Or maybe he needs to send a private message to Halver Smith."

"You may not be far from the truth there," Grandstaff replied. "The smart money is betting that Hobart wants to be the next prime minister. He may want your perspective on a Nationalist administration."

The outer office of the Chancellor of the University of Luna was an airy place filled with wall hangings, green growing things, and aluminum furniture finished to look like wood. The chancellor's secretary, a decorative blonde, sat at a horseshoe desk and worked on her computer console. At the same time, Thorpe and Grandstaff sat in the waiting area and leafed through recent issues of *The Transactions of the Society of Lunar Educators* and *Solar System Higher Education Review*. And though Grandstaff appeared to be reading the impenetrable jargon, Thorpe's attention kept wandering in the receptionist's direction. Twice she had caught him staring at her. Each time she had responded with a distant, professional smile. Thorpe was considering how to open a conversation when a chime sounded. She picked up her earphone, listened for a few seconds, then nodded. She turned to them. "The chancellor will see you now."

Thorpe and Grandstaff were greeted by a man with bushy eyebrows and an unruly mop of white hair. He exuded confidence as he strode across his office to greet his visitors.

"Hello, Willem," he said to Grandstaff. "I haven't seen you around the health club lately. Where have you been working out?"

Grandstaff shook the chancellor's outstretched hand. "Please, Robbie, you don't want to give Mr. Thorpe the idea that I lie around the sauna all day. He might report me to Mr. Smith. I'd have to go back to working for a living then."

The chancellor turned to Thorpe. "I'm Robert Cummings, Chancellor of the University."

Thorpe shook hands and allowed himself to be directed to a plush chair in front of Cummings's desk. The top of the desk held an intercom, computer screen, and gold picture frame. In the frame were holograms showing a middle-aged woman and three children.

"Is this your family?"

"It is indeed!" the chancellor boomed. "Those pictures are quite old, however. The five-year-old girl is getting married next month, and my eldest son just presented me with my fourth grandchild. I'm happy to say that Ingrid, my wife, is still as beautiful as ever. Are you married, Mr. Thorpe?"

Tom shook his head. "I've spent most of the past decade on *The Rock*. Not much opportunity to meet the right woman, I'm afraid."

"That will make you a popular man in Luna City. Government service seems to attract young women. And since many of our young men are off working in the ice mines, the situation bodes well for the single male."

"If I'd known that, I'd have come to Luna earlier."

The chancellor offered his visitors refreshment. When all three had low-gravity cups filled with steaming liquid, he leaned back in his chair. "I'm always glad to be of assistance to Citizen Grandstaff, Mr. Thorpe. I must tell you, however, that he has not told me why you wanted this conference."

Thorpe leaned over to retrieve his briefcase, opened it, and withdrew the Astronomical Union's announcement of the coming close encounter with Jupiter. He handed it over to Cummings, who perused it without comment.

"As you can see, Mr. Chancellor, Farside Observatory discovered this object six weeks ago. The observatory is, I believe, a branch of your university."

The chancellor nodded. "Semiautonomous. If you wish anything of the observatory, you will have to speak with Director Meinz."

"I will be at the observatory next week. As head of the observatory's parent organization, we felt that you would like to be briefed concerning our intentions."

"By all means."

Thorpe repeated the cover story he had been given. The gist of it was that Sierra Corporation was actively considering the exploitation of the comet nucleus if its postencounter orbit proved to be economically viable. He went on to explain the legal requirements for ownership of the comet. Halfway through his presentation, the chancellor hunched forward. It had just occurred to him that there was money to be made.

When Thorpe finished, Cummings asked, "Are you saying that you want to *buy* this comet from the university?"

"It's much too early for that, sir. There are too many unknowns to make an accurate projection of the post-Jupiter orbit. Also, we have yet to receive data as to the asteroid's size or composition. All of these factors weigh heavily on the profitability equation. I've been sent to purchase an option against *future* exploitation rights. If the comet later turns out to be commercially viable, we will be willing to negotiate a long-term mining lease at that time."

Cummings frowned as he slowly stroked his chin. "It seems to me that you are being hasty about this, Mr. Thorpe. Why risk anything until your questions are answered? Why not wait until after the close encounter?"

Thorpe smiled. "If we wait, then our competitors will also see the commercial possibilities. By taking a small risk now, we establish a strong bargaining position later."

"It would seem to be in our university's interest to enhance the competition, not limit it," the chancellor replied. "Why should we give SierraCorp a monopoly position?"

"You shouldn't, Mr. Chancellor. If you are certain that the postencounter orbit will fall within certain highly restrictive tolerances, then your best negotiating stance is to wait and hold an auction. If, on the other hand, you are uncertain as to what that orbit will be, then you'd best hedge your bet. Secure whatever benefit you can get out of it now. The longer you wait, the more chance the observatory's rights-of-discovery will be rendered worthless by new data."

"And if they turn out to be worth a great deal, SierraCorp wins and we have sold a valuable resource for a pittance."

"Not at all," Thorpe responded. "Our option will not specify the final lease price. If someone offers you more, then take it. All we ask is that we be allowed to match anyone else's final bid."

"How much are we talking about for an option?"

Thorpe named the figure that Halver Smith had authorized to begin the bidding. The university chancellor's eyes grew momentarily larger. "That is very generous of Mr. Smith."

"We want you to know that we are serious," Thorpe replied with his most sincere look.

"How do we proceed from here?"

"I will travel to Farside Observatory to confirm the data I have in my possession. I'll need to know the comet nucleus's composition and size. We are interested in certain organic materials found in comet nuclei. If we discover that material in this particular nucleus, then I'll be ready to sign a letter of intent on the spot."

"Ah, yes," Cummings replied. "I may have given you a wrong impression earlier. While Farside Observatory is autonomous in many things, matters such as these require university concurrence. It's a matter of legality, you understand."

"Of course," Thorpe responded. "Once the director and I have signed the letter of intent, I will return here to obtain your signature as well. That is the proper procedure, is it not?"

"Most proper, Mr. Thorpe. I'll get a message off to Director Meinz this afternoon. I'm sure that you will find him most helpful."

CHAPTER 5

Had it been visible from space, Luna City would have looked like nothing quite so much as a giant bull's-eye. Since it was underground, however, the city's shape was apparent only to someone who took the time to study a map. Tom Thorpe did just that as he plotted the route from his hotel to John Hobart's apartment.

Luna City was situated 200 kilometers southwest of Copernicus Crater. The site had first been occupied in 2005 by one of the United States' early lunar settlements. The colony had expanded a decade later with the discovery of subsurface ice deposits. Later, automatic tunnel-boring equipment had carved out six concentric rings 500 meters below the surface. As soon as each tunnel was sealed and pressurized, it was occupied by new immigrants from Earth.

As the population grew, those first six tunnels had been widened, cross-connected, and added to. Eventually five additional habitat levels were carved from the lunar bedrock. Each new level was carved out of bedrock one hundred meters below its predecessor, and with one or two more concentric rings. The sixth and most recent level included a total of twelve rings in all.

Tom Thorpe stood in front of a public screen and punched in his destination. A ruby-red line marked the route to Hobart's apartment. A moment later he found himself holding a three-dimensional guide map on which the city's truncated conical shape was apparent. Confident that he could find his destination—or at least find his way back to his hotel if he got lost—he stepped out onto the Grand Concourse.

The Grand Concourse was a spiral gallery cut into the side of the large manmade cavern that dominated the city center. The cylindrical cavern was more than one hundred meters in diameter and extended 500 meters from floor to domed roof. The cavern functioned as the city's air reservoir and social center. An artificial sun hung suspended from the apex while the green of a park spread across the cavern floor half a kilometer below. Lining the long walkway were the entrances to theaters, restaurants, hotels, specialty shops, bars, and sidewalk cafés. The concourse rose twenty meters in each turn, with five complete turns between main levels.

It was 1900 hours when Thorpe stepped out onto the concourse from the lobby of his hotel. The artificial sun had been turned down to a pale blue color to simulate terrestrial twilight. In another hour it would be switched to the deeper blue of night. Multicolored lights had been turned on up and down the spiral ramp, causing the wispy clouds that floated through the cavern to fluoresce in the twilight. Twin streams of Lunarians moved upramp and down as young couples and families strolled leisurely past shop windows.

Thorpe's hotel was midway between levels Four and Five on the west side of the central cavern. John Mahew Hobart's apartment was on Level Three, 150 meters overhead, and in the northeast quadrant of the fourth concentric ring. Thorpe had

briefly considered strolling up the concourse to Level Three, but
had given up the idea when a quick calculation informed him that
the distance along the spiral walkway was more than two kilometers. His injured leg had begun to ache as it always did by day's
end, and even in lunar gravity, Thorpe was not confident of his
ability to climb that far.

Instead he located a public airlift and let himself fall forward
into the vertical shaft. Rising air tugged at his clothes. Had he
been on Earth, he would have crashed into the impellers located
200 meters below. At one-sixth his Earth weight, however, he
was wafted upward by the high velocity air. He wobbled as he
fought to maintain proper position—spread-eagled, back arched,
stomach pushed out as far as it would go. He watched the lighted
level indicators sweep past. When he reached Level Three, he
grabbed for the polished railing that ran around the shaft's periphery and nearly missed. Once he had it, he swung his body out of
the airstream and landed lightly on the third-level landing stage.
He then walked down a short corridor and back out onto the
concourse. As he left the lift enclosure, his ears were still ringing
from the noise.

Consulting his map, Thorpe found that he was still on the
wrong side of the central cavern. He eyed one of the foot bridges
that the city planners had installed across the chasm. The bridge
did not look substantial enough to hold a man's weight, let alone
the combined load of the stream of humanity currently moving
across it. Despite his years on *The Rock*, Thorpe felt trepidation
as he stepped out onto the slowly oscillating bridge. He crossed
without looking down.

Ten meters upramp from the bridge he found a large corridor
with the sign NORTHEAST RADIAL displayed in glowing white letters. He stepped on one of two moving slidewalks and allowed
himself to be carried outbound. The fourth circumferential ring
was a kilometer distant from the Grand Concourse. He reached it
in ten minutes. Once there, he stopped a passerby and asked if
she knew where he might find the residence of John Mahew
Hobart. Five minutes later Thorpe found himself in a short cross
corridor whose furnishings marked it as one of the richer sections
of the city.

*   *   *

"Ah, Mr. Thorpe, glad you could come!" Hobart enthused when he greeted the SierraCorp representative at the door.

"I'm a little early," Thorpe replied. "I wanted to give myself some time in the event I got lost."

"Think nothing of it. I'm pleased that you made it at all. We have stories of tourists who have been lost for days. Come in and meet my wife and the other guests."

Hobart's home had been sculpted to resemble a natural cave on Earth. Mostly it was open space, with conversational groupings clustered in various natural-looking chambers, each separated from the others by a thin screen of artificial stalactites and stalagmites. Likewise, passages to other rooms were disguised as natural openings. Soft, indirect lighting illuminated the space from behind sculpted walls. Hobart led Thorpe past a small pond filled with lilies and goldfish to where several people stood clustered around a well-stocked bar.

"Thomas Thorpe, I would like you to meet my wife, Nadia. Nadia, this is Mr. Thorpe, operations manager for *The Rock*."

"Hello, Mr. Thorpe," Mrs. Hobart said, holding out her hand. She was a handsome woman in her late forties. Her black hair was streaked with gray, but otherwise she could have passed for a decade younger than her true age. Her evening gown bared more flesh than it covered but was conservative by Lunarian standards. "I'm pleased you could come."

"I'm grateful that you could have me," Thorpe replied.

Hobart got him a drink and introduced him to the rest of the guests. It quickly became apparent that the occasion was a gathering of the Nationalist Party of Luna and its faithful. Just as the introductions were concluded, a soft chime sounded, and Hobart excused himself to answer the door.

"So, you were involved in moving *The Rock*?" one of Hobart's other guests asked. Thorpe turned to the man who had been introduced as Harold Barnes, an official of the Bank of Luna.

Thorpe nodded. "From the first scouting expedition until six weeks ago, when I was injured in an accident."

"Yes," the banker's wife said from beside him. "John told us what happened. You must have been terrified!"

"Not at the time. I remember worrying that we would fall behind our production schedule."

"How unspeakably brave!" the matron cooed.

Thorpe laughed. "I've had the shakes plenty since, I can assure you."

"Just how much *did* it cost to move *The Rock*?" Barnes asked.

"A lot!" Thorpe responded. "You would have to ask Halver Smith for the exact figures."

"I doubt he would tell me."

"I doubt he would," Thorpe agreed.

Barnes was unfazed by the answer. "My bank has studied the economics of asteroid capture. They estimate it to be ten times as expensive as a similar project on Luna. Why is that?"

"Lots of reasons," Thorpe replied. "*The Rock* masses three hundred billion tons. A propulsion system to move that much mass doesn't come cheap. Then there's the time involved in the project. It took four years, you know. That bears on the cost of money, insurance, and wages. Finally, there's the fuel cost. We ate up nearly ten kilograms of antimatter getting *The Rock* into Earth orbit."

"*Ten* kilograms, did you say? That's quite a lot, isn't it?"

Thorpe nodded. "About two years' production for one of the big power satellites."

"It was my impression that *The Rock* orbited quite close to the Earth. Almost hit it, in fact! Why so much antimatter?"

"It's true that *The Rock*'s initial orbit occasionally brought it quite close to us. However, it was also inclined ten degrees to the ecliptic."

"The what?"

"The plane in which the Earth orbits. Change-of-plane is the most costly of all space maneuvers. Eighty percent of the antimatter we burned went to realigning *The Rock*'s orbital plane. After that, getting from solar to terrestrial orbit was easy."

"In my business, Mr. Thorpe, we are often asked to consider financing such ventures. Would you recommend such a project?"

Thorpe shrugged. "Like most things, it depends."

"Depends on what?"

"First I'd have to see the orbital mechanics involved. How much delta V—that's velocity change—is required over what period of time? Then I'd take a hard look at the company's technical expertise. Finally—"

"Harold Barnes!" someone behind Thorpe said. "Are you pumping our guest for free advice?"

Thorpe turned to see Mrs. Hobart standing behind him. She came forward and grabbed him gently by the arm. "You will have to excuse him, Tom. Compared to a Lunarian, a Scot is a spend-thrift, and our bankers are the worst of the lot. Harold here will pump you for free advice all night long if you let him. Harold, one more offense and I'll have to banish you from my parties."

Barnes bowed to his hostess. "A fate worse than death, Nadia. I will abide by your proscription."

"In the meantime, I need to borrow our guest." She led Thorpe to where the two of them could sit on a park bench next to the indoor pond. "I apologize for not having seen that earlier. I'm afraid Luna is still a frontier, and some of the social graces tend to be lost on us."

Thorpe smiled. "Not as much of a frontier as where I come from. Your home is lovely."

"Thank you. John had it built special. I am a native of Earth, and in the early years of our marriage I used to complain about being forced to live in a cave. This—" She let her arm sweep around the living area. "—is his revenge."

"It's still beautiful."

"We like it. I see you've finished your drink. Would you care for another?"

"Perhaps a glass of wine. I have to navigate back to my hotel tonight."

Nadia Hobart got up and returned with a glass of white wine, then asked Thorpe how he was enjoying Luna City. He explained that he had not seen much yet, but that he had several days in which to sightsee. She suggested a list of sights within the city and recommended a tour operator who would take him to the Tranquility Monument. They were still discussing the local points of interest when the cook announced that dinner was served.

After dinner Hobart invited Thorpe to his study with two other men. One turned out to be Harold Barnes, the banker.

"Bourbon, Mr. Thorpe?"

"Just a small one."

"It's quite good," the M.P. said as he filled a small glass, with long sides to control the liquid in the Moon's low gravity. "We distill it ourselves. It would make an excellent export item if it weren't for certain reactionary elements on Earth who forbid it."

Thorpe nodded. Earth's import restrictions were an irritation for all the space habitats. Surrounded as they were by an inexhaustible supply of vacuum, space distillation was easy and cheap. Fearing the competition, Earth's distillers had long ago banded together to outlaw the importation of extraterrestrial liquors.

When each man had a glass in hand, John Hobart turned to his guest. "How goes the comet-buying business?"

"I beg your pardon," Thorpe replied as he fought to keep his expression neutral.

His attempt at nonchalance was met by a broad smile. "Come now, Mr. Thorpe. Surely you must realize what resources I have at my disposal. Your appointment with Chancellor Cummings was recorded in the university computer. It didn't take my search routine long to find it. After that, I merely phoned the chancellor and asked what you wanted. Tell me about this comet."

Thorpe gave the Lunarians the same story he had told the chancellor.

"Do you really think this interloper from the deep black is suitable for mining?" Hobart asked.

Thorpe shrugged. "No way to tell until we see the postencounter orbit. We also need to know the composition and size. Our decision depends on whether certain minerals are present in the comet. Still, it's enough of a possibility that Mr. Smith doesn't want to pass it by."

"I got the impression that Willy Grandstaff was surprised when I invited you here tonight."

"He said that such an invitation is most unusual."

"That it is. I almost didn't issue it. I made it to the spaceport tube station before turning back to find you. My associates and I have been discussing an idea for quite some time. We'd like your opinion."

Hobart leaned back in the lounger and clasped his hands across his midsection. "Some people have likened Luna to a giant mining concern. We tunnel everywhere. We tunnel after ice deposits, are forever hollowing out new living volume, and dig for those metals we need for our industries. We get our metals from the same source as Sierra Corporation. We mine asteroids for them. The difference is that your asteroid is free flying, while ours crashed down on the Moon billions of years ago.

"Because of all this tunneling, we find ourselves perennially short of heavy-mining equipment. Despite all our efforts, the equipment manufacturers never seem to catch up. As a result, we are forced to ration the machinery we devote to ice mining, habitat construction, and metals extraction. In order to increase the production of one commodity, we have to cut back in the other two areas.

"Ice is critical to us, Mr. Thorpe. The health of our economy depends on it. It is the source of our water, air, and much of our chemical fuel. At the moment, our inability to expand ice production is stifling our economic growth."

"Build more heavy machinery."

"That requires additional factories, which require additional resources we don't have. What do we do without while we're building the factories? No, we need something which will boost ice production over the short term and give us the time to make long-term investments."

"A good trick if you can do it."

"We think we've found a way," Hobart said. "It has occurred to us that if we were to stop all metals extraction, we could devote that equipment to ice mining."

"But then you'll need another source of metals."

"It has been suggested that *The Rock* could be that source."

"You want us to supply you the way we supply Earth?" Thorpe asked.

"Precisely. And we'll pay for the metal in ice."

"At what rate of exchange?"

"One to be worked out," Harold Barnes said. "Ten tons of iron for every ton of ice would be a reasonable exchange."

"You're talking a hundred thousand tons of ice a year. *The Rock* doesn't need that much. What do we do with the surplus?"

"Sell it to the other habitats," Barnes said. "Believe me, it would make quite a profitable sideline."

"What about your own ice exporters? This will put them out of business."

"We'll see that they are compensated for the loss."

"It's an intriguing offer," Thorpe said. "There's only one problem."

"What is that?" the fourth man asked. Thorpe remembered that he had been introduced as an official of the miners' union.

"How do we get the iron down to you? We use aerodynamic braking for deliveries to Earth. Since Luna doesn't have an atmosphere, that won't work. Nor can we use rockets to land the cargoes. It wouldn't be economical."

"We have a great deal of empty territory, Mr. Thorpe," the union official said. "Why not just drop it into some remote crater?"

"You don't know what you're asking," Thorpe replied. "You can't just drop a million tons of iron moving at a few kilometers per second onto the Moon! You'd spray chunks of Luna all over the place, not to mention the pieces that would go into orbit."

"What if you drop your ore body into deep regolith? Wouldn't that be akin to a water landing?" Hobart asked.

"I suppose if the material were loosely packed in the first place. We could give the ore bodies a wider frontal area to spread out the load. But where would you drop it?"

"Are you familiar with the Orientale Basin?"

"I've heard of it."

"The basin is a large mare on Luna's western limb. A large meteor struck there four billion years ago. Since Orientale was never flooded with magma, the basin floor is composed of loose ejecta from the impact. It is four kilometers deep in places. The compaction quotient is such that it should act almost like a liquid during any such impact."

"What about material splashing?" Thorpe asked. "With your weak gravity, no telling where the loose rocks would come down."

"That, of course, will have to be studied in more detail," Hobart agreed. "Is SierraCorp interested in such a proposition?"

"More than interested," Thorpe replied. "Tell you what. I will report this conversation to Mr. Smith and get back to you after my return from Farside Observatory. Fair enough?"

"Very fair, Mr. Thorpe. We, in turn, will refrain from discussing the idea with Señor Sandoval of System Resources until we hear from you. After all, an asteroid in hand is worth more than one in transit. More bourbon?"

Thorpe looked down at his glass, which was nearly empty. "Perhaps one more, Citizen Hobart. We'll drink to a profitable enterprise for all concerned!"

"No, Mr. Thorpe," Hobart said. "We will drink to the Republic of Luna. May it ever be strong!"

CHAPTER 6

Tom Thorpe sat beside the teenage driver in the control cab of the rolligon and watched as the vehicle's powerful headlamps illuminated the lunar night. Despite the panoramic view, there was not a great deal to see. It was three days after local sunset, and the Farside landscape was as dark as the blackest night on Earth.

It had been twelve hours since the Circumlunar Monorail had deposited Thorpe at Hadley's Crossroads, and four hours since the rolligon had begun the 120-kilometer journey to the observatory. He had seen little since leaving Hadley's except the constantly changing pattern of tire tracks left over from previous trips.

With nothing interesting in view, Thorpe had used the time to organize his thoughts. The morning after the dinner party, he had summarized Hobart's proposition in a long cable to headquarters. He had then booked a seat on the day tour to the Tranquility Monument, where he had viewed another set of tracks—the strange, corrugated bootprints laid down by Armstrong and Aldrin more than a century earlier. The marks of their sample scoops were as distinct as the day they had been made; yet the blue field and red stripes of their flag had faded almost to invisibility.

Upon his return to Luna City, Thorpe was surprised to find an answer to his cable waiting at his hotel. Upon decoding, it read:

AM MOST INTERESTED IN TRADING IRON FOR ICE. CONTINUE YOUR PRESENT ASSIGNMENT, BUT OBTAIN FURTHER DETAILS. OBVIOUSLY, I PICKED THE RIGHT MAN TO SEND TO LUNA. THIS MUST BE WHY THEY PAY ME THE BIG BUCKS!

Halver Smith

That had been the end of Thorpe's vacation. He had spent his remaining days in Luna City studying the economics of ice mining and the selenology of the Orientale Basin. What he learned encouraged him. There was no obvious reason why iron could not be delivered to the Moon in million-ton lots.

Thorpe was suddenly shaken out of his mood as the rolligon rounded a corner and started to slide in the direction of a steep drop off.

"Isn't it dangerous to drive this fast at night?" he asked after the teenage driver had regained control. Like Thorpe, the driver was encased in a lightweight vacuum suit. His suit was metallic blue, although the original hue was hardly recognizable beneath a thick layer of soil. Thorpe's own suit was Day-Glo orange and bore the emblem and registration number of Vern's Suit Rental, Hadley's Crossroads, Luna. It, too, was heavily soiled. Its interior smelled of too many unwashed bodies.

"Better driving at night than in the daytime," the driver responded in his clipped Lunarian accent. "Hate to get caught by a solar flare without my lead underwear."

"That isn't what I meant. Shouldn't you slow down?"

"Naw! I've driven this track a hundred times. Know it like the back of my hand. Oof!"

Thorpe felt his stomach try to climb into his throat as the rolligon hit a bump and bounced two meters into the black sky. They were in zero gravity for two seconds before the vehicle landed with a thump and a spray of dust. The driver turned his head and grinned. His cowlick was clearly visible against the background of the instrument lights. "Sorry about that one, boss. Thought I was over far enough to miss it. That mogul near tipped me over last trip!"

"Then slow down, damn it!"

"Nothing to worry about, boss. The track is smooth as glass from here on in. Observatory's just over that next hill."

Thorpe sat up straight to gaze forward. They had been seeing the lights of Farside Observatory's surface installations sporadically ever since they had climbed over the crater's rim. True to the driver's word, as soon as they topped the hill, a cluster of white lights appeared in the middle distance.

"How far?" Thorpe asked.

"This here mound is called Twelve Klick Rise."

"Twelve kilometers?"

"Little less now. Call it eleven and a half."

"Where are the telescopes?"

"See the main beacon?" the driver asked, referring to the strobing red light mounted on a tower in the center of a cluster of glowlamps.

"Yes."

"*The Big Eye* is to the left of that. You can't see it because it's mostly painted black."

Thorpe settled back in his seat, disappointed. He had expected the big telescopes to be gleaming under floodlamps. But, of course, there was no reason to illuminate them against the lunar night, and every reason not to. A stray beam directed into the mirrors could well destroy an astronomical observation.

They continued down the track and within fifteen minutes pulled up to a Quonset-style surface building covered with a thick layer of lunar soil. The driver spoke briefly into his radio, and a heavy pressure door swung open. The driver pulled his vehicle inside. The door closed, and the rolligon was buffeted by air as the surrounding volume was pressurized.

Thorpe felt his suit go limp around him, but waited to remove his helmet until the driver signaled that it was safe. The air was cold and had a metallic taste.

"End of the line, Mr. Thorpe," the driver said, laughing. "Hope I didn't scare you too much."

"Good thing I went to the head back at the crossroads. That last bump would have made me wet my pants for sure." Thorpe unbuckled his seat belt and got to his feet. The misery of the ride was beginning to fade slightly.

"Come on, let's get you below. You can leave that suit in the locker room. I'll be down to pick it up after I hook up to the lox tanks and make arrangements to get my cargo off-loaded. Approach control said Director Meinz will meet you below."

"Thanks for the ride," Thorpe said, gathering up his kit bag from behind the seat. "It was an experience."

The teenager grinned. "Wait till you see me on the return, when I'm running light. I'll really show you some fancy driving!"

"Mr. Thorpe? I'm Hermann Meinz, Director of the Observatory. This is Niels Grayson, Senior Staff Astronomer."

Thorpe shook hands with the two men he had found waiting as

he exited the lift from the surface. The director was a thin man. His face gave the impression of having been stretched too tightly across his skull. He was hairless save for a fringe of white running around the back of his head. Thorpe estimated that the director was in his seventies. Grayson was in his mid-fifties, dark, and muscular.

"You'll want to get out of that suit," the senior staff astronomer said. "Use the Number Three cubicle."

Thorpe thanked Grayson and turned to the indicated suiting cubicle. He stripped off the suit and abandoned himself to an orgy of scratching before sponging down and donning singlet, shorts, and slippers. Finally he combed his hair, gathered up his kit bag and the vacsuit, and returned to where the reception committee awaited him.

"Shall we adjourn to my office?" Director Meinz asked.

"By all means," Thorpe replied. He hung the suit on a hook where the rolligon driver could find it, then followed the astronomers down a long corridor past a series of emergency pressure doors.

As they walked they passed offices filled with computer terminals and photo interpreting equipment, storerooms, and work places. Despite its isolation, the observatory appeared to have all the amenities, including a fully-equipped gymnasium.

Professor Meinz's office was dominated by a wall-size mural showing the hundred-meter-effective telescope with the sun behind it.

"Chancellor Cummings has briefed us on the purpose of your visit, Mr. Thorpe," the professor said after inviting the other man to sit. "I must say that I am surprised that Sierra Corporation is interested in Comet P/2085 (G)."

"Is that the comet which will pass close to Jupiter?"

"It is. I was even more surprised to discover that Farside Observatory has a commercial interest in the matter."

Thorpe shrugged. "Mr. Smith had our legal department research the history of the Space Claiming Act. The provision giving discoverers sole rights for a decade was intended to protect the scientific value of newly discovered bodies. I don't think the prospect of licensing a commercial developer was ever considered. Whether they thought of it or not, you own the rights and can do with them as you will. We hope you will option them to us."

"Why, Mr. Thorpe?" Niels Grayson asked. "Even if it achieves the most desirable orbit possible, the comet's velocity at perihelion will be on the order of fifty kilometers per second. That hardly makes it an attractive candidate for capture."

Thorpe had an answer ready. "I never said anything about capture, Professor Grayson."

"But the chancellor told us . . ."

Thorpe nodded. "He told you that we want to capture this comet and bring it into high Earth orbit. That was an assumption on his part, one that I didn't correct. If our competitors learn of our interest, perhaps they, too, will reach the wrong conclusion."

"Then I truly don't understand," Grayson said.

"What makes this particular asteroid potentially valuable is not its velocity, but the plane of its orbit. The asteroid will leave Jupiter very nearly in the ecliptic. That is correct, isn't it?"

Grayson nodded. "Within plus or minus two degrees."

"That is what caught Mr. Smith's eye. For some time he has been evaluating an inexpensive method for placing loads into modified Hohmann transfer orbits. To work, they have to be launched from the ecliptic. If we can satisfy that one criterion, we can ship refined organics profitably across interplanetary distances."

"I know of no such work being done," Meinz said sharply.

Thorpe smiled as he had been told to do. "I'm sorry, but I'm not at liberty to discuss it. Trade secret."

The director muttered something about foolishness, then leaned back in his chair. Grayson turned to Thorpe. "I understand that you need additional information before you can make a decision."

"I need to know something about the size and composition of the comet nucleus. Neither was discussed in the Astronomical Union announcement."

"That is because the nucleus is obscured by the surrounding gas cloud. We can't see it yet."

"Not at all?"

"Not with the equipment we've been using."

"That implies that you haven't been using the proper equipment," Thorpe said, gesturing at the mural behind Meinz's desk.

"If you refer to *The Big Eye*, you are correct."

"May I ask why not?"

"The problem is one of access. There are quite a number of

important observing programs in progress at the moment. Even with its multiple object capability, there are only so many directions *The Big Eye* can look at any given moment. I'm afraid it's booked solid for the rest of the year."

"How long would it take to scan for the comet nucleus?"

"One to four hours, depending on viewing conditions inside the coma."

"Surely there must be some slack in the schedule. No one works *that* close to the margin. What do you do if you have a mechanical problem?"

"We reshuffle as best we can," Meinz replied. "And if we come up with any spare time, we have a long waiting list. I'm afraid P/2085(G) doesn't even make the list."

"It could be worth a substantial sum to the observatory. Doesn't that give it priority?"

Meinz cleared his throat. "Point well taken, Mr. Thorpe."

"So how about it? Is SierraCorp's offer worth an hour of *The Big Eye*'s time?"

Meinz did not answer for nearly a minute. Finally, he leaned forward. "It will take a few days to arrange, but we'll see if we can't free up the hundred-meter compound for an hour or so."

"Excellent," Thorpe replied. "Now, if you don't mind, I'd like to turn in. I've been awake for twenty hours straight."

"By all means," Meinz replied. "Professor Grayson will show you to your quarters."

Thorpe slept in late the next morning. It was not often that he allowed himself the luxury. However, save for a tour of the observatory that afternoon, he had nothing scheduled. By the time he had bathed, shaved, brushed his teeth, and dressed, it was nearly 1000 hours.

He managed to locate the staff lounge after getting lost twice. The lounge was empty save for one man working with a hand computer and a pile of printout forms. Thorpe noticed that he was typing one-handed. It took him a moment to realize that the man was missing his right arm. He could not help thinking that had things gone a little differently with his accident, he might have been missing a limb himself.

Thorpe nodded to the man, then proceeded to the food dispenser. Thirty seconds later he found himself holding a covered tray on which rested two pieces of toast, a sealed carton of orange juice, and a large mug of coffee. He carried the food to a table near the main entryway and sat down to enjoy his breakfast.

"Mr. Thorpe?"

The husky contralto voice caught him with a mouth full of toast. Thorpe glanced up to see a tall blond woman standing over him. Her hair was fluffed up around her heart-shaped face in a manner typical of low-gravity environments. The next thing he noticed was the deep blue of her eyes, the upturned nose, and the wide mouth fixed in a friendly smile. Like him, the woman was wearing singlet, shorts, and Moon slippers. On her the outfit looked good. Thorpe hurriedly swallowed and nearly choked as he scrambled to his feet.

"Why, hello!"

"You *are* Mr. Thorpe, aren't you?" the woman asked, her expression turning to one of mild concern.

"That's me."

"Hi, I'm Amber Hastings. Professor Grayson won't be able to guide you today after all. He's tied up in a meeting. He asked me to extend his apologies and to take over for him. I hope you don't mind."

"The day I mind a beautiful woman, is the day I'll lie down so they can throw dirt over me."

"How gallant!" she said. Despite her attempt at sophistication, Thorpe noticed a sudden reddening of her complexion at the compliment. "Mind if I sit down?"

"Please do."

She folded her long legs beneath the table and sat across from him.

"Care for a piece of toast?" he asked.

"No, thank you. It's only two hours until lunch. I don't want to ruin my appetite."

"I thought of holding out, but I'm famished. It must have been the ride in the rolligon."

Amber laughed. "Everyone feels the same way. It's the natural response to having survived the trip."

"I can believe that," Thorpe agreed. "Especially considering the way that young man drives!"

"Oh, you had Varl for a driver? Consider yourself lucky. Compared to his sister, he's the soul of caution."

"You can't be serious!"

"Absolutely. In fact, I'll be going home on leave come the

sunrise run. I just pray Varl will be at the controls. I understand you're here to rent our comet."

He nodded. "If the answers to a few questions come back positive. In fact—" Thorpe stopped and stared at his guide. "Hastings? Of course, you're the astronomer who first discovered it, aren't you?"

"Actually, the observatory computer discovered it. I just reported it."

"I should have recognized your name right off," Thorpe said. "Somehow I had the impression you were a man."

"I'm not."

"So I see," Thorpe replied, using a tone that implied much more.

"Keep it up and you'll turn my head."

"That's the idea."

Neither of them spoke while he finished his juice and coffee. As soon as he had drained the last of the black liquid, Amber suggested that they begin the tour immediately, go until lunch, and then pick up again in the afternoon. He agreed readily. As they left the cafeteria, Thorpe missed seeing the one-armed man write something in his notebook.

Amber led him down two levels and along a corridor until they came to what was obviously a control room.

"This is where we run *The Big Eye*," she said, gesturing to a horseshoe-shaped console. "That is, this is where we direct the computer which controls the telescope."

"Why isn't anyone here?"

"We're on night-operations schedule at the moment. The only thing that can go wrong at night is that one of the telescope segments might drift out of calibration. If that happens, the computer signals the duty staffer, and he attempts to correct the problem. If he can't, he calls maintenance."

"I suppose you shut down during the day."

"Oh, no! Luna has no atmosphere to scatter light, so the sun doesn't faze us at all. We are *very* concerned that *The Big Eye* might transit across the sun when changing positions, however. If Sol is ever allowed to occupy the telescope's prime focus—even for an instant—the heat flux will destroy the telescope. We've got all sorts of safety interlocks built into the system to prevent that from happening. Even so, one of us is always on duty here whenever the sun is up. In fact, I was on day duty when the computer first notified me that it had discovered the comet."

"Discovered how?"

"It caught the coma in a photograph."

"May I see it?"

"Certainly," she replied.

She had him stand to one side while she sat in the operator's chair. A few deft strokes on the keyboard caused the large view-screen to fill with stars. One of them looked different from the others.

"Even though this is our first view of the comet, it is also our best. That's because this picture comes from *The Big Eye*. The numbers across the bottom indicate the date and time, the fact that 102 mirror segments were active, and that the Number Two collector and photointensifier were in use."

"Any evidence of the nucleus itself?"

"Not in this view, but then that particular combination isn't very sensitive to that sort of thing." Amber let her fingers dance across the keyboard, and the scene was replaced by another. It showed the same starfield, but the view was less detailed, as if taken from a greater distance. "This is our second view, taken three weeks later. It's the one that I used to make the preliminary estimate of the comet's orbit. Of course, we've been refining that first estimate on a weekly basis ever since."

"Yes, I know," Thorpe answered. "I have copies of all of the Astronomical Union's updates. I'd be interested in what you've learned that isn't in the reports."

"Not much," Amber responded. "We've seen traces of all the usual constituents: water vapor, carbon monoxide, methane, nitrogen, hydrogen cyanide. That doesn't surprise us. Most of the long-term cometaries show similar patterns of volatile outgassing."

Thorpe nodded. "Professor Grayson mentioned that last night. He also said that you couldn't put a figure to the object's size yet."

"Not yet. It could be anywhere from a small snowball to a large moon."

"I imagine you astronomers will learn quite a lot from the close encounter with Jupiter. After all, this sort of thing doesn't happen very often!"

"It happens more often than you might think."

"Oh?"

"I don't mean that we see asteroids or comets zipping to within two million kilometers of Jupiter every day. This will definitely be the closest encounter ever observed by human beings. But old Jupe has quite a reach on him. He's responsible for the orbits of about half the periodic comets in the Solar system. Believe me, on the scale of the universe, this is pretty small potatoes. If it weren't, they'd assign someone more senior than a junior staff astronomer to follow up. In fact," Amber predicted, "I'd be willing to bet that ten years from now, no one will even remember Comet P/2085(G)."

Later, Thorpe would have reason to regret not taking that bet.

CHAPTER 7

The main control room for *The Big Eye* was crowded with onlookers as a study of Cepheid variables in the Andromeda Galaxy slowly wound to an end. The Andromeda study was the last of three concurrent observation programs that had been running, three in a never-ending stream of demands for the big telescope.

As the time-remaining clock clicked off the last few minutes, Amber Hastings worked steadily at putting the final touches on the comet-viewing program. Unlike the sixty-centimeter telescope, *The Big Eye* would study the comet in wavelengths extending from the near infrared to the far ultraviolet. The telescope would remain split into three sections for the first thirty minutes. Each would be optimized for a different portion of the spectrum. Then *The Big Eye*'s 400 active segments would be combined into a single powerful instrument. The remainder of the viewing program would be spent trying to pick out the tiny spark of the nucleus amid the general haze of the coma. If that proved impossible, Amber had provided an option for detecting the nucleus's presence.

The region through which Comet P/2085(G) was currently passing was one of the most thickly populated in the heavens.

Amber had arranged the coma observations to take advantage of that. By analyzing the spectra of stars shining through the gas cloud, she could map the coma's structure. That would allow her to make deductions concerning the nature of the unseen nucleus. And, should the nucleus happen to occult one of the myriad background stars, that would give her a direct measure of its size.

"Viewing program recorded and locked in," Amber reported as she finished her work. "Two minutes to go before we take control."

Hermann Meinz nodded. He, Grayson, and Tom Thorpe all stood in a loose clump behind Amber. Several other members of the observatory staff stood patiently behind a rope barrier. Even John Malvan, the government auditor, had taken time off to watch the excitement. Thorpe had met Malvan at a dinner party thrown by Niels Grayson and his wife two evenings previous.

"Hello," Thorpe had said after being introduced. "I saw you the first morning I was here. You were in the lounge working on some papers."

Malvan nodded. "It's about the only place I've found where I can spread out properly. I must say that I was pleased to hear of SierraCorp's interest in leasing the comet. The royalty payments will go a long way toward ending the observatory's financial problems."

"I imagine they will," Thorpe replied, feeling guilty. Had Halver Smith truly intended to mine the nucleus, the yearly payments would have exceeded the observatory's operating costs. Too bad there would never be a production lease. Still, the option payment was more than generous. It would alleviate the current crisis.

"Observation program is ending," Amber announced to her audience. "Stand by to reposition telescope."

Galaxy M31 faded from the screen, to be replaced by a panoramic view of *The Big Eye*. It was still night topside, but light amplification circuits showed the telescope as a fuzzy green image. As the telescope pivoted, the movement was less a turning of the main structure than a group of independent movements by its mirrors. It was almost like watching something alive stir from a long sleep.

Two minutes later Amber announced that the telescope was locked on target and that data was flowing. Simultaneously, a crowded starfield appeared on the main screen. There were so many stars that it was difficult to spot the hazy patch of light that was their target.

"What's happening?" Thorpe whispered after ten minutes with no apparent activity.

"We're taking data," Grayson said in a normal voice. As he spoke, a low tone sounded.

"What was that?"

"The computer has enough information to reconstruct the coma's structure," Amber answered over her shoulder. She typed a command into the control board to put an image up on the screen.

The screen showed a diagram that bore a striking resemblance to the contour lines on a map. The pattern of concentric circles overlapped several background stars.

"The nucleus is at the center of the isophote rings," Grayson said, pointing to the diagram.

"The what?" Thorpe asked.

"Lines of constant brightness. I think we're going to get lucky. The pattern center is damned close to that Magnitude Eight star."

Almost as if his words were a signal, Amber exclaimed, "I've got occultation!"

Thorpe looked up to see an electronically generated box flash on the screen where the star had been. It was gone, covered up as the comet's invisible nucleus interposed itself between star and telescope.

"Occultation has ended," Amber reported fifteen seconds later.

"Damn, that took a hell of a long time," Grayson muttered beside Thorpe.

"What does that mean?" Thorpe asked.

"It means that the nucleus is larger than any of us thought," Director Meinz replied.

"How much larger?" Thorpe asked.

"A hell of a lot larger," Grayson responded.

A sudden silence descended over the control room as Amber went to work converting the occultation time into a size measurement.

Tom Thorpe used the lull to consider the import of the information. If the nucleus were larger than a few kilometers, there would be no possibility of nudging it from its postencounter orbit. The energy required would be prohibitive. And that would be Halver Smith's defense against stock manipulation. Should anyone be foolish enough to announce a capture program, it would be a simple matter to discredit them with a few well-placed calls.

Somehow the thought of saving Sierra Corporation the cost of the exploitation option did not make Thorpe as happy as it should have. After pondering that for a moment, he concluded that he was feeling let down. It had been exciting to watch the data pour in and to have the comet's cloak of mystery peeled away. Something inside him wanted the excitement to continue. For the first time he understood what drove astronomers to spend their lives peering into the deep black. The years of lonely observation could be made worthwhile in a single moment of discovery.

The end of the hour came quickly. As Amber turned control back to the computer, onlookers began drifting away, leaving the principals clustered around the control station. One of the few onlookers to remain was John Malvan.

"It will take quite some time to reduce all of this data," Amber said, looking at Thorpe, "but I can give you some preliminary conclusions. I make the nucleus's diameter to be between four hundred and five hundred kilometers. It is definitely a volatile-rich comet nucleus, although one that appears remarkably solid. Does that sort of body meet SierraCorp's specifications?"

Thorpe opened his mouth as he prepared to deliver the bad news, then closed it again. An odd thought had just occurred to him. He struggled to keep a straight face as he asked Amber to amplify on her findings.

She explained that the nucleus was large enough that it was probably a solid body rather than the loose conglomeration of snowballs that characterize most cometary nuclei. Their coma observations proved that the nucleus was mostly water ice in composition, although with all of the other impurities common to comets. Since the nucleus was a solid body, it would be unlikely to break up under Jupiter's gravitational influence.

"Well, Mr. Thorpe," Director Meinz said. "Are you prepared to sign a Letter of Intent?"

Thorpe paused and appeared to be struggling with a decision. After a minute he looked at Meinz. "I will need much more detailed data on the composition, Mr. Director."

"You'll get as much as our computers can wring out of sixty minutes of observations by the system's largest telescope."

"Very well," Thorpe said. "We'll take a chance. Shall we say five minutes in your office?"

"That will be fine, Mr. Thorpe," Meinz replied, trying mightily to disguise his relief.

At the back of the control room John Malvan frowned. Something was bothering him, and he could not figure out what it was.

Halver Smith sat and stared at the flames flickering in his library fireplace. He was old-fashioned enough to want to burn natural wood, and rich enough that he could afford it. He had long maintained that neither gas nor synthetic celluloid could ever compare with the crackling fire and pungent odor of real pine. That night he watched the flames in the darkened room and contemplated the future.

As he had explained to Tom Thorpe two weeks earlier, SierraCorp was facing a short-term liquidity crisis. Only Smith knew how critical the situation really was. As business schools the world over taught, there were only five ways in which capital could be obtained. It could be earned, borrowed, withdrawn from savings, obtained through sale of assets, or received as a gift. *The Rock*'s capture had been largely financed through borrowing and gifts—which was all the sale of stock really was. For a long time it had seemed that those two sources would be sufficient. Once the banks saw projections of asteroidal iron sales, they were generous with easy credit. The same projections had insured that stock sales were brisk. A public fascinated by the project had snapped up the stock issues almost before they were released.

The price of SierraCorp shares had nearly doubled in the five years it had taken to move *The Rock* to Earth orbit. Their value had risen another thirty percent on the day the first ore body splashed down off the coast of Brazil. And the stock had not been hurt by glowing press reports concerning the amount of iron that SierraCorp would be delivering.

Three years later reality had taken hold as actual production figures displaced fictional ones. With the continued progress of the Avalon Project, the bloom had further gone off Halver Smith's rose. For the first time, SierraCorp's stock began to slip in value. The decline of the stock had triggered the banks to reevaluate their attitude. Suddenly, Sierra Corporation's line of credit was no longer unlimited. Requests for loan extensions were denied while new loans were negotiated for shorter periods at higher rates.

Nor were the investors and banks Smith's only problem. The same politicians who once had spoken in support of space iron were muttering about the loss of jobs at home. The same surface mining operations that had once been polluters of the air and water had become home-grown industry. Talk of protectionism was in the air. Both United Europe and the North American Union had laws pending to tax space iron. Two African nations had banned the import of space iron altogether.

Smith's immediate problem was how to refinance some of the long-term notes that were coming due. If he could refinance at reasonable rates, it would give *The Rock* time to reach full production, thereby ending the liquidity crisis forever. It was the skittish financiers who most worried Smith. That was the reason he had dispatched Tom Thorpe to the Moon. Better to waste a little money now than to risk a panic in asteroid mining stocks when someone announced the formation of a capture program.

As he sat and gazed into the fire, Smith considered his remaining sources of ready cash. With investment and borrowing cut off, and with no savings worthy of the name, there was only one option left. He would have to sell off assets.

The only facility that would bring a high enough price was the Sierra Skies Powerstat. Smith had acquired Sierra Skies to provide *The Rock* with a ready source of antimatter on its long flight to Earth orbit. The station would bring a good price, but its sale would be a danger signal to every financial analyst in the system. Once word got around that Halver Smith was shedding assets, it could well trigger a feeding frenzy by banks and investors. As Smith considered the problem of raising money without seeming to need it, he was interrupted by one of his servants.

"What is it, Emil?" he asked, squinting into the sudden bright light from the hallway as the servant opened the library door.

"The night operator at headquarters is on the screen, sir. She asks if you will take a phone call from the Moon."

"The Moon? Who?"

"Thomas Thorpe, sir."

"I'll take it in here."

"Yes, sir."

Smith turned on the light next to his chair and was momentarily dazzled. He swung the phone screen into place and activated it. The features of one of the operators at Sierra Corporation headquarters faded into those of Tom Thorpe.

"Hello, Thomas. Where are you calling from?"

Three seconds later Thorpe's features came alive. "Good evening, sir. Farside Observatory. I hope I didn't disturb you."

"Not at all. What news?"

"Both the observatory director and I have signed the Letter of Intent."

"Good!" Smith replied. "Give me the details."

"Please go to scrambler."

Smith blinked, then reached out and engaged the scrambler. There was a moment of interference that quickly cleared.

"Scrambler engaged. Now what the hell is this all about?"

"Matters have changed, sir. I had to make a quick decision. I hope it was the right one."

"Explain!"

Thorpe described all that he had learned at the observatory, including the fact that the comet nucleus was 500 kilometers in diameter.

"Say again, please," Smith ordered.

"That is five hundred—five zero zero!—kilometers in diameter."

"Why did you sign the letter? Surely you must know anything that large can't be moved!"

"Agreed, sir. We did a little calculation. The nucleus masses at least six-to-the-sixteenth-power tons. That's *sixty million billion tons*!"

"So why do it?"

"Because, sir," Thorpe said, "that's sixty million billion tons of *ice*! Water ice, methane ice, ammonia ice."

"So?"

"I've been studying the economics of ice mining. There is a very large market for it everywhere in space. I remembered something you wrote in your thesis on asteroid mining. You said that the early mines in the asteroid belt would not have failed if their product had been worth just five times more than it was."

Smith nodded. "I remember the paragraph well. So what?"

"So, ice is ten times more valuable than iron! By your calculations, it's the one thing that can be shipped interplanetary distances at a profit. Anyway, I took a chance that you might want to get into the ice-mining business. You can always say that I exceeded my authority and denounce the whole deal."

There was a long pause while Smith adjusted to the fact that he was the proud owner of an interplanetary iceberg. He had read somewhere that all the water on Earth massed 1.2 billion billion tons. That meant that twenty such icebergs would fill every ocean on the planet. What, by the fickle gods of Wall Street, was he going to do with that much ice? It was sheer lunacy to think of taking on another major enterprise with Sierra Corporation's finances in their current sad state.

Yet, this could also be the miracle he had been hoping for. What was needed was a new factor in the equation, something to stir the pot. If Sierra Corporation were suddenly to announce a new asteroid mining venture, it would breathe new life into the investors and banks. He would, in effect, be changing the subject. An expedition to the comet would be necessary, of course. Anything less would appear phony. Still, initial exploration need not be expensive. If, like the option payment, they kept Smith's creditors at bay for a while longer, the money would be well spent.

"Did you hear me, Mr. Smith?" Thorpe asked anxiously from 400,000 kilometers away.

Smith's grim features slowly dissolved into a smile. "I heard you, Thomas. Don't worry, I'll hold up my end. I'm not sure exactly what we're going to do with our prize, but I'm willing to invest in an expedition to look it over. You may have just solved more problems than you know!"

At the same time Thorpe was on the phone to Halver Smith on Earth, another call was made from Farside Observatory. John Malvan was attempting to get in touch with John Hobart. After fifteen minutes of working his way up through levels of subordinates, he finally found himself face to face with the leader of the Nationalist Party of Luna.

"Yes, Citizen Malvan? My secretary said that this is a matter of utmost urgency to the Republic."

"Yes, sir."

"You look familiar. Do I know you?"

"I'm an auditor for the Committee on Scientific Appropriations. We met at a party about a year ago. I doubt that you would remember me."

"You used to be an ice miner, didn't you?" One of the talents that had served Hobart well in politics was an almost photographic memory for peoples' names and faces. "Minus an arm, as I recall."

"Yes, sir."

"I remember you," the politician responded. In truth, that was about all he remembered, but long practice had taught him to leave the impression that his memory of a caller was complete. "What can I do for you, citizen?"

"They've made a discovery here at the observatory that I think you should know about, sir." Malvan went on to detail essentially the same information that Thorpe had given to Smith. When he finished, he said, "I thought you ought to know about this."

"And you say the director of the observatory has already signed this Letter of Intent?"

"Yes, sir. I remember it bothered me at the time, but I hadn't thought it through."

"I can still intervene. An ice asteroid five hundred kilometers in diameter, you say?"

"Yes, sir. Then you agree that this might be important?"

"You were right to call me. Keep your ears open and keep me informed. Copy down this number!" Hobart held a card on which his private phone number was printed. The call would be automatically routed to his office, home, or personal phone day or night.

"I'll keep you informed," Malvan said when he finished copying the number.

"Good-bye, Citizen Malvan. And thank you!"

John Hobart sat and stared at the phone screen for long seconds after it went blank. The ramifications of the comet were both frightening and exciting. They would have to be studied before anything final was allowed to happen—which meant that a certain chain of events had to be stopped immediately.

Hobart reached out and pushed the buzzer for his secretary.

"Yes, sir?"

"Please get Chancellor Cummings on the phone, Miss Cates. I want to speak to him about a matter of some urgency."

CHAPTER 8

"Attention, all passengers! Sunrise in thirty seconds. Take all necessary precautions."

The announcement echoed through the Circumlunar Monorail as the string of stubby cylinders pierced the darkness of the long lunar night. Tom Thorpe searched the horizon for some sign of impending dawn. At first there was nothing but dark beyond the triple-pane window. A moment later the train topped the scarp it had been climbing, and the sun was a full hand's width above the horizon. The transition from pitch-black to blinding light was nearly instantaneous.

Thorpe grunted in pain as twin daggers thrust themselves into the backs of his eyes. He quickly averted his gaze, but not fast enough to prevent green afterimages from swimming in front of him. "Damn, that was fast!"

"That's why they warn you," Amber said from beside him. "I should have said something. I saw you staring out the window, but didn't realize that you weren't aware of what was coming. I assumed you knew the danger because of your work on *The Rock*."

Unlike Earth, where dawn was heralded by a gradual brightening in the eastern sky, sunrise on any airless body was a more violent affair. The only warning came when higher elevations were illuminated by the sun. In cases where no higher ground was visible, the onset of each day was like switching on a light, especially at 300 kph.

Thorpe peeked out through slit eyelids, then slowly opened his eyes fully. After staring at the back of his own hand, he let his gaze sweep the interior of the passenger module. The one thing he avoided was the window and the furnace landscape beyond. Just thinking about it made his eyes water. "I don't think I damaged anything."

"I can ask the steward for an ice pack if your head hurts."

"Not necessary. Besides, I'd just as soon not admit to such a fool stunt. He might think me a tourist."

She laughed. "A fate worse than death!"

Having finished his business at Farside Observatory, Thorpe had arranged for passage on the predawn rolligon to Hadley's Crossroads. He had been surprised to discover Amber Hastings already aboard when he climbed through the open hatchway into the big vehicle's passenger cabin.

"What are you doing here?" he had asked as he took the seat next to hers.

"I'm going home on leave!"

"That's right. You mentioned that, didn't you?"

She had nodded, the gesture barely visible through the helmet of her vacuum suit. "I worked late last night to clean up all the loose ends from the comet. I didn't want to have to wait another two weeks for the next run."

"Glad you're here. Having someone to talk to will take my mind off Varl's driving."

Thorpe quickly discovered that Amber did indeed take his mind off the journey. He became so absorbed in her company that he barely noticed when the rolligon became spaceborne for nearly five full seconds.

They had confined their conversation to small talk at first, but matters had quickly turned more personal. Thorpe found himself telling her the story of his life. She reciprocated with tales of what it was like to grow up in the underground warrens of Luna. Afterward they sat in silence for long minutes until a wild maneuver by the rolligon's driver touched off a round of jokes. By the time they reached Hadley's Crossroads, they were nearly choking on laughter inside their suits.

They had been lucky in that they only had to wait two hours for a monorail to Luna City. Fifteen minutes out of Hadley's the speeding train intercepted the terminator, giving Thorpe his painful lesson. Ten minutes after that Amber pointed to a jagged mountain that rose above the horizon.

"See that peak over there?"

Thorpe glanced across the stark landscape at the distant peak and nodded.

"That is Devil's Scarp. They lost a scouting expedition back there just after the turn of the century. Five men vanished without a trace."

"How can anything vanish on the Moon? They must have left tracks."

She shook her head. "They were using a moonjumper. Last word was that they were setting down near the scarp."

"Landing accident?"

"Probably."

Thorpe nodded. He had seen the rocket craft that served the same function as aircraft did on Earth. A moonjumper looked a lot like the Apollo lunar modules, or the landing craft that had ferried Thorpe to the Luna City spaceport. Four splay-footed legs surrounded a rocket motor with a pressurized cabin on top. The jumpers did not fly like aircraft. Rather, they launched themselves into ballistic paths, then slowed their plunge with rockets for landing.

"And no one found any remains?"

Amber shook her head. "No trace. Some think that they set down on a slope and started a slide that buried them. Me, I often wonder if they aren't just sitting out there waiting for someone to come along. Maybe in a billion years . . ."

"I take it that Luna isn't that well explored," Thorpe said.

"It's hardly explored at all. Especially here on Farside. Oh, we have orbital pictures, of course. That isn't the same as ground exploration. Remember, Luna's surface area is thirty-eight million square kilometers. That's roughly one-quarter the land area of Earth. Our population is only ten million, and even the simplest trip outside requires careful preparation. You can see the problem."

"You've done remarkably well, considering the amount of time people have lived on the Moon. Look at Earth. It was only a couple of hundred years ago that human beings finally explored it all. Even now there are parts of the deep oceans that no one has ever visited."

"Earth," Amber said wistfully. "I'd like to see it someday. Especially the oceans. It must be frightening to actually be in water over your head!"

"You'll probably get a chance to find out for yourself before long."

"Why do you say that?"

"You are the discoverer of Comet P/Hastings, aren't you?"

Amber groaned. "Please, that joke isn't funny!"

"It's no joke. I talked to Niels Grayson before we left. He said that the System Astronomical Union has tentatively chosen that name. I understand that it's a long tradition to name comets after their discoverers."

"I'm *not* the discoverer! The observatory computer found the damned thing. All I did was punch a few buttons." She told him of her problems when she had been asked to name the comet.

"You can't fight it, you know."

"Fight what?"

"Fame and fortune. The media won't let you. I can see the stories now: 'Beautiful Young Astronomer Discovers Spectacular New Comet!'"

"That is precisely why I don't want the damned thing named after me," Amber replied. "It's going to be a circus once they discover just how spectacular it's likely to be. For someone so new to the profession to gain such notoriety is damaging. Look at Clyde Tombaugh. He discovered Pluto when he was my age, then went on to do some really first-class work on galactic clusters. No one remembers that later work. All they remember is Pluto!"

"Maybe the comet will be a dud," Thorpe said facetiously. "That way no one will notice."

Amber shook her head. "It will be hard *not* to notice this one, Tom. With its mass, it will sprout a tail a billion kilometers long. Worse, the orbital period will be less than a decade. In the years it sweeps close to Earth, it will likely extend across the entire vault of the sky!"

"Just how close is it likely to come?"

She shrugged. "No way to tell until after the encounter with Jupiter."

"No chance of it running into anything important, is there?"

"No chance at all," she said, laughing. "A planet is just too small a target."

"Then how do you explain all the shooting stars in Earth's skies over the years?"

"Simple. There are an awful lot of them! The ecliptic is fairly crowded with the flotsam left over from the Solar system's formation. The vast majority of that debris is too small to be dangerous. The Earth is struck by something as large as a kilometer about once every million years."

"Yet Comet Hastings will orbit in the ecliptic."

"*Near* the ecliptic," Amber replied, her manner suddenly serious. "If its orbital inclination is more than plus or minus three thousandths of a degree, it can never, ever run into the Earth. And please don't suggest that it can, not even in jest! Every reporter in the system will want my opinion on the coming apocalypse."

"I promise," Thorpe said, raising his hand in the three-fingered Boy Scout sign. Amber dissolved into laughter. Thorpe joined her. Suddenly their conversation of the last few minutes seemed unbelievably silly.

The main transportation hub for Nearside was the Luna City Spaceport. In addition to its being the jumping-off point for the ships of deep space and the local suborbital craft, all surface routes converged there. The main station for the Circumlunar and Tycho monorails was a sprawling complex in the spaceport's northeast quadrant. The train on which Tom Thorpe and Amber Hastings were passengers passed through the big airlock at Luna City Station some nineteen hours after departing Hadley's Crossroads. Twelve of those hours had been spent in transit. The rest were the result of numerous stops to discharge and take on passengers and cargo.

Unlike the high-speed machines of Earth, the Circumlunar monorail lacked any hint of aerodynamic sleekness. Its shape was dictated not by the wind, but rather by reliability and maintainability considerations. Not even the engineers who had designed the monorail modules thought the result beautiful. To Thorpe's eye, the chain of cars looked like six beer cans strung together by a slightly drunken model builder.

By the time the train arrived at Luna City Station, Thorpe and Amber had been in each other's company for more than twenty-five hours. That included six hours in which they had snuggled together under a single blanket and tried to sleep. There were few better ways to get to know another person, especially one of the opposite sex.

"Home at last, Thomas!" Amber said as the distant sound of expanding air reached them through the monorail's hull. The sound brought with it a sudden swirling of expansion fog against the cabin windows.

Thorpe admired her form frankly as she got out of her seat and stretched to get the kinks out of her muscles. She then turned to the overhead rack where the hand luggage had been stowed.

"Here, let me help you with that," Thorpe said as he hurriedly got to his feet. She handed him two pieces of hand luggage and his briefcase containing the partially executed Letter of Intent. He juggled all three pieces until they were comfortable, then followed her toward the airlock at the back of the module.

The air outside had the cold, metallic taste of having just come from high-pressure storage. Amber led the way to an escalator that passed into an upward-sloping tunnel. Half a minute later they entered a large dome with windows set around the perimeter. Thorpe had been there before—it was Luna City's main transit hall.

As they moved toward baggage claim, Amber led Thorpe to one of the windows and pointed to a series of towers that marched across the lunar plain.

"The mass driver," she said. "My father used to bring me here to watch the cargo pods. I'd never seen anything go so fast in my whole life. Here comes one now!" Amber pointed at the most distant tower.

A stubby cylinder appeared in the distance, shot across the gap between two towers, and raced for a third. At each tower it picked up momentum. Within seconds it had closed the distance to the transit hall, flashed by, and was gone.

Thorpe's attention was diverted as he caught sight of Willem Grandstaff's reflection in the window. SierraCorp's lunar representative was just emerging from a tunnel leading from the Luna City tube station. Grandstaff halted, scanned the crowd, saw Thorpe, and waved. Thorpe waved back, and Grandstaff started across the open expanse between them.

Thorpe turned back to Amber. "Are we still on for tonight?" Amber had a twelve-hour layover between the monorail's arrival and the departure of the moonjumper for Miner's Luck.

"I wouldn't miss it! Formal dress?"

He shrugged. "Any way you like."

"Definitely formal, then. I'll meet you in the lobby of your hotel at 2000 hours."

"I can pick you up."

Amber shook her head. "I doubt you could find my friends' apartment," she said. "They live in one of the new residential rings down on Sixth Level. You'd get lost for sure. No, I'll see you at your hotel."

At that moment Willem Grandstaff reached the two of them. Thorpe introduced him to Amber and made sure that Grandstaff knew she was the discoverer of the comet.

"Good afternoon, citizen," Grandstaff said, bowing deeply. "I understand that your discovery is quite a find."

"It's big!" Amber said with a laugh. "How suitable it is for your purposes, I can't say. I only hope that Halver Smith isn't wasting his money."

Grandstaff laughed. "Mr. Smith seldom *wastes* money. He has been known to make some very long-term investments, however."

Thorpe checked the chronometer hanging at the apex of the dome. It was 1500 hours on a Friday evening. Their appointment with Chancellor Cummings was for 1600. If they were late, it would be Monday before he could get his Letter of Intent signed.

"We'd better hurry," he told Grandstaff. "We've got an appointment in an hour."

"Plenty of time, Mr. Thorpe," the representative replied. "The university is only fifteen minutes from here by tube."

Amber waited on the platform of the tube station while Grandstaff and Thorpe entered one of the small cars that shuttled between the spaceport and Luna City. She waved as the car accelerated away from the platform and entered a brightly lit tunnel. Thorpe waved back, twisting in his seat to do so. He watched her out of sight, then turned to face forward.

"What news from Earth?" he asked.

"Mr. Smith has been running financial simulations ever since you reported to him. He's very excited about it. Once we have the exploitation rights sewn up, he will begin preparations to float a new issue of Sierra Corporation stock." Grandstaff went on to explain Smith's plan to reinvigorate SierraCorp's finances. "I wouldn't be surprised if Mr. Smith offers you command of the expedition!" he finished.

Grandstaff's account caught Thorpe by surprise. He had not talked to Smith since that night he called from the observatory. Thorpe had been both relieved and gratified when the SierraCorp chairman had backed his signing of the Letter of Intent. He had assumed Smith had seen the same commercial potential that he had. It was a shock to learn the big boss was using the comet's future notoriety to sell stock. Was that not precisely what he had sent Thorpe to Luna to prevent?

"Are you sure about all of this?" Thorpe asked.

Grandstaff nodded. "I received a long coded telex yesterday. Mr. Smith was emphatic that we are to obtain that option as quickly as possible. He authorized doubling the payment if necessary. Is something the matter?"

"Nothing," Thorpe replied. He settled back in his seat to consider how best to make his case to Smith that Comet Hastings was far more than an expedient financial ploy. With proper support, vast mountains of ice could be en route to Luna and the space habitats within a few years.

Ten minutes after leaving the spaceport, the car pulled into the university tube station. The car entered a loading area, and Thorpe climbed out while Grandstaff settled his account with the machine.

On the way from the station to the chancellor's office, they passed serious-faced students hurrying between classes. At the midpoint of their walk they came to a large cavern at the center of the university complex. The cavern reminded Thorpe of a miniature Grand Concourse. A small artificial sun was suspended from the roof, illuminating a forest of green arrayed up each of the high walls. The Office of the Chancellor was not far from the cavern.

When they arrived, they were ushered in by a blond receptionist.

"Ah, Mr. Thorpe, welcome back!" Cummings said as he advanced across the room to shake Thorpe's hand. "I understand you had a successful trip!"

"It was certainly an interesting one, Mr. Chancellor."

"You have the Letter of Intent with you, of course."

Thorpe took the letter out of his briefcase and passed it across the desk. "All that is required is your signature, after which we will transfer the funds to the university bank account."

"Everything certainly appears to be in order," Cummings said after a full minute of studying the document. He did not, however, reach for a pen.

Grandstaff prodded him gently. "If you will add your signature, Mr. Chancellor, we won't take up any more of your valuable time."

"I would very much like to do that, Willy. The university needs the money. Unfortunately, I cannot."

"I don't understand," Thorpe said.

"Gentlemen, I was informed this morning that an emergency bill has been introduced into Parliament that will make the Comet Hastings discovery rights the property of the Republic. Under the circumstances, I can't very well sign away those rights. To do so could cost me my appointment as chancellor."

"What's Parliament's interest in this?" Grandstaff asked. "Who introduced the bill?"

"John Hobart. He has plans for the comet. Rather than use it as a source of organics, he proposes to ship it in quantity to Luna and alleviate our water shortage." Cummings shrugged. "So you see, gentlemen, my hands are tied."

Thorpe and Grandstaff quizzed the chancellor gently for another ten minutes before excusing themselves. Both men hid their disappointment until they were outside the university's jurisdiction.

"Well, what do you suppose happened?" Grandstaff asked.

"Someone figured out what we were up to and got word to Hobart."

"Someone at the observatory?"

"Who else?"

"Any ideas?"

Thorpe shrugged. "It could have been anyone."

"Miss Hastings?"

"I doubt it," Thorpe replied. "If she had a hand in this, I think she would have given me a hint on the trip here. No, it was probably Director Meinz or Niels Grayson. They must have begun thinking in nonastronomical terms and realized just how valuable that much ice might be."

"Mr. Smith is counting on us to obtain those rights for him. What we need is some method of placing a legal claim on the nucleus. It wouldn't have to be a very strong claim, just one good enough to make the Republic amenable to reason."

Thorpe thought for a moment, then brightened. "I may have just the thing!"

CHAPTER 9

The Grand Concourse was a mass of milling humanity as Tom Thorpe and Amber Hastings made their way upramp against a Friday night crowd. The reason for the general downslope motion could be heard wafting up from the park below. The Luna City Philharmonic, assembled on the cavern floor 200 meters below, was playing a medley of songs dating from the days of the revolution.

As they strolled, Thorpe could not help stealing sidelong glances at his companion. The Amber Hastings he had left in the tube station had been rumpled. Her bloodshot eyes, smudged face, stringy hair, and wrinkled clothing were testimony to the long hours spent in transit. The Amber Hastings who had arrived at his hotel was a woman transformed. Gems were sprinkled through her blond tresses, which were piled atop her head. Her face was thinner than it had been, and her red-lined mouth wider. Her skin glowed with the inner radiance that could only have been produced by the most expensive cosmetics.

Her face and coiffure were accentuated by her jumpsuit. The black fabric was a random pattern of opacity and translucence that sparkled with her every movement. The deeply plunging bodice accentuated her barely concealed breasts, while the costume's back was virtually nonexistent. Slits in the fabric gave glimpses of Amber's long legs, which were sheathed in a pair of flare-topped boots. A belt of golden links, along with matching necklace and earrings, completed the outfit.

"My God, when you said formal, you meant it!" was the first thing Thorpe said to her.

"Like it?" she asked, pirouetting for his inspection. "I borrowed it from my college friend, the one I'm staying with."

"It's beautiful! I had no idea you would go to all this trouble. All I have is a tunic and shorts."

"No one looks at what a man is wearing."

"Not while he's in the same room with that outfit," he agreed. Thorpe liked the way she blushed at his compliment.

"I asked the hotel concierge for a few suggestions concerning restaurants," he said. "Only I'm not sure the ones he recommended are fancy enough."

"I've already input our reservation request at Luigi's," she replied. "The city central computer has us down for 2030 hours."

"Where is this restaurant?"

"Upramp about a kilometer from here."

"Come on then," he said, offering her his arm. "Let's start hiking."

Luigi's turned out to be an auditorium-sized cave decorated to resemble a forest clearing on Earth. The sky overhead was black, with myriad stars sprinkled across it. Low on the horizon, a yellow harvest Moon was rising through a gap in the trees. Somewhere in the background they could hear the sound of rushing water, and with it the chirp of insects and the croaking of frogs.

"Beautiful!" Thorpe whispered to Amber as the maitre d' led them to their table.

"I thought you would like it. It's the best simulation on Luna."

Halfway across the clearing a distant white city came into view. The city was situated on a series of hills across a broad river valley. It shimmered in the moonlight without a trace of artificial illumination save for the flickering yellow glow of oil lamps behind many windows. A carpet of dirty white rocks on the hillside turned out to be herds of sheep bedded down for the night. Near each was the campfire of the herdsman.

The maitre d' seated them at their table and then withdrew. Whoever had designed the restaurant had somehow managed to maintain the panoramic view while masking out all save the closest tables. Thorpe sat and gazed in admiration around him. After a moment, though, he chuckled.

"What's the matter?" Amber asked, following his gaze.

"That's a mistake over there," he said, pointing. "That square building on the first hill is the Parthenon, while the circular one in the distance is the Colosseum."

"So?"

"So, one is in Athens and the other in Rome. They're a good thousand kilometers from one another."

"Right next door to each other considering how far both are from here."

"I guess that's right," Thorpe agreed.

They began dinner with champagne that had never been anywhere near France. Afterward they ordered. Thorpe had the veal Parmesan, and Amber chose the scallops tortellini. While they waited, they switched to red wine and ate hot buttered bread sticks.

Dinner went quickly as Thorpe told Amber more stories about life on *The Rock*. Before he knew it, he was finishing a bowl of spumoni while Amber sipped the last of a cup of tea. Music wafted through the restaurant, and couples began to drift toward a dance floor that moments earlier had been a mountain meadow.

"Care to dance?"

"I'd love to."

They danced together through three different tunes with hardly a word between them. Thorpe was acutely aware of Amber's warmth and the smell of her perfume. She fitted herself to him and lowered her head to his shoulder. He let his hand drop to the small of her back, where he lightly caressed her bare skin. He could sense her smile rather than see it.

They continued that way until the music dwindled into inaudibility. With the halt, Thorpe sighed deeply. "I could do this all night, but I think we need to discuss business."

Amber lifted her head from his shoulder. "Business?"

"Come on, let's go back to the table and I'll explain."

They returned to their seats, where Thorpe signaled for more wine. When their glasses were again full, he broached the subject about which he had been thinking furiously since leaving Chancellor Cummings's office.

"I've been in contact with Earth," he lied. "Mr. Smith has had the legal department researching the Space Claiming Act."

"So?"

"So, the law states that rights-of-discovery shall reside in the individual/organization first reporting the discovery."

Amber nodded. "Which is why you and Director Meinz signed that Letter of Intent."

"Precisely. When I left Earth, the legal department was of the opinion that all rights belong to the observatory. They aren't so sure anymore. They think you may also be entitled to rights-of-discovery."

"Me?" Amber asked, startled. "But I didn't do anything. The computer discovered it. All I did was file the sighting report."

"That may be all that is required. The question is whether the slash in individual/organization means *and* or *or*."

"But I'm on the observatory's staff. How can I have any claim on an observatory discovery?"

"I'm not saying that you do. I'm saying that the legal department thinks you *may* have one. You know how lawyers are. They're paid to anticipate the worst. They have advised Mr. Smith that things will be cleaner if we include you in any agreement we reach with the observatory."

Amber's brow knit in confusion. "I don't understand."

"It's simple really. The Sierra Corporation is ready to pay you 100,000 selenes if you will sell us an option on your First Discovery Rights."

"How much?"

"One hundred thousand selenes."

Amber blinked. She then reached for her wineglass and drained it in a single gulp. "Did you say . . . one hundred . . . *thousand*?"

"I did."

"For what?"

"Your signature on a Letter of Intent similar to the one that Director Meinz has already signed."

"But that's silly! I don't *have* any rights-of-discovery."

"Whether you do or don't is a matter for the lawyers. In the meantime, wrapping up this loose end is worth the price to Mr. Smith. Believe me, he can afford it."

She refilled her glass and took another sip of wine. "When do you propose bestowing this windfall?"

"Right now." Thorpe reached into his coat pocket and extracted two identical sets of papers, each wrapped in the light blue backing of legal documents. He handed one to Amber and kept the other. "I didn't want to bring this up tonight, but this would seem my last opportunity. After all, you're going home tomorrow, and I'm headed back to *The Rock*."

When she had finished reading, Amber looked up. "This is insane!"

He shrugged. "My advice is to take the money before the lawyers change their minds."

"But it isn't right!"

"I don't see you twisting my arm."

She chewed on her lower lip and gazed down at the letter Grandstaff had drawn up earlier in the day. "Maybe I should have a lawyer look at this."

"Suit yourself. I would point out, however, that it is virtually the same agreement Director Meinz signed. All it does is give us the exclusive right to negotiate for an exploitation charter. Should you conclude that someone else has made you a better offer, we ask the right to match it. Oh, and should either of us become convinced that the other is negotiating in bad faith, the aggrieved party has the right to petition the International Court of Arbitration."

"That's all it does?"

"That's all. I'd be willing to repeat what I just said before witnesses, if you like."

"It's not necessary," she replied.

"I think it is. Waiter!"

The waiter appeared, Thorpe explained his need, and a few minutes later they had four witnesses—two waiters, a waitress, and a cook. He repeated what he had told Amber about the Letter of Agreement. Afterward he asked Amber and the witnesses to sign the document and then used one of the restaurant's hand terminals to punch in generous tips for the four employees. When the round of signatures was complete, Thorpe folded each of two copies of the contract. One he gave to Amber and the other he returned to his jacket pocket.

"Thank you for your services," he told the hovering witnesses. When they had dispersed, he asked Amber for the number of her bank account. He then used the terminal to punch in a transfer of 100,000 selenes. When he finished, he handed the instrument to Amber to verify the transaction.

She looked at him, wide-eyed from the credit balance that showed on the tiny screen. "That's all there is to it?"

"That's it." Thorpe said. He lifted his glass. "I think this calls for a celebration, don't you?"

"You lied to me!"

Tom Thorpe gazed at Amber's angry features staring out the phone screen and carefully considered his reply. As he did so, he found it particularly difficult to concentrate. One reason lay in the dull throb behind his temples caused by the previous evening's festivities. A more serious impediment was the way his train of thought short-circuited as he remembered how lovely Amber had looked and how happy she had been.

Following Luigi's, they had made their way back to his hotel via several of the Grand Concourse's bars. The concert in the park had long since ended, giving Amber no shortage of strangers willing to toast her good fortune. Somewhere between the third and fourth stops Thorpe had taken her into his arms for a first tentative kiss.

Later they had sought out a dark corner to try again, and their explorations were carried out with an intensity that neither could deny. Afterward it had seemed only natural that Amber accompany him back to his room. The rest of the night had been a kaleidoscope of intertwined limbs, seeking mouths, and passion. Eventually they had fallen asleep in one another's arms. Thorpe had awakened just before noon to discover Amber gone and a note on the nightstand:

Darling,
I thought about waking you, but decided that one of us should get some sleep. It's 0600 hours and I have a moon-jumper to catch. I had a wonderful evening. I hope you will write me at the observatory once you're back on *The Rock*. Perhaps we can take our vacations together next year. If you aren't interested in continuing our relationship, I'll understand. You were wonderful!

Love always,
Amber

Thorpe had spent what was left of the morning nursing his hangover and trying to get over the feeling that he had lost something important. As soon as he was able to speak coherently, he put through a phone call to Halver Smith on Earth. Grandstaff had already informed the home office of the attempt by the Luna parliament to freeze them out. Thorpe told his chief about the agreement with Amber Hastings. He then went on to detail his plan to thwart Parliament. Smith listened quietly, asked a few questions, then gave his approval to proceed.

Five minutes later the phone in Thorpe's room beeped again. He reached out to answer it and found himself face to face with an angry Amber Hastings.

"You lied to me!" she repeated. "I just called Director Meinz. He says that Chancellor Cummings refused to sign your letter. You tricked me. Why?"

"Where are you calling from?" he asked to buy time.

"The spaceport. My flight was delayed. I remembered some things at the observatory and decided to check in. That's when Meinz told me. Why did you lie to me?"

"I never told you that Cummings had signed the letter."

"You let me believe he had."

Thorpe sighed and nodded. "That I did. I felt bad at the time, and even more so now. My only defense is that what I did was necessary."

"Necessary for what?"

Thorpe told Amber about the bill that had been introduced in Parliament nationalizing Farside Observatory's claim. "What else was I to do?" he asked when he was done.

Amber's anger cooled visibly as he spoke, to be replaced by an emotion he could not identify. "But how can the paper I signed possibly change anything?"

He opened his mouth to answer, but was interrupted by a tone from the phone. A line of text scrolled across the base of the screen informing him that John Mahew Hobart was waiting to talk to him.

"Did you tell Director Meinz about our agreement?" he asked.

Amber nodded. "Not more than ten minutes ago."

"Care to bet who he called as soon as you hung up?"

"I don't understand."

"Never mind. Bad joke. Hold on a moment, I have another call."

He switched over to find himself looking at the leader of the Nationalists. Hobart's features were distorted from being thrust too close to the phone pickup. He, too, looked mad.

"What the hell is this I hear about you making some kind of a deal with Amber Hastings, Thorpe?"

"You hear correctly."

"What are you up to?"

"I'm protecting my company's interests, Citizen Hobart, just as you are protecting those of the Republic. Care to discuss the matter?"

Hobart blinked once, thought it over, then pulled back from the phone. His transformation of mood was as quick as any

Thorpe had ever seen. "I would be very interested in discussing it. When and where?"

"This evening. You choose the place."

"My apartment at 1800."

"Fine. Do you mind if I bring Miss Hastings along?"

"Bring anyone you like."

"I'll see you then."

Hobart switched off, causing Amber's call to automatically reconnect. He told her of his conversation with Hobart. "Shall I pick you up?"

"I can find my own way."

"Very well. See you then."

"You're damned right you will!"

When Amber was gone, Thorpe turned away from his screen and reviewed what had just happened. It was, he decided, the best he could have expected. He had never been one to agonize over what might have been. He turned his attention to marshaling his arguments.

"Hello, Mr. Thorpe. Nice to see you again," Nadia Hobart said as she ushered Thorpe into her home. "John is in his study."

"It's a pleasure to see you again, Mrs. Hobart. I hope I'm not intruding."

"Nonsense," she replied as she gave him an appraising look. "When you marry a politician, you learn that a great deal of work gets done outside office hours. Now, if you will follow me . . ."

She led Thorpe to the same room where John Hobart had outlined his plan to trade iron for ice. When they arrived, Thorpe found Amber already there. She was seated in one of Hobart's easy chairs, sipping from a high-rimmed glass of rose-colored liquid. Hobart strode across the room in the easy, space-devouring glide of a native Lunarian. "Ah, Mr. Thorpe. Welcome!"

"Hello," Thorpe replied as he grasped the M.P.'s hand. "Hello, Amber."

"Tom," she responded with an almost imperceptible nod of her head.

"I asked Miss Hastings to show up early. I wanted to find out precisely what happened," Hobart explained. "Refreshments?"

"Please," Thorpe replied. He took a seat next to Amber's. "I'm sorry you missed your flight."

"No problem," she replied. "I'm scheduled on tomorrow's jump to Miner's Luck."

Hobart handed Thorpe a low-gravity glass similar to the one Amber held. It was filled with clear liquid. "I believe you expressed appreciation for our Lunar vodka the last time we met."

Thorpe took the drink, sipped from it, and pronounced it excellent. Hobart took his own seat and smiled in Thorpe's direction. There was very little humor behind the smile.

"I now know *what* happened, Mr. Thorpe. However, I can't figure out *why* it happened. Other than to enrich Miss Hastings's bank account, I see no purpose in your actions. Care to enlighten us?"

Thorpe shrugged. "I arrived in Luna City to find my company about to be frozen out of its interest in Comet Hastings. I acted to establish a legal claim which we can pursue in court if necessary. Naturally, we'd prefer a compromise."

Hobart studied his opponent for long seconds. "Why do you think you've established a claim?" he asked finally. "Since Miss Hastings possesses no rights-of-discovery with regard to this comet, she can't very well sell them to you."

"I think she does have them," Thorpe replied.

"That and a deciselene will get you a pint of air at any dispensary in this city. The fact remains that the Space Claiming Act gives all rights for a period of ten years to the discovering institution. That, Mr. Thorpe, is Farside Observatory, Luna."

"The Space Claiming Act speaks of the discovering 'individual/organization.' That is Amber and Farside Observatory."

"Don't be ridiculous," Hobart replied. "She's an employee of the University of Luna, paid with public funds and utilizing public-owned equipment. The rights-of-discovery are the exclusive property of the Republic and its citizens."

"Then perhaps you should call it Comet Farside Observatory."

Hobart smiled in spite of himself. "Touché! Perhaps we should. What are your intentions in this matter?"

"To come to an amicable agreement, if possible, Citizen Hobart; or to assert Miss Hastings's rights in court, if necessary."

"How can you assert a right that even she doesn't believe she has?"

Thorpe shrugged. "That is a matter for the courts to decide."

"Do you really think there's any court on Luna that will go along with such an outlandish contention?"

"I doubt it," Thorpe replied. "However, since Comet Hastings is nowhere near cis-Luna space, your courts lack jurisdiction. The matter will have to be referred to the International Claims Court in The Hague."

Hobart was quiet for a moment, then understanding slowly dawned on him. "And how long is the backlog in the Hague court these days?"

"Just under twelve years."

Hobart nodded. "By which time the observatory's rights-of-discovery will be totally useless. The comet nucleus will go to whoever first establishes a permanent presence on its surface."

"Precisely."

After a long pause Hobart continued. "You spoke of a compromise, I believe."

"I did."

"What exactly did you have in mind?"

"A joint expedition to explore the nucleus following its encounter with Jupiter," Thorpe replied.

From their reactions, he could see that the suggestion had caught both Hobart and Amber off guard. The M.P. blinked in surprise, while Amber shifted nervously in her chair.

"I beg your pardon," Hobart said.

"We're assuming a great deal based on one telescope observation. What if the ice proves to be less extensive than the astronomers believe, or if the postencounter orbit predictions are wrong? I am suggesting that the Republic of Luna and Sierra Corporation jointly send a ship to take a good look at the prize."

"What sort of arrangement do you have in mind?"

"Sierra Corporation will provide the ship, most of the crew, and some of the scientific personnel. You will provide your own people to fill out the roster, also someone to look after your interests. Finally, we split all costs equally."

"What's to stop us from mounting such an expedition on our own?" Hobart asked. "Luna has ships too."

"Of course you do. And most of them are busy doing important things. Divert them and you are liable to suffer those economic consequences we discussed the last time I was in this room. Also, we would be forced to get a restraining order to stop you. Now, if SierraCorp provides a suitable ship, there will be no adverse impact on your economy. Besides, we have expertise that you need. It is, after all, our business!"

"Who represents SierraCorp on such an expedition?" Hobart asked.

"That is up to Mr. Smith," Thorpe replied. "However, I plan to request that he consider me for the job. Perhaps Amber could represent Luna."

"What about it, Miss Hastings?"

"Sorry, but I must decline."

"I understand," Hobart said. "It will be a long voyage, possibly one filled with hardship. You are probably wise not to go."

"You don't understand at all," Amber replied. There was a sudden light behind her eyes, as if she had made an important decision. "I plan to go, all right. But I'll look after my own interests when I do. After all, if Thomas is right, I own half a comet!"

PART 2

ENCOUNTER
WITH
JUPITER

CHAPTER 10

Having crossed the orbit of Saturn, the planetoid made straight for the largest of Sol's children. One hundred eleven times it had swept in toward the Sun. Always before, fate had placed Jupiter far distant from its path. Not this time. On this approach the planetoid was aimed directly at the world which more than any other gathered wandering bits of flotsam to its breast.

Tom Thorpe floated in front of the phone screen in the crouching position the human body always assumed in the absence of gravity. In that position he appeared at ease. Nothing could have been further from the truth. It was all Thorpe could do to keep his anger under control as he waited for the space-to-ground circuit to clear.

"Mr. Monet's office," a young woman answered after a few seconds delay.

"Is he there?"

"Who may I say is calling?"

"Tom Thorpe."

"And the subject, Mr. Thorpe?"

"The Comet Hastings Expedition."

"Please wait a moment."

Thorpe found himself gazing into a computer-generated light pattern that was supposed to be soothing. In his case it was not working.

"Ah, Mr. Thorpe," Nathan Monet, Sierra Corporation's comptroller, said as he came on the screen. "What may I do for you?"

"You can tell me why your people turned down my order for antimatter, Monet!"

"We in the comptroller's office feel that you were being somewhat . . . shall we say, overzealous?"

"What the hell are you talking about?"

"To be blunt, Mr. Thorpe, my analysts have checked, and find that your request for fuel is far in excess of what you really need. Your own mission plan calls for the expenditure of 4.5 grams of antimatter and eight million kilograms of monatomic hydrogen. Yet you requested nine antimatter grams. That is exactly double your projections."

"I know that," Thorpe growled.

"If I may remind you, Mr. Thorpe, my department has been charged with insuring that we obtain maximum efficiency out of our limited funds. Furthermore, Mr. Smith has requested all divisions to tighten their belts."

"Tighten someone else's belt. I need that antimatter!"

"We feel that five grams would be more than sufficient for your needs," Monet said.

"That's only ten percent above our rock-bottom needs."

"Eleven percent. My people have checked industry practice, and ten-percent energy reserves are quite common."

"On the milk run to Luna Equatorial Station. Damn it, we're going out to chase a comet! We have to assume that things won't go precisely as we planned them."

"A good manager doesn't allow such deviations to occur, Mr. Thorpe. My staff assures me that our allocation is more than fair."

"Your staff isn't risking their collective asses. I am. So is every man and woman spacing with me. Either we get the full nine grams, or we don't leave orbit."

"My God, man! Do you know what antimatter closed at on today's market?"

"I know what my life is worth. More importantly, I know what Mr. Smith will say if he has to settle this argument."

The comptroller stiffened. "You are, of course, free to take the matter to him. I doubt he will approve squandering the corporation's funds."

Thorpe took a deep breath and decided to approach the problem from another direction. "Look, the price of antimatter is expected to rise steadily for the next couple of years, right?"

"That is correct. Apparently, the Avalon Project is expending far more energy than was originally appreciated."

"Then we merely sell any excess on the open market when we get back. Even figuring the cost of money, we should be able to break even. We might even turn a profit."

The comptroller looked thoughtful. Thorpe could see that he was mentally balancing immediate costs against future benefits. Finally he said, "We'll certainly consider that option, Mr. Thorpe. No promises, of course."

"When will I have your decision?"

"At the mission briefing."

"Fine. See you the day after tomorrow."

As soon as the screen went blank, Thorpe muttered an obscenity and turned to face the hatchway behind him. Lifting his feet, he sought a firm purchase on the bulkhead and pushed off for the freighter's control room. Karin Olafson, captain of the independent space freighter *Admiral Farragut*, looked up as he sailed through the control-room hatch. She could see from his expression that things weren't going well.

"I take it the battle with the bean counters is yet to be won," Olafson said. She was a stocky woman with close-cropped blond hair, a ready smile, and a motherly manner. At age forty-five, she was nearing the end of her active career as a ship's master. That was one of the reasons she had chartered her ship to Halver Smith for the next three years. The money would go a long way toward a comfortable retirement. The idea of adventure had also appealed to her.

"I think I scored some points," Thorpe replied as he moved to the acceleration couch next to the one the captain occupied. He grabbed hold of the armrests and levered himself to a sitting position. "He doesn't want to escalate the fight to Mr. Smith. He knows he'll lose. It was just a matter of finding a way for him to dismount his hobby horse gracefully."

"And did you?"

"We'll find out at the mission briefing."

"I hope so. I don't relish embarking on a three-year voyage with only ten percent energy reserves in my toroid."

"You won't have to, Captain. What about the rest of your preparations?"

"You get us that antimatter and we'll be ready for launch. As you saw during your approach, we've got the telescope affixed to the bow."

"Any problems with that?"

"The damned thing's so heavy that we had to weld it directly to the thrust-column butt plate. Where the hell did you get that antique, anyway?"

"Out of a museum, of course."

The six-mirror instrument had been the first compound telescope ever built. It had seen active use at Mount Hopkins Observatory for seventy-five years before retirement. Since then it had been one of the prime exhibits in the University of Arizona's Museum of Astronomy. Obtaining it had proven childishly easy. Thorpe had merely mentioned that it would be used to study the approach of Comet Hastings to the Jupiter system. The museum's board of governors had then voted unanimously to loan the 4.5 meter-effective-diameter instrument to the expedition. They had replaced the telescope's antique controls with modern electromechanical actuators and removed its heavy azimuth mounting pedestal. Even so, it was large enough to cause Captain Olafson concern about her ship's structural integrity.

The telescope had been Thorpe's idea. It was his way of making peace with a certain lady astronomer.

Amber Hastings lay by the pool with her eyes closed and let the warmth of the sun soak into her skin. On the table beside her lay a computer terminal keyed into the big machine in Halver Smith's basement. She had been Smith's guest for several days while she slowly became accustomed to Earth's gravity. In between sightseeing trips she worked on the operational plan for the expedition to the comet that bore her name.

It had been eight months since the observatory computer had first called her attention to a patch of haze in the sky, and half a year since Luna and SierraCorp had agreed to fund their joint expedition. A great deal had happened in those six months.

SierraCorp had chartered a converted freighter to transport a dozen scientists and their equipment to Jupiter. Once there, the ship would take on additional reaction mass at the scientific station on Callisto and await the arrival of the comet. Following the comet's passage through the Jovian system, they would rendezvous with the nucleus and spend the next eighteen months exploring its surface. They would ride the comet through perihelion, then abandon it as it approached the orbit of Venus outbound.

"Taking a break from your studies?" a voice asked.

Amber opened her eyes to see Halver Smith standing over her. He was attired in a frayed pair of pants and wore a shirt with several ragged holes in it. From the stains on his clothing, it was obvious that he had been digging in the dirt.

"The sun is so warm that I thought I would take a nap," she said, squinting up at him.

"You haven't forgotten to put on your lotion, have you? People with your complexion sunburn very easily, you know."

She shook her head. "I'm lathered up from head to toe with sunscreen."

"I'm going riding. Care to come along?"

She blinked in surprise. "Me? On a horse?"

"Why not?"

Upon her arrival at the estate, he had taken her on a tour of the facilities. It had been at the stables that she had seen her first live horse. The big beasts had fascinated her, although it had taken all of her courage to stand close enough to stroke the silky brown flanks of one. The thought of actually climbing up on a horse sent shivers down her spine.

"But what if I fall off?"

He shrugged. "Then you get up and get right back on again. I've fallen dozens of times."

Amber did not know what to make of that statement. Such a fall must surely be fatal in Earth's gravity.

"It would be an experience to tell my grandchildren, I suppose."

"That it would. Come on. If a fat old man can ride a horse, anyone can."

Half an hour later Amber found herself following Smith along a bridle trail that meandered through the woods of his estate. She had decided that she was not going to die, and was beginning to enjoy the experience, terrifying though it was.

"By the way," Smith said as they rode across a broad meadow filled with small yellow flowers, "Tom Thorpe is coming home."

"Oh?" Amber asked as she tried to keep any hint of emotion out of her voice. Despite her stormy parting with Thorpe, she had found herself thinking about him more and more over the past six months. Whenever she remembered his infectious grin, it was hard for her to stay mad at him.

Smith seemed not to notice the sudden flush that came over her at the mention of Thorpe's name. He continued almost without pause. "He sent word that he will be in this evening. He's got a lot to do before the meeting, so I doubt we'll be seeing him before then."

"Too bad."

They rode in silence for another few minutes until Smith spoke again. "Would you mind if I ask you a personal question?"

"Depends on the question, Halver," she responded. Somehow it seemed strange to call one of the ten richest men in the system by his first name.

"What happened between you and Thorpe on Luna?"

Amber felt her cheeks begin to redden. "What do you mean?"

"I mean that he hasn't been the same since he got back. He does his job, but he doesn't seem as happy as he once did. Sometimes people will catch him staring off into space, brooding. I've talked to his friends on *The Rock*. They all agree that he's never been particularly introspective before."

"Why do you think the change has anything to do with me?" she asked.

Smith smiled. "By the time you reach my age, young lady, you learn to recognize the symptoms."

"Symptoms?"

"I think our Mr. Thorpe is in love. Any idea who the lucky woman might be?"

Amber did not answer. She did not have to. Her suddenly flaming skin did it for her.

When viewed from space, *Admiral Farragut* looked like something a child would build out of construction sticks. The long-range freighter was a collection of geometric shapes some 150 meters long. The vessel was comprised of three distinct sections, each of which could be detached from the ship should the need arise.

The engine module was a maze of spherical tanks and interconnected piping at the ship's stern. Eighteen large spheres—hydrogen tanks arrayed in three clusters of six—nearly obscured the central cylinder which was *Admiral Farragut*'s main source of power. A blackened exhaust nozzle jutted from the antimatter thrust chamber, and high temperature radiators could be seen poking out between the fuel tanks.

In front of the long-range tankage, the freighter's heavy thrust keel became visible for a few meters before disappearing into the large cylinder that was the freighter's cargo module. The ship's cargo holds were all built into the forty-meter-diameter cylinder on which clusters of oversize reaction-control jets had been mounted. Those jets not only controlled *Admiral Farragut*'s attitude in space, but would be used to land the cargo module on the comet nucleus.

The freighter's forward section contained the habitat sphere, a twenty-meter-diameter module that included all of the control systems used to fly the ship and also provided a living environment for passengers and crew. The control room was located at the very center of the sphere, with living quarters, supply bins, tankage, auxiliary power system, and work spaces surrounding it. The sphere, which would also be detached and landed on the comet nucleus, possessed its own reaction-control jet clusters and landing jacks.

Finally, the open framework of the compound telescope jutted forward from *Admiral Farragut*'s prow. Because the telescope was rigidly welded to the freighter's hull, it would be pointed by aligning the entire ship. Since the ship would coast for ninety-nine percent of the voyage, that was not a problem.

Tom Thorpe watched the freighter drop away as his ferry craft began the long fall back toward Earth. He saw none of the ugliness that would have been apparent to someone accustomed to the sleek aircraft of Earth. In space, form followed function, and it was function that determined beauty. If *Admiral Farragut* could get him where he wanted to go, Thorpe would gladly overlook its aesthetic imperfections.

John Malvan was also en route to Earth. Like Amber, he had found that the discovery of Comet Hastings had meant an unexpected change in his life. A week after he had reported his suspicions regarding Tom Thorpe's mission to John Hobart, Malvan had received orders to return to Luna City to meet with the M.P.

"Good of you to come, John," Hobart had said at their first meeting. "Did you have a pleasant journey?"

"Tolerable," Malvan said with a shrug.

"I imagine you're wondering what this is all about."

"Yes, sir."

Hobart explained the deal he had made with Thorpe. He finished by saying, "How would you like to represent Luna on this expedition?"

"I beg your pardon?"

"We would like you to represent Luna's interests on this expedition. It will mean a jump of three grades and a nice boost in salary. More importantly, it will gain you friends in Parliament, not the least of whom will be myself."

"Why me?" Malvan asked.

"Why not? You were an ice miner before your accident and have worked as a field auditor since. You're honest, a hard worker, and a patriot. Who else would have warned me that this planetoid of ice was headed our way?"

Malvan shrugged. "I thought it my duty."

"You thought correctly. You prevented a great injustice. I only wish we had been able to save the full rights for Luna. Now we need someone who will protect our interests."

"Don't you trust Halver Smith?"

"In truth, I do. It is to their benefit to cooperate with us. After all, who else will buy their ice? But I learned long ago to hedge my bets. If we find that we can't deal with SierraCorp, then we will have to develop the comet alone."

"How do we do that if they own half of it?"

Hobart looked at Malvan with serious eyes. "That is the sort of hypothetical question a politician never answers. Just remember, we are a sovereign nation and they are not. We are not bound by terrestrial law, and they are. That comet is important to us, more important than any convention regarding the ownership of astronomical bodies. If we find our interests threatened . . . well, let's remember that sovereign nations sometimes resort to military means to secure their interests."

"Are you saying . . ."

"I'm not saying anything," Hobart replied. "I'm merely trying to explain the importance of this expedition. Will you accept the commission I am offering you?"

Malvan was silent for nearly a minute. Finally, he said, "Put that way, Citizen Hobart, I don't see how I can refuse."

Malvan had spent the next six months learning everything he could about comet nuclei and the economics of ice mining. He had also studied SierraCorp extensively, even to the point of reading the classified economic intelligence sent to Luna City by its diplomats on Earth.

He had left Luna City a week prior to the final mission briefing, proceeding first to Luna Equatorial Station, then to Newton

Station in geosynchronous orbit. His schedule called for a three-day layover at Newton, an inconvenience that bothered him not at all. Of all the transit stations, Newton offered the greatest array of diversions for travelers. Malvan spent the three days preparing for the long journey to come. That his prepartions consisted of visits to the gambling decks and sojourns with female entertainment specialists was no one's business but his own.

By his third night aboard, however, Malvan was looking forward to a quiet evening in which to rest and recuperate. He began by searching out a small bar frequented mainly by station personnel. He ordered his drink from a well-stocked liquor dispenser, moved to an empty table, and sat down. He quietly nursed his drink for half an hour as he watched the bar fill up following the end of day watch.

He was about to leave when a pretty young woman in the uniform of the station staff approached and asked if she could share his table. He gestured and told her that he would be honored by her presence.

His table mate introduced herself as Barbara Martinez and explained that she was a computer programmer for Sky Watch. By the time Malvan had explained who he was, the two of them were on a first-name basis. They talked together for an hour. Then, despite his vow that he would spend his last evening aboard quietly, Malvan found himself suggesting that Barbara join him for dinner. She quickly accepted the offer.

During dinner they had talked mostly about the coming expedition and what it would be like to ride a comet on its journey around the sun. Barbara, it turned out, knew a great deal about comets. She was an astrogeologist who had done her doctoral thesis on comet formation. She told him how she envied him. During the dessert course she invited him to visit her compartment.

Their lovemaking bore no resemblance to the impersonal gymnastics he had experienced with the professional joy girls. Rather, it had been a quiet, relaxed striving with one another; the sort of thing that took place between long-time friends. Sometime during the night Barbara sat up in bed while still astride his loins and looked into his eyes. "Will you remember me when you are out at the comet?"

He had smiled. "I'll remember this night fondly forever. It isn't often a man of my age gets the opportunity to make love to a young, beautiful woman. I still don't know why you picked me up at the bar."

"Does it matter?"

"Not especially. Still, one can't help but be a little suspicious at such good fortune. About the only thing that would kill my mood is if you told me that I remind you of your father."

She laughed. "Hardly. My father is at least a decade younger than you are."

He groaned. "Now that was uncalled for!"

"Are you really interested in why I sought you out?"

He nodded. "I think my ego can take it."

"You'll think me awful."

"Try me and see."

"It was your arm," she said, gesturing toward the stump where his right arm should have been. "To be honest about it, I was curious. I wondered what it would be like making love with a one-armed man."

"And how was it?"

She shrugged, moving her entire body in a way that caused a delicious stirring deep within Malvan. "About the same, I guess. How did you lose it?"

"Mining accident. I got caught by a slide while we were drilling for ice under Mare Nectaris. I was lucky. The two men working by my side were killed."

"Do you ever wish it hadn't happened?"

"Not much point in that, is there? Besides, I've learned to cope." He accompanied his words with a loving tweak. Her squeal cut off further conversation, and they returned to the business at hand. Later, they slept. In the morning she fixed breakfast and accompanied him to the door when it was time to leave.

"Will I see you again?" she asked.

"I should pass this way in about three years. I will be happy to look you up if you like."

She sighed. "I'll probably be an old married lady by then. Still, you never can tell. Look in the station directory. If you find my maiden name listed, give me a call."

"I'll call whichever way it works out. If you're married, I'll invite you and your husband out for the best dinner in Newton Station. If you're single, we'll repeat last night, assuming I'm still up to it."

She laughed. "After a three-year voyage? I'd be willing to lay odds on that!"

"You could be right. What if I bring you a piece of comet?"

"I'd like that."

CHAPTER 11

The prelaunch briefing for the Comet Hastings Expedition was held in the San Francisco headquarters of Sierra Corporation. In a city where real estate had been overvalued for two centuries, Halver Smith's solution to the problem of lebensraum was unique. The Great Earthquake of 2016 had forced authorities to raze the old federal penitentiary on Alcatraz Island. For half a century the rubble lay undisturbed, save by goats grazing at the island's hardy grass. Smith had purchased the island at auction during one of the city's periodic fiscal crises in the early seventies and had proceeded to build his corporate headquarters there.

SierraCorp Headquarters was dominated by a tall needlelike spire that soared half a kilometer above San Francisco Bay. During the area's frequent bouts with fog, it could be seen thrusting up out of the thick blanket of white. Four large domes, each a headquarters for a different SierraCorp division, surrounded the central tower. The island, much of which had been turned into a park, was connected to the mainland by an underwater tunnel.

Amber Hastings kept close watch on the crystalline buildings as Smith's private jumper swooped toward a rooftop landing on the central spire. Even before the machine stopped oscillating, Smith had thumbed the hatch open and stepped out. Amber gathered up her folio case and followed. A stiff, cold wind caught her unaware. She stiffened with shock as a thousand pinpricks assailed her body, and felt a moment of panic as the world spun around her. The next she knew, Smith had steadied her with a firm grip and was leading her toward a downward-sloping stairwell.

"Something the matter?" he yelled above the keening of the wind when they had gained the shelter of the stairs.

She blinked at him as she tried to calm her racing heart. "Sorry. For a moment I thought I'd fallen down an airlift. I guess I had an attack of vertigo."

Smith pushed his tousled hair back into place. "My fault. I didn't think to warn you. It can't be blowing more than thirty or forty kph up here. I call that a gentle Frisco breeze."

"One of the reasons I came to Earth," she responded with a shaky laugh, "was to experience weather. I guess that was it!"

"A very mild form, I assure you. Follow me and we'll get you inside."

He turned and led her through two sets of doors whose arrangement reminded Amber of an airlock. Beyond lay a glass-enclosed observation deck that completely circled the tower.

"Come here, and I'll show you something you didn't see on the approach!"

Amber followed Smith around the central stairwell to the other side of the deck. As she walked, she noticed that the entire building thrummed from the force of the wind. It made her wonder just how sturdy a structure it truly was. All such questions were instantly forgotten as she was treated to a sudden panoramic view of the Golden Gate Bridge five kilometers distant.

"It's beautiful!" she said, her voice hushed in reverence. "It looks just like the view wall in the Forty-Niner Bar and Grill in Luna City."

"This is no view wall," Smith replied. "It's the real thing."

"They certainly knew how to build for eternity, didn't they?"

"That they did, although the bridge requires continuous work to keep it in repair. There are half a dozen robots whose only task is to keep the ironwork free of corrosion. Considering the care it gets, it should stand for centuries. That is, unless someone tears it down first."

"Oh, they wouldn't!"

"There have been suggestions to do just that. Big as it is, the bridge is too small for the larger surface craft to pass under it. The shipping people have suggested replacing it with a tunnel."

"That would be a tragedy!" Amber said. Like most Lunarians, she knew Earth as a collection of scenes purveyed by view walls. The old bridge was one of her favorites and, to her mind, a landmark as permanent as the pyramids.

Halver Smith noted the sudden look of distress on her face and smiled. "Don't worry, no one will touch it if I have any say in the decision. Now then, we'd best be getting to our meeting. Wouldn't do to have the boss late for his own briefing."

Smith led her to a lift at the center of the observation deck. Thirty seconds later she found herself in a large rotunda on the ground floor. The man-made cavern had been finished in polished marble and was illuminated by light that filtered down through translucent windows. No sooner had she stepped from the lift than she heard her name called. The voice was familiar.

She turned to see Tom Thorpe striding purposefully across the floor of the rotunda. He carried a large bunch of red flowers cradled in the crook of his arm. Suddenly all the things Amber had thought to say to him vanished. They stood in awkward silence for long seconds.

"Hello, Thomas," she said finally.

"Hello, yourself."

"Are those for me?"

He grinned and handed over the flowers. "Sorry, I nearly forgot I had them."

She buried her nose in their blooms. "Umm, roses! My favorite."

"It's good to see you again."

"And you."

"What say we have lunch after the briefing to bring each other up to date?"

"All right."

At that moment Thorpe seemed to see Halver Smith for the first time. "Uh, everyone's in the conference room, sir. We're ready to start."

"Good! Let's get to it. We've a lot of ground to cover." Without looking back, Smith walked toward one of the sets of double doors that punctuated the rotunda's perimeter.

The conference room was circular, as was the double concentric ring of small tables at its center. There were two chairs at each table, with each person's place marked by a color-coded name card—blue for expedition members, white for others. Thorpe directed Amber to the seat next to his own. Amber, glancing at the blue tag with her name on it, commented on the foresight of whoever had arranged the seating. Thorpe merely grinned. She took her place and gently laid the roses down in front of her.

Smith took his own seat. By the time he withdrew several note cards from his pocket, the sudden scraping of chairs had passed and everyone was in their proper place.

"Good morning, ladies and gentlemen," Smith began in a loud, clear voice. "As most of you know, I am Halver Smith, your host. If I haven't had the opportunity before, let me now welcome you to San Francisco and Sierra Corporation Headquarters. A few housekeeping items before we get started: These briefings are scheduled to last all week. Our purpose here is to resolve any outstanding issues regarding this expedition, so don't hesitate to speak up if anything is bothering you. Rest rooms may be found outside the door and to your right. Also, I'm told that the kitchen staff will arrive with coffee, tea, rolls, and fruit in another few minutes. This is to be a working meeting, so don't hesitate to get up and walk around if you feel the need."

Smith glanced once again at his notes and continued. "Now then, a few introductions before I turn the meeting over to those who will do the actual work. First, the woman who made all of this possible, Amber Elizabeth Hastings of Farside Observatory, Luna. Amber, please stand and take a bow!"

Amber rose to a round of applause. She smiled self-consciously, acknowledged the accolades, then quickly sat down. Smith went on to introduce Roland Jennings, the Republic of Luna's consul-general. The consul made a quick speech emphasizing the spirit of cooperation between the Republic and Sierra Corporation. Jennings then introduced John Malvan, Luna's representative on the expedition. The auditor did not bother to stand. He acknowledged the introduction with a casual wave.

When the consul finished, Smith introduced Tom Thorpe; Karin Olafson, *Admiral Farragut*'s captain; and several of the scientists who would be on the expedition. The chief scientist was to be Professor Chen Ling Tsu of the University of Hong Kong, expert in the field of asteroid formation and structure. His deputy, and Amber's new boss, was Cragston Barnard from the University of Luna City. Barnard's wife, Cybil, was also going along, in the capacity of ship's doctor. As Smith's introductions continued around the table, it became apparent that the expedition would be fairly evenly divided between SierraCorp employees and Lunarians. Smith concluded the introductions by saying, "We will now begin the formal briefings. I give you Thomas Thorpe!"

Thorpe rose from beside Amber. "We are about to embark on an epic voyage, ladies and gentlemen," he began. "It will be a voyage lasting three years. Our first stop will be Callisto Scientific Station, where we will await the comet's passage through the Jovian system. That will be the last time we are in contact with civilization. Should anything go wrong after Callisto, there will be no one to help us. Whatever the problem, we will have to handle it ourselves.

"As you have undoubtedly noticed, this expedition is composed of equal numbers of terrestrials and Lunarians. In such diversity lies our greatest strength. We cannot allow that strength to be transformed into weakness by interplanetary parochialism, factionalism, or partisan Earth/Moon politics. I therefore ask each of you to temporarily suspend whatever allegiances you bring to this expedition. For the next three years you must consider yourself citizens of space and of *Admiral Farragut*. By this, I do not mean that Citizen Malvan cannot report to his principals on Luna, nor I to mine on Earth. I *do* mean that each of you must place the needs of the expedition first. Is there anyone here who feels that they cannot abide by these rules?"

When no one spoke, Thorpe nodded. "Very well. We will have Articles of Organization ready for your signatures this afternoon. Now then, I fear I've talked too much. So, if no one has any objections, I will ask Miss Hastings to brief us on the latest findings regarding the comet. Amber?"

"Holocube down, please," Amber said to the empty air. There was a brief whirring sound as a large transparent cube appeared from out of the ceiling. "First slide, please."

The cube filled with a starfield and a view of Comet Hastings taken by *The Big Eye* less than two weeks earlier. The comet's coma was still only a dim smudge of light.

"You are all familiar with the comet's basic statistics," Amber said as she glanced around the tables. "The nucleus is nearly spherical, with a diameter of five hundred kilometers and a mass of some sixty million billion tons. Measurements of the rate at which the coma is building indicate the nucleus's temperature to be in the range of ten degrees Kelvin. That is very cold for an object a billion kilometers from the sun."

"Any new data on the comet's composition?" Professor Chen asked from his seat half a dozen places to Amber's right.

She turned to look at him. "We still show the spectral lines for water, ammonia, cyanogen, and a few other impurities in the comet's coma. We cannot, of course, use coma measurements to determine the percentage of stony material in the mix. If other comets are an accurate guide, there ought to be some."

"Any evidence of free oxygen, nitrogen, or helium?"

"We've seen hydrogen and oxygen in the coma in excess of that which resulted from photodisassociation of water molecules, and there are traces of nitrogen. We have not detected any helium. That is hardly surprising since any pools would have boiled away during previous solar passages." Amber turned her attention back to the general audience. "I'm afraid that most of the details of the nucleus's composition will remain a mystery until we actually get there."

Amber ordered her second slide displayed. The holocube changed to show a three-dimensional diagram of the asteroid's projected path through space. The orbit was a single white line leading to Jupiter, and a fan-shaped rainbow of color extending away.

"We have been watching the comet very closely these past six months and have quite a good projection of its current orbit. It will sweep in from deep space to cross Jupiter's orbit two hundred days from now. The distance at closest approach will be approximately two million kilometers. Jupiter's gravitational pull will swing the comet through approximately twenty degrees of angle. The multicolored lines represent the possible range of postencounter orbits."

"Those postencounter orbits fan out across four degrees of arc, Miss Hastings," Chen Ling Tsu said. "Surely you can pin them down closer than that!"

"I wish we could, Professor Chen. Unfortunately, there are certain limitations involved in observing an object so distant. To improve our data will require observation of the comet at close range for several weeks."

Amber continued to answer questions regarding the mechanics of gravitational capture for twenty more minutes. When one of the SierraCorp technical experts asked how *Admiral Farragut* was to be landed on the nucleus, she smiled. "That is Captain Olafson's department. I will now turn the briefing over to her."

"How was I this morning?" Amber asked that afternoon as she and Thorpe enjoyed a late lunch.

"You were fine," he assured her.

The first day's briefings had ended early in order to give participants time to prepare for the second day's session, which would be the start of four grueling days devoted to a detailed review of every aspect of the mission plan. Thorpe used the respite to show Amber the San Francisco waterfront. It was nearly 1500 hours when they boarded a replica of a nineteenth-century stern-wheeler for lunch. The needle shape of SierraCorp Headquarters and the Golden Gate Bridge were clearly visible through the restaurant's windows.

"I hope I wasn't too technical."

Thorpe laughed. "Even your consul-general understood what you were talking about. I've met the man. Believe me, orbital mechanics is not his specialty."

"Who was that little man you were arguing with during the break?"

"That was Nathan Monet, SierraCorp comptroller."

"Does he always scowl like that?"

"He does when he doesn't get his own way. Monet and I have a running dispute over *Admiral Farragut*'s fuel load. He wants to allocate the bare minimum necessary to perform the mission. I want sufficient reserves to take care of the unexpected. I thought I had him talked around to my point of view, but the damned bean counter is as stubborn as he is myopic. Mr. Smith finally told him to give me what I want. That was the reason for the scowl."

They talked for ten minutes about inconsequential matters. Finally, Amber cleared her throat. "Why did you invite me to lunch today, Tom?"

"Since when does a man need a reason for asking a beautiful woman to lunch?"

"You're stalling!"

"All right," he said. "I asked you out so we could talk about what happened on Luna."

She shrugged. "A man and a woman drank too much and spent the night enjoying one another's bodies. It happens all the time."

"Is that all it was for you? Mere exercise?"

She smiled humorlessly. "Isn't that supposed to be my line?"

"It's a serious question. I would like a serious answer."

"The truth?" she asked. "I have trouble remembering my feelings that night. It's as though it happened to another person. I remember that I was feeling giddy even before we started hitting the bars. Later, I felt . . . content. It seemed so right at the time, even though I knew our relationship was strictly temporary. Later, I found that I couldn't forget you. Waking or sleeping, you have been much on my mind of late, Thomas Thorpe."

"It's been the same with me. You don't suppose it could be love?"

"I don't see how," she replied. "We've been alone together, what? A day and a half? You can't fall in love that quickly, can you?"

"I don't know. I haven't much experience."

"Me, neither."

"Did you know that I have your picture in my kit bag?"

"You do?"

He nodded. "I clipped it from a newsfax story about the comet. You know the one. They superimposed your face over a shot of *The Big Eye*."

Amber blushed. She did indeed know the story. They had made her out to be a combination of Albert Einstein and Corbel Van Dyke, with a little Sir Isaac Newton thrown in. She had been kidded about it unmercifully for weeks.

"So, what do we do now?" he asked.

"If this were Luna, I'd suggest that you move in with me to see if we felt the same after a month or so."

"Earth customs aren't very much different."

"Too bad we're not staying on Earth or Luna."

"I don't follow you."

"You said it just this morning. We are soon to become citizens of *Admiral Farragut*. That changes things."

"How so?" he asked.

"On board ship, it will be impossible to keep an affair quiet. Everyone will know about us the moment we go to bed together."

"So what?"

"So I don't want people to think I owe my position on the expedition to the one I assume in your cabin each night."

"Damn it, Amber, you discovered the comet. Why would anyone think that?"

"I just know they would. It's human nature. If eighteen of us are going to live cheek to cheek for the next three years, I'd rather not start out as grist for the gossip mills. Nor should you. It could seriously affect your ability to lead. I think it best that I merely be one of your crew. If we still feel the same when we get back, we can do something about it."

"You expect me to see you every day and pretend that I'm not attracted to you? What kind of an iron man do you think I am?"

"The kind who will respect my wishes."

"I'll have to think about it," he said after a long pause.

"Fair enough. In the meantime, what's for dessert?"

CHAPTER 12

Amber floated alone before the forward viewport of the orbit-to-orbit transfer vehicle. In front of her lay the great rectenna of the Sierra Skies Powerstat. The rectenna, a flimsy construct of metal wire and structural composite some five kilometers in diameter, would have been invisible except for a spider web of maintenance lights. The lights made it appear a disembodied plane floating alone in the vast blackness of space.

Ten kilometers aft-orbit lay the powerstat itself. Like the half dozen other power stations that orbited 37,000 kilometers above the equator, Sierra Skies was a collection of intricate mechanisms flying in loose formation. The habitat cylinder was rotating slowly in the undimmed sunlight, its red-and-white-checkered hull bright against the black of space. Around the habitat lay six large fusion generators, giant spheres from which emanated long towers adorned by paddle-shaped, white-hot radiators. The radiators glowed. Each generator produced 1200 bevawatts of electrical power. Half of that output was transmitted by a low-density microwave beam down to Earth, to be distributed across United Europe. The rest was used to synthesize antimatter. The antiprotons were manufactured in particle accelerators, then cooled, converted into antihydrogen, and stored in superconducting magnetic traps.

The overall efficiency of the process was less than ten percent, but antimatter was by far the best power source yet devised for spacecraft. The dual nature of the powerstats' business had long been the subject of controversy. Was it more important, the argument went, to deliver energy to Earth, or to synthesize antimatter for the ships of deep space? To those who lived beyond the atmosphere, there had never been any argument. A steady supply of antimatter was as necessary to their lives as oxygen or ice.

Because of the disagreement over just how much antimatter was to be allocated for the Comet Hastings expedition, *Admiral Farragut*'s final fueling had been delayed until just before launch. All expedition members had been ordered to report aboard ship at the Sierra Skies Powerstat. They had been trickling up from Earth for nearly a week. Amber was the last to arrive, having waited for the latest observation reports from Farside Observatory.

"Captain says we'll be under power in three minutes, ma'am," a voice said from behind Amber's back. She glanced over her shoulder to see Terence Sweeney, the grizzled flight engineer of the orbit-to-orbit craft. She had not heard him come up from below.

"Does that mean I will have to return to my seat, Mr. Sweeney?"

"Not at all," he said with a chuckle. "It's just a little side thrust to make sure we miss the rectenna. Make sure you hold on when the buzzer sounds. You could sprain something if you're floating loose when the jets pop."

"Understood," she said, returning to her sightseeing. The Earth was a mottled beach ball below her, with Ireland and Great Britain two large ships plying the blue waters off the coast of continental Europe. Beyond Earth was Luna. Seeing that sparked pangs of homesickness. It would be three years before she looked again upon her home. Suddenly the thought of the expedition seemed far less glamorous than it had at first.

The warning buzzer sounded on schedule. It was followed

fifteen seconds later by two long coughs from the orbital ferry's reaction jets. Simultaneous with the sound, a plume of vapor flashed past the port, sending a million scintillating particles wafting through the darkness.

After the course correction, nothing happened for twenty minutes, as the tiny cluster of structures continued to grow in the viewport. When the powerstat filled half the port, the flight engineer again entered the small compartment.

"Captain says that since you're our only passenger, he's gotten permission to divert to your ship and make a direct transfer. That ought to save you an hour or so."

"Thank the captain for me, Mr. Sweeney. How long until we get there?"

"Fifteen minutes. The powerstat management gets a bit tense if we come in much faster than a crawl."

"When will we be able to see *Admiral Farragut*?"

"You can see her now."

"Where?"

The engineer pointed to one of two large irregular constructs attached by a series of cables to one of the fusion generators. "There, tucked in close to the Number One accelerator module. See it?"

She followed his finger. "That little thing?"

"Not so little," he replied. "It just looks that way because the accelerator is so damned big."

Amber gazed at the ship, which was still smaller than a fingernail held out to arm's length—it was difficult to make out details other than the spherical hydrogen tanks, cylindrical cargo module, and crew module up front. But as she gazed across several kilometers of vacuum, there seemed to be an open framework of pipes on the prow that she did not recognize from the old photograph that had been included in the mission plan.

"What's that, Mr. Sweeney?"

"What's what, Miss Hastings?"

"That mechanism on the ship's bow?"

"Don't know," he said, squinting at it. He turned in midair, kicked off against a bulkhead, and arrowed out of sight. He was back in fifteen seconds with a pair of binoculars. He used them to study the freighter. Finally he handed them to Amber. "Damned if I recognize it. Looks like some sort of docking mechanism, or maybe an extension of the thrust frame."

Amber raised the binoculars to her own eyes and dialed for maximum magnification. One of the things that had fascinated her on Earth had been the way the atmosphere softened things at a distance. No such effect was evident in space. She quickly found herself staring at the ship as if she were hanging a few dozen meters away. She swept the binoculars forward along the freighter's flanks, noting the lighted viewports in the crew module. Then she had the mysterious prow ornament centered in her field of view.

The angle of the sun made viewing difficult. Even so, it took less than a minute for her mind to sort out the confusing patterns of light and shadow. She gasped as recognition hit her.

"What's the matter, Miss Hastings?"

"It's a telescope, and a big one! Looks like at least a four-, possibly a six-mirror compound instrument. Now where the hell did they get something like that for this expedition?"

Sweeney shrugged. "Why don't you ask them when we get there?"

"I will."

Ten minutes later Amber had no need to ask where Thorpe had obtained the telescope. During the orbital ferry's approach they had passed directly over the bow-mounted instrument. She recognized it immediately as the MMT—Multi-Mirror Telescope—known affectionately to four generations of astronomers as the "Big Ugly Six-Pack." Because of its archaic mirror design and its mass, no one had ever made a good case for transferring the Six-Pack to orbit. But the freight had finally been paid, and Amber suspected that the telescope would never be returned to Earth. Despite its age, it was still a superb optical instrument. It would make a welcome addition to Farside Observatory's suite of observational tools.

A sudden clanging announced the orbital ferry's successful docking with *Admiral Farragut*. Amber took the noise as her signal to swim back into the main passenger cabin and collect her baggage. Her two suitcases and overnight bag seemed a pitifully small collection with which to begin a three-year journey. Her personal spacesuit, delivered several weeks before, was her only other possession. Because of the sudden health of Amber's bank account, both vacuum suit and the ship coveralls in her luggage were the best money could buy.

She towed her suitcases to the airlock just as Sweeney opened the inner door. Stretching beyond the open outer door was a short docking tube. The big freighter's airlock was also open, giving the impression of a deep well. A gray-haired man hovered to one side of the freighter airlock and craned his neck to look up at Amber.

"Good-bye, Mr. Sweeney," she said, shaking hands with the engineer. "Thanks for the ride."

"You're welcome, Miss Hastings. I'll tell my wife and kids about you some night when the comet is high in the sky."

She laughed. "You do that, Mr. Sweeney."

She picked up her bags and slowly levitated them to align with the center of the docking tube. Then she kicked off from the after bulkhead, intending to sail unaided from one ship to the other. But as she sailed through the ferry's outer coaming, her right shin banged against one of the airlock hinges. The sudden pain caused globular tears to form in her eyes as her body spun sideways and momentarily bounced off the accordian-pleated fabric of the docking tube.

"Damn!" she muttered as she rubbed the injured leg and fought to extricate herself. She made very little progress until a strong hand grabbed her right ankle and began pulling her down toward the freighter. Embarrassed, she let her rescuer do all the work while she concentrated on retrieving what little was left of her dignity.

"Hello, there!" the white-haired man said when he had pushed her through the airlock and cycled both doors closed. "Hurt yourself?"

"My pride more than anything. Thanks. I thought I could handle myself better than that."

"No problem," he responded. "It's the legs that get in the way out here. Damned things were never intended for snaking through holes, you know. By the way, I'm Kyle Stormgaard, chief engineer of this rust bucket."

"Amber Hastings."

"Figured it had to be you," he said, grinning. "The missus told me that you were a looker. Besides, you're the last to come aboard."

"The 'missus'?"

"Captain Olafson. We like to think that we own this bucket, although the Bank of Montevideo might have other opinions."

"She's your wife?"

"Going on twenty-five years," he said proudly. "About the same amount of time we've been spacing together, in fact."

"You must be very close."

Stormgaard laughed. "Believe me, Miss Hastings, by the time this trip is over, *you'll* think that you're married to me—me and everyone else aboard. A spaceship is no place for either a claustrophobe or someone with a privacy fetish."

"I'm a Lunarian, Mr. Stormgaard. I know I don't suffer from claustrophobia. I'll let you know in a few months about the other part."

"Fair enough," he said. "Come on, and we'll stow your gear in your cabin. You can sleep there tonight. Tomorrow, of course, you paying passengers go into the tanks."

Amber shivered. The mission plan called for nearly everyone to spend the outbound trip in cold sleep. That was the only thing that made sense on such a long journey. It minimized the quantity of consumables required and reduced the strain of enforced idleness. To Amber, however, a cold-sleep tank bore too great a resemblance to a coffin. She was looking forward to the experience about as much as she might have looked forward to a trip to a dental plastician.

Stormgaard, who had been gathering her scattered luggage, noticed the look on her face. "What's the matter?"

She explained her aversion to cold sleep.

"You've got nothing to worry about," he assured her. "You won't feel a thing while you're under, won't age a day, and most importantly, won't have to listen to my jokes for another six months. I grant you that waking up is no picnic, but the pain and the nausea are over quick. Me, I'm looking forward to it."

"You're going into the tank too?"

"Sure," he replied. "There are six of us in the crew. We've split ourselves into three pairs. Each pair will be awake for two months and asleep for four. There isn't a whole lot that can go wrong with a ship coasting through the vacuum, you know. I'd much rather spend the time sleeping. Come on, and I'll show you to your quarters. Dinner's at 1800 hours, and the captain doesn't like anyone to be late."

Thorpe strapped himself in the observer's chair in *Admiral Farragut*'s control room and watched as final preparations were made for getting under way. The control room was a dome-shaped compartment dominated by a full circumambient screen on which could be displayed any combination of televised views and computer-generated charts. With the dome switched to the hull cameras, the control room's four acceleration couches appeared to be floating in space.

Thorpe felt as if he were in a planetarium. The great glowing ball of the sun hung low in front of him, while a crescent Earth stretched beyond the dome's horizon at his feet. Luna was out of sight somewhere aft. The cluster of reactors and habitat cylinder that made up the Sierra Skies Powerstat were clearly visible above the lighted limb of the Earth. And despite the pressure of the Sun, the stars glowed in all their electronically enhanced glory. The Milky Way was a silver band arching across the dome.

"Sierra Skies control, this is *Admiral Farragut*. How do you read?" Captain Olafson's voice asked from somewhere behind Thorpe. The freighter had departed the power station half an hour before with a single pop of the ship's reaction jets. They had been drifting slowly away from Sierra Skies ever since.

"Hello, *Admiral Farragut*. We read you clearly."

"We just passed out of the inner zone. Request permission to accelerate to mid-zone speed."

"Stand by, *Admiral Farragut*." There was a thirty-second pause while the controller reviewed the ship's flight path. Ten years earlier a ship had departed one of the powerstats only to find that its orbit took it directly through the delicate power rectenna. Ever since that incident, approaches and departures had been tinged with paranoia. "All right, *Farragut*. We check you as being clear of the inner zone. You may accelerate as planned. You are reminded that it is a violation to light off your main drive until you are one hundred kilometers distant."

"Understood, Sierra Skies. We will observe the hundred-klick rule!"

"Good luck on your mission, *Admiral Farragut*!"

"Thank you, Sierra Skies control. Please arm the reaction-control system, Kyle." This last was addressed to the chief engineer, who occupied the acceleration couch beyond the captain's.

"Aye aye. RCS armed."

"Warn the crew, Mr. Rodriguez."

The third control-room crewman, who monitored all ship's systems except the engines, reached out and touched a control. His voice echoed through each of the compartments.

"Attention, all hands. RCS maneuvering is about to commence. You have fifteen seconds to secure for maneuvering."

Captain Olafson waited the fifteen seconds, then did something to her lapboard that caused a series of aiming circles to be superimposed on the overhead dome. There followed a brief sputtering of jets, and the outside universe began to rotate slowly. At thirty degrees the captain triggered another brief burst, and the circles stopped precisely on the bearing called for in the flight plan. The next time the jets fired, they did so for more than five minutes. Thorpe felt a tiny tug as he sank into the padded surface of his acceleration couch.

At the apex of the dome a flight-status display appeared, showing a slow increase in the distance between the freighter and the powerstat, as well as an increasing rate of separation. When their speed relative to Sierra Skies reached 500 kph, Captain Olafson shut down the reaction-control jets.

"Final check. Mr. Rodriguez, make the announcement."

"Attention, all hands! Stand by for final readiness check."

Suddenly the dome no longer showed surrounding space. A dozen internal views appeared overhead. Each was from a camera mounted in a passenger cabin. The freighter's initial acceleration would be less than one-quarter of a standard gravity, but experience had taught Captain Olafson caution. People had been known to break their necks when caught off guard by the onset of acceleration.

She quickly ran down the list of passengers, asking each if he or she was ready to space. For the most part the screens showed *Admiral Farragut*'s passengers and crew strapped into their bunks. It was not until the captain turned her attention to the Barnards' cabin that she noticed that the ship's surgeon was missing from her assigned station.

"Where is your wife, Professor Barnard?"

"She's in the dispensary rearranging her medicines," the Lunarian professor replied.

Karin Olafson switched to a view of the dispensary. She found Cybil Barnard seated with one foot wedged beneath a shelf, happily rearranging medical supplies.

"We're ready for launch, Doctor!"

The ship's surgeon jumped and looked up quickly to where the camera's active light glowered at her like a baleful red eye. "You should give a person warning before you do that, Captain."

"Why aren't you in your cabin?"

"I have work to do here."

"You reported ready for space before we left the powerstat. Was that incorrect?"

"No, but I have things to organize."

"When will you be ready to start cold-sleep processing?"

"As soon as you have things stabilized, Captain. The more we can get into tanks while we're under boost, the better it will go."

"Very well. Now please return to your cabin and strap down. It wouldn't do to have our ship's surgeon break a leg during launch."

"I will as soon as I get things stowed here."

"Now, Doctor! That's an order."

The pert blonde in the white coverall gulped and reddened slightly. "Aye aye, Captain. I'll be strapped down in two minutes."

The captain continued her survey of the passengers and crew. When the remainder of the eighteen men and women aboard had been heard from, she began a methodical search of the cargo module. Cameras mounted high on the bulkheads stared down at the expedition's equipment. Everything appeared secure.

The visual inspection continued into the power module. There would be no access into that module throughout the journey except in the event of an emergency. Even so, Captain Olafson's gaze swept the spaces, looking for loose tools left behind by careless workmen. Next she surveyed the ship's eighteen spherical hydrogen tanks. Had any tank been leaking, the computer would have already sounded the alarm. Even so, the captain used the visual check to look for wisps of vapor. Only after the visual inspection did she ask for a computer check of ship's status.

"I've got green lights across the board, Captain," Rodriguez reported.

"Very well. Mr. Thorpe, do I have your permission to launch?"

"Permission granted."

"Stand by for launch sequence. Close all pressure doors. Bring the thrust-chamber magnetic field to full strength. Stand by for reaction mass and antimatter injection. Two-minute warning, Mr. Rodriguez."

"All hands. Prolonged acceleration to commence in two minutes. I repeat. Acceleration at one-quarter gravity in two minutes! Stand by."

"How long until we reach injection speed, Captain?" Thorpe asked, referring to the velocity that would place them in a flat hyperbolic orbit for Jupiter. A minimum-energy orbit would have taken three years and brought them to the giant planet long after the comet's departure. They would cross the 800-million-kilometer gulf between planets in only six months. To do so, their speed would be far in excess of local system escape velocity. If anything happened to the ship's engines en route, they would continue outbound forever.

"We'll be under power for three hours thirty-six minutes, Mr. Thorpe. I plan to watch everything closely for an hour, then order cold sleep operations to commence. Have I your permission to proceed?"

"Uh, yes," Thorpe said as he realized that he was being dressed down for interrupting the captain at a critical moment. "Proceed."

"Very well," Captain Olafson said. "Mr. Chief Engineer, give me first antimatter injection in ten seconds. Mr. Rodriguez, sound the klaxon."

A raucous alarm suddenly sounded through the ship. Then Captain Olafson herself made the final announcement.

"Attention, all hands. Stand by for full power, Ten . . . nine . . . eight . . . seven . . . six . . . five . . . four . . . three . . . two . . . one . . . now!"

A gentle hand pushed Thorpe down in his couch as a 100,000-degree flame erupted from the magnetic nozzle at *Admiral Farragut*'s stern.

They had begun their long voyage to Jupiter!

CHAPTER 13

Being resurrected was not all that it was cracked up to be. It *hurt* . . . horribly!

As she struggled back to consciousness Amber Hastings concentrated on her pain. It was the one reality in her universe, and, in a way, welcome—for if she felt pain, she must be alive. Besides the pain, there was the cold. A thousand frigid knives cut into her flesh wherever it contacted bare metal.

She opened her eyes fully for the first time. Two centimeters above her face was a structure of curved glass, which alternately fogged over and then cleared. She watched the cycle with half-hearted interest. The fog always seemed to thicken with the onset of an ache in her ribs and dissipate with its easing.

She forced herself to breathe deeply. The glass became more fogged, but her tired brain began to respond to the increased oxygen supply. She remembered where she was and why.

Hers had been the sixth name called after *Admiral Farragut*'s departure. She had reported to the axis shelter behind the control room, where Dr. Barnard had injected her with a golden fluid, made her strip naked, and helped her into the glass and metal interior of the tank. By the time Amber had been wired into the plumbing—a thoroughly degrading process—she had barely been able to keep her eyes open. The last thing she remembered was the gurgling sound the oxygenated fluorocarbon made as it poured into her lungs. She had tried to cough it up, but found she could not. Then unconsciousness had taken her.

Having oriented herself, Amber groped for the cover release lever. It took three tries before she could summon the strength to pull it. She watched the glass cover slide away from her face. She lay still, exhausted, her breath coming in ragged volleys. But she did not have long to rest. As soon as the cover retracted, a crewman appeared and helped her to sit up.

A sudden attack of vertigo led to a spasm of the dry heaves. When they were over, she slumped down to rest her forehead on the top of the tank. She held that position until black spots no longer swam before her eyes. Finally, she felt good enough to sit up and look around.

"Feeling better?" the crewman asked.

"A little," she answered. Her voice was a harsh rasping sound in her ears. "I'm sorry, but I don't remember your name."

"Spacer First Class Bernardo Velduccio, Miss Hastings."

"Did we make it, Mr. Velduccio? Are we at Jupiter?"

"We're about a week out."

"Who's awake?"

"The full crew, Mr. Thorpe, the Barnards, John Malvan, and now you."

"And the comet?"

"We can see it with the naked eye. It's a small patch of fog beyond Jupiter."

"I want to see it for myself," she said, straining to rise out of her tank.

"Not quite yet," he replied as he gently pushed her back down. "First I have to get an I.V. started. After that, the doctor wants to examine you. Then you will want to shower and put on clean clothes. Believe me, you shouldn't rush the decanting process. It will just make you weak and prolong your pain."

Amber leaned back against the padded end of the tank. Somehow the metal had lost its earlier coldness. At the mention of clean clothes, she was reminded that she wasn't wearing anything. She wondered how she could be sitting up, naked, speaking calmly to a stranger. She decided that the machine must be feeding drugs into her system that, among other things, short-circuited the modesty reaction.

Fifteen minutes later she had recovered sufficiently to climb out of the tank under her own power. After a hot shower she dressed awkwardly with Velduccio's help, then let him tow her toward the dispensary. *Admiral Farragut* was in zero gee, making the movement both harder and easier than it would have been under gravity. Tom Thorpe was waiting for them when they arrived.

"Any problems?" Thorpe asked Velduccio as he helped guide Amber to a gurney. The two men strapped her down. Each wore ship boots to keep them attached to the deck underfoot.

"None," the spacer replied. "She bounced back as fast as anyone I've ever seen."

Amber, who felt weak as a baby, looked up at Thorpe. He had changed since she had last seen him. His tan was faded, and he had lost weight. She was not sure, but she thought there was more gray in his hair, too. She wondered how she must look to him.

"Hello," she said weakly. "I half expected to see your face the moment I opened the tank."

"The captain ordered me to stay away. She said I'd just get underfoot and impede progress. How do you feel?"

"About the way I look," Amber replied. "I don't think I want to die anymore, but I'm not that interested in living either."

"You sound great! I could barely talk when they brought me in here."

"How long ago?"

"A week."

"How are things going?"

"Fine. We're right on schedule and in contact with Callisto Station. We'll be there in another week. Two weeks after that the comet will pass through the Jupiter system and we can finally get to work. By the way, there are six months' worth of messages for you from Farside Observatory. I glanced through them. They've refined the orbital parameters quite a bit. The captain wants you to look over the data to help with the mission planning after Callisto."

Amber struggled to sit up. "I'll do that immediately." She found a gentle hand on her shoulder restraining her. She glanced up to see Cybil Barnard.

"Plenty of time for that later," the doctor said. "Right now you get a full checkup followed by eight hours of sleep. Mr. Thorpe, please leave me alone with my patient."

"I'm going, Doc."

"And tell my slave driver of a husband that his assistant will be indisposed until tomorrow. Now then, Amber, please roll up your sleeve."

Amber sat in *Admiral Farragut*'s telescope control room and watched a close-up of Jupiter on the screen. The current view reminded her of the first picture she had ever seen of the planet.

Jupiter's face was a series of alternating white and pink bands of cloud. At their boundaries the bands devolved into complex eddies of dark red and pale yellow. Other strips were banded by blue or gray boundaries. Many of the eddies were larger than the Earth, yet on Jupiter were the least of the planet's features. The whirlpools and cyclones were the true landmarks of the Jovian atmosphere.

As she scanned the King of Worlds, Amber noticed that the cross hairs at the center of the screen were slowly drifting to the right. She reached out and used a joystick to correct the movement. From far off came the quick popping sound of reaction control jets as they responded to her command.

The cross hairs centered themselves near a black dot which was itself moving across the face of the planet. Estimating the angle of the sun, Amber searched and quickly spotted what appeared to be a distortion of the Jovian atmosphere. The distortion was Jupiter's moon, Io, transiting the face of its parent world. The black spot was its shadow.

"Looking at Jupiter again, I see!"

Amber turned around to note Cragston Barnard behind her. Her ex-professor from the University of Luna City smiled as he pulled himself to sit beside Amber. Barnard had the gangly, slightly awkward build common among Lunarians. Except for a too prominent nose, he was quite handsome and had been the subject of considerable speculation among his female students when Amber was at the university.

"Ready to begin observations of the comet?"

"Ready," she replied. "Just thought I would check out the big fellow while I waited for you."

"It's enough to take a person's breath away, isn't it?"

Amber nodded. "That it is."

Barnard punched several commands into the computer that controlled the telescope. "Before we get to work, what say we take a look at Callisto? It should be rounding the planet just about now."

Amber moved the telescope cross hairs to coincide with the predicted position of Jupiter's outermost Galilean moon.

"Increase magnification to one hundred," Cragston ordered as the reaction-control jets popped to halt the rotation they had put on the ship.

Amber responded and was rewarded with the sight of a round world only slightly off center in the viewscreen. Callisto was the size of Mercury and peppered with impact craters. The craters were unlike those of Luna or Mars, however. Where Luna's craters had central peaks, Callisto's were uniformly flat-bottomed. Some even had depressions in their centers. The lack of structure was the result of Callisto's surface composition, which was mostly water ice. Beneath the icy crust lay a subterranean ocean of liquid water, an ocean 200 times deeper than any found on Earth.

That Callisto was inhabited became obvious within seconds. A bright green dot appeared near the moon's equator.

"Apparently," Barnard said, gesturing toward the screen, "the scientific station wants to talk to Captain Olafson. Shall we listen in?"

"Only if you want to be on bread and water for the rest of the trip," Amber joked. "Come on, let's get to the comet observations."

Captain Olafson leaned back in her acceleration couch and worried as she gazed at Jupiter in the overhead dome. Her view of the planet was unmagnified, making the King of Worlds slightly smaller than Luna when seen from Earth. Three of the Jovian moons were lined up on one side of the planet. Two were large enough to show visible disks, while the third remained a close-in point of reddish light. But what worried Karin Olafson was neither the planet nor its moons. Her mind was occupied with the Jovian system's well-known radiation hazards.

Like Earth, Jupiter possessed a magnetic field, which trapped particles of the solar wind and concentrated them to form radiation belts. Because Jupiter's magnetic field was far stronger than Earth's, its radiation belts were far more extensive and powerful —10,000 times more powerful in places. When the first space probe, Pioneer 10, had traversed the Jovian system, it had been exposed to radiation a hundred times the level required to kill an unprotected human being.

Earth's Van Allen radiation belts were often described as circling the planet's waist like an old automobile tire. In truth, however, the toroidal region of radiation was far from symmetrical. The solar wind and the sun's magnetic field combined to thin the radiation above the daylight hemisphere, while extending it for several planetary diameters over the night hemisphere. The image she visualized was of a boat riding at anchor in the swift river of the solar wind. The current raised a small bow wave, but caused a lengthy wake to stream away from the stern.

So it was with Jupiter. The planet's radiation belts were only a few planetary diameters thick above the side facing the sun, but streamed away for millions of kilometers on the night side of Jupiter. The practical result was that for twelve days out of sixteen, Callisto orbited in a region of low radiation. For the rest the moon was wreathed in a deadly, invisible fog. It was that fact more than any other which made navigating the Jovian system so worrisome for ship captains.

Captain Olafson's first problem involved the approach to Callisto. In six days they would drop to within a million kilometers of Jupiter while decelerating. Once slowed, they would swing around the giant world to overtake Callisto from below and behind, then rendezvous with the moon high above the daylight hemisphere and the radiation belts. But in crossing behind the planet, *Admiral Farragut* would plunge through the heart of one of the most powerful of the Jovian radiation regions.

The freighter's hull shielding was adequate for most purposes but wholly incapable of protecting the crew from Jove's version of the Van Allen belts. Luckily, the ship's designers had provided for such an eventuality. Radiation protection had been the reason they had located the control room at the center of the habitat module and surrounded it with the heavy girders of the thrust frame. Behind the control room was an equally well-shielded compartment, the ship's "storm cellar," to which the crew could retreat during solar flares. For the Comet Hastings expedition the storm cellar had been fitted with cold sleep tanks. And while the passengers and crew mostly lived and worked on the outer decks, they would return there during the transit through Jupiter's radiation belts.

The passengers and crew would be well shielded, if somewhat crowded, during the transit. But the ship's delicate electronic modules would not be protected. They would have to survive the exposure to radiation—and not just once.

The mission plan called for *Admiral Farragut* to plunge three times through Jupiter's radiation belts. The first exposure would come as they made the approach to Callisto; the second when they accompanied the moon on its transit of the night hemisphere; the third as they left the system in pursuit of the comet. The ships that normally plied the Jovian system were specially designed to survive such high radiation doses. Karin Olafson's ship was not.

"Message laser coming in from Callisto," Rodriguez said from beside her. The two of them were the only people currently in the control room.

"Patch it into my station."

The message was an update on local conditions and a proposed flight plan change that would marginally lower the exposure problem. Because the time delay between ship and station was still sixty-six seconds each way, she did not expect a two-way conversation with anyone on the ground. Anything longer than fifteen seconds tended to be so annoying that people avoided conversing. Still, she took the trouble to record a long message thanking the station crew for their efforts. Theirs was a lonely existence, and a little courtesy went a very long way out there in the deep black.

CHAPTER 14

Tom Thorpe hovered in front of the port and stared at the heavily cratered surface of Callisto. *Admiral Farragut* was in an equatorial orbit a mere fifty kilometers above Jupiter's eighth-most-distant moon. Directly below Thorpe was the large ringed basin called Asgard, with its concentric ripples of ice where an ancient asteroid had crashed through the crust. The crater had filled with water, which quickly froze over to heal the wound. Despite its prominence, Asgard was a phantom crater, more visible from orbit than from the ground, a level place in a world covered with impact craters. An even larger asteroid strike had taken place at Valhalla, 3500 kilometers to the southwest. The Valhalla Basin was where Callisto Scientific Station was located. Thorpe gazed down at the crater that was not really there and thought of all that had happened during the previous ten days.

Admiral Farragut had followed its flattened hyperbolic orbit to within a million kilometers of Jupiter before Captain Olafson had fired the engine. After so many months the sudden return of gravity had been a shock. The engine had thundered for less than two hours before once again falling silent. By the time weightlessness returned, the freighter had added its own name to the list of Jovian satellites.

It had taken three days for the ship to climb away from Jupiter and overtake Callisto at an altitude of 1.8 million kilometers. For half that time everyone had crowded into the storm cellar. Captain Olafson had remained at her station the entire time they had been in the radiation belt. Like everyone else, Thorpe noticed her worried look and hoped it was merely caused by professional diligence.

Eventually everyone had been allowed to return to the outer decks and had swarmed to the viewports. Thorpe would never forget the sight of a crescent Ganymede silhouetted against the darkened disk of Jupiter's night hemisphere.

Following their arrival, Captain Olafson had given the order to revive the remainder of the sleeping expedition members. The seven still in their cold tanks would be disappointed at having missed the entry into the Jovian system. But with Comet Hastings arriving in twelve days, their disappointment would not be long-lived.

The Asgard Basin slipped from sight. A few minutes later the outer edge of Valhalla began to intrude on the cratered landscape. Thorpe's sightseeing was interrupted by the sound of a buzzer. Reluctantly, he turned away from the viewport to answer the sound-only intercom. "Thorpe, here."

"We've been invited down to the scientific station, Mr. Thorpe," Captain Olafson's voice said. "They want to discuss refueling and to coordinate observations of the comet during its close encounter."

"They're providing transport?"

"Of course."

Thorpe nodded. *Admiral Farragut* carried two small moon-jumpers in its cargo hold, but they would not be of any use at Callisto. Their propulsion systems lacked the power needed to land on the large moon.

"Have you broken out the trade goods yet?"

"I have Rodriguez and Schmidt doing that now."

Refueling *Admiral Farragut* would be a formidable task for the scientific station. Eight million kilograms of hydrogen was not easy to lift. And even though the station was being paid handsomely for their services, Halver Smith had suggested a cargo of delicacies to insure their enthusiasm. The "trade goods" were several cargo containers packed in the manner of Christmas food assortments.

"How soon before their ship arrives?"

"They'll launch as we sweep over Valhalla this trip and rendezvous two hours later. That will leave us half an hour to the first landing window. They're sending one of their auxiliary craft, so there will only be room for three of us this first trip. Any suggestions as to the third member of the ground party?"

Thorpe had a strong suggestion as to who he would *like*. To state it, however, would violate his pact with Amber. He replied with studied nonchalance. "I suppose we'd best take someone from the astronomy department. Professor Barnard is the obvious choice."

"Not available. He's helping his wife with the decantings. It will have to be Amber."

"Fine," he replied, hoping his voice did not betray his attempt at Machiavellianism.

There was a moment of silence on the other end of the intercom that made him think that Captain Olafson had no trouble seeing through his little ploy. "Very well, Mr. Thorpe. I'll see you at the Number One airlock in two hours. I'll take care to notify Miss Hastings."

The ship that came up to get them was less a spacecraft than a collection of components strung along a thrust frame. At the bow was a flight cabin barely large enough for the vacsuited pilot. It reminded Thorpe of the bubbles used on some of the early helicopters. Behind the cabin three acceleration couches straddled the thrust girder. No attempt had been made to enclose them; the passengers were exposed to space. Behind the passenger seats was a crossbar on which cargo could be hung. Finally, there were six cylindrical reaction-mass tanks, an antimatter toroid, and a magnetically shielded mixing chamber affixed to the aft end of the girder.

Thorpe's first sight convinced him that he was looking at an orbit-to-orbit scooter. Upon closer inspection he noticed the stubby landing gear that made the contraption resemble a four-poster bed; a series of underjets were mounted on swivels. The contrivance did not look safe to Thorpe.

"Are you sure this thing will fly?" he asked the pilot as he clambered to his seat.

The pilot chuckled. "Not to worry, chief! Callisto may be as large as Mercury, but its density is only about one-third that of the inner planets. That gives it a surface gravity one-fifth standard, or slightly more than Luna's."

"It will be nice to get back to normal gravity," Amber said from her own place astride the scooter's rail.

"Oh, you a Lunarian, ma'am?"

"Yes."

"Me too. The name's Jarrod Whitehead, from Tycho Terrace. Master pilot, jack-of-all-trades, chief cook and bottle washer."

"I'm Amber Hastings. I was born and raised in Miner's Luck."

"I've got a cousin who used to live around there. Name's Ivan Starkol. Now he runs a vacuum-equipment shop out of Luna City South. Ever hear of him?"

"No, sorry."

"Just as well," the pilot replied with a laugh. "Rumor in the family is that old Ivan would sell Grandma if he thought he could make a ten-selene profit."

"I'll remember that next time I'm in the market for a suit."

"Say, that's a right pretty one you've got on. Boeing Mark Twelve, ain't it?"

"It is."

"Care to sell?"

"Sorry, but I'm going to be needing it."

"Yeah, I suppose you will. Oh well, I probably couldn't afford it anyway."

"Do you make this trip often?" Amber asked.

"Not often to orbit," the pilot replied. "Mostly I fly point-to-point on Callisto. Of course, I'll be getting lots of practice with you folks. The director wants me to run a daily shuttle service between *Admiral Farragut* and the station. Got that cargo secured back there, Captain?"

Karin Olafson, who had been supervising the placement of the two pods of trade goods, waved in the gesture that substituted for a nod in a vacsuit. "All secure, Master Pilot."

"Then I'd suggest your people get back inside the ship. I'm

ready to cut loose and start my deceleration program."

"Rodriguez, Schmidt, Velduccio, back inside!" While the three crewmen cycled through the freighter's airlock, Karin Olafson strapped herself into the third seat on the scooter.

The trip down to the surface gave them a panoramic view of Callisto. The scientific station was largely invisible, save for a collection of communications gear and a series of spherical storage tanks on the surface. A hundred meters from where the scooter touched down, a Quonset hut led to a lift leading down to the subterranean base, an arrangement not unlike the entrance to Farside Observatory.

Whitehead climbed out of his flight cabin as soon as they touched down and immediately strode aft to assist Amber in dismounting the scooter. Thorpe clambered awkwardly down without assistance, surprised at what six months in cold sleep had done to his coordination. Captain Olafson followed him.

"You can leave the cargo," Whitehead informed them. "We'll have a crew up in a few minutes to off-load it."

Karin Olafson scanned the field. Her features were silhouetted through the bubble of her helmet. Thorpe could see her frown. "Where are your ships?"

Only then did Thorpe realize that, except for their own ungainly steed, the landing field was empty.

"Ah, I'm afraid you've caught us with our pants down," Albert Kaffin, director of Callisto Scientific Station, said upon being asked the same question. The three expedition members were seated in the director's office a hundred meters below the surface. They sat on individual stone benches in front of a tablelike desk of the same material.

"I beg your pardon, Mr. Director?" Karin Olafson asked in a surprisingly mild tone. Thorpe had to admire the way she was holding her temper.

"I'm afraid our normal refueling vessels aren't here at the moment."

"Where are they?"

"Down at Io."

"And what are they doing there?"

Kaffin, a small man with a perpetually pinched expression and a receding hairline, squirmed uncomfortably behind his desk. "We have a number of instruments on the Ionian surface with which we monitor conditions there. The moon is really quite a fascinating place, you know. It's attached to Jupiter via a plasma tube which is the source of much of the planet's decametric radio emissions. Io is locked in orbital synchronism with both Europa and Ganymede, and then there are the volcanoes, the sulfur halo, the tidal heating . . . But then, you aren't interested in a catalog of the moon's abnormalities, are you?"

"No, sir," Thorpe replied. "We're interested in the whereabouts of our refueling ship, for the use of which your organization was paid in advance."

"I know very little about the Earthside arrangements. I'm merely the silly bugger who has to make good on promises made half a system away. Now then, if I may continue my explanation?"

"Go ahead," Karin Olafson ordered.

"This station maintains an extensive instrument cluster on the Ionian surface to monitor a number of scientifically important data. Three weeks ago we lost contact. At first we believed it to be a communications breakdown. Electronics don't last long in that environment once the shielding fails. Because there are so many important investigations in progress, I immediately dispatched our two ships to investigate. I was confident that they would both be back in time to service your vessel.

"You can imagine my chagrin when my people reported that instead of a telemetry malfunction, they had discovered the cluster buried beneath a sulfur flow. It seems a new volcano has recently erupted near the site, and they tend to be the messiest with regard to sulfur discharges."

"So you lost some instruments," Karin Olafson replied. "How difficult can it be to plant another set and get those ships back here?"

"Oh, the ground cluster isn't lost, Captain, merely buried. The sulfur that flows from these volcanoes is tepid by human standards. Most flows emerge around twenty degrees centigrade. That won't harm the instruments. As for replacing them, I'm afraid we can't. They are one-of-a-kind prototypes. No, we have to dig them out and move them to another observation area."

"Fine, you can do that once my ship has been refueled."

"Come now, Captain. You know how expensive it is to move around the Jovian system. To recall my people and then send them back would be grossly expensive in terms of both reaction mass and antimatter."

"But why two ships?" Thorpe asked. "Wouldn't one have been entirely adequate for the task?"

"Oh, no!" Kaffin replied. "Surely, Mr. Thorpe, you must realize that Io orbits inside the radiation belt. It possesses the most hostile environment of any place in the system. We never send a single ship to Io. What if it were to become disabled? No, one ship lands while the other orbits overhead as a safety measure. That rule is inviolable."

"And how soon will they be back?" Karin Olafson asked. All the while the director had been speaking, her complexion had been going from pale pink to crimson.

"I'm afraid the excavation and relocation will take at least another month. Working as they are with remote excavators, it's impossible to hurry. To do so would risk damaging the instruments."

"Damn it, we can't wait here another month!"

"You can still catch the comet. I grant you that it's an imposition, but it hardly constitutes a crisis."

"It *is* a crisis, Mr. Director. My ship isn't shielded against radiation the way yours are. Frankly, I'm already worried about my control and communications circuits. We've figured a certain number of failures into the plan and carry spares. Now you're asking me to orbit this ice ball for a month longer than planned? That's at least two more trips through the radiation belts, possibly more if we're delayed further. Would you have us wait until every piece of electronics aboard is radiated into so many bits of inert silicon?"

Kaffin leaned back in his thronelike chair and sighed. "We thought that might be your attitude. That is why we've gone to the trouble of preparing another option."

Tom Thorpe trudged across the mixture of rock and dirty ice that was Callisto's surface.

"Better stop here," Jarrod Whitehead cautioned. The pilot was Thorpe's guide. The two of them were striding across the flat plain of the Valhalla Basin two kilometers north of the scientific station.

Overhead, Jupiter was three-quarters full. The Great Red Spot was near the terminator, having just crossed over from night into day. Except for variations in color, the great storm had not changed much since human beings had first turned their telescopes skyward.

Thorpe halted next to where the Callistan pilot had stopped. He glanced across the plain in front of him.

"Where is it?"

"You can't see it from here," Whitehead replied. "It's over the horizon. This is as close as you want to get, though. Wait, the director's calling me on the other channel. I'll be right back."

Thorpe watched the pilot's lips move through his visor as he conversed with the scientific station. The only sound that came to Thorpe was the distant hissing of the stars and galaxies. After a minute Whitehead returned to the communications channel the two of them were using.

"The director's started the thirty-second countdown. Make sure your feet are well apart and your legs flexed."

Thorpe turned to gaze in the same direction as his guide. Thirty seconds went by. He was about to ask what had gone wrong when there was a sudden thump against the soles of his boots. He rode out the shock with flexed knees. A moment later a geyser erupted from somewhere over the horizon.

The fountain was typical of a low gravity, airless world. It spewed upward like a giant flower, spraying thin fog toward the heavens. In that first instant of eruption Thorpe had an impression of a large cylindrical object racing skyward. It had receded too fast for the eye to follow.

"Hot damn, it works!" Whitehead exclaimed. "I had my doubts there for a moment."

Thorpe nodded. He had had his own doubts when he first heard the proposal. The director's plan involved launching a series of cylindrical tanks containing liquid hydrogen. Up to six cylinders at a time were to be loaded into a vertical shaft left over from the early explorations of the moon. A small toroid containing a few milligrams of antimatter would then be dropped to the bottom. The toroid would release its charge of antimatter on impact. The matter/antimatter reaction would flash ice into steam, and the resulting explosion would hurl the stacked fuel cylinders upward at greater than escape velocity. *Admiral Farragut* would then chase the cylinders down and transfer their vital cargoes to its own tanks.

"What do they say about the speed?" Thorpe asked.

"Radar clocks it at five kilometers per second," Whitehead replied. "It has definitely broken free of Callisto and is in orbit about the big guy! Of course, when we get six tanks stacked one atop the other, launch velocities will be slower. They should still be adequate, though."

"And how long to reload?"

Whitehead's grimace was visible through his visor. "That's a problem. We just fired our only tank. We'll have to make more."

"How the hell are you going to do that? Surely you don't have that much sheet metal just lying around free!"

"We don't make them out of metal," the pilot said. "We cast them from ice."

"You're kidding!"

"Not at all. Ice is a dandy structural material under Callistan conditions, and casting the tanks is easy."

Thorpe grinned sheepishly inside his suit. "And with liquid hydrogen inside, I guess they aren't going to melt anytime soon."

"You can believe that, chief!"

"How do you keep them from tumbling after launch?"

"We don't," Whitehead replied. "The tanks are four meters in diameter by one hundred meters long."

Thorpe nodded. "Of course, they're self-stabilizing! They orbit with one end facing Jupiter."

"It helps to launch them with as little tumble as possible, of course," the pilot said. "Otherwise it might take a damnably long time for the tank to reach stability."

"So how long to begin launching in earnest?"

There was a moment's pause before Whitehead said, "We ought to be able to launch three times during any twenty-four-hour period."

"Six tanks per launch . . ." Thorpe's words drifted into inaudibility as he did a fast calculation in his head. "I make it a week to fully replenish our fuel stocks."

"I'd make that two weeks," the pilot responded. "Remember that Callisto orbits through Jove's radioactive tail in another six days. All activity on the surface will have to stop then."

"May I see the shaft?"

Thorpe followed Whitehead to the source of the geyser. The pilot cautioned him to be careful as they approached the edge. Thorpe saw the reason as he directed his helmet light into the hole. No matter how far he narrowed the beam, he could not see the bottom.

"How deep is this?"

"Three point seven five kilometers," Whitehead responded.

Thorpe looked up and blinked in surprise. "What the hell were you guys trying to do?"

"This is a test bore to check out surface conditions. You should see the real thing. In fact, I'll show it to you if you have the time. It's fifty kilometers southeast of here. As of last week, it was down to a depth of fourteen kilometers."

"Don't tell me you've found gold on this rock?"

The pilot's chuckle was a deep burbling sound in Thorpe's earphones. "Not hardly. No, we're trying to penetrate the crust and break into the subterranean ocean. That's one of the reasons we located the station at Valhalla. The crust's only about fifty kilometers deep under our feet. It's a couple of hundred kilometers everywhere else."

"Why drill through the crust?"

"We don't drill these things, we melt them. As for why, that's easy. We think there may be life down there. We've found some highly tantalizing hints. So, what do you think of our cannon?"

Thorpe let his lamp play across the walls of the bore. Here and there, rivulets of water melted by the recent explosion had already refrozen.

"My compliments," he said. "Jules Verne would have been proud of you!"

Whitehead's guffaw echoed through Thorpe's helmet. "I guess he would, at that!"

CHAPTER 15

Three days after *Admiral Farragut*'s arrival at Callisto, most of the station staff and the ship's crew were engaged in refueling the freighter. Both Captain Olafson and Tom Thorpe had returned to the ship to direct operations while other expedition members took their places on the moon. Amber Hastings and the station's scientists were concentrating on plans to track the comet through its close encounter with Jupiter.

"The trick will be coordinating your telescopic observations with our ground-based radar," Radha Rajapur, Callisto's chief astronomer, explained. The two of them were studying the latest plot of the comet nucleus's predicted orbit through the Jovian system. "If we can do that, then we can annotate your observations with precise position and velocity information on a second by second basis."

"That shouldn't be too difficult," Amber replied. "With the comet passing inboard of Callisto, you people will have the best seats in the house."

Rajapur, a small Indian with piercing black eyes, nodded. "We have been most fortunate. I will have to burn incense to the Goddess of Luck next time I am home."

As the discussion continued, Amber reflected that the ancients may not have been far wrong when they had thought comets a potent omen. One single point of light in the sky had most certainly altered her own life. Even a year earlier she would have told anyone who suggested that she would ever visit Jupiter that they were crazy. Now she was planning the first look at what would almost surely be the most spectacular comet in history.

Comet Hastings was far from spectacular at the moment, however. The gaseous coma had grown to only a few thousand kilometers, and would likely undergo a significant change during its trip through the Jovian system. By studying the interaction of coma and cis-Jupiter space, the scientists at Callisto Station hoped to learn as much about their own backyard as they did about the comet.

Amber had studied comets extensively since her discovery. She knew that they did not usually form a tail until they were within 2.5 Astronomical Units of the sun. Some astronomers were betting that Comet Hastings's large nucleus would cause it to grow a tail early. They cited the case of Comet Humason in 1962, which had developed a pronounced tail at 2.6 A.U. An opposing camp maintained that the massive nucleus would retard tail formation. They pointed to the vast heat sink that the nucleus represented. Even that group conceded, however, that once the nucleus heated up, it would produce a spectacular tail that would grace Earth's skies every seven years for centuries.

Nor were close approaches to Jupiter all that uncommon. In 1886 Comet Bennet had actually approached to within 400,000 kilometers of the planet, dipping well inside the orbit of Io. The comet had been observed to split into several small pieces following the encounter. In fact, most of the periodic comets had at one time encountered the King of Worlds. Their orbits bore the indelible marks of Jupiter's influence.

After four hours of discussion, Amber and the Callisto scientists had worked their plans to the point where they could begin actual preparations. They had established a rigid observational timeline, with targets of primary and secondary importance marked to the millisecond. By following the plan, both *Admiral Farragut* and Callisto Station would be assured that they were observing the same phenomenon at the same time.

"I'd say that about does it," Amber said when they had completed their timeline.

"Agreed," Rajapur replied. "I suggest that we adjourn for a few hours. I believe, Amber, that you are to be the guest of honor at the gala banquet tonight!"

Amber nodded. "Since the captain and Tom Thorpe have abandoned us, I guess I'm elected."

Callisto Station had been excavated from ice and stone one hundred meters below the Valhalla Basin. Since ice was an excellent sealing material, the station purposely maintained its corridors at temperatures below freezing, heating only the individual compartments where people lived and worked. As Amber walked back to her quarters, snuggled inside an electrically heated "snowsuit," she heard her name echo through the long corridor. She turned to see John Malvan hurrying toward her. The one-armed ex-miner had arrived on the previous day's shuttle flight. He moved in the distance-eating, low gravity stride of a native Lunarian.

"Hello, John!" she said. "I haven't seen you since you landed. Where have you been keeping yourself?"

"I've been letting the station people show me around, and bringing Luna up to date on our progress."

"Why not use the radio aboard ship?"

Malvan shrugged. "They've got enough problems chasing fuel cylinders." Left unsaid was the fact that Malvan was also demonstrating his independence of Tom Thorpe and Captain Olafson.

"What have you seen?"

"Quite a lot!" he replied. "I just returned from a visit to the hole they're boring through the crust. Have you seen it?"

"No. I've heard it's pretty deep."

"Deeper than anything we've ever tried on Luna. God, what I wouldn't have given in the old days to find ice deposits like the ones they've got on this moon. There's more ice in the crust than rock."

"I know what you mean," Amber replied. "If we had even half the water they waste here, Luna would be swimming."

"Where are you headed?"

"Back to my rooms to get cleaned up for the big banquet."

"Mind if I walk with you?"

"Not at all. What's on your mind?"

"Seeing all this ice has gotten me to thinking."

"About what?"

"I've been wondering why Sierra Corporation is interested in Comet Hastings."

Amber laughed. As she did so, exhalation fog swirled around her like smoke. "The same reason Luna is interested in it! They want to mine the ice and make a fortune."

"But if mining ice is their goal, why not Callisto? I've asked Director Kaffin. He says that they'd be happy to have someone start a commercial operation here. It would triple the number of ships which call each year and reduce the cost of operating this station."

Amber stopped and turned toward Malvan. "Mining Callisto has been tried. The economics were against it."

"Precisely!" Malvan replied. "So what makes Comet Hastings any more attractive? It can't be the distance. You yourself say the comet's postencounter orbit will take it beyond Jupiter. So, why not Callisto instead?"

"You can ask the same thing about Luna. Why do we want it?"

"We want it because *they* want it. Everybody knows Halver Smith is an expert. If he thinks he can make it pay, then he probably can."

She nodded. "Tom said they have some inexpensive method for getting their cargoes into transfer orbits."

"What method? Has anyone explained it to you?"

"No, it's a trade secret."

"Why? Everyone will know how they do it the first time it's used. Why the big secret?"

"You've obviously thought this through. Make your point."

"I think they're planning to capture the comet and put it in orbit about the Earth."

"Impossible! The damned thing masses sixty million billion tons. It would take all the energy the human race ever produced and then some to get it into Earth orbit."

"Not if they plan to slice off a small piece and orbit that while they stick the Republic with the useless remainder."

"They can't do that. It would violate the agreement."

"How? We agreed to share the nucleus equally. They will have one percent and we will have ninety-nine. What court would fault them for their generosity?"

"Then we slice off a chunk of our own," Amber replied, "and take it to Earth orbit."

"Sure, the next time the comet enters the inner system. How long will that take?"

"Seven years."

"In the meantime, Halver Smith has a monopoly on ice production and charges anything he damned well pleases."

"Do you have any proof that's what they're planning?" Amber asked.

"No. It's just a scenario at the moment. With your help, I may be able to get proof."

"I won't spy for you!"

"I'm not asking you to spy. I'm asking you to keep your eyes open. If you happen to hear anything about SierraCorp's plans for the nucleus, I'd like you to tell me."

"Why should I?"

"Because you are a patriotic Lunarian and I'm the official representative of your government. Think about it. Now, if you'll excuse me, I've promised some of the station staff that I will sit in on their bridge tournament."

With that he turned and walked away. Amber watched him go. When she had finished her meeting with Rajapur and his colleagues, she had been tired but happy. Now she was frightened. Despite the warning Thorpe had given them at the outset, politics was raising its ugly head.

"There she is, Mr. Thorpe. Stand ready with the fueling line!"

Thorpe perched in the space between two of *Admiral Farragut*'s white-painted hydrogen tanks, feeling like a fly caught on a billiard table. He gazed out into space toward Jupiter, with the still-large half disk of Callisto to his left. Far off in the distance, just above the planet's ruddy limb, he could see the cylinder that was their prize. As Jarrod Whitehead had predicted, it orbited with one end pointed at the planet, held there by the force of Jupiter's tides. Captain Olafson, too, was taking advantage of the tidal force. As *Admiral Farragut* slowly closed on the icy fuel tank, the ship's bow pointed directly toward Jupiter's heart.

"Uh-oh," Thorpe muttered, wishing he could rub his burning eyes inside his helmet. "This one's got some spin on it!"

As he watched, the pattern of black stripes around one end of the cylinder slowly changed position. Thorpe chinned the timer in his helmet and waited until the same pattern recurred.

"I make it one point five revolutions per minute, Emilio."

"I concur, Mr. Thorpe," Rodriguez said. "Any suggestions?"

"This is one we buck upstairs." Thorpe reported his discovery to Captain Olafson.

"It's too risky," she decided. "You'll tangle the fueling line. Come back in and we'll abandon this one."

"Let's not be hasty," Thorpe replied. "This is the last of the second batch. It isn't as though we have another candidate readily available. Why not finish the approach and give us time to look the situation over?"

"I'll not take unnecessary risks."

"Agreed, Captain. But it won't hurt to look."

"Very well. Are you two anchored out there?"

"Anchored," they answered in unison.

"Very well. Stand clear of the jets."

The flare of reaction-control jets signaled the start of the final approach to the cylinder. So far they had been forced to abandon two of the free-flying tanks. One had gone tumbling out of control, and the second had split open during launch. Thorpe did not want to give up a third unless absolutely necessary.

The captain brought the ship's stern to a halt some fifty meters from their quarry. Looking down from his perch, Thorpe could see the bronze-colored vent valve that was their goal. The valve rotated slowly as the cylinder spun about its axis. If they hooked up to it, the rotation would knot the fueling line within a few minutes.

"What if we spin the ship, Mr. Thorpe?" Rodriguez asked. "We can line up our stern with the cylinder's axis and match its rate of rotation. That way we can hook up without winding the line into a knot."

"What about the loop?" Thorpe asked. Whatever slack they maintained in the line would cause it to bow. That would not be a problem while the line was empty, but as soon as it filled with hydrogen, the swinging mass would cause both the spinning ship and the fuel cylinder to wobble. If it got bad enough, they might collide.

"Run a safety line over and have the captain pull it taut with the jets. We can hang the fuel line from it and keep it from bowing."

Thorpe thought about it, then broached the subject with the captain over the radio link.

"Have you any idea how hot our exhaust nozzle is?" she responded. By "hot," she meant radioactive.

"All right, if we can't go over the stern, we'll go over the bow. Turn the ship head on to the cylinder. We'll lash the fueling line to handholds all the way forward. You match the tank's rotation, we jump across, and all any of us have to worry about is getting dizzy before we finish the job."

Once again there was a pause in the conversation as the captain considered the suggestion. "It just might work. I'll move in close, say to within twenty meters."

"The line ought to reach," Thorpe agreed.

"Secure while I turn the ship!"

The banquet was held in the main hall of Callisto Scientific Station, where a large gallery had been carved from the ice and then insulated with heavy translucent panels.

"I understand from Dr. Rajapur that you two have just about finished planning your observations," Director Kaffin said to Amber midway through the meal.

"Yes, indeed," Amber replied. "Between our two sets of instruments, we will observe the comet across the full range of the electromagnetic spectrum."

"I'm sorry I wasn't able to attend your meetings. The refueling has been taking most of my time."

"How's it going?"

"We just launched our third set of six. Captain Olafson has notified us that we can stop after tomorrow's series of launches. That's very good news. The launch crews are exhausted."

"I hear the same thing from the ship," Amber said. "Luckily, chasing the comet doesn't require the same amount of reaction mass that the run out from Earth did."

Admiral Farragut's original design had included only a single hexagram of hydrogen tanks around the ship's power module. That capacity had been tripled for the Comet Hastings Expedition—to a total of 72,000 cubic meters. Those two extra rows of white spheres, plus the antimatter plasma the ship had taken on at the Sierra Skies Powerstat, gave the converted freighter the ability to change its velocity by a hundred kilometers per second. Virtually all of that delta V capability had been required to reach Jupiter six months after launch. To replace all the hydrogen they had used on the outbound leg would require the launch of more than one hundred fuel cylinders.

Fortunately, chasing the comet as it left the Jovian system required far less acceleration. Two dozen cylinders would provide sufficient reaction mass to continue the mission. Allowance for unavoidable wastage brought the number of tanks to be launched to thirty. Once at the comet, of course, *Admiral Farragut*'s crew would have two years in which to refine the reaction mass they would need to return home.

"Perhaps you would explain the significance of what you and

Dr. Rajapur are doing," Kaffin said. "My board of directors will be interested."

"Certainly. Your ground-based radar will track the comet through the system. It will provide us with our first position determination for calculating the comet's new orbit."

"Have pity on me, Miss Hastings. I am merely a poor biochemist with a knack for administration. I know very little about orbital mechanics."

"An orbit has six classical elements, Mr. Director. These are its semimajor axis, eccentricity, inclination to the ecliptic, longitude of the ascending node, argument of periapsis, and time of periapsis passage. It isn't necessary for a layman to understand all of that. It's enough to know that we need three good position readings, or two positions and a time, to fully define the orbit. Your radar sightings will give us the first of these as the comet leaves the Jovian system."

"But surely your ship can do just as good a job."

"No, sir. You see, a spacecraft in flight seldom knows precisely where it is. Your station, on the other hand, occupies a known point on a moon that has been tracked for centuries. At any instant in time, we know where Callisto Scientific Station is with absolute precision. Your radar measurements will tell us where the comet is with respect to Callisto, which in turn will allow us to calculate the nucleus's position."

"My old physics teacher told me that there is no such thing as absolute precision, Miss Hastings."

Amber laughed. "Believe me, on the scale we're talking about, this will come damn close!"

"And how do you plan to get your second 'absolutely perfect' position reading?"

"We plan to match velocities with the comet and follow it for a month."

"You just said that you won't know where you really are. How will you know where the comet is?"

"Farside Observatory will transmit a modulated laser beam in our direction periodically after we leave Jupiter. By noting the arrival time of that beam, we will be able to measure the distance between *Admiral Farragut* and Luna to within a few tens of meters. Do that half a dozen times and you have an orbital prediction almost as good as the one we have for Callisto. Naturally, we'll cross-check using Mars, Venus, and Jupiter sightings, as well as your station's laser beacon."

"It sounds very complicated."

"It isn't really. It's just time-consuming and requires a degree of precision that isn't often needed, not even in astronomy."

Kaffin picked up his ornate wineglass, a product of local manufacture. It showed the nymph Callisto being changed into a bear. "My compliments to you, Miss Hastings, and my very great wishes for your success!"

CHAPTER 16

Admiral Farragut's second passage through the radiation belts of Jupiter was far less comfortable than the first had been. For one thing, it took longer. Being in orbit about Callisto meant sharing the moon's leisurely orbit around the big planet. At Callisto's distance from Jupiter, the passage took seventy hours.

Nor were three days' isolation in the storm cellar the only difference. Since everyone had been awakened, there were seven more living, breathing bodies crammed into the restricted space. To make room, most expedition members kept to their cold-sleep tanks unless they had duties that required them to move about. Meals were untidy affairs where everyone tried to keep their food from the path of errant elbows, knees, and backsides. Amber began to notice the odor of too many people and too much machinery in too close proximity. Adding to her discomfort were cooking odors and the unsavory aroma that emanated from the compartment's single toilet.

The last eight hours had been the worst. Everyone watched the chronometer as it counted down the minutes to freedom. Captain Olafson's announcement that the outside radiation detectors had fallen silent was followed by a loud cheer. The echoes had barely died away when a stream of unkempt bodies headed for the outer decks.

Captain Olafson gave her passengers and crew one hour to recover from their ordeal. By the end of that time nearly everyone aboard had damp hair, a new jumpsuit, and smelled of soap and lotion. Strapped into her couch in the control room, Karin Olafson monitored water consumption. The return to normal usage was her signal to sound First Acceleration Warning. Fifteen minutes later *Admiral Farragut* dropped away from Callisto for the last time. The freighter was en route to its assigned station just beyond the orbit of Ganymede.

"Communications check, time check," Amber said into her headset.

Seven seconds later Radha Rajapur's voice came back to her: "We read you clearly. At the mark, the time is 21:16:00. Mark!"

Amber glanced at the chronometer, added the three-and-a-half-second communications delay, and nodded. A voice time check was no substitute for the radio timing signals traveling continuously between ship and station. Still, it served to confirm that the computers had indeed achieved synchronization.

She acknowledged Rajapur's message, then turned to Cragston Barnard beside her. "The communications link is properly established, Dr. Barnard."

"And the data links?"

Amber keyed in a series of commands to her computer terminal and watched the response on an auxiliary screen. "All data links are operating normally," she said after a few seconds.

"Record cubes?"

"On line. We have triple redundancy across the board."

"Attitude program?"

"Loaded in and ready to run."

"Very well. Let's take some manual observations while we're waiting for the automatic program to start. Call the captain and have her relinquish control to us."

Amber signaled the control room and passed on Barnard's request. A few seconds later the captain announced that the ship would be undergoing quick changes of orientation and that passengers and crew should move about with caution. That done, she told Amber that she was free to rotate the ship.

Two quick bursts of the attitude-control jets brought the telescope to bear on the comet. Another command set the instrument's field of view to maximum. The comet's ghostlike coma filled the screen. For the past two weeks the milk-white ball had grown progressively brighter. The comet had been inside the Jovian system for quite some time, having passed inside the orbits of Himalia and Leda just as *Admiral Farragut* had entered the trailing radiation belt. Now that it was less than five million kilometers from the big planet, its visible coma had grown to nearly one-quarter of a million kilometers.

"Let's take a string of observations at all wavelengths. It looks like we're getting some disturbance along the leading edge."

Amber ordered that the comet be recorded across the full spectrum, then looked up at the screen. Sure enough, the uniform gas ball was beginning to grow tendrils around the edges. Compared to interplanetary space, the Jovian system was thick with atoms, molecules, and bits of gas and dust. The micrometeoroid count alone was several orders of magnitude higher than in open space.

As the gas of the comet's coma penetrated ever deeper into the system, it suffered from increasingly frequent collisions with Jovian flotsam. The result was a distinct flattening of its leading edge. What had been a nearly perfect sphere was quickly turning into a blunt teardrop. A tenuous shock wave of excited particles took form 100,000 kilometers in front of the nucleus. The behavior of that shock wave would tell the watching scientists as much about cis-Jupiter space as it would about the structure of the nascent comet.

When the multispectral photographs were completed, Barnard ordered that they take their first close look at the nucleus. Although the comet was still a number of hours away, the time had come to observe surface details. Once the comet sailed past Jupiter, it would be between the ship and the sun. To the astronomers aboard *Admiral Farragut*, the nucleus would appear a tiny crescent shape, a bare sliver of light with too little surface illuminated to make out details.

As Barnard expanded the telescope's magnification, the ball of light swelled until its edges overflowed the screen. With the increase in magnification came a decrease in the amount of light being gathered. Automatic contrast controls compensated for much of the loss, but were unable to counteract a slow dimming of the screen.

After thirty seconds they reached maximum magnification. In the center of the screen was a tiny disk. Barnard did something to improve the contrast, and the object developed a pattern of splotches where none had existed before. There was also a suggestion of rays emanating away from the nucleus into the surrounding gas cloud, as if invisible rivers of matter were boiling off the ball of ice.

"There's your namesake, Amber. Glad you came along?"

She hunched forward intently, bringing herself into contact with the seat belt which kept her from floating away. After half a minute spent studying the image, she sighed. "There have been times in the past week that I've wondered about that, Crag. But now . . . I wouldn't have missed seeing this for anything!"

While Amber and Barnard busied themselves with observations, most of the other scientists looked over their shoulders via the ship's intercom. Karin Olafson took the time to confer with her husband in the control room. The subject was their ship's health following its second transit of Jupiter's radiation belts.

"Think she'll hold up for one more dose, Stinky?"

Chief Engineer Stormgaard nodded slowly. As he did so, the captain could see the scar at his temple where, years earlier, he had been gashed by an exploding impeller. Since that time, the scar had been a reliable indicator of his mood. When Kyle was calm, the scar was nearly invisible, but when he was angry or worried, it stood out in livid contrast. To her relief, she could barely see it.

"We've come through in remarkably good shape," he responded. "We'll have a fair number of electronic modules to replace after we're safely away from here, but nothing we can't handle."

The two of them were loosely tied to their respective couches by safety belts, but otherwise floated free below the dome. The control room was their favorite place aboard ship. Many a time they had made love in the couches there with a vast Earth and a limitless black sky above them. As they floated, they held hands with the unconscious ease of those long married.

"What about these damaged engine-control circuits? Shall we replace them before we begin chasing after the damned comet?"

Stormgaard shook his head. "Not unless we plan to make another orbit around Jupe. Schmidt or Rodriguez would have to suit up and go outside. I'd hate to be out there when the astronomers decide they want to take a look in some new direction."

Karin nodded. The possibility of a crewman being blasted by an attitude-control jet was too great to allow anyone outside during telescopic observations. Before anyone left the security of the habitat module, she planned to have the jets under her personal control.

The schematic diagram on an auxiliary screen showed a series of colored rectangles connected by complex patterns of lines. Each rectangle had at least one arcane code; some had several. Nor was the diagram static. Even as they watched, one of the blocks changed color and took on a new code. The captain was relatively adept at reading the symbols, but the chief engineer was the expert in their family.

Kyle Stormgaard had long ago made the science of electronics his personal specialty, even to the point of studying its history and evolution. The history of electronics, he had often expounded to his wife, was a paradoxical evolution. Devices of exponentially increasing complexity had somehow bred ever simpler levels of utility. When the field began, each functional element had been represented by a single discrete device. Resistors, capacitors, inductors, vacuum tubes, diodes, and transformers had all been laboriously assembled by hand. Later, hand wiring had been replaced by printed circuit boards and vacuum tubes by transistors. In just a few decades transistors had given way to the plastic cockroach shapes of integrated circuits, and then to the short-lived surface-mount technology.

Then, early in the twenty-first century, someone had invented the ultimate integrated circuit, one that could be programmed to simulate any other. Which function the circuit performed was controlled by software. Once those "virtual functions" had been programmed into the circuit, they could be changed from moment to moment. Thus was born the "electronic function module."

Instead of thousands of specialized chips, *Admiral Farragut*'s electronic suite consisted of a few dozen devices for power handling which were coupled to millions of identical modules. The ship's central computer kept track of what went where on a second-by-second basis, programming and reprogramming the modules as the need arose. The system had the advantage of being inherently fault tolerant, redundant, and self-healing.

That they had dared to enter the Jovian radiation belts at all was due to the basic tolerance of the function modules. When a module was damaged, the ship's computer automatically compensated for the loss by reprogramming other modules. The ship would go on functioning until so many modules were damaged that the computer lost its ability to heal the damage. Precisely when that point would be reached was what worried Karin Olafson.

"What say we have a pull-and-plug party as soon as we're lined up with the departing comet?" the captain asked.

"Good idea. We can look over the hull and see what kind of a scouring we've been taking while floating around in this pea soup."

"How long to put us back into full service?"

Stormgaard glanced at the readout that carried the running tally of inactive modules. "Forty hours if we rely on the crew. Perhaps as few as twelve if we call on the passengers to help."

Karin nodded. "All except the astronomers. Something tells me that they are going to have their hands full for the next month!"

Twelve hours later Amber and Barnard were more than busy. They were frantic! Things were happening almost too fast for human comprehension. Though the pace made little difference to the computer, it was frustrating everyone trying to follow the action.

The telescope had just finished a series of detailed examinations of the comet's coma in the infrared spectrum. Multiple collisions with the dense Jovian medium were beginning to heat up the dust and gas. The observations would later be paired with Callisto's radar maps to form a minute-by-minute examination of the ways in which the passage had affected the coma's structure.

"Stand by," Barnard muttered to no one in particular as the series came to an end. Latest readings put the comet's periapsis at 1.62 million kilometers and the time of closest approach fifteen minutes in the future. "We're about to get our last photos of the nucleus for the next month or so."

Amber nodded. The screen finished flicking from point to point within the gassy coma. Although rigidly mounted to the ship's bow, the telescope had a limited ability to shift its view, which it accomplished by adjusting the collecting mirror at the center of the honeycomb skeleton. To point at the nucleus, however, required a ten-degree rotation of *Admiral Farragut* around its yaw axis. Everyone onboard was jolted first by a single long burst from the reaction jets, then again a few seconds later as the computer halted the ship's rotation.

The nucleus stood out in the center of the screen as the vibrations set up by the rough handling quickly died away. The nucleus had turned into a miniature planet three-quarters full. The comet head was seamed, as if by giant cracks. A large circular crater was also partially in view. The cracks and crater suggested that Comet Hastings had collided with some other body in the recent past—sometime in the past few billion years. Such a collision could well have sent the giant ice ball reeling sunward for the first time.

One thing Amber noticed immediately was that the comet's surface remained indistinct, softened as if by atmosphere. The effect was the result of 100,000 kilometers of gas and dust. Even though the coma was a very good vacuum, it obscured the nucleus's smaller details and softened the lines of the larger.

"Check with Callisto and see how they're doing," Barnard ordered.

For the tenth time in the hours since going to automatic, Amber signaled the scientific station. Once again the delay in receiving a response was seven seconds.

"Callisto here, *Admiral Farragut*," Rajapur replied. "Go ahead."

"How are your observations coming?"

"Wonderfully," Rajapur enthused. "You should see the swirl patterns we're getting between the coma and the local medium! You can actually see the lines of force that make up Jupiter's magnetosphere. We'll be able to plot the local field gradient in more detail than we've ever managed before."

"And your range data on the nucleus?"

The expected pause lengthened to nearly fifteen seconds.

"Had to get the latest projection," he explained when he returned. "You can tell your people that we have it pegged within a few wavelengths on our high-frequency radar. We've been continuously illuminating it with the comm laser as well. The returns are somewhat hit and miss, but by the time it leaves the system, we should have the orbital path plotted to within a few centimeters. How go things down below, *Farragut*?"

Amber described their own readings to Rajapur. When she was finished, the two of them exchanged a few other pieces of data before signing off. The full contact, including communications delays, had taken five minutes.

Ten minutes later the image on the screen had changed perceptibly. No longer three-quarters full, the small moon was half full and shrinking. Barnard intently watched the streaming numbers in the lower-right corner of the screen.

"That's it!" he announced. "The nucleus just passed periapsis. Signal the captain to make the announcement."

A few moments later Captain Olafson's voice echoed throughout the habitat module: "Attention, all hands! Dr. Barnard has just announced that the comet has reached minimum distance from Jupiter. It is now headed out of the system."

The cheering was audible even through the closed hatch of the telescope compartment. Amber and Barnard ignored the noise. They still had work to do.

Four hours later a bleary-eyed Cragston Barnard gazed at the tiny crescent shape on the screen, then turned to Amber with the lopsided grin that she remembered from her university days. "That about does it. Put her on automatic and let's get something to eat."

Amber leaned back in her own seat and stretched to get the kinks out of aching muscles. The tension of the past several hours had given her a stiff neck, and she was on the verge of exhaustion. It was a good exhaustion, though, the kind that followed something strenuous that had been particularly well done.

"How long shall we keep observing?"

"Another two hours at least," he replied. "I want to get a good set of pictures of the coma backlit by the sun. We can put them together in a stop-action series and actually see the turbulence building in the gas field. After that, we'll give control of the ship back to Captain Olafson so that she can start us after the nucleus."

Amber groaned.

Barnard frowned. "What's the matter?"

"It's time to go back into the storm cellar!"

He nodded. "Unless you want to get out your lead under-wear."

She unhooked her seat belt and floated into the air. "You go get something to eat without me. I want to get cleaned up while I still have the chance."

CHAPTER 17

Jupiter barely showed as a disk aft, while the comet was a hazy patch of fog forward. For three weeks *Admiral Farragut* had chased that patch of haze and watched it grow steadily as they drew ever nearer to the fleeing quarry.

Thorpe glanced at the nebula as he floated free of the Number One airlock, then concentrated on pulling himself along a series of handholds that had been welded to the hull. When he reached his destination, he attached his safety line to a padeye, then pivoted to watch his student practice her first egress.

"Okay," he called over his suit radio. "You can start out now. Be sure you have a firm grip on the next handhold before you let go of the last."

As he watched, a lime-green arm appeared in the open airlock and groped for a handhold. As soon as the gloved hand had a firm grip, a helmet and armor-encased torso followed.

"How am I doing?" Hilary Dorchester asked as she pulled herself to where Thorpe bobbed at the end of his safety line.

"Not bad," he admitted grudgingly. "Make sure you get that line snapped to something before you let go. Free maneuvering is a lesson we'll get to later. I don't want to waste fuel retrieving you if you float away from the ship."

"Yes, boss!"

Hilary Dorchester was the expedition's low-temperature chemist. A buxom brunette in her early thirties, she had been the last to be revived after they had reached Callisto. Despite her position as "tail-end Charlie," or possibly because of it, she had lost no time in suggesting to Thorpe that he would be welcome in her bed on a continuing basis. Thorpe had politely turned down the invitation, and Hilary had accepted his decision with cheerful good manners. Subsequently, she had alternated her free time between Leon Albright, the expedition's geologist, Dieter Schmidt of *Farragut*'s crew, and lately, John Malvan.

Such arrangements of convenience were fairly common in space, and in fact Thorpe had enjoyed something similar with Nina Pavolev. Two people usually set up housekeeping as a defense against the constant danger of their daily lives. Sometimes they grew to love each other, sometimes not. In either case it was a good adaptation to an alien environment while it lasted. Considering the fact that there were but two unmarried women on the expedition, Thorpe would have had difficulty explaining his rejection of one of them. If pressed, he would have stammered that Amber would never have approved.

"All right," he said after Hilary had secured herself to the ship's hull. "We're going to start with a few basic exercises. I want you to get used to the effort required to move around in a vacsuit. Remember, that isn't a light summer frock you're wearing!"

She grinned behind her helmet visor. "I would never have chosen a frock that made me look this fat!"

Admiral Farragut had barely ended its final swoop around Jupiter when Captain Olafson ordered everyone but the astronomers to assist in replacing radiation-damaged modules, a number of which were located back along the freighter's thrust frame and could only be reached from outside. It soon became obvious that the expedition was woefully short of people who could handle themselves in vacuum. So while they tailed the comet, Captain Olafson had asked her husband and Tom Thorpe to teach the groundhogs the basics of living and working in a pressurized balloon.

In the past two weeks Thorpe had conducted a total of eight tours outside the ship. His technique was always the same. Two hours of lectures inside, followed by a gingerly exit onto the hull, then half an hour of familiarization. Once a student felt comfortable in the suit, Thorpe would lead them back along the habitat module toward the cargo bay. There they would open one of the oversize hatches and descend into the unlighted cylindrical cavern. Finding one's way amid the clutter of the dark holds was good practice for working on the night side of an asteroid. Such experience would come in handy when his fledgling vacuum monkeys began their explorations of the comet nucleus.

Later he planned to teach them to fly.

"How are things going, Mr. Malvan?" Kyle Stormgaard asked as he strapped himself down across from the ex-miner. The chief engineer and Luna's representative had gotten to know one another during the refueling operations off Callisto. Malvan had volunteered for outside duty, but had been turned down because of his handicap. He had nevertheless helped the spacers get into and out of their suits, and had generally taken some of the load off their shoulders. During that effort, he and Stormgaard had discovered a common passion for bridge. They played whenever they could get a foursome together. At other times they squared off at chess.

"Hello, Kyle!" Malvan replied as he secured the small chess computer to the table in *Admiral Farragut*'s wardroom. "Ready to be humbled?"

"The day a one-armed Lunatic can humble me, I'll turn in my master engineer's certificate!"

"That's too bad. I don't know what we're going to do without you for the rest of the trip."

With the start of the game came a halt to the banter. Both men played intensely through the opening moves, each pushing the other without letup. Only after each had irrevocably committed to a strategy did Malvan break the silence.

"I've often wondered, Kyle. Just why did you and Karin sign on for this expedition?"

The engineer considered whether or not to trade one of his own knights for Malvan's bishop, decided in favor of it, and made his move before answering. "The money's good, and Halver Smith financed an overhaul before we left. Besides, Karin and I wanted to do something different before we retire."

Malvan chuckled. "Did it for the adventure, eh?"

"Who knows? Maybe the scientists will name a crater after us. How about you?"

"Me?" Malvan asked. "I'm just a bureaucrat who decided it was safer for his career to come along than not." Malvan explained the circumstances of John Hobart's request that he be

Luna's representative. While they had been in cold sleep, Hobart was elected prime minister of the Republic.

"You must have wanted to come along, at least a little."

"The idea wasn't without its attractions," the Lunarian admitted. "I never really enjoyed my job as an auditor."

The chief engineer moved one of his pawns so as to threaten Malvan's queen. As expected, the pawn did not last long, but its sacrifice paved the way for a deep penetration by Stormgaard's king's rook. "Did you get your report off today?"

Malvan nodded. "Right on schedule, as usual."

Each Monday morning, ship's time, Malvan requested a secure communications link to Luna. He always transmitted a coded report detailing the events of the previous week. Included were factual events, shipboard gossip, and Malvan's own suspicions and surmises. The week after they had left Callisto, he reported his suspicions about SierraCorp splitting off a chunk of the comet and moving it to Earth orbit. So far his reports had brought nothing from Luna except routine acknowledgments.

"Rodriguez tells me that you transmitted twenty thousand bytes this morning," Stormgaard said. "Beats me how you find that much to say week after week."

Malvan moved his queen to threaten Stormgaard's rook, and the engineer quickly withdrew it three squares. "Not a whole lot else to do on this tub except write my reports. Still, I often wonder if I'll ever have anything truly worth reporting."

"Don't worry," the engineer replied. "Something will come along. Things always seem to happen in space."

Three weeks in front of her computer screen had given Amber a new respect for the ancient astronomers who had tracked comets across the heavens. With three sightings and only pencil and paper, they had accurately predicted the return of a comet eighty years into the future. To do that required a calculation that was relatively simple in theory, but mind-numbingly complex in practice. Even with computers, plotting a track through space required long hours and inhuman patience.

Amber and Cragston Barnard had spent much of the first week after the comet's encounter with Jupiter reviewing their data. Telescopic and radar observations had had to be correlated. When they had their own observations keyed to those of Callisto, they transmitted the entire batch to Luna. After that they had turned to discovering new facts about the comet.

Barnard had assigned himself to study the nucleus's physical features, while giving Amber the job of plotting the orbit. For his own task he relied on the observations they had taken just before the nucleus zipped past them at Jupiter. By the second week following their departure, the senior astronomer had produced a general map of the daylight hemisphere. The map showed several craters of differing size, plus a suggestion of fault lines criss-crossing the surface. The fault pattern appeared to be related to the large impact crater they had seen on the nucleus's limb.

While Barnard worked to map the nucleus, Amber continued her own task. It was essentially the same work she had performed at Farside Observatory. She used the radar measurements from Callisto to calculate the comet's location at its closest approach to Jupiter. By triangulating Callisto's data with their own, she was able to establish periapsis within a few hundred meters. She established that as her starting point for the comet's postencounter orbit.

With a single anchor point established, she turned to determining her own position in the cosmic scheme of things. Eighteen days after leaving Jupiter, she turned the telescope on Luna's tiny image and computed her distance from home. The ship's computer repeated that calculation more than a thousand times during the half hour in which *The Big Eye* transmitted the beam. In so doing, it defined a tiny chord of *Admiral Farragut*'s orbit about the sun. That in turn gave Amber an accurate prediction of their flight path for the next month. She punched up the ship's orbit on her screen. The nominal path was a ruby-red line surrounded by a sharp cone of ghostly blue. The cone represented the ever-increasing positional error over the next thirty days. Amber gazed at it and nodded in satisfaction. It was by far the best orbital projection they had ever had.

Having established where *Admiral Farragut* was, Amber set out to compute the position of the comet nucleus. At twenty-one days out of Jupiter the freighter finally pulled to within radar range of the fleeing planetoid. Amber used the radar return signal to give her a position vector. Since she knew *Admiral Farragut*'s own position, she was able to convert it into a vector describing the nucleus's position with respect to the Sun. By plugging that datum into the computer, plus the time since periapsis, plus the periapsis position, she was able to project the comet's orbit about the Sun.

It was nearly midnight ship's time when she finished her final calculations. She had just completed entering the last of the data when she was startled out of a warm intellectual fog by the sound of a voice behind her.

"Good evening. What's got you up at this time of night?"

She turned to see Tom Thorpe lever himself through the open hatchway. Despite her fatigue, she smiled.

"Hello. I might ask you the same. Aren't you supposed to take Hilary outside again tomorrow? You should be getting your rest."

Thorpe ignored the sarcasm in Amber's voice when she mentioned Hilary, and decided to change the subject. "How are things going?"

"Better than expected, actually," she told him. He moved forward, anchored one foot beneath the computer console and began massaging her shoulders. She sighed and closed her eyes. "I just finished up my second position point. I think we've got its orbit tied down pretty closely now. Oh, that feels good!"

"Glad you like it. Mind if I ask a question?"

"Go ahead."

"Will the tail stretch across the sky the way the news commentators have been saying?"

She shrugged. "That depends on two factors: brightness and distance. I can't help you on the first. The big versus cold argument is still raging. As to distance, that I *can* figure out!"

"Don't bother if it takes a long time to set up."

"No problem. I only have to push a button and let the computer do the work." Amber turned around. The movement put a temporary stop to his massaging. As his hands left her shoulders, she felt disappointment; but she was also relieved. She was not ready to follow where his touch might have led.

She typed a command into her workscreen. The display changed to show a schematic of the Solar system. The comet's orbit was superimposed over those of the planets and crossed each of them at an approximate thirty-degree angle. At the bottom of the screen were numbers showing the positions of each of the planets and Comet Hastings as the comet swept in toward perihelion. While Thorpe watched the display, Amber watched the numbers. The comet circled the Sun, the tiny representation of its tail swiveling to always point away into space. When the comet symbol had passed the orbit of Earth, Amber turned to Thorpe and whistled softly.

"What's the matter?" he asked.

She looked at him with wide eyes. "Earth is going to get a better look than I thought."

"It's going to be close?"

"Not on the inbound leg. Earth will be in another quadrant of the sky as the comet moves inbound. But eighty-six days later it will pass *very* close to Earth on the outbound leg!"

"How close?"

"I make it a near miss. No less than one planetary diameter, no more than two and a half. The planet will pass well inside the coma and tail. If the people predicting massive boil off are right, there ought to be a milky-white glow from horizon to horizon!"

"Too bad we'll have to abandon the nucleus before then," Thorpe said. "It ought to be an impressive sight. You could wave to the folks at home as you go by."

At his comment Amber's face took on an odd look. "Hmmm, I'd forgotten about home . . . Luna, that is!"

"What about it?"

"This orbital tracking model I'm using doesn't incorporate it. We don't usually include satellites because they take up too much processor time. Moon and asteroid gravitational pulls are usually insignificant. This time there could be a minor effect. Wait a minute while I plug Luna into the program."

Amber turned back to her work station and deftly broke into the program code. She modified it with sure, quick keystrokes. When next she ran the calculation, the visual display was gone, leaving only columns of numbers to march up the screen. When the calculation finished, Amber broke into the code once again to check her work. She ran the program a second time, taking great care to make sure that her comet-position data was correct. The slower speed at which the numbers appeared on the screen indicated to Thorpe that she had also substantially reduced her iteration interval.

When she had run through the program twice, she looked up at Thorpe. There were tears in her eyes.

"Well?" he asked. "Did Luna make a difference?"

"Luna will be in its first quarter during the encounter," Amber replied with a quaver in her voice. "That means that the axis of the Earth-Moon system will be lined up almost perfectly with the nucleus's orbital path. I'm certain it will miss Luna, although it will be damned close! My figures show no more than five thousand kilometers to spare, possibly a lot less."

"But it *will* miss?"

Amber's response was a nervous nod.

"Then why so glum? It ought to be a spectacular sight!"

"I should think so," Amber replied, her voice suddenly dead of all emotion. It was as if she had become part of the computer herself. "Luna's gravitational field isn't much, but at that range it doesn't have to be. The nucleus's orbit will be deflected ever so slightly; just enough that it will strike the Earth a glancing blow somewhere near the sunrise terminator. What happens after that depends on how inelastic the collision is. The nucleus could bury itself in the Earth, or it could bounce and continue its journey, or it may just loop into a high ballistic lob and come crashing down halfway around the world several hours later.

"It really doesn't matter, of course, since the initial impact will kill everyone and everything on Earth!"

PART 3

THE IMMOVABLE
OBJECT

CHAPTER 18

Jupiter was astern, and the sun was taking a steady toll on the planetoid of ice. Most of the surface volatiles had long since boiled away. Only in the deepest crevices were oxygen and hydrogen snows still to be found. The craters and plains were being continuously scoured by an ever more energetic solar wind. Even though the surface temperature was still well below their freezing points, water, methane, and carbon dioxide all began to sublimate under the bombardment. That new spate of outgassing added to the cloud of vapors that would soon begin to form the comet's tail.

Halver Smith stood on the balcony of his estate and listened to the muted party noises emanating from inside the big house. The occasion was his annual New Year's Eve gathering for SierraCorp executives and their guests. As he breathed the cold night air, he let his gaze drift outward. Holiday lights flowed through the valley below like a river of fireflies. A crescent moon cast the entire scene in silver, throwing the first tendrils of the night's fog into stark relief. In another hour Smith's mountaintop estate would be surrounded by a sea of silver fleece.

As he watched the fog, he mulled over the events of the twelve months just past. On balance, it had been a pretty good year. Not only was production up for all operating units, but the worrisome load of short-term debt he had carried a year earlier had largely been wiped out. For that he had to thank Tom Thorpe. Stock sales had soared almost from the moment the Comet Hastings Expedition had been announced. It seemed as if everyone who had bet *The Rock* would be an expensive flop was afraid to let a new, similar opportunity pass.

At the thought of the expedition, Smith let his gaze drift up toward Jupiter. It had been a month since the comet had transited the Jovian system. As expected, the story had been a two-day media sensation that was promptly forgotten. People would not think of the comet again until it became visible in the night sky of Earth.

There was a sudden increase in the party noise behind him. Smith turned to see a woman silhouetted against the light. He smiled as he recognized Anna Voltuna. The two of them had gone to college together. It had been Anna who introduced Smith to Victoria, who later had become his wife. Several times the three of them had gone sailing on the *Sierra Seas*, and Anna had often stayed with Victoria when Smith was away on business. After Victoria's death, she had helped him pick up the pieces of his life.

"So there you are!" she exclaimed upon spotting him at the far end of the balcony. "I've been looking all over for you. Are you alone?"

"Who did you expect to find with me?"

"Come now, Hal! I saw that buxom blonde hanging off your arm earlier this evening. It's well known that men of your age and social standing have a certain... vulnerability, shall we say?"

"Is that why you were so cautious? You thought I might be feeling up some young thing out here?"

Anna laughed. "I wouldn't have put it so crudely, but yes! It would have been an encouraging sign, too. You work too hard! All you ever think about is that damned asteroid of yours. You should have more fun in your life. If a fling would help relax you, then I'm all for it."

"I'll keep that in mind the next time I'm propositioned. Did you come out here just to lecture me on my love life?"

"Not exactly," she said, shivering. "I had a couple of reasons. The first is that you still owe me a kiss from Christmas."

"So I do. And the second?"

"Your man Jarmon's looking for you."

"Did we run out of champagne?" The question was rhetorical. Halver Smith's wine cellar was renowned on three continents.

She shook her head. "The night communications supervisor called from headquarters. They've got a message for you from space."

"From *The Rock*?"

Anna shrugged. "You know I can't tell one planet from another. Jarmon seemed excited. He told me the message is in your private code. He's checking the back of the house. I remembered seeing you head this way, so I decided to track you down."

"Thanks," he said. "It's probably *The Rock*'s manager complaining about the comptroller again. Those two have been going at it for months. You will excuse me, won't you?"

"Not until I get my kiss."

"Right," he said with a grin. He moved to enclose her in his arms, and for a few moments they were twenty again. After a long moment, he broke the kiss. "Sorry, but I'd best find out what's up."

"You are coming back to the party, aren't you?"

"If I can." With that, he took Anna by the arm and escorted her inside.

It took him five minutes to track down his butler among the throngs of party goers. He eventually found Jarmon in the back bedroom, where an all-night poker game was in progress.

"You have a message for me, Jarmon?"

"Yes, sir. The duty communicator at headquarters forwarded a long, coded communiqué. The authenticators indicate that it is one of your personal codes."

"Who sent it?"

"Mr. Thorpe aboard *Admiral Farragut*, sir."

Halver Smith's eyebrows lifted in surprise. In the eight months since the expedition had left Earth, Thorpe had had no need to communicate with him directly. That he did so now could only mean trouble. Something must have gone wrong with the ship.

"Where is this message now?"

"In your personal file in the household computer, sir. Where do you want to take it?"

"My study, I think. Go clear out anyone you find. Do it quietly. Any rumors that get started tonight could cause our stock trouble tomorrow."

"I'll take care of it, sir."

Smith circulated through the crowd for five minutes, bantering with his employees, friends, and neighbors. At the end of that time Jarmon sought him out and loudly announced that an old friend was on the phone wanting to wish him a happy New Year. Smith made an excuse and followed the butler to his study.

"Nicely done. Any problems?"

"No, sir. The room was empty. I took the liberty of activating the antieavesdropping equipment to standby and closing the privacy curtains."

"Thank you. You may return to your duties. If anyone asks, give them the friend-on-the-phone story."

"Yes, sir."

As soon as Jarmon closed the door, Smith activated a control that sealed the room. At the same time a quiet buzzing emanated from the walls and ceiling, insuring that any eavesdropping device would return only white noise.

He sat down at his work station and keyed for his personal data file. Sure enough, at the top of the list was a message from Thorpe. Smith's eyes swept the file log and noted that the message had been transmitted in two parts. The first was in text format; the second, and largest, in binary. As Jarmon had indicated, the message authenticators showed the file to be encrypted in one of Smith's personal codes.

At the last keystroke the screen cleared. The message appeared to be a technical report on the comet's orbital parameters. Smith began to scan rapidly, intent on discovering what Thorpe considered so urgent that he had to bother the big boss with it. He got as far as the end of the second paragraph:

. . . this analysis indicates that the comet nucleus will impact the Earth at 20:12:16, 17 July 2087. Such an impact will, of course, destroy all life on Earth.

Smith stopped, blinked, and went back to the beginning. He reread it slowly, letting his eyes move from word to word rather than down the screen in his normal fast scan. It was the slowest he had read anything since the sixth grade. He could not help himself. He kept stumbling over unbelievable statements written in a dry, matter-of-fact style.

. . . velocity and position accurate to six decimal places . . . sixty million billion tons . . . will arrive with a ten-kilometer-per-second differential with respect to the Earth . . . glancing blow on the leading terminator . . . behavior unknown postimpact . . . assumptions should be checked by experts . . .

As his palms suddenly became clammy with sweat, Smith performed a trick he had learned in college. He willed himself to be totally accepting, shutting off the voice inside his brain that kept screaming that it could not be so. With the effort of will, his thoughts took on a dreamlike quality. It was almost as if it were someone else reading Thorpe's catalog of horrors. Only when he reached the end of the report did he sit back to consider what, if true, was surely the Earth's death warrant. After an indeterminate time he refocused his eyes and quickly scanned the report's various appendices. Most were technical supporting evidence.

A second after he keyed acceptance of the binary attachment, his screen flashed to display a diagram of the Solar system. In addition to the orbits of the planets out to Jupiter, the schematic showed a long ellipse with a tiny comet symbol slowly moving sunward. In a little over a minute the comet swept in from the outer system, rounded Sol, and began to move back out again. The blue-white marker that represented Earth moved to intercept it.

The screen flashed to show the Earth and Moon in close-up.

As Smith watched, the comet swam slowly toward Luna. The two passed one another by less than a lunar diameter.

The comet approached Earth from below and behind, closing at an angle of approximately thirty degrees. As the tail swept across the planet, the tiny dot representing the nucleus moved in front of it. The two markers merged as one. The display froze, save for a single blinking word etched in scarlet letters:

IMPACT!

Halver Smith played the projection through twice more. The result was the same each time.

As he scanned through the attachments to the report, he found a list of recommendations as to how things should be handled from that point on. By and large, they were common sense things to do if faced with the end of the world: 1) get independent confirmation, 2) quietly notify the authorities, 3) avoid public panic, and 4) work to avert the catastrophe. At the bottom of the page was a short note in Tom Thorpe's handwriting:

Mr. Smith,
    Identical report and recommendations forwarded to Prime Minister Hobart, Republic of Luna.
                                                            Tom

Smith frowned. He would have preferred to be the sole recipient of this news—at least for the time being. Still, he could not blame the expedition's Lunarian contingent for warning their own people. Luna's inhabitants had as much stake in what happened to the Earth as the average terrestrial. After all, they were dependent on the Mother World for much of what they needed to live. They would not long survive its destruction.

Like Halver Smith, John Hobart was in a state of shock after decoding the apocalyptic announcement. Since Luna was on Universal Time, it was already New Year's Day there. Like Smith, he had decoded the message at home and then watched the terrible words march up his computer screen. He had then keyed for the graphic display that showed the comet colliding with the Earth. He had watched the collision ten times when his screen beeped for attention.

"Sorry, Prime Minister," the duty operator at the capital said as soon as she saw his face. "I have Halver Smith on the line from Earth. He claims it is very important that he speak to you. He's listed as a V.I.P., so I thought I'd better check."

Hobart blinked. The note from Malvan had told of a copy of the report being forwarded to the SierraCorp chairman on Earth.

"All right. Put him through. Then I want this line sealed."

The phone screen cleared to show Smith staring out at him. The terrestrial tycoon's round face was accentuated by the distortion of the phone pickup. Smith's features remained frozen, as if he were in a trance—an effect caused by the three-second delay between Earth and Luna. Finally, recognition showed in his eyes and he began to speak.

"Good morning, Citizen Hobart."

"Hello, Mr. Smith. Where are you calling from?"

"San Francisco."

"It must be very late there."

"A little after midnight," Smith confirmed. "Uh, have you received a confidential communiqué from your representative aboard *Admiral Farragut*?"

"I have. I was just now looking it over. I must say that I found it quite distressing."

"No more than I. How credible do you think this is?"

"I'm not sure." He noticed that Smith had avoided any direct mention of the subject. He approved of such circumspection. The news was not the sort one trusted to a communications beam, not even a sealed one.

"I plan to have the figures checked before I go any further," Smith said. "I have an acquaintance at the University of California who can be counted on to keep a secret."

"For my part, I plan to bring in the director of Farside Observatory. He, too, will be sworn to secrecy. Any suggestions as to what we do if this information turns out to be correct?"

"Kanzler is a member of the System Council. I thought I would ask for an audience with the chief coordinator. Do you agree?"

"I agree that the System Council is a good place to begin. Luna reserves the right to act independently if it must."

"As will every nation on Earth. That is why the council must coordinate the response."

"I have no argument with you, sir," Hobart said. "It's just that political considerations may dominate this crisis."

"One good way to prevent that is to make sure the lid stays on until we confirm we have a problem. I understand that Farside Observatory is the receiving point for all raw data on the comet."

"That is correct."

"It's important that they not pass it along. We don't want some independent researcher stumbling on to this until we're ready."

"We won't be able to keep it quiet for long," Hobart warned.

"We won't have to," Smith answered. "Either we prove there's nothing to worry about, or else I arrange an audience with the chief coordinator of the council."

"How long do you plan to wait?"

"Ten days."

"All right," Hobart responded. "I'll endeavor to keep the lid on at this end. If I haven't heard from you within ten days, I will be forced to go public with what I know."

"Fair enough."

After a few more exchanges, Smith signed off, and John Hobart sat gazing at the blank phone screen. Finally, he sighed and signaled his private secretary at home.

"Yes, sir?" she asked when she came on the phone.

"Do you remember a government report about a year ago, Amalthea? It surveyed Luna's dependency on Earth imports?"

"Yes, sir."

"Do you remember who authored it?"

"I believe it was Dr. Jinsai at the university. The title was 'A

Study of Strategic Dependencies in the Lunar Economy.'"

"Get Jinsai on the phone and ask him if he will favor me with a visit at my home. Today, if at all possible. I may have some work for him."

CHAPTER 19

NEWS ITEM:

UNIVERSAL FAX, DEN HAAG, UNITED EUROPE— 15 JAN 2086 (FOR DISTRIBUTION TO UNEUR, NORAM, LUNA, XTERR)

HALVER SMITH, WELL-KNOWN AMERICAN ENTREPRENEUR, IS VISITING THE HAGUE TODAY. HE WILL BE SEEING CONSTANCE FORBIN, CHIEF COORDINATOR OF THE SYSTEM COUNCIL IN HER NEW RIDDERZAAL OFFICE. ALTHOUGH THE SUBJECT OF THEIR DISCUSSIONS HAS NOT BEEN RELEASED, SOURCES WITHIN THE COUNCIL BUREAUCRACY INDICATE THAT SMITH WILL ATTEMPT TO ENLIST THE CHIEF COORDINATOR'S SUPPORT FOR AN INTERNATIONAL AGREEMENT ON EXTRATERRESTRIAL TARIFFS AS THEY APPLY TO METALS OBTAINED VIA ASTEROID MINING. NO POSTMEETING ANNOUNCEMENT IS EXPECTED.

END

Constance Forbin sat in her fiftieth-floor office and gazed out over The Hague. In the distance was the ancient center of the city, including the Binnenhof and the Hofvijver pond. The pond was invisible behind the rows of stately buildings, but the bare limbs of the trees that bordered the waterway reached toward the leaden sky like a randomist sculpture from the early years of the century. The previous night's heavy snow littered the streets and parks of the once-capital of the Netherlands and lay in deep mounds where it had slipped from the steeply pitched roof of the ancient castle. In a dozen places within the Old City, flashing yellow lights marked the location of robot snow equipment. The plows had been out all night fighting a losing battle to keep the streets clear. Now that the snow had stopped, they would quickly dig the city out. Within forty-eight hours the streets would be cleared of any trace of the blizzard just past.

Constance Forbin was a fifty-year-old with a distinguishing streak of gray in her otherwise ebon hair. Her suit was severely cut in a style that flattered what even Constance admitted was a figure that flirted with dumpiness. She smiled as she gazed down at the park that fronted the New Ridderzaal Tower. In the summer it was an area of verdant green, alive with flower beds and the simple greenery with which the Dutch landscaped their country. At the moment it was an unbroken field of white that resembled the salt-encrusted sea bottom that the whole area had once been. Two children were cutting diagonally across the park, breaking trail as they pulled a sled behind them. Closer to the office tower, a crowd of pedestrians surfaced all at once from the local underground transport station. The majority of the bundled-up commuters hurried across the windswept street and into the warmth of the Headquarters Building of the System Council for International and Interplanetary Affairs.

The council had been founded at the turn of the century as one of the last creations of a dying United Nations. Its mandate had been to look into matters that might be important a century later. The council's job was to study trends, predict where they might lead, and offer recommendations as to what, if anything, ought to be done about them.

Despite the dissolution of its parent, the council had prospered. Even though its efforts continued to be financed by the major terrestrial nations and the Republic of Luna, the council was beholden to no one. Service with the council was by invitation. The council's normal operating mode was to appoint a small study group of experts knowledgeable in a field. The groups were kept small for the sake of efficiency, but were large enough to prevent intellectual inbreeding. Group discussions were usually held via teleconferencing and computer networks, although face-to-face meetings were also common.

When a study group finished its assignment, its recommendations were sent to a central data base. There they would be displayed for a full year, giving each of the council's ten thousand "advisors" opportunity to comment and criticize. Only after all suggestions and objections were resolved was a recommendation given the imprimatur of the entire council. In keeping with the organization's quasiofficial status, such recommendations were not binding on anyone. Yet most were immediately adopted as official policy by the various nations. Such was the clout of the System Council.

Constance Forbin did not belong to the council, per se. She was, in fact, one of its employees. She and 3000 other staffers assisted the working groups with administrative details, allowing the deep thinkers to remain free to think. As chief coordinator, it was her job to see that assignments were equitably made, differences of opinion properly debated, and minority views given a fair hearing. She also administered the various supranational service agencies that the council had come to control over the years, chief among which were Sky Watch and the Earthquake Prediction Bureau. And, of course, it was the chief coordinator's duty to deal with the public.

Constance's enjoyment of the winter scene was suddenly interrupted by the buzzing of her intercom. "Professor Hardesty is here, Mrs. Forbin."

"Please send him in."

The door opened and a stoop-shouldered man with a permanent limp moved through it. "Happy New Year, Constance. And how is the chief coordinator this fine winter morning?"

"Not bad, Franklin. How is the Senior Administrator for Sky Watch?"

"Couldn't be better," he replied. "I came in last night to beat the storm, and spent the whole evening watching it snow. I'm a native of Southern California, and it always seems unnatural to see white flakes fall from the sky."

"You should live here as I have for the past twenty years. The novelty wears off quickly. It's too bad about the clouds. The weather people thought it might clear up today. Looks like they were wrong."

"Do them some good. We've got a contingent of weather types aboard Newton Station. They spend entirely too much time being pleased with themselves. They could all benefit from a stiff jolt of humility. Now then, why couldn't we handle this via the usual computer hookup? What's so important that I had to come down personally? This gravity hurts my leg!"

"I don't know. You have heard of Halver Smith, haven't you?"

"Of course. His ore barges are one of my major headaches. Do you have any idea how much calculation time we eat up figuring out clear lanes for Smith? The last time he delivered one of his million-ton monstrosities, my people came damned close to penetrating the safety zone of one of the big comm stations. I wrote up several reprimands over that incident. What about Smith?"

"We're meeting him in a few minutes," Constance replied.

"Why?"

"I wish I knew. Professor Kanzler of the University of California set up the interview. He called me at home, told me that it was imperative that I talk to Smith, and asked that you be present in person. Kanzler was very emphatic that the meeting not be put out over the air."

"That doesn't tell us much. Still, Erwin's a good man. I doubt he'd ask if it weren't important."

"That was my thought," Constance confirmed. "I only wish he'd been more frank with me. He was obviously excited about something. I had the impression of some other emotion just below the surface. It was almost as though he's frightened of something."

Halver Smith sat in the back of the hotel limousine and gazed out at the snow-covered streets. Despite the bone weariness brought on by two weeks of tension, he gazed in wonder at the tidy Dutch city under its blanket of new-fallen white. He had found himself doing a lot of gazing in wonder lately—ever since Professor Kanzler had confirmed Amber Hastings's prediction. It was not certain that Comet Hastings would strike the Earth, but it was a strong enough possibility to be worried about.

The knowledge that the planet could well be doomed had hit Smith like an intravenous drug. It was as if each of his senses had been honed to new sharpness. Suddenly there was beauty in almost any scene. Every breath brought a new perfume to savor. Food tasted better. In the past several days Smith had watched a child play with a ball, stopped to observe the liquid curves of a pretty young woman as she walked down the sidewalk, and admired the way a hawk had cavorted in the air currents outside his penthouse office.

"Mr. Smith?" an earnest young woman in the livery of the council's uniformed staff asked.

"Yes," he replied as he brushed his windblown hair back into place.

"I'm Miss Voorstadt. Coordinator Forbin is waiting for you in her office. Will you please follow me?"

"Of course."

The guide led him to a central bank of elevators, and in a matter of seconds Smith found himself on the fiftieth floor. It was only a dozen steps to the coordinator's outer office. The coordinator's secretary buzzed her boss and then told him to go in.

Constance Forbin met him at the door. Her handshake was surprisingly firm. She directed Smith to a seat in front of her desk and introduced him to Franklin Hardesty, Sky Watch administrator.

"Good of you to interrupt your busy schedule to see me, Madame Coordinator," Smith said. "You, too, Mr. Hardesty."

"Isn't Professor Kanzler with you, Mr. Smith?" Hardesty asked.

"I'm afraid not. His doctor won't let him fly." Smith tapped his tunic where an inner pocket lay. "He did send along a recording with his views."

"His views of what?"

"Now, Franklin," Constance Forbin said. "Let us welcome our guest before you begin to grill him, shall we? Coffee or tea, Mr. Smith?"

"No, thank you. I just finished breakfast. I'm afraid I haven't adjusted to the change in time zones yet."

"I didn't have that problem," Hardesty replied. "Newton Station is on Universal Time, which is also the next zone west."

"Yes," Smith responded. "Professor Kanzler said that you would have come down from orbit. I hope we haven't unduly inconvenienced you."

"Depends on what you have to say."

"I'm sorry for the mystery. I believe you'll agree that my news is best shared in private once you hear it."

"Then shall we begin?" the coordinator asked.

Smith picked up the briefcase, laid it flat on his lap, then removed two thick sheaves of paper bound in individual security cases. He keyed passwords into the thin keypads on the front of each booklike case. At the final digit the covers sent an electrical charge through the special paper inside, breaking down the coating which would otherwise burst into flame upon exposure to light. Assured that the reports were safe, he unzipped the cases with a flourish and handed one to each of his listeners.

"Coordinator Forbin. Administrator Hardesty," Smith said. "If nothing is done to prevent it, the Comet Hastings nucleus will strike the Earth on July seventeenth of next year. I'm told by experts that the impact will kill everyone on Earth."

There was an uncomfortably long silence, which Constance Forbin was the first to break. "You came here, Mr. Smith, *to announce the end of the world*?"

"I'm afraid that I did."

"Have you any idea how many people have made that same claim over the centuries?" Hardesty asked. His tone made clear his opinion of Smith's announcement.

"Millions."

"Why should we believe you any more than one of them?"

"I can prove my claim."

"How?"

"With the evidence I just gave you."

While the two leafed through the reports, Smith summarized the data for them. He described the comet's close encounter with Jupiter and the postencounter orbit into which it had been thrown. He spoke of the near miss of Luna which would result in the nucleus being diverted into the Earth.

"And you believe this?" Hardesty asked after Smith had finished. The Sky Watch administrator was gazing at an orbital chart showing the relative positions of Comet Hastings and Earth over the next eighteen months.

"I was hesitant at first. That is the reason I contacted Professor Kanzler. He has done an independent study of the data. He agrees that a collision is a very real possibility."

Hardesty gazed at Smith for long seconds, then shook his head emphatically. "What you are suggesting is just too fantastic. Either this is the greatest three-corner billiard shot of all time, or else God is trying to tell us something. Frankly, I don't like either hypothesis very much."

"The figures are there before you."

"Figures have been cooked up for hoaxes before."

"Why would I perpetrate such a hoax?"

"A good question," Hardesty replied. "I've followed your career, Smith. I know that you have gained a great deal from the publicity generated by this expedition to the comet. Perhaps you are trying to drum up interest. If that is your game, you are destined to lose. Manipulating astronomical data isn't as easy as stock prices."

"Then you can check the accuracy of this?" Constance asked as she waved the report at Hardesty.

"Easily. In fact, I've thought of a quick check of Mr. Smith's veracity that we can perform ourselves right in this office."

"What is that, Franklin?"

"To strike the Earth, the comet must orbit in the same plane. If the two orbits are not coplanar, they can never intersect. That is the reason Halley's Comet represents no threat to us. Its orbit is highly inclined to the ecliptic and does not intersect Earth's orbit at all."

"Is that correct, Mr. Smith? Must the orbital planes be lined up for a collision to take place?"

"Essentially, yes," Smith replied. "There is one special case where it can happen, but that has no bearing on the situation at hand. Comet Hastings does indeed orbit in the same plane as the Earth."

"So you say," Hardesty replied. He slapped the diagram he had been studying with his open palm. "This picture suggests that all of the planets orbit in the ecliptic. That, of course, is false. Most have orbits inclined to that of the Earth. Jupiter, for instance, moves as much as seventeen million kilometers above and below the ecliptic as it travels about its orbit."

"What has that to do with Mr. Smith's claim, Franklin?"

"Comet Hastings passed within a few planetary diameters of Jupiter less than a month ago. That puts Jupiter in the plane of the comet's orbit. If it was not passing through the ecliptic at the time of the close encounter, then Mr. Smith is perpetrating a hoax. The alignment must be perfect, by the way. If the Big Boy was even a few seconds of arc above or below the ecliptic, the comet will miss."

Constance Forbin smiled. "Well, then, let us find out where Jupiter was."

Hardesty rose from his chair and limped over to where the coordinator's work station sat next to her desk. A few seconds spent punching keys brought a frown to his face.

"Well, Franklin?"

"Jupiter's current declination—its position with respect to the ecliptic—is minus 0.002 degrees of arc."

"When did it actually cross the ecliptic?" Smith asked quietly.

"One month ago," Hardesty conceded.

"Then Mr. Smith's claim is correct, Franklin?"

"It's possible. Still not very likely, however. You can't imagine how minuscule a target Earth is when one considers the immensity of space."

"Is that true, Mr. Smith?"

"Absolutely, Madame Coordinator. Professor Kanzler wants me to emphasize that we can't guarantee the comet nucleus *will* hit the Earth at this time, only that it *may*. We will need far more precise measurements of its orbital parameters to be sure. He suggests that we get them as quickly as possible. Obviously, we have to find out for sure before it's too late to do anything about it."

Donald Callas sat in his office on Avalon asteroid and stared at a black sky filled with diamond sparks. One spark in particular drew his attention. It was an oddly elongated blob bright enough to leave an afterimage. Callas turned down the overhead glow panels and rummaged in the lower drawers of his desk for his binoculars. A moment's fiddling with the optics showed the elongated star to be two spheres hovering close to one another. The smaller of the two was very nearly eclipsed by the larger, which was dazzling blue-white. Callas sighed as he gazed at the Earth and the Moon from across a ten-million-kilometer gulf of space.

It had been five years since Callas had last set foot on Earth. It seemed like a lifetime. In those early days Avalon had moved just outside of Venus's orbit, occasionally dipping to within two million kilometers of Earth's stillborn twin. It had been Callas's job to nudge the big asteroid into a more useful orbit for mining. Half a decade and a dozen kilograms of antimatter later, Avalon orbited 140 million kilometers out from the sun. The asteroid's orbit meant that it periodically overtook the Earth. Avalon and the Earth-Moon system had been in conjunction twice since orbital modifications had begun. Each time Earth and Luna had grown larger, brighter, and more beautiful in Avalon's black sky.

Two years hence, Avalon would approach Earth from below and behind, moving with enough velocity to curve around the planet in a gentle S-shaped curve. There would follow a complicated maneuver in which Earth and Luna would capture the way-ward asteroid. Avalon's initial orbit about Earth would be highly elliptical, extending nearly to Luna in one direction and looping down to geosynchronous altitude in the other. The months and years that followed capture would be devoted to circularizing the asteroid's orbit. None of those postcapture operations would be of the slightest concern to Donald Callas, however. His contract would be fulfilled the moment Avalon completed its first full orbit of the planet. Once around the Mother of Men, and he would return home a rich man, never to leave again.

Callas gazed for another few minutes at the beautifully blue-white world low above the asteroid's barren horizon. Finally, he lowered the binoculars with a sigh and ordered the lights full up. The stark blackness beyond the thick windowpane receded. He returned to viewing the endless progression of shortage reports which were his personal purgatory.

CHAPTER 20

John Malvan floated into *Admiral Farragut*'s wardroom and pulled himself to the food dispenser, where he selected coffee, toast, and orange juice. The machine delivered a covered break-fast pack, which he tucked under the stump of his right arm. Then, turning, he found Hilary Dorchester watching him from across the compartment.

"You're the first person I've seen smile since we got the bad news," he said. "What's so funny?"

"Nothing's funny," she replied. "I was just watching the way you handle yourself without weight. I'm still as clumsy as a new-born babe."

"You weren't clumsy last night," he said.

"How gallant of you to notice, sir! But I still wonder if I'll ever be able to handle myself as well as you do."

He shrugged. "It's all a matter of technique. You'll catch on."

"Do you really think so?"

"Everyone does eventually," he said, securing the breakfast pack to the table and unplugging the coffee bulb from its receptacle. He took a long, slow sip of the black liquid and sighed. "That's what I need in the morning! I can't face depilating without my coffee, let alone the end of the world."

"Any word from Earth? Have they even acknowledged our warning?"

"Not yet. Personally, I think they decoded the data, decided that we are all drunk out here, and forgot about it."

"Do you really think so?"

Malvan was surprised at the intensity of her question. He grinned. "No, of course not! Give them time. It must be difficult to organize things without causing a public panic."

"This sneaking around is all wrong!" Hilary hissed. "We should be shouting the news to anyone who will listen."

Malvan shook his head. "Sorry, but that's precisely what we *shouldn't* be doing."

"If the comet is really going to hit Earth, the people there have a right to know. They should have some say in how things are handled."

"Why?"

"Because their lives are at stake!"

Malvan sighed. "Did you ever see a run on a bank, Hilary?"

"How could I? It's been fifty years since the last bank failed."

"On Earth, maybe. They still happen with depressing regularity on Luna. The institution I have in mind was a regional savings-and-loan. Somehow a rumor got started that the president had invested heavily in a local tunneling project which had a blowout and lost a lot of air. The rumor wasn't true. The bank had only a modest interest in the tunnel. It didn't matter. Within half an hour they had to take their computer offline because panicky depositors had drawn down their reserves to nothing. Shutting down was a mistake. No one ever trusted them after that. The bank failed, and the president killed himself."

"What's that to do with the comet striking Earth?" Hilary asked.

"Panic does funny things to people. If they stampede over the prospect of losing a little money, what do you think will happen when you announce the end of the world?"

"Surely you aren't suggesting that we *never* tell them?"

"We'll tell them. But the public mood has to be carefully prepared. They have to be in the proper frame of mind to prevent a panic. That takes time and careful preparation. If nothing else, the riot police have to be mobilized in advance of the announcement, not after."

Hilary opened her mouth to respond, then closed it again as the public-address system in the overhead came alive.

"Attention, all hands! This is the captain speaking. Muster in the storm cellar in fifteen minutes. I repeat, the axis shelter in fifteen minutes!"

"Well," Malvan replied with a grin. "I would say that we've finally heard from Earth."

Amber Hastings arrived to find the axis shelter crowded. She carefully threaded her way to her customary spot atop her own cold-sleep tank and sorted through her notes while the others found their own anchor points. The hatch leading to the control room opened and Captain Olafson floated through, with Tom Thorpe close behind.

"Everyone here?" the captain asked as she steadied herself with a handy stanchion. There was a brief pause while she counted heads. "All right, let's begin. One hour ago we received a long communiqué from the Chief Coordinator of the System Council. They are forming a working group to coordinate all activities with regard to the comet. We work for them now. Our new orders were included in the communiqué. Listen up!"

She took a message flimsy from her pocket and began to read aloud:

DATE: 20 January 2086
    TO: Captain Karin Olafson, ISF *Admiral Farragut*; Thomas Thorpe, Leader, Comet Hastings Expedition
FROM: The Honorable Constance Forbin, Chief Coordinator, System Council
SUBJECT: Revised Expedition Orders

1.0   Pursuant to the Space Emergency Treaty of 2056, as amended by the Mexico City Compact of 2073, ISF *Admiral Farragut* is hereby placed under the authority of the System Council. You are directed to obey all lawful orders emanating from this office and from Council Working Group No. 7490.

2.0 Any and all previous contracts, agreements, or understandings between *Admiral Farragut*, its owners, passengers, and crew, the Sierra Corporation, and the Republic of Luna, are null and void.

3.0 You are ordered to proceed at your best pace to the Comet Hastings nucleus. You will survey that body from space and report your findings. You will initiate landing operations only upon receipt of orders and if you consider such an action to be safe.

4.0 You will monitor the nucleus's position and velocity throughout your approach. You will acquire data needed to further refine the comet's orbital parameters.

5.0 You will conduct direct observations of the nucleus's terrain and internal structure and will report all such to CWG-7490.

6.0 You will assist in any orbital modification efforts that may be judged necessary to insure the safety of Earth.

7.0 You will affix a security classification of TOP SECRET to all information regarding the Comet Hastings nucleus, and will transmit such information only when properly secured. No public release of information regarding any aspect of your work is to be made. All such will be coordinated through this office.

8.0 Good luck, *Admiral Farragut*. We're all counting on you!

> Constance Forbin
> Chief Coordinator
> System Council

Captain Olafson looked up as she finished reading. "We have been making a slow approach to the comet nucleus in order to conserve fuel. That will now change. In precisely one hour this ship will accelerate at one-half gravity for twenty minutes. We will make rendezvous with the nucleus in five days' time, and will begin observing its surface as soon as we are within observation range. Are there any questions or objections to these orders as I have read them?"

"What's this stuff about all contracts between ourselves and Sierra Corporation being null and void?" Bradford Goff, the expedition's heavy-equipment specialist asked. "Surely they aren't telling us that our employment contracts are abrogated!"

Tom Thorpe shook his head. He had anchored himself beside the captain and had watched everyone's reaction as she read the orders. "Included with the orders was a message from Mr. Smith. He confirmed that control of the expedition has passed to the System Council. He emphasized, however, that our personal contracts will be honored in full."

"What about these 'orbital modifications' we're supposed to assist with?" someone asked. "What are they talking about?"

Captain Olafson turned to Professor Barnard. "Is the astronomy department prepared to answer that question?"

Barnard gestured toward where his assistant perched on her cold sleep tank. "Amber has been studying the possibilities. I'll let her explain."

Amber glanced up from her notes and found everyone's eyes on her. She had had enough time to run a few simple calculations, and was not happy with the numbers. Still, the mood aboard ship had been black ever since the comet's likely collision with Earth had become common knowledge. Amber resolved to put the best face possible on the situation. She cleared her throat and began to speak with as much confidence as she could muster.

"I suppose the Earth seems a fairly large place to those who live on it," she began. "I know I have always found it to be an impressive sight in the Nearside sky. Yet on the scale of the Solar System, it is actually quite tiny. The Earth has an equatorial diameter of only 12,756 kilometers. That is barely one-eleventh Jupiter's diameter and one-hundredth the diameter of the Sun. The Earth orbits the Sun at a speed of 29.8 kilometers per second. If you divide the planet's diameter by its speed, you discover that the Earth travels its own length every seven minutes. In other words, it is a small, rapidly moving target.

"As everyone who has traveled in space knows, the way to avoid a collision is to change the orbit of one of the colliding bodies. Modifying an orbit requires energy proportional to the momentum change needed. Momentum, of course, is dependent on the object's mass and velocity. Unfortunately, the comet nucleus has a great deal of mass. We would have no trouble changing the comet's orbit if only we had a few decades to work at it. With the nucleus orbiting near Jupiter every seven years, it's likely we wouldn't have to do anything. Jupiter's gravitational reach would soon warp the comet's path away from Earth's orbit. No, our problem is the next eighteen months. Even if we used our largest and most efficient propulsion engines, we could never divert it into a safe orbit in time."

"Then Earth is doomed!" Hilary Dorchester said from where she sat next to John Malvan.

"Not necessarily," Amber replied. "You see, it isn't really necessary to alter the comet's orbital track. We can also avert a collision by merely altering its schedule! That is much easier to do."

"Of course," Professor Chen said. "If we can cause the comet to arrive at the collision point early, there will be no collision!"

"Precisely."

"How early?"

"Based on existing data," Amber replied, "I calculate that we need to gain three minutes over the next eighteen months. That includes the foreshortening caused by the nucleus's oblique approach to Earth."

"That doesn't sound bad at all," Chen replied. "What's that in velocity? Anyone bring a calculator with them?"

"It works out to an increase of 0.0005 percent in the nucleus's speed. If we can increase its current velocity by just five centimeters per second, it will miss Earth by a thousand kilometers."

There was a moment of silence, then a roar as a dozen competing voices offered suggestions for accelerating the nucleus. Seeing that the excitement was contagious, Amber gave up trying to explain that even though the number was tiny, sixty million billion tons gave the task a Herculean dimension.

"Amber, wait up!"

Amber stopped and spun in midair in the slightly awkward motion of a zero-gravity turn. Tom Thorpe came swarming up behind her.

"Hello," she said as he overtook her.

"Hello, yourself. Where have you been hiding? I hardly ever see you anymore."

"Professor Barnard and I have been busy. We're double-checking all of our past work."

"Still looking for a dropped decimal point?"

She nodded.

"You're not going to find it, you know."

"I know. It's just that I can't get over the feeling that it's my fault."

"Your fault? Why?"

"The comet bears my name," she said, a trace of bitterness in her voice. "Just think of the billions of people who will curse me once they find out. Damn it, I told them I didn't want it named after me!"

"Come on," he soothed. "Nobody is going to blame you. This is an act of God if there ever was one."

"Ever heard of shooting the messenger who brings the bad news?"

He gazed into her eyes for a long moment. "This is really getting to you, isn't it?"

She sighed. "Maybe just a little. I haven't been sleeping very well."

"Have you talked to Dr. Barnard about it?"

Amber shook her head. "She'd just prescribe sleeping pills. I don't need that."

"I've got a bottle of brandy that I keep in my cabin. What say we have a drink?"

"Does Captain Olafson know about this bottle?"

"Does she tell me everything?"

For the first time in weeks Amber laughed. "That's what I thought."

The two of them moved a quarter of the way around *Admiral Farragut*'s habitat module to Thorpe's cabin. Despite his status as leader of the expedition, his quarters were identical to everyone else's. Optimized for zero gee, they held a desk, two chairs, a sleeping net, an entertainment console, and a variety of recessed lockers for personal effects. A hatch opposite the airtight door led to a second compartment containing a zero-gravity toilet, sink, and shower.

Amber brushed past Thorpe, giving him a strong whiff of her perfume. She headed to the far chair and strapped herself in. Thorpe closed the door, then moved to one of the lockers in the overhead. He returned with a bottle, two drinking bulbs, and a syringe. The bottle was obviously from Earth and lacked the specialized contrivances designed for handling liquids in microgravity. Thorpe handed the bulbs to Amber before deftly inserting the syringe through the cork and filling it with fluid. He then injected the liquid into one of the bulbs before repeating the operation for the other. He stowed the bottle and syringe before accepting one of the bulbs.

"Skoal!"

Amber smiled, then sipped carefully from the bulb. She savored the mild burning the liquid caused as it flowed across her tongue and down her throat. A few minutes later she was feeling warm all over. "This is excellent."

"It should be," he replied. "It came from Halver Smith's private stock."

"Ah, to be rich!"

"You *are* rich, or at least well off. Remember, you have progress payments piling up from your discoverer's rights."

"Too bad I'll never have a chance to spend the money."

Thorpe frowned, then made a show of attaching his drinking bulb to the nearby steel bulkhead. The bulb's magnetic base held it in place. "Maybe we should talk about it."

"About what?"

"Whatever's bothering you. I'd say that you've figured out the energy required to accelerate a five-hundred-kilometer ball of ice by five centimeters per second."

"How did you know?"

"I move asteroids for a living, remember? How bad is it?"

"Bad," she replied. "Everyone seems to forget that the nucleus masses sixty million billion tons. That's *one-twentieth the mass of all the water in all the oceans on Earth!*"

"It's a lot," he agreed. "So how hard will it be to accelerate it that tiny bit?"

"I figure the job will take 125 billion tons of reaction mass and a quarter ton of antimatter."

"And that is what has you worried?"

She sipped from her bulb, then nodded. "You know it's a good year when the human race manages to synthesize even twenty-five kilograms of antimatter. How are we going to get *two hundred fifty* in the next eighteen months?"

"Don't worry about it. It's not our problem."

"*Not our problem!*"

"That's exactly what I said. Our job is to survey the nucleus and report what we find to Earth. Others will have to figure out how to avoid a collision. If we try to do their jobs in addition to our own, we won't do either very well. This is one time you have to concentrate on what you're doing and hope the other fellow does the same."

"So your suggestion is that I forget what I've learned?"

"Don't forget it. But don't let it eat at you either. You're vital to Earth just now. All of us are. If you don't believe me, just think of how helpless you would feel if you were back at Farside Observatory. We are humankind's eyes and ears. We report what we see when we get to the nucleus. Everything else is a sideshow just now."

"But what if they can't speed the nucleus?"

He shrugged and made a show of plucking the drinking bulb from the bulkhead. "In that case, we eat, drink, and be merry. For tomorrow..."

CHAPTER 21

"All right, let's pull back to wide angle."

Amber touched a control, and six ancient mirrors moved to a new focus in their hexagonal frame. The small spherical object that had been centered in the telescope's field of view quickly contracted to invisibility, to be replaced by a glowing cloud. The comet's coma had thickened since the nucleus had departed Jupiter, and would continue to do so for the next year or so. Friction from the solar wind would begin to produce a recognizable tail about the time the nucleus reached the Asteroid Belt.

Admiral Farragut had entered the prototail five days earlier. In the month since Jupiter they had chased the ice asteroid thirty million kilometers to sunward. Never had it appeared as more than a brilliantly lit crescent. Their attempts to map the surface by recording features as they rotated through the crescent had proven unsatisfactory. Close observation of the nucleus's surface continued to be thwarted by the cloud of gas and dust that surrounded it.

"Wide-angle view," Amber responded as the screen stabilized.

"Maximum contrast," Cragston Barnard ordered.

The screen changed again. The filaments of a frozen explosion flowed into view. The curved features were too dim to be seen normally; only the computer's ability to differentiate minuscule differences in brightness made them visible. They radiated outward from the nucleus, clearly marking its position even though it could no longer be seen.

"No doubt about it," Barnard said after taking several photometric readings of various regions of the coma. "The nucleus is outgassing much faster than predicted."

"Yet the percentage of volatiles in the cloud is holding steady," Amber responded. "They should be increasing."

The older astronomer shook his head. "Everything we see indicates that, except for its size, the nucleus is a normal deep-space chunk of ice. No, we've overlooked something, and I think I know what it is."

"What's that?"

"Internally generated heat from the tidal stresses of the close approach to Jupiter."

"Gravity flexing?"

Barnard nodded. "Getting that close must have strained its equilibrium some. Heat generated in the interior is just now making it to the surface."

"Could be," Amber agreed. "Gravity flexing keeps Callisto's interior liquid, and look how far from Jupiter it is."

Barnard pointed to a particularly bright streamer. "Look at that jet! It must be bubbling up from a major flaw in the surface."

"That big crater we saw during the flyby?"

He nodded. "Or deep faults radiating around it. A really big crack might act like a heat well."

"It would have to be pretty deep," she cautioned.

Barnard shrugged. "As you would expect, considering the size of the hole left behind."

"It will be interesting to see if you're right when we get closer."

"Care to lay a small wager on it?"

"Not on your life, boss! You've been right too often lately."

As she operated the telescope's controls, Amber hummed to herself. Her mood was totally different than it had been after she had discovered the awful truth about her namesake. The cause for her change in attitude was obvious to everyone aboard ship. Amber was in love!

She and Tom had had a second drink that day in his cabin. Halfway through it they had started reminiscing. The conversation had drifted to the bargain they had made in San Francisco. By the time the third drinking bulb was drained, Amber found herself agreeing that it was stupid of them to waste time when the end of the world was at hand. They had laughed about it.

Then the laughter had abruptly stopped. A long look had turned into an embrace. Hungry lips had sought others, and Amber felt herself wrapped in strong arms. What happened next had been as natural as breathing. There had even been a funny moment when, midway through their act of love, they had been forced to scramble for safety belts as acceleration alarms hooted throughout the ship. *Admiral Farragut*'s engines came to life, and they finished under half a gravity of acceleration.

Later, they had slept the night in one another's arms and made love again in the morning. At breakfast she had announced to the entire wardroom that she was moving in with Tom. Somehow, no one seemed surprised.

"All right," Barnard said, stretching beside her and jolting her from her reverie. "That's enough for this session. Program in the coma observations and switch the system to automatic. I won't need you again until First Watch."

"Are you sure, Crag?"

"I'm sure. I got the impression at lunch today that our leader is unhappy with my monopolizing your time. After you finish your programming, I don't want to see your face back here until morning."

Karin Olafson lay in her acceleration couch and watched the comet nucleus on the viewdome. The endless fog was beginning to be dispelled. She had strained her ship's fuel reserves to arrive a month early, yet only in the last few hours had they been able to see their destination with the unaided eye.

"What's the range, Mr. Rodriguez?"

"Five thousand kilometers and closing, Captain."

"Please ask Professor Barnard if he has enough approach data. I'm ready to turn the ship."

"Aye aye." There was a brief murmuring sound as Rodriguez contacted the astronomy compartment. Then he said, "Ready whenever you are, Captain."

Karin glanced over her shoulder at her husband. "Ready to turn the ship, Mr. Chief Engineer?"

"Ready, Captain."

"All right. Stand by for the announcement." She keyed for the general circuit on the ship's intercom. "Attention, all hands! I am turning the ship for braking. Beware of Coriolis forces and moment arm accelerations. Turning maneuver in thirty seconds!"

Karin fired the attitude thrusters on schedule. The habitat module vibrated with the sound of the firing. The sound had not yet died away when the sky began to rotate on the dome overhead. She watched the viewdome compass grid closely. When it showed the ship a few degrees short of its turn, she fired the thrusters again. A second *whump!* brought the rotation to a halt. At the dome's zenith lay a small banded world of almost intolerable brightness. At a range of thirty million kilometers, Jupiter was half the size of Luna as viewed from Earth. Its bright light shone through the coma, giving it the look of a full moon on a hazy night.

"Aft view, Mr. Rodriguez."

Once again the overhead dome cleared to show the crescent image of the nucleus. It appeared much as it had throughout their month-long stern chase, except that the crescent was no longer soft-edged and gauzy. The ice nucleus had become a small planet with a sharply defined limb and a darkened hemisphere. The darkened portion glowed dimly by Jupiter light.

The captain pointed out the phenomenon to Thorpe, who was strapped in beside her. "Looks like we'll be able to work right through the local night."

"How close are we going to pass abeam of the comet, Captain?"

"What's the matter, Mr. Thorpe? Don't trust my flying?"

"Just curious."

"We'll be three hundred kilometers distant at closest approach. I've got all my side cameras operating, so we should have a good view of the sunlit side. That big crater will be fully illuminated.

When we reach a distance of two thousand kilometers to sunward, I'll bring her to a halt."

Thorpe nodded. There would be no need for a stabilizing orbit around the ice mass. Given the meager gravitational pull of the low-density nucleus, it would take the better part of a year for the ship to fall two thousand kilometers.

Captain Olafson watched the ice asteroid change perspective as they made their approach. Their closing speed—purchased at the cost of a significant percentage of their remaining reaction mass—was five kilometers per second. As they drew even with the comet nucleus, she would decelerate at a full two gravities for four minutes in order to bring *Admiral Farragut* to rest at the desired distance. After that there would be several days of observations before they chose a landing site.

Once they had permission from Earth, they would detach the habitat module and set it down on the surface. Next the cargo module would be landed under automatic control. The engine module would be left in orbit high above the nucleus, where it would act as a communications relay. Once they had their hydrogen distillery set up, they would ferry each of the spherical tanks down to the surface for refilling.

Slowly, the asteroid grew until it was as large as a planet. As they reached the point of closest approach, Karin Olafson keyed the intercom. "All hands, prepare for heavy acceleration! Two gravities in two minutes. Make sure that you are strapped down tight. I repeat, two gravities in two minutes. Drop whatever you are doing and get into acceleration couches now! Report status when ready."

She waited until everyone on board had reported their readiness for acceleration. As she had done before launch, she visually inspected their condition as well as looked over her ship. Then she checked the readiness of the control-room crew.

"Mr. Chief Engineer!"

"Ready for acceleration, Captain."

"Computer check, Mr. Rodriguez."

"Green lights across the board."

"Close all pressure doors. Bring the thrust-chamber magnetic field to full strength. Stand by for reaction mass and antimatter injection."

"Standing by, Captain," Chief Engineer Stormgaard said.

There was a long pause.

"First antimatter injection in thirty seconds. Mr. Rodriguez, sound the klaxon."

The acceleration alarm sounded throughout the ship.

"Attention, all hands. Stand by for full power, Ten ... nine ... eight ... seven ... six ... five ... four ... three ... two ... one ... now!"

Barbara Martinez walked slowly down the long corridor of Newton Station and wondered what she had done to deserve a summons to a private meeting with the senior administrator of Sky Watch. Grade Six computer programmers did not often meet privately with El Patrón, and when they did, they usually did not enjoy the occasion.

She reached the S.A.'s office and checked her appearance in the full-length mirror provided for the purpose. What she saw was a trim, black-eyed brunette, with a ready smile and a mouth slightly too large for her face. She studied her features with the detachment of someone confident about her appearance. The powder-blue of her uniform set off the slight duskiness of her complexion to good effect. Satisfied, she signaled her presence.

There came a muffled command to enter, which she did. Franklin Hardesty sat hunched over a report that bore the scarlet TOP SECRET cover page. In addition to the security rating, the report bore the logo of the System Council. The council had performed classified studies in the past, she knew, but those had usually involved sociologically sensitive subjects. To her knowledge, Sky Watch had never dealt with anything more classified than tide schedules.

Hardesty glanced up and closed the report at her entrance. "Please be seated, Miss Martinez."

"Thank you, sir."

The senior administrator maintained his office on Gamma Deck where local gravity was barely one-third standard. He claimed that the higher gravity on Alpha and Beta decks made his leg ache.

"I've been looking over your file, Miss Martinez. I understand that you trained as an astrogeologist."

"Yes, sir. I did my doctoral thesis on cometary formation."

"Why aren't you working in that field?"

She shrugged. "Where does an expert on comets go to get a job? Except for this recent expedition to Comet Hastings, there haven't been many opportunities for a person with my specialty."

"I take it that you are following the progress of the expedition."

"When I can. They've been pretty quiet since the comet left Jupiter. A stern chase is a long chase, I guess."

"I understand that you know one of the expedition members."

She nodded. "John Malvan. I met him when he was passing through last year. He promised to bring me back a chunk of the comet."

"Malvan is Luna's official representative on the expedition, is he not?"

"Yes, sir. Mind telling me why you're asking all these questions?"

"Sky Watch has been tasked to support one of the council working groups. They need our very best people. I'm thinking of nominating you."

"A study project, sir? Concerning the comet?"

"I'm sorry, but that's as specific as I can get. The job involves an extended stay on Earth. Interested?"

"Yes, sir!" Like most of the Sky Watch personnel, Barbara had long since exhausted the entertainment opportunities Newton Station had to offer. Despite the high pay and luxurious living quarters, it was impossible not to notice that she was living her life in a curved sewer pipe. An extended vacation on Earth was just the thing for her.

"If chosen, you will be asked to maintain rigid secrecy. You won't be able to tell anyone what you are doing, and there will be restrictions on your freedom of movement."

"For how long?"

"It could be for some months. Still interested?"

"You say that this is important?"

"It's vital."

"Then I'm interested."

Hardesty nodded. "Pack your bags and be ready for the noon ferry. You are to report to Room 1012 in our Denver headquarters at 0800 local time tomorrow. They'll have additional orders for you there. Any questions?"

"No, sir."

Hardesty stood up and stuck out his hand. "Good luck. We'll be counting on you."

* * *

Halver Smith hurried through the bracing wind to the main building of what had been a teacher's college in New Mexico. Snow lay everywhere except along the walkways between buildings. Pipes running through the concrete kept the snow melted from the walks. Beyond the red brick buildings with their green copper roofs lay a saw-toothed mountain range.

The abandoned college had come into Smith's possession five years earlier, and when Constance Forbin had explained the need for a secure site to house the new working group, he had offered the campus. It had taken a small army of workmen two weeks to get it properly equipped. The dormitories were still undergoing refurbishment.

Despite having his suit heater turned to high, Smith was shivering by the time he entered the administration building. After being identified by a security guard, he was allowed to ascend to the second floor. The project manager's secretary informed him that Director Warren had someone in his office but that he would be free in a few minutes. Smith spent the time warming himself by an old-style radiator.

When the director's door opened, a pretty young woman walked out. Smith noticed her because her hair was so dark it shone with a blue sheen. She had a look on her face that Smith recognized. It was the dazed expression of someone who had just learned the truth about the comet.

"New fish?" he asked as she brushed past him without seeing him.

Her eyes sought him out, then seemed to focus. "Beg your pardon?"

"I asked if you are new here?"

She nodded. "I'm just down from Newton Station."

"And Director Warren has just told you what's going on."

She nodded again.

"In my experience, it takes about a week to regain one's composure."

"I'll remember that."

Smith watched her out of sight. He did not envy her at all. She still had the orientation briefings to sit through. Most people needed a few stiff drinks by the end of their briefing sessions.

"Hello, Clarence," he said as he entered the director's office. "I see you've been spreading happiness again."

Clarence Warren was a forty-year-old former professor who

looked right at home in his new office. Overweight, he had a tendency to waddle when he walked.

"Good afternoon, Halver. Yes, I always try to break the news to the new recruits personally. I find their reactions tell me something about their personalities. What can I do for you?"

"I understand that the first pictures are in. I thought I would pop over and look at them."

"Why, for God's sake? Morbid curiosity?"

"Moving asteroids is my business, remember?"

"Right," Warren replied. "I sometimes forget that you started the whole industry. I've got the mapping shots around here somewhere."

Warren reached into his desk and pulled forth a set of fully annotated photographs of the sort astronomers used. The holograms had been enhanced to show detail and elevation. Looking at them was like looking down on a miniature Luna.

The first photograph showed the nucleus in full sunlight. The overall color was the tan-gray of Luna except where recent craters had dug through the eons-long accumulation of cosmic dust. The most prominent feature was a giant crater that extended for nearly one-quarter of the ice asteroid's diameter. The crater was surrounded by a series of concentric ring walls and possessed a central peak that had slumped downward over the centuries until it was barely a hillock.

Radiating outward from the crater were a series of dark rings, which were no doubt physical flaws in the surface, Smith decided—giant crevasses left over from the collision that had formed the crater.

The central crater was not the only such on the surface. As in the case of most of the airless bodies in the Solar system, the surface was covered with overlapping craters down to the limits of camera resolution. There were also puzzling dark linear markings, similar in appearance to the crevasses emanating from the central crater but not like them. Peering closely at the photograph, Smith discovered what looked like a shadow.

"These look like mountain ranges," he said, pointing the features out to Warren.

"Those," the project director replied, "are rock outcroppings. As we expected, the whole nucleus is a seventy-five/twenty-five percent ice-rock mix. Some mechanism has caused rock ridges to form in two places. As you say, they're mountains of a sort."

Smith continued to gaze at the object that had recently become so important in his life. Other photographs showed other aspects, including the side directly opposite the big impact crater. Additional crevasse features showed that the collision that had dislodged the ice asteroid from the Oort Cloud had nearly ripped it asunder. The entire interior appeared to be a series of faults.

"May I have a set of these, Clarence?"

"If you'll sign for them," the director replied. "Got any idea how we're going to shove that much mass out of our way?"

"Not yet," Smith said. "Maybe I'll come up with something after I've studied these photos for a while."

"Any idea where we should have them land?"

"Certainly," he said. "The crater's the logical place."

"Why?"

"Easy. That's the key to the nucleus's structure. If we're going to turn it, that's where it will have to be."

CHAPTER 22

REPORT NO. 165B
PHYSICAL PARAMETERS OF THE COMET HASTINGS NUCLEUS

... the nucleus measures 496 km equatorial by 475 km polar, with a rotation of 16 hours 49 minutes 7 seconds. Its mass has been computed to be 6.0212×10^{16} tons. Its surface gravity varies from 0.662% gee at the pole to 0.605% gee at the equator.

The nucleus's primary topographic feature is the large impact basin dubbed Ground Zero Crater (GZC). (See Report No. 122D, "Topographical Feature Names on the Comet Hastings Nucleus") The inner ring wall of GZC is 125 km in diameter and rises 0.7 km above the elevation of the crater floor. This postmelt plain is typical of impact-crater formation on predominantly icy bodies. As in the case of ice moons in the Jupiter and Saturn systems, the floor of GZC exhibits a phantom ring structure which marks the different solidification rings in the surface ice. Beyond the GZC wall may be found a series of concentric crevasselike faults which show up as sharp shadow demarcation lines in low sun-angle photos. Spectrographic analysis of the gas emanating from these fault regions indicates that internal heating is indeed taking place in the core of the nucleus. (See Report No. 97A, "Internal Heating of the Nucleus Due to Tidal Stresses Sustained During Jupiter Flyby")

Other macro structures in the topography of the nucleus include two outcroppings of rocky material. These have been dubbed the Little Alps Mountains (LAM) and Low Sierra Mountains (LSM). The LAM formation predominates in the Western Hemisphere (the hemisphere antipodal to GZC) and the LSM predominates in the Eastern. The LSM outcropping extends to within 5 km of the GZC wall. No clear explanation has been advanced as to the reason for this proximity.

Extensive cratering of the surface follows the icy-moon norm. Weathering of all craters is apparent and can be attributed to repeated entries by the nucleus into the middle Solar system during perihelion passages on its preencounter cometary orbit. The degree of "slumping" to be seen in crater walls can be used to accurately measure crater age to within ± one cometary orbital period (± 9 million years). These measurements tentatively confirm that GZC is the oldest major crater on the nucleus's surface.

Additional conclusions that can be deduced from the extensive antipodal fracturing directly opposite GZC is that the nucleus's interior was substantially damaged by the original collision. This is further attested to by. . .

Summary Prepared by:
L. T. Chen, Astrogeologist
C. J. Barnard, Chief Astronomer
A. E. Hastings, Principal Astronomer

2 February 2086

*   *   *

Tom Thorpe lay in the observer's couch in *Admiral Farragut*'s control room and watched the Comet Hastings nucleus on the overhead viewdome. The nucleus was larger than he had ever seen it. What had once been an invisibly small dot of light now filled half the sky as the habitat module dropped with glacial slowness toward its landing point. Thorpe knew the slow approach was the safest, but chafed at the enforced inactivity. He was anxious to get to work after ten days spent mapping every square centimeter of the nucleus's surface.

The ship had initially hovered 2000 kilometers to sunward of the ice asteroid. From their "high noon" vantage point they had trained the bow telescope and two panoramic mapping cameras on the target. Over the next four days—six full revolutions of the nucleus—they had mapped the surface in visible light and several different wavelengths of ultraviolet and infrared. As they watched the nucleus rotate beneath them, they had slowly come to realize just how big a world it really was. With a diameter of nearly 500 kilometers, the ice asteroid had a surface area of 250,000 square kilometers—making it larger than either Rumania or Idaho. On the trip out from Earth, Thorpe had fallen into the habit of thinking of it much as he thought of *The Rock*. No such equality existed. *The Rock*'s largest dimension was less than one-hundredth the nucleus's diameter.

At the end of four days they had transmitted their data to Earth via secure data link and then moved the ship to hover directly over the ice asteroid's south pole. There they had hovered for another full revolution as they photographed the south polar region. They had then repeated their observations above the north spin pole.

The landing site finally selected and approved by Earth was located ten kilometers inside Ground Zero Crater. Not only did the smooth plain invite a landing, but the crater's formation had been the last catastrophic event in the ice asteroid's history. Indeed, much of its current structure was the result of the collision that had originally dislodged it from the Oort Cloud.

The site was also near the "Badlands," a region of particular interest to Professor Chen. The Badlands were a region of jumbled topography where the Low Sierra Mountains jutted quite close to the rim of Ground Zero Crater. Superimposed on the two dissimilar terrains were ring after concentric ring of fault lines and crevasses. Out of those deep cracks boiled the invisible wind that was steadily building the surrounding coma.

When everything was ready, Captain Olafson had lifted the habitat sphere clear, parked it a safe distance from the remainder of the ship, then repeated the performance with the cargo module. When all had been checked and double-checked, she had begun their slow descent to the surface.

As Thorpe lay in his couch, an actinic spark high above him caught his attention. He ordered his observer's screen to focus on that section of the sky and was rewarded with a view of the barrel-shaped cargo compartment silhouetted against the black of space. In a change of plan, they had decided to send the cargo module ahead of them. It would touch down a minute or so before the habitat module, veryifying that the floor of Ground Zero Crater was as solid as it appeared.

"Crater in sight," Emilio Rodriguez announced to the control room as soon as the ring wall began to protrude above the horizon.

"I see it," the captain responded. "Continue the approach."

Karin Olafson sounded more relaxed than she felt as she lay in her acceleration couch. Her eyes scanned her displays in quick succession while she held a side controller in her right hand, ready to instantly wrest control from the autopilot should that prove necessary.

"See anything dangerous, Mr. Chief Engineer?" she asked several minutes later when Ground Zero Crater filled the overhead viewdome. For the descent, the dome was displaying the view below the habitat module.

Kyle Stormgaard's voice issued from an overhead speaker. "Go for the primary, Captain. It's as smooth as a baby's behind."

The chief engineer was space-suited and perched in an open airlock. He had a hand controller and would take over the ship should the ship's cameras fail during the critical landing phase. He was scanning the landing site with high-powered binoculars, searching for hazards.

"Mr. Rodriguez, do you confirm that?"

"Confirmed, Captain. Radar indicates an ice surface flatness of 0.04 and a thickness of at least several hundred meters. Thermal scanning indicates the surface temperature is rock steady at 124 degrees Kelvin."

"Very well. Watch out for powder as the cargo compartment

touches down, Kyle. We might want to take a wave off if visibility drops too low."

"Understood, Captain," came the quick response.

As Thorpe watched on the viewdome, the distant cargo compartment dropped the last few dozen meters toward the asteroid's surface. A quick flicker of its powerful attitude-control jets was sufficient to halt its downward slide. It hovered in vacuum for long seconds before slowly dropping the last three meters to the ground. The big compartment oscillated slowly a few times on its landing jacks and then stabilized.

"Cargo compartment is safely down. No evidence of surface dust."

"Hold on, people, we're going in."

The rest of the landing was an anticlimax. The large, spherical, habitat module resounded with a couple of quick bursts from the attitude-control jets, then there was silence. Nearly half a minute later Thorpe felt something push him gently down into his seat. A strange brown-gray landscape lay visible on all sides, while overhead a shrunken Sun stared down from out of an ebon sky. Captain Olafson immediately began calling out shutdown procedures.

Thorpe exhaled loudly. Only then did he realize that he had been holding his breath. After a moment spent gazing around the viewdome horizon, he began clawing at his straps, suddenly anxious to be free. After eight months and nearly a billion kilometers in transit, *Admiral Farragut* had finally arrived!

"They're down," Franklin Hardesty announced.

"Are you sure?" Constance Forbin asked.

The head of Sky Watch nodded. "Newton Station just received the confirmation report from Captain Olafson. Both the habitat and cargo modules have been successfully landed, and operations are under way to anchor them to the ice."

"Good news," the chief coordinator said.

"Damned good news!" Hardesty replied.

The two were in a secure meeting room in the New Ridderzaal Tower, hosting a conference of the major nations of Earth. The North American Union was represented, as was United Europe, the Democracia de Sud America, the African Union, Greater China, India, and Australasia. Constance Forbin had revealed the secret of the wayward comet on the first day of the conference.

To her surprise, the assembled functionaries had taken the news with relative calm. Whether the response was due to their lack of understanding of the danger or because their espionage services had penetrated council security, she had no way of knowing. Nor did she consider the question important. The secret had been a fleeting one at best. Matters had progressed to where it was necessary to inform the public. If they were to have any chance of diverting the comet, they would have to begin preparations on a scale that would be obvious to all.

"Now that your people are on the ground, what do they propose to do?" the North American representative asked. He was a tall man with a permanent scowl.

"Explore, of course. There is a great deal that can only be learned by close observation."

"To what end?"

"If we are to accelerate the comet and cause it to miss the Earth, we will have to know where to push. That requires a good model of its internal structure. We'd hate to see it come apart at the first shove."

The representative of United Europe was a small woman with a gap in her teeth which showed whenever she talked. "I would think we would want precisely that. Blow it to atoms, I say!"

Franklin Hardesty shook his head. He was seated next to Constance Forbin at the midpoint of the conference table. "The nucleus is much too big to be destroyed by explosives. First of all, there probably isn't enough antimatter in the Solar system to do the job. Secondly, even if we had the required power, we still wouldn't want to smash it. That would shatter it into a billion chunks the size of small mountains. Can you imagine what would happen to Earth if one of those chunks were to hit us?"

"So instead we wait for it to fall on us in one piece?"

"The New Mexico working group is analyzing the problem," Constance Forbin assured her. "They have all of *Admiral Farragut*'s space observations. They will have a recommendation on how best to proceed in a few weeks."

"In the meantime, what about all of these cargo vessels you want us to pay for?" the Indian Subminister of Space Affairs asked. Mr. Jaharawal was a small, dark man who punctuated his speech with a variety of annoying sounds.

"What about them?"

The first day of the conference had been taken up with a review of the data that proved that the comet would strike the Earth. The second had begun plans to modify three large bulk carriers into heavy-equipment transports. The ships would be equipped with high-efficiency engines, massive tanks, and enough reaction mass to match orbits with the nucleus in only three months.

"We don't know that these expensive ship modifications are necessary," the subminister continued. "To go ahead without a clear plan is a foolish expense."

"The need for heavy lift is obvious," Franklin Hardesty responded. "Would you have us wait until every detail is finalized before getting to work?"

The subminister refused to be cowed. "My nation hasn't the resources to provide either the System Council or Sky Watch with an unlimited budget. We cannot afford to have you committing funds like a drunken spacer."

"May I remind my esteemed colleague that the comet is destined to strike a few thousand kilometers from his own coastline?" the representative of United Europe said.

"That will make no difference to the average Indian come the next election. They already grumble about the cost of this international debating society Mrs. Forbin runs. How many more rupees will you usurp for your theoretical studies?"

"As many as necessary to save the Earth, Mr. Minister. As for the transports, if we don't begin the work immediately, they won't be ready in time to do us any good."

"Whether we succeed," the dark-skinned, ash blonde who represented Australasia said, "depends on properly marshaling public opinion. What progress is being made for the public announcement?"

"Considerable," Constance replied. "We've formed another council working group. This one is composed of specialists in mass psychology. The key, they believe, is to raise the public's level of concern without actually frightening them. It's been suggested that we not tell them the whole truth right away."

"And do they have a suggestion for how this can be done?"

"Yes, they do. In fact, they have come up with something quite ingenious."

* * *

Transcript of *The Weekend Roundup With Ric Thompson*, Trans-Earth Communications Network, 12 February 2086.

(Trans-Earth Network logo fades to closeup of Ric Thompson, network anchor)

THOMPSON: Good evening, ladies and gentlemen. This is Ric Thompson with *The Weekend Roundup*, your compendium of the week's happenings. This was the week that saw the announcement by the System Council that next year's spectacular Comet Hastings sky display may be even more spectacular than anyone imagined. The comet, it seems, will pass very close to Earth on its way back into deep space. Although the comet head is expected to miss us by several thousand kilometers, scientists point out that there is some margin for error in their calculations.

As a precaution, the System Council has announced that they will coordinate a program to prepare a series of nuclear charges with which to destroy the comet should that prove necessary. To discuss these matters, we have tonight an interview with the comet's discoverer, Miss Amber Hastings. Before we begin, a clarification is in order regarding this interview.

Miss Hastings is aboard the research vessel *Admiral Farragut*, which recently landed on the comet's surface. Because the communications delay with the comet is still some forty minutes, it was not possible for the interview to take place in real time. Therefore, we transmitted a series of questions which were posed to Miss Hastings via computer simulation. The simulation then adjusted itself to her answers just as a human interviewer would. I must emphasize that she did not know the questions in advance. In this way we obtained the same reaction as we would have had I been in the room with her. Miss Hastings's answers were then edited together with my questions to produce the following interview.

(The scene changes to show a rear quarter view of Ric Thompson. He is looking at a screen out of which Amber Hastings is staring.)

THOMPSON: Good evening, Miss Hastings. I hope that we haven't caught you at a bad time.

HASTINGS: Not at all, Ric. I'm on my way to suit up and begin the day's explorations, but I can always find time for the press.

THOMPSON: What is the surface of a comet like?

HASTINGS: The nucleus reminds me a great deal of my home on Luna. The ice is gray-brown from billions of years of collecting cosmic dust as it orbited the sun. We are quite close to the rim of the largest crater here, and we can see the top of the ring wall peering over the horizon to the north. The sun is a bright star in the sky. Its image is softened by the comet's coma.

THOMPSON: Coma?

HASTINGS: The envelope of gas and dust which surrounds the main nucleus. It's that bright circular ball you see in pictures of comets.

THOMPSON: I understand that this nucleus is something of a wayward meteorite, and that it will pass close to Earth late next year. Is that true?

HASTINGS: *(Nodding)*

Our calculations show that there is a good chance of that happening.

THOMPSON: How close will it come?

HASTINGS: *(Hesitates a moment)*

That is difficult to answer. There are quite a number of imponderables involved. We believe that the comet will approach Earth to within one planetary diameter, at least.

THOMPSON: How far is that in kilometers?

HASTINGS: A planetary diameter is 12,500 kilometers.

THOMPSON: *(Laughing)*

Well, that doesn't sound so bad. I wish I could miss my mother-in-law by twelve thousand klicks!

HASTINGS: It is *very* close by the standards of the Solar system.

THOMPSON: Yes, I suppose it is. You astronomers are used to working with really big numbers, aren't you? I understand that the System Council is making plans to blow the comet up should it come too close. Care to comment?

HASTINGS: You will have to ask them that. It's been nearly nine months since I was on Earth, and as you might expect, I'm a little out of touch.

THOMPSON: There is one thing that I've been curious about, Miss Hastings. I suppose if the comet were to hit Earth, it would cause a great deal of destruction.

HASTINGS: A very great deal, Ric.

THOMPSON: It would look something like a nuclear bomb going off, wouldn't it?

HASTINGS: Yes.

THOMPSON: I've been wondering . . . What would it *sound* like?

HASTINGS: *(Blinking in surprise)*
I beg your pardon?

THOMPSON: I've heard that some meteors produce a sonic boom as they pass through the atmosphere. Others make a ripping noise. If this comet nucleus of yours were to land in someone's front yard, what would our viewers listen for?

HASTINGS: It would be difficult not to hear it, Ric. A meteor strike the size of Comet Hastings would arrive with the sound of a billion thunderclaps!

THOMPSON: Strike like thunder, eh? Then we'd best all hope nothing like that ever happens. Thank you, Miss Hastings. And now, we have to take a break for a commercial.

(Close-up on Ric Thompson. Fade to commercial.)

Amber and Tom Thorpe lay together on the floor of their cabin. Even though the nucleus's gravitational pull was less than one percent, it was still too much for them to hang from a hook on the wall as they had done in zero gee. People who tried sleeping vertically found their sleep disturbed by dreams of falling. They watched the replay of Amber's interview with TECN. When Thompson reached the question of what the nucleus would sound like as it crashed to Earth, there came a strangling noise from Amber.

"They were supposed to cut that out!" she exclaimed as the interviewer's question and her answer went out over the air. "The council ordered us to play down the prospect of a collision."

"I would say someone decided that a good interview was more important than following orders."

"Damn it," she swore. "That computer must have asked me a hundred questions. I was getting tired and couldn't believe the inanity of asking what it would sound like! I just fired back the first thing that came to mind."

"It isn't your fault. They're the ones who mucked it up. I'll bet the System Council is fit to be tied."

"They'll probably want my ass for this!"

Thorpe smiled and ran his hand over the subject in question. "They'll have to fight me for it."

CHAPTER 23

NEWS ITEM:

UNIVERSAL FAX, DEN HAAG, UNITED EUROPE—21 FEB 2086 (FOR DISTRIBUTION TO AUSL, CHN, NORAM, SOAM, UNEUR, LUNA, XTERR)

SOURCES CLOSE TO THE ADMINISTRATION OF THE SYSTEM COUNCIL HAVE ALLEGED THAT THE COMET HASTINGS ICE ASTEROID, WHICH HAS BEEN REFERRED TO IN RECENT PRESS REPORTS AS THUNDERSTRIKE, WILL COLLIDE WITH THE EARTH ON 17 JULY 2087. A SPOKESMAN FOR THE CHIEF COORDINATOR'S OFFICE DECLINED TO COMMENT OFFICIALLY BUT STATED ON BACKGROUND THAT SUCH SPECULATION IS "PREMATURE AND IRRESPONSIBLE." WHILE ADMITTING THAT THE POSSIBILITY EXISTS, THE SPOKESMAN REPORTED THAT EFFORTS ARE UNDER WAY "TO INSURE AN ADEQUATE MARGIN OF SAFETY WHEN THE COMET REACHES EARTH NEXT YEAR." AS EVIDENCE OF THIS CONTENTION, THE SPOKESMAN POINTED TO THE CRASH EFFORT TO MODIFY SEVERAL LARGE ORBITAL CARRIERS FOR TRANSPORTING MEN AND EQUIPMENT TO THE COMET. THE SHIPS, HE CLAIMED, WILL BE

204 MICHAEL McCOLLUM

READY FOR SPACE BY APRIL 1, A FULL SIXTY DAYS AHEAD OF
SCHEDULE.

END

Barbara Martinez sat at her work station and watched numbers
scroll up the screen. The glowing figures reflected the results of
the working group's latest simulation. Barbara did not have to
plot the data to know that they had suffered another failure. No
matter what combination of propulsion schemes they tried, it
seemed impossible to change the nucleus's velocity by even the
most insignificant fraction of a percent. The ice asteroid was just
too damned massive to be budged!

"Well, pulsing the antimatter stream doesn't seem to make any
difference," she said to Gwilliam Potter. "We'd still require more
antimatter than we can produce in a decade. So much for the
theoreticians' latest brainstorm."

"Just as I told you before you started," Potter replied. He was
a British European who had shared Barbara's office for the past
two weeks. Barbara had found him to be urbane, funny, and just
a bit too pessimistic.

"So what do we do now?"

He shrugged elaborately. "You'd best ask the big thinkers
about that. I think we're going about this all wrong."

"How so?"

"Just look at the simulations we've been running. They're all
variations on existing techniques. Hell, Halver Smith pioneered
most of them. We've tried injecting antimatter directly into the
ice and boiling it away. We've tried pulverizing the damned stuff
and running it through surface-mounted reaction jets. We've even
thought of using those three converted bulk carriers as spacego-
ing tugs. So far nothing has even come close to what we need."

"So tell me something I don't know."

"While you've been playing with your figures, I've been
working on an idea of my own." He gestured toward his workscreen, on which was displayed a view of Ground Zero Crater
and its surroundings.

"And I thought you were merely goofing off because you
didn't want to help me with the coding."

Potter grinned. "There's that, too."

"What have you got?"

"In every attempt to date we've tried to obtain thrust by accelerating small masses to high velocity."

"How else can we get propulsion efficiency?"

"Maybe we need the economy of scale more than efficiency."

"I don't follow."

"What if we impart a small velocity to a really big mass?"

"Isn't that what we're trying to do to the whole asteroid?"

"That comment, my dear office mate, is a null set of the zero equals zero variety. I'm suggesting that we break off a major chunk of Thunderstrike and toss it away at relatively low speed —one hundred meters per second, for instance."

"I wouldn't let the director hear you call the nucleus by that name," Barbara warned.

"Why not? Everyone else calls it that. Is it my fault that the press has figured things out and are now camped on the director's doorstep?"

"You're still the one Warren will chew on if he hears you use that word."

"I don't plan to use it around him," Potter said.

"Never mind. What about your idea?"

"Have you ever noticed all of the fracture rings that surround Ground Zero Crater? It almost reminds you of a cork pushed into an eggshell, doesn't it?"

"I imagine the Earth will have a similar mark if the nucleus collides with it."

"I'll bet it will," Potter agreed cheerily. "Looking at all of those faults got me to thinking. What if we could somehow push the cork back out again?"

"Great idea. How do you plan to do it?"

"Did you ever own a pellet gun?"

Barbara shook her head. "My father wouldn't allow it. He said no daughter of his was going to kill helpless birds."

"My father said the same thing. A friend had one, though, and the first thing I did was shoot out the picture window in the living room. Have you ever noticed the way glass breaks when it's struck by a pellet?"

"Sure. There's a small entry hole, then a big chunk taken out of the back."

Potter nodded. "The technical term for the phenomenon is 'spalling.' The initial impact sets up a compression wave through the glass. When that wave reaches the other side, it's reflected as a tension wave. Glass is almost infinitely strong in compression, but very weak in tension. The result is that the reflected wave breaks off a piece and sends it flying. Interestingly, the spalled chunk recedes with the same energy the pellet originally imparted to the glass. The same principle was once used to penetrate armor plate with a shaped charge."

"Your point?"

"Simply that the spalled chip carries away the energy of impact. If we could use the fault pattern around Ground Zero Crater to spall off a really big piece of Thunderstrike, what sort of velocity could we achieve?"

"Let's say you could get one hundred meters per second separation speed. I still don't . . . Oh!"

Potter smiled broadly. "The lady begins to understand. If we time it such that the spalled-off chunk is aimed back along the orbit, conservation of momentum will kick Thunderstrike forward just a little. With luck, we might even pick up our elusive five centimeters per second on the first try."

"How large a chunk can we get?"

"Ground Zero Crater is 125 kilometers across and our laser drills can get down twenty kilometers or so. That's a couple of thousandths of the asteroid's total mass. If we got a separation speed of more than fifty meters per second, it ought to be enough."

"What if it isn't?"

"Then we repeat the operation as many times as necessary, or until we run out of time or antimatter. We could peel the asteroid like an onion if we had to."

"There's still the problem of how we break off a really big chunk."

"We'll need big bombs planted at just the right places in the fault system," Potter replied. He pointed to his workscreen. "If I were doing it, I would sink my shafts here, here, and here. If we set the bombs off together, we ought to be able to cleave the ice like a diamond cutter working on a gemstone. What do you think?"

Barbara gazed at the places he had indicated on the screen. They were all points where the fault lines were particularly close together. "I think it will require a lot of analysis, but that it might have possibilities."

"Should I mention this to the director?"

She nodded. "Just as soon as we work up a few numbers. It sounds good, Gwilliam. I think you've discovered the solution to our problem!"

"If not," he said, "we're going to send those poor fools aboard *Admiral Farragut* down a lot of cold holes for nothing."

Nadia Hobart answered the door on the second chime and found a red-faced, rotund man standing in the corridor outside. She smiled at the familiar visitor and invited him inside. "They're in the den, Harold. They just started."

"Thank you, Nadia," Harold Barnes replied. "And how is Luna's First Lady this evening?"

"Still not comfortable with people calling me 'First Lady.'"

"You'll get used to it. You're a natural for the job. Just don't let those leeches down in Administration run your life. Do things because you feel comfortable doing them, not because some protocol officer thinks you should."

"Thanks, I'll remember that," she said as she led Barnes through the simulated cavern of the living room.

"How is John? I haven't seen him since the victory party election night."

Nadia Hobart bit her lower lip, a nervous habit she had picked up as a farm girl in Kansas. "I'm worried about him, Harold. He's working too hard. First the election, and now this comet thing. He'll wear himself out within a year if he doesn't slow down. You're his friend. You could talk to him after the meeting."

"I can try. I'm not sure what good it will do. Truth is, Nadia, we've all been working hard on this feasibility study John ordered. Thank God, it's almost over."

"What have you found out?"

Barnes sighed. "That we're in better shape than I would have thought possible. The import duties Parliament passed last decade worked better than anyone expected. We're much more self-sufficient than we were. I'm convinced that we can survive without Earth, but only if we prepare now."

"What needs to be done?"

"Where does one start? We desperately need stockpiles of semifinished manufacturing stock—things like germanium wafers, seed crystals, superconductor doping powders. We need to improve our stockpiles of terrestrial genotypes, too. The back-order rate at our life banks is nearly thirty percent! We've never upgraded a lot of our equipment-operating software, and many of our financial records are stored in Earth data bases."

"Have you told John these things?"

"Haven't had the chance. The bank just finished the report this afternoon."

"Hello, Harold!" John Hobart boomed out. "What haven't you told me?"

"The results of the survivability study."

"We'll get to that. You know my guests, I believe." Despite his hearty manner, it was easy to see that Hobart was a tired man. He had dark bags under his eyes, and his face had developed a whole new set of worry lines during the past month.

"Professor Jinsai and I see each other at the Chamber of Commerce luncheon every Wednesday, and, of course, Advisor Sturdevant and I go back years together. I don't recognize this other gentleman, however."

"Professor Albert Portero, astrophysicist from the university, I'd like to introduce Harold Barnes, First Vice President of the Bank of Luna."

"Professor Portero."

"Citizen Barnes."

"Pour yourself a drink, Harold. Professor Portero was just explaining tektites to us."

"What, by Tycho's frosts, is a tektite?"

Professor Portero, a thin-faced man with a nervous way of moving his hands, replied, "A tektite is a piece of glass formed by impact heating during a meteor strike, Citizen Barnes. They come in a variety of shapes and sizes. Most are microscopic, although some as large as a ten-selene piece have been discovered. Their presence in a particular region marks the landing site of ejecta thrown up during meteor crater formation. On Earth tektites are found in localized regions known as 'strewn fields.' Lunar tektites tend to be scattered evenly across the surface due to the Moon's lower gravity and lack of atmosphere. Although tektites are generally found on the same body where they were formed, a number of Earth-formed tektites have been found on Luna, and vice versa."

"Meaning," Hobart put in, "that ejected material has occasionally achieved terrestrial escape velocity and landed here."

"Correct," Portero replied. "Most Earth-formed tektites on

Luna are similar in composition to those found in the Australasian strewn field. That particular field is the result of a giant meteor strike into the Pacific Basin 750,000 years ago."

"How did that strike compare with a Comet Hastings strike?"

Portero's laugh was a short bark. "There is no comparison, Prime Minister. Comet Hastings will be more violent by several orders of magnitude!"

"Then we can expect a considerable fountain of ejecta to be launched into space?"

"Considerable," Portero agreed. "And since much of that material will attain Earth orbital speed, we can expect Luna to intercept debris for decades following impact. Our simulations suggest that the amount of mass which will eventually fall on Luna will exceed a million tons."

There was a low whistle from Barnes. "A million tons!"

"Much of that will be in the form of micrometeoric dust," Portero explained. "As such, it will not present a major hazard to us. However, we can expect larger pieces to fall from the sky as well. These bigger rocks will devastate large areas of the Moon."

"How big?"

"That's difficult to say without a better understanding of the impact dynamics. I would venture to guess that we will end up with several more craters the size of Copernicus."

There was sudden silence in the study. Copernicus Crater was nearly a hundred kilometers in diameter. The violence of that strike had sprayed ejecta for hundreds of kilometers in every direction. The shock wave alone would devastate millions of square kilometers.

"How soon after the collision with Earth will we be in danger?" the prime minister asked.

"Ejecta will begin arriving within forty-eight hours of Earth's destruction. Meteors will continue falling for centuries unless we do something about them."

"What can we do?"

"We can establish a warning system like Sky Watch," the professor of astrophysics replied. "We'll have to track the larger chunks, then move them to safe orbits. I doubt that we'll be able to get them all, but we can certainly reduce the danger."

"What about those we don't stop?"

"I suppose we'll have to disperse the population," Advisor Sturdevant replied. Alex Sturdevant had been John Hobart's close friend and advisor for nearly twenty years. His position in the new government was as powerful as it was unofficial. "That way we won't lose everything if a piece of Earth comes crashing down on Luna City."

"Can we do that, Professor Jinsai?" Hobart asked. "Can our economy stand the disruption?"

The professor of economics shrugged. "What other choice have we, Prime Minister?"

The shrunken Sun stood in the black sky as Amber Hastings made her careful way toward the gaping hole in front of her. The Sun was behind her, casting a black shadow at her feet and turning the crevasse into an ink stain on the landscape. Despite the numerous spikes that soled her boots, she slipped like a skater teetering at the edge of control as she negotiated a slight incline.

"You'd best plant an anchor before you go any farther," Kyle Stormgaard advised over their private communications channel.

"Putting one down now." Amber detached a meter-long baton from her equipment belt and touched the dirty gray surface. A small explosion erupted from the baton's muzzle, driving a steel piton into the ice. A safety line connected the piton to Amber's equipment harness. "Anchored."

Beside her, *Admiral Farragut*'s chief engineer put down his own anchor. The two explorers then moved cautiously toward the lip of the crevasse.

Surface explorations had been under way for two weeks, and the confidence of the exploration teams had grown with each day spent on the ice. At first their activities had been confined to off-loading heavy equipment from the cargo module and bringing the hydrogen-cracking system online. The latter task involved activating the expedition's power reactor and running power cables to a heavy-laser drill out on the ice. The drill was to bore a test hole several kilometers deep. The bore would not only allow them to map the way ice composition changed with depth, but would provide feed stock for the hydrogen-cracking unit.

It had taken the better part of a week for the shaft to reach a depth of two kilometers. Ice samples taken from the wall of the test bore showed the nucleus to be a fairly typical denizen of the Oort Cloud. Like most cometary nuclei, Comet Hastings was composed of clathrate ices—frozen H_2O with other compounds interspersed within the ice's crystalline structure. At various depths they found high levels of ammonia, carbon monoxide, carbon dioxide, formaldehyde, hydrogen cyanide, methane, and nitrogen mixed in with the water ice. Also present were varying concentrations of meteoric dust.

Even before the drilling began, it became obvious that the nucleus was far from geologically stable. During the encounter with Jupiter the asteroid had been subjected to powerful tidal stresses which in turn had generated waste heat. That heat was making its slow way to the surface. As the near-absolute-zero ice warmed, its expansion triggered internal jolts which resulted in surface tremors. Most were too weak to feel. Occasionally they were strong enough to knock the laser drill out of alignment. Each time that happened, work had to be halted while the laser was realigned.

Not until end of watch on their seventh day aground did they experience a really large tremor. Karin Olafson was in the ship's control room when she was nearly pitched out of her couch. The tremor lasted less than a minute but was sufficiently strong to break the habitat module free of one of its anchor chains. When the quake was over, the captain wasted no time ordering the surface crews out to repair the damage. They had worked most of the night to reanchor the habitat and cargo modules and to stabilize them with guy wires.

Another delay had been caused by the expedition's two moonjumpers. The tiny flying machines were standard models used on Luna—their underjets proved too powerful for the nucleus's gravitational field. A quick burst from the jets would send the little craft high into the sky, and landing was little more than a controlled crash. After a few test flights the small flying machines had been grounded until their thrusters could be derated.

With the return of the moonjumpers to service, the exploration teams began to venture outside the vast crater. Their first destination was the Badlands, where they found a landscape as rugged as anything in the Solar system. Mountains, thrust upward at impossibly steep angles, were cut by long valleys that ran outward from Ground Zero Crater. Cutting across the mountains and valleys were the crevasses formed during the impact of a billion years earlier. With Earth's suggestion that it might be possible to spall off a large chunk of the nucleus, the crevasses had become a prime object of study.

"What do you think?" Amber asked Kyle as the two played

their suit lamps along the opposite wall of the crevasse. The lamps revealed a narrow canyon with vertical walls. The bottom was impossible to see hidden in shadow and too far away for their lamps to illuminate.

"It's deeper than I thought it would be," Stormgaard replied. "I wonder if we brought along enough line."

"There's only one way to find out."

Amber and the chief engineer had been assigned the job of planting a seismograph in the bottom of the crevasse. It would have been a simple matter to fly down with their suit jets. However, a miscalculation in the confined space could send them tumbling out of control, and a suit malfunction could leave them stranded. Climbing ropes were a lot more trouble, but ultimately safer.

Amber sank two more pitons into the ice, then fastened two coiled safety lines to them. She tossed the lines into the crevasse and watched them sink lazily from sight, uncoiling as they went. While Amber rigged the lines, the chief engineer planted a communications repeater at the lip of the crevasse. He pointed one of the device's horns downward and oriented the other toward where the power section of the *Admiral Farragut* hovered above the nucleus's north pole. When finished, he straightened up and asked Amber if she was ready.

"Ready," she replied.

"Let's do it, then."

They each hooked a line to their suit harnesses, then casually stepped over the precipice. It took Amber eight seconds to fall her own length, by which time she had taken up the slack in her line. After that it was a simple matter of falling into the dark while keeping a gloved hand around the line to regulate her speed.

The greatest danger in working in the nucleus's low gravity was that it promoted overconfidence. At two-thirds of one-percent standard, the nucleus's gravity made a person feel certain about surviving a kilometer-long fall. They could. But such a fall would end on the hard ground at forty kph—an impact more than sufficient to puncture a suit or break a neck. As Amber descended, she kept a running tally of the number of seconds it took to traverse the distance between marks on the line. Every once in a while she gripped the line tighter to slow her fall.

The descent proved uneventful until the very end. Amber had

intended to land lightly on the icy floor of the crevasse. As she touched down, the solid surface gave way, sending her into the cold ice up to her waist. She shouted a warning to Stormgaard, who halted his descent in time. He played his light over the sparkling surface while Amber extricated herself by pulling herself hand over hand up the line.

"What caused this?" she asked when she hung once more on Stormgaard's level.

"Must have been the microquakes," the chief engineer replied. "Loose material dislodged from the walls collects here in the bottom of the crevasse."

"I wonder how deep it is."

"No way to tell," he responded.

Amber kicked at the snow. "What are we going to do? We can't very well anchor the seismograph in this powder."

"No problem," Stormgaard replied. "We'll plant it on the crevasse wall. Come on, let's get to it."

They worked for fifteen minutes making sure that the small orange box was firmly affixed to the icy wall. When they were through, Stormgaard directed Amber to check the communications link with the ship.

"Hello, *Admiral Farragut*. This is Team Three. Can you hear me?"

"Hello, Team Three. This is Base. We read you loud and clear. Where have you two been?"

"Down a hole, Base. Have you been trying to get us?"

"Affirmative. Be advised that we were rocked by a Force Four Tremor about a minute ago. It's a surface wave traveling south to north. Take precautions. It's headed your way."

The two explorers glanced at each other and then at the pile of detritus at their feet. Together they triggered their suit jets and began an emergency ascent, trailing their safety lines behind. They were a hundred meters above the floor when the ice wall beside them began to shake.

"Keep away from the wall," Stormgaard warned as they were suddenly engulfed in a blizzard.

It was over in seconds. Amber emerged into the clear again to see Kyle's brightly lighted suit a dozen meters to her right. She began to feel calm again. She called the ship to tell them that they had come through the temblor okay. There was no answer, save her own echo.

"Think the communications relay could have been dislodged?" she asked, worried.

"Could be," Stormgaard responded. He shut off his suit jet and let his momentum carry him up as he craned backward to turn the beam of his helmet lamp upward. His sudden oath caused Amber to do the same.

High overhead a solid wall of falling ice was slowly closing on them.

CHAPTER 24

The Comet Hastings nucleus bulked large in the black sky as Tom Thorpe clambered among the struts and braces that supported *Admiral Farragut*'s Number Three hydrogen tank. Around him lay a forest of insulated pipes and electrical wiring. He pulled himself to where several pipes came together in a complex mechanism that transferred hydrogen from the tank to the ship's engines. He closed a valve, then triggered the control to release the latches that secured the tank to the thrust frame. Bracing against a handy strut, he placed his backpack against the tank's outer layer of insulation and pushed. Slowly, the 4000-cubic-meter sphere separated from the orbiting power section.

"Here it comes," he radioed Dieter Schmidt in Moonjumper One.

"I see it."

The jumper was an ungainly construct. Its transparent body was mounted on four heavy landing legs with oversize pads for feet. Surrounding the cabin were a series of struts and braces, which held all manner of gear, everything from thruster clusters, to communications antennas, to a variety of flight sensors. Nestled between the landing feet was the small craft's oxyhydrogen rocket engine with its oversize exhaust nozzle. Moonjumpers were designed for ballistic point-to-point travel on Luna and had never been intended for orbital operations. However, the jumper made an ideal orbital transfer vehicle in the weak gravity of the nucleus.

Thorpe and Schmidt had the task of ferrying one of *Admiral Farragut*'s tanks down to the surface. There it would be filled with hydrogen from the cracking system, then returned to the ship. The cycle would be repeated until each of the ship's eighteen tanks were filled.

As Thorpe watched, Schmidt moved the jumper close to the slowly receding sphere. The crewman used the remote manipulator to remove one of four thruster packs that the jumper carried clipped to its forward basket. He attached the pack to a thrust pad on the tank's equator, then moved ninety degrees around the snow-white sphere and repeated the maneuver. He repeated the procedure twice more. When all four packs had been attached, Schmidt moved the jumper to a safe distance and turned control over to the thruster packs' master autopilot. The thrusters emitted simultaneous bursts of flame, and the tank's slow drift toward the comet nucleus accelerated perceptibly.

Thorpe watched the tank out of sight while Schmidt maneuvered the jumper close to the orbiting power section. Thorpe used his suit jets to cross the ten-meter gulf of vacuum, then squeezed in beside the jumper pilot. "Let's go home."

They followed the free-flying tank as it made its way toward Ground Zero Crater. They were ten kilometers above the Little Alps Mountains when Thorpe's suit radio began beeping.

"Thorpe here," he answered.

Cybil Barnard's anxious voice echoed in his earphones. "Thomas?"

"I'm here."

"We may have an emergency."

"Who?"

"It's Amber Hastings and Kyle Stormgaard."

Thorpe's stomach underwent a sudden fear contraction. "What about them?"

"They aren't answering. They called in about twenty minutes ago, received a tremor warning, then went off the air. We've been trying to contact them without success."

"Could they have had a radio failure?"

"Possible, but we think you'd better check on them."

"Agreed. Where are they?"

"Cervantes Crevasse, sixty-five north by sixteen east. They've got the other jumper."

"We'll check it out." He turned to Schmidt. "Let's change our landing site. Home on Jumper Two's signal."

Schmidt swept a hand over the control board, and their earphones came alive with the reassuring *dit-dit-dah* of the other jumper's beacon.

The universe suddenly tilted as Schmidt altered their trajectory. Five kilometers in front and below, the tiny white sphere continued on its way toward the crater base. Ten minutes later they were sweeping across the rugged terrain of the Badlands, searching for the red beacon that would mark the other landing craft.

"I've got it," Schmidt said, pointing toward a black gash in the surface of the comet.

Thorpe nodded. He, too, had seen the beacon. "See if you can set us down next to it. Keep clear of the crevasse."

"Will do."

The landing was agonizingly slow. By the time their footpads touched down, Thorpe was already unstrapped from his seat and halfway out the hatch. He jetted across the gap between jumpers without bothering to touch down. When he arrived, he anchored himself to the vehicle and looked around. After a moment he noticed the multiple sets of scuff marks in the thin layer of frost that overlay the harder ice of the asteroid's surface. The scuff marks led off in the direction of the crevasse.

"They headed for the crevasse," he reported before jetting in that direction. As he flew, Thorpe reeled out a safety line behind him. He braked his flight at the edge of the crevasse, grounded, and looked around. What he saw caused his heart to skip a beat.

There at the edge of the deep cut were several anchor pitons. Brightly-colored safety lines extended from two of them, leading down into the crevasse. He stepped to the edge and angled his suit lamp down to follow the lines. There, at the limit of his light, the safety lines disappeared into what appeared to be a snow bank.

"Oh, my God!"

"What's the matter?" Schmidt asked.

"They've been caught in an avalanche. Their lines disappear into a mound of loose ice."

"Don't sound so worried," Schmidt answered. "I come from

avalanche country on Earth. People there are buried for hours and still survive. In this gravity they shouldn't have been hurt unless a big solid chunk fell on them. They'll be all right if we can dig them out before they run short on breathing air."

"You're forgetting something," Thorpe replied. "This snow is near absolute zero. Their suits were never designed to be submerged in it. If we don't reach them quickly, they'll freeze to death!"

Barbara Martinez lay strapped into the acceleration couch of the ground-to-orbit shuttle and gazed out the viewport at the immensity of space. She had not expected to see a black daytime sky quite so soon. Yet less than a month after she had left Newton Station, she was back in space without ever having had the opportunity to sample the fleshpots of Earth. She gazed past the wing at the limb of the Earth and consoled herself with the knowledge that the situation was temporary.

The Thunderstrike Project, as the New Mexico study group had come to be called, needed someone to brief the officers who would take the bulk carriers out to meet the comet. A quick check of the roster had shown Barbara to have more space experience than anyone else on the team.

"They didn't even give me time to pack," she muttered as she searched for the ships that were her goal.

Gwilliam Potter's idea for modifying Thunderstrike's orbit had become official policy. It had been adopted after a week-long critique by three groups of project scientists. After its validation, director Warren had hailed the idea for its simplicity. Even those who worried that they would be unable to blast a large enough piece of the nucleus free agreed that the idea was theoretically sound. Potter's supporters pointed to the extensive network of faults that underlay Ground Zero Crater to answer their concerns.

That Thunderstrike's underlying structure had been shattered was obvious to everyone. Rings of crevasses surrounded the crater out to a distance of seventy kilometers. Seismic readings had confirmed that those splits were manifestations of a deep fault system. If sufficient explosive power could be properly applied, humanity might well finish the sundering begun by some nameless asteroid a million millennia earlier.

For explosive power they would use antimatter bombs at the bottom of deep bore holes. The "bombs" were actually standard antimatter storage rings to which small packets of chemical explosives had been affixed. When the explosives were detonated, each storage ring's magnetic field would fail, releasing a full kilogram of antimatter into the surrounding ice. The resulting energy release would be channeled into the fault system, hopefully setting off a titanic steam explosion beneath several square kilometers of the asteroid's surface and causing it to split open like a ripe melon, ejecting Ground Zero Crater and its surroundings into space.

"We're coming up on *Goliath* out your port, Miss Martinez," the shuttle's pilot announced over his intercom.

"Thank you, Captain," Barbara replied. She scrunched down to press her cheek against the cool viewport. There, low against the planet, she caught sight of a triangular constellation of strobing lights, beacons of the ships that would transport men and material to the comet.

Goliath, Gargantua, and *Godzilla* had been built to haul bulk material between Luna and the space habitats in the days before the Luna City mass driver had been erected. Since the mass driver had rendered them obsolete, they and their five sisters had been placed in orbital storage, where they had remained for nearly thirty years before the Thunderstrike Project took them over. For the past two months 500 skilled workers had worked round the clock to modify them for the coming mission. The old chemical engines had been ripped out and the latest antimatter-powered converters installed. Inside their layers of protective magnetic fields the antimatter chambers operated at temperatures approaching a million degrees centigrade. Where it had taken *Admiral Farragut* six months to reach Jupiter, *Goliath* and her sisters could make the same journey in only twelve weeks.

The winged shuttle fired its attitude jets as it approached *Goliath*. The bulk carrier was a large sphere 150 meters in diameter. Most of that, Barbara knew, was internal tankage for reaction mass and consumables. Much of the heavy cargo was to be carried externally, welded to hardpoints all over the ship. As they made their approach, Barbara saw everything from medium crawlers to large laser-drill rigs arrayed around *Goliath*'s hull. The arrangement gave the ship a messy look and probably played hell with the captain's center-of-gravity calculations, but made off-loading equipment at the nucleus relatively easy.

Two quick spurts from the attitude-control jets and the shuttle had matched velocities with the big bulk carrier. Five minutes later a flexible transfer tube snaked its way toward the shuttle's midship airlock. Barbara collected her notes and made her way aft. A crewman helped her through the airlock and into the tube. When she entered the larger ship, she found a four striper waiting for her.

"Welcome aboard *Goliath*, Miss Martinez. Glad you could join us. I'm Captain Palanquin."

"Good morning, Captain. Is everyone here?"

Palanquin nodded. "In the wardroom. Follow me, and we'll get the briefing started."

Barbara followed the captain through one of the ship's main circumferential corridors. Shipyard workers were everywhere, working in what to Barbara's eyes was utter chaos. The vessel had an unfinished look about it. There were the scars of welding torches on bulkheads and decks, loose cables strung along passageways, and the smell of paint in the air. The section of the ship through which she was led was being converted to bunk rooms for the heavy-equipment operators. The bunks were stacked four high.

"How many men will you be transporting to the comet, Captain?" she asked, suddenly aware of the magnitude of the effort.

"About a thousand," he said. "*Goliath* will be the habitat ship, while *Gargantua* and *Godzilla* will be used for heavy equipment and consumables transport."

The wardroom was crowded with ship's officers. Not only were *Goliath*'s senior officers in attendance, so too were the captains, first officers, and chief engineers of the other two ships. Barbara arranged her notes on a podium and gave the record tile she would be using to a spacer. When all was ready, she asked for the lights to be turned down.

"Good morning, ladies and gentlemen," she began. "My name is Barbara Martinez, and I'm a computer programmer with the Thunderstrike Project. I'm here to brief you on what we have learned about the comet nucleus and to answer your questions."

Barbara called up her first graphic, a full view of Thunderstrike as seen from space. She explained what the comet nucleus was and why it was dangerous, then reviewed its surface features. When she reached Ground Zero Crater, she explained Gwilliam Potter's plan for spalling off a large chunk in order to change the comet's orbit. When she finished her explanation, a grizzled space captain raised his hand.

"Yes, sir. You are?"

"Captain Jacques Marche, of *Godzilla*. These antimatter bombs which each ship is to carry—how many of them will there be?"

"As many as possible, Captain. At the moment we have budgeted thirty-eight kilograms of antimatter for the explosives. You will appreciate that we had to strip every stockpile in the system to get that much."

"Will it be enough?"

"We believe so. Not all of it will be used for the first shot. If the comet doesn't split off a big enough chunk on the first attempt, we'll try several more times. The System Council has ordered all of the orbiting power stations to full antimatter production, even if they have to cut back on power delivered to Earth. That will make a few more kilograms available before I-Day."

"I-Day?"

"Impact Day!"

"I understand we'll be arriving at the comet a full year ahead of that date," another captain said.

"That is correct. We hope to have the first charge set to blow by I minus 250. We'll shoot every thirty days after that if it proves necessary."

"I'm concerned about my ship. I'm being asked to run my tanks dry on the outbound journey. Why not arrive a little later and save some fuel for emergencies?"

"We've got to get to the nucleus as quickly as possible," Barbara replied. "The closer Thunderstrike gets to Earth, the more difficult it will be to make it miss."

Amber fidgeted in her sleep and wondered why it was so cold. She must be back in the cold-sleep tank, she decided. She reached out to search for the manual override. It was not there. She felt as if her limbs had been wrapped in heavy gauze. The cold got suddenly worse, and a great throbbing began somewhere inside her skull. She opened her eyes and gazed upward. A frost-white glaze reflected her instrument lights a centimeter in front of her face.

Frost-white glaze!

Her mind snapped back to the moment when she and Kyle had stared stupidly up at a layer of ice falling slowly toward them.

"Don't panic," Stormgaard had advised. "Swing your light west while I try east. See if you can spot the edge of the slide."

She did as she was told. The whole north wall of the crevasse appeared to have caved in. Amber saw nothing but overhead ice for as far as her light extended. The view reminded her of pictures she had seen taken by divers beneath Earth's polar ice caps. She reported her observation to Stormgaard.

"Same here," he said. "We'll have to butt our way through. Jets to full. Arms at your sides. Don't worry about cracking your helmet. It's tougher than you are."

Gulping, she had followed his direction, and they had soared upward toward the descending icefall. Amber remembered the loud *crack!* as her helmet struck the descending layer of dirty white. Despite Stormgaard's assurances, she waited for the wind that signaled the start of explosive decompression. The helmet held, but the blow rattled her teeth. The icefall was not solid but composed of fist-sized chunks. She could tell that she was making progress upward by the battering she was taking. It was like being pelted with rocks. Then the pelting stopped, and the ice falling past her faceplate slowed. Suddenly, the ice was stationary around her. She was being dragged backward by the general fall.

"Kyle, I'm stuck!" she radioed. Her call went unanswered. Either her antenna had been carried away or else Stormgaard was blocked by too much ice. Amber considered her predicament. The icefall would reach the bottom of the crevasse in another few seconds, and when it did, there would be a terrible crunch. She had to extricate herself before that happened.

Then everything went black until she woke from a dream that she was back in cold storage. She focused her eyes to gaze at her helmet chronometer. It had been an hour since she and Stormgaard had entered the crevasse and approximately half that time since they had begun their panicked ascent. Half an hour. Had they missed her yet? Was anyone worried? Perhaps they were already above, digging furiously to reach her. If so, they had better hurry.

She tried to move her arms and legs and discovered that she was held fast. That puzzled her at first, then frightened her. What if she had broken her neck? Then reason took over. If she were paralyzed, she decided, she should not be able to feel her fingers and toes. All of her digits either ached or tingled. It almost felt like the time she had developed frostbite as the result of an experiment in chemistry class.

Frostbite!

At the thought she leaned her head forward to chin her heater control, only to find it already operating at full. Suddenly the reason for her immobility became clear. With the nucleus's low gravity and the loosely packed material around her, she ought to be able to move. The fact that she could not budge pointed to a sinister possibility.

Compared to the temperature of the surrounding ice, Amber's body was practically incandescent. Her vacuum suit was intended as much to protect the local environment from the heat she radiated as it was to keep her warm inside. While she lay unconscious, her suit had melted the ice and submerged her in a pool of water. As the exterior of the suit had cooled, however, the water had turned back into ice. By the time Amber woke, she was frozen fast in the center of a block of ice of indeterminate thickness.

It was only then that she began to be afraid. In the back of her mind she had been thinking about her air, food, and water. Now she knew that none of these were important. All that was important was the cold. Already she could feel it seeping into her extremities, slowly making them numb. In another ten minutes she would lose all feeling in her limbs. No more than half an hour after that, they would be frozen solid, dead appendages attached to a rapidly cooling torso.

She knew that it did not matter how quickly rescuers arrived from the ship. Already it was too late. By the time they dug her free, she would be frozen as solid as the block of ice in which she was embedded. At the sudden realization that she was facing death, Amber began to sob softly. The sound echoed through her helmet, mocking her.

CHAPTER 25

Tom Thorpe anchored himself on the edge of the crevasse and watched Jumper One lift into the black sky. The jumper's exhaust was a stiff wind that sent flurries of ammonia snow swirling about him. The storm quickly fell to a whisper as the tiny spacecraft dwindled toward the southern horizon. A moment later Jumper Two took off on autopilot and buffeted him again as it raced after its departed twin. Mission rules called for the jumpers to be manned whenever possible as a precaution against computer failure. The critical need at the moment, however, was to get the maximum number of rescuers to the scene as soon as possible. Sending Jumper Two back on automatic doubled the available transport and more than made up for the minor risk they were taking.

With the departure of the jumpers, Thorpe turned his attention to the crevasse. He and Schmidt had taken turns tugging on the two safety lines in the hope that they could haul the two avalanche victims to the surface. After some initial movement, both lines had gone taut and remained solidly anchored. Schmidt had wanted to use the jumper winches, but Thorpe had vetoed the idea as too dangerous. If a line snapped, they would have no hope of finding Amber or Stormgaard in the icefall. By using the red-and-yellow cables to guide their digging, they had a chance. And even if the safety lines remained intact, there was no guarantee that the same would be true for their two friends. Dragging Stormgaard and Amber up through that collection of ice blocks could easily puncture their suits or snap their necks.

Thorpe paid out his own tether and slipped over the lip of the crevasse. He reached the bottom within two minutes and began digging frantically at the point where one of the safety lines disappeared into the ice. Surface operations on the nucleus had quickly taught them that one man could do the work of a dozen in the nucleus's gravity field. Thorpe grappled with chunks of ice larger than himself, heaving them mightily in all directions. Despite their low weight, they retained full mass and inertia, causing him to strain for each new conquest. Within minutes he was perspiring heavily inside his clammy vacuum suit.

He worked without thinking, afraid to dwell on what Amber was probably feeling. He dug with the strength and speed of a madman, moving quickly despite the constrained motions that his suit forced upon him. He had followed the red-and-yellow safety line through the icefall and had cleared a hole nearly three meters deep when he realized that he could no longer feel his fingers. He ignored the numbness until his fingers' weakness forced him to halt his digging.

"Thorpe, are you down there?"

The radio call caused him to glance up toward the crevasse's rim. The sun was low on the horizon, causing the rim to appear a river of fire in an otherwise black universe. Standing there, illuminated by the light, were two figures in vacuum suits. One was John Malvan.

"I need some help down here!" he yelled. Until that moment he had not realized how hard he had been breathing.

"On my way." Malvan dropped into the crevasse with surprising swiftness. He used his suit jets to accelerate his fall, and then again to brake his descent. The Lunarian skated across the jumble of ice blocks to where Thorpe still stood in the depression he had created. Malvan, the ex–ice miner, took in the scene with a practiced gaze. "What's the situation?"

Thorpe hurriedly explained what he had found, then pointed to the slack safety line he had been trying to dig out of the ice. "I can't work my hands anymore. You'll have to dig."

"You're wasting your time. We'll never get them out this way."

"I don't have time to argue," Thorpe growled.

Malvan was nonplussed. "Neither do I. This is no job for brawn. We have to work smarter."

"What do you suggest?"

"They're sending it down now."

Thorpe leaned back to gaze upward to where an assemblage of parts was being lowered to the crevasse floor. He recognized one of the expedition's high-pressure oxygen tanks, a stiff coil of high-pressure tubing, and several sections of straight pipe.

"What are you going to do with that?"

"Use a miniature version of what Earth hopes to do to this asteroid."

"You aren't going to try and blast them out?"

"In a matter of speaking. I'm going to inject compressed gas down into the ice mass to break it up."

Thorpe nodded inside his suit. Air at one standard atmosphere exerted a million dynes on each square centimeter—several tons when applied across the area of the large ice blocks he had been manhandling. In the nucleus's low gravity field, even a few hundredths of an atmosphere should be sufficient to scatter the icefall with the efficiency of a chemical explosion.

Thorpe clambered up out of the hole he had made while two figures drifted down into the crevasse. He was not surprised to see that one of them was Captain Olafson. The other was Cybil Barnard, the ship's doctor.

"Which is which?" the captain asked as soon as she grounded. She was looking toward where the two safety lines disappeared into the icefall.

"I don't know," Thorpe replied. "I've been digging here because this was the first one I came to."

Karin Olafson fell forward and caught herself on outstretched arms in a low gravity push-up. She studied the line where it entered the ice. She then moved over and repeated the maneuver at the other line. Then she straightened her arms and pushed herself erect. "You're right. There's no way to tell. How long has it been?" The question, spoken in a different voice, was obviously not addressed to Thorpe.

Chen Ling Tsu's scholarly voice immediately echoed over the intercom circuit. "Fifty-seven minutes."

"Time's a'wasting. Let's get them up."

John Malvan was already at work assembling sections of long hollow tube. He worked deftly, despite his handicap. When the tube was ten meters long, he carried it and a tripod into the pit. The tripod was equipped with explosive anchors to attach it to the nucleus, and a drive mechanism that grasped the long tube and pushed it into the ice. It took several attempts before Malvan found a place where the tube would penetrate deeply. When only a meter or so projected from the ice, he dismounted the tripod and handed it to Karin Olafson. Malvan then attached the high-pressure hose to a fitting at the end of the tube. Thorpe attempted to help, but found that his hands were useless inside their gloves. They were beginning to ache in the warmth from his suit heater.

The four of them climbed out of the pit and moved the high-pressure tank a hundred meters distant down the crevasse.

"Watch out for flying debris!" Malvan warned as he turned the valve on the air tank. Nothing happened for a moment. Then the ice bellied up in a slow explosion all around the buried tube. They waited for the larger pieces to settle before rushing back into the swirling fog that obscured the center of the explosion.

"Here's one!" Cybil Barnard yelled.

Thorpe scrambled through the fog until he came across the doctor's form. She was bent over what at first appeared to be another block of ice. Only on closer examination did he realize that the block was man-shaped.

"Who is it?" Captain Olafson asked over the radio.

Thorpe felt the knot in his stomach tighten as he leaned over to shine his light on the figure. The sarcophagus of glaze ice was remarkably clear. It reflected his light, but let him see enough to note the white beard.

"It's your husband!" Thorpe yelled.

If the captain felt relief at the news, she did not show it. She merely ordered them to get him out of the pit. Thorpe helped the doctor move Kyle Stormgaard to the crevasse wall.

"Is he alive?" Thorpe asked as the doctor shone her light into the chief engineer's faceplate.

"I don't know," she said. "We need to get him back to the ship." At her order, the work party on the rim took up the slack in Stormgaard's safety line. The doctor followed her patient toward the surface. She used her suit jets to keep him from banging against the crevasse wall.

Malvan retrieved his tube and moved up the canyon with it, searching for another point to probe. Debris from the explosion complicated the job. He set up his tripod and drove the tube into the ice once more. They retreated, and Malvan turned on the air again. The explosion was less violent than the last, but still sufficient to open a large crater.

The three of them waded into the cloud they had just created. An agonizingly long minute passed before Captain Olafson called out that she had found the safety line. She pulled it taut and followed it to its end. The line disappeared into the icefall.

"Damn, she's still buried."

"She can't be down too far," Malvan replied. "This is about the level we found Kyle at. Shall we blast again?"

"First let's try pulling her to the surface," Thorpe said, reversing his previous decision. He was acutely aware of the time that had elapsed since Amber had been buried.

The three of them lined up on the safety line and anchored it to their equipment belts. They strained for ten seconds before the line moved. Thorpe knelt down and gazed at the ground. A cylindrical block of ice had been raised a few centimeters. It took a moment to recognize the shape.

"Here she is!"

Unlike the ice that encased the chief engineer, Amber's sarcophagus was opaque. There was no seeing her face through the faceplate of her suit.

"How do we get this off?" Thorpe asked, referring to the opaque coating.

"We don't," Malvan replied. "We'll get her back to the ship first."

"But she's liable to freeze!"

Thorpe felt an arm on his shoulder, a gesture difficult to execute in a vacuum suit. "Courage. She's been in there a long time. A few more minutes won't make any difference one way or the other."

"Let's get this meeting started. We've a lot to cover today!"

Constance Forbin stared down the long mahogany table at the double row of faces turned in her direction. Seated before her were the twelve most powerful people on Earth—not the richest or best known, but definitely the most powerful. It was a measure of the extent of their power that few members of the public realized such power even existed. To enforce their decrees, the twelve could order the arrest of anyone. Neither warrant nor charge were required.

The Special Board of Managers had been appointed by the System Council to coordinate the diversion of Thunderstrike. That their mandate was limited solely to matters involving the comet did not detract from its sweep. With regard to the planetoid of ice, their word was law.

"We'll have a report from Director Warren first. How did last week's avalanche affect your operation in New Mexico, Clarence?"

"Not as badly as it might have. It's a shame about Amber Hastings, of course, but the survey crews are nearly back on schedule."

Constance Forbin nodded. "I suppose we should have expected a few casualties. Have you chosen the points in the fault system where you want the antimatter charges placed?"

"The primary list is ready for peer review, and my staff is compiling the list of secondaries now."

"Any surprises?"

"Two substitutions from the preliminary recommendations we reviewed last meeting. Neither was a particular surprise."

"And the crew briefings? How are they going?"

"Barbara Martinez just returned from her orbital tour. She brought back a long list of additional equipment the space crews want to take along."

"What sort of equipment?"

"Mostly space parts and other things they may need out there. Apparently, they didn't think much of our ground-based recommendations."

"Will any of these requisitions push back the fleet's launch?"

"Unlikely," Warren replied. "Almost everything will be in orbit by the middle of next week. That will give them time to load it aboard the ships and redo their weight and balance calculations."

"Keep me advised. We *must* launch on schedule. Lord Blenham, your report, please."

The white-haired European leaned forward to rest his elbows on the conference table. It was Blenham's job to orchestrate the Thunderstrike public relations campaign, something for which he was uniquely suited after a lifetime spent on London's Fleet Street.

"Actually, Madame Coordinator, the campaign is going quite well; possibly too well."

"What do you mean by that?" the Australasian representative asked.

"I mean that we have allayed the public's fear to the point where they are totally unconcerned about the comet. They are practically soporific on the subject. Thunderstrike barely makes it to the list of the top ten public worries in the latest polls. At our direction, the news people have taken to calling the nucleus a 'wayward meteor,' or 'a bit of space flotsam.' Most people have no idea of just how large and dangerous it is."

"Then you've done your job properly, Blenham," one of the other managers remarked. "The primary goal is to avoid a public panic."

"That is what we told ourselves at the time. Last week's accident got me to wondering about the wisdom of our approach."

"In what way?" Constance Forbin asked.

"I think we may have overplayed our hand. The vast majority believe that we will divert the nucleus on schedule and that they can go about their individual lives without worry. What happens if something happens to shake their confidence?"

"What can go wrong?" the North American manager asked.

"How should I know? My field is crowd psychology and public relations. Still, the way we're marketing this whole effort seems wrong to me. We should be playing up the drama—humanity striving against a hostile universe, that sort of thing. As long as our public posture maintains that diverting this comet is routine, we leave the populace in a fragile emotional state. One major setback and they'll panic."

"Do you have anything more concrete than a hunch on which to base this position?"

"I do," Blenham replied. "I had my people run a full simulation on a second-order setback. The resulting opinion swing was forty percent negative!"

There were a number of low whistles around the table. To cause four out of ten people to suddenly change their opinions about anything usually took an act of God. On the other hand, Constance Forbin remarked, that was precisely what they were facing!

Amber stirred in her sleep, vaguely aware that something was wrong. She lay in that half dream state characteristic of the time just before waking, luxuriating in the peaceful feeling it gave her. Slowly, almost grudgingly, she came fully awake to find Cybil Barnard leaning over her.

"Hello," the doctor said. "How are you feeling?"

Amber stretched and found her muscles curiously limp. "Fine. I just had the most awful dream . . ." It was then that she realized the significance of having the doctor standing over her. "Oh!"

"You've been a very sick woman," the doctor responded. "You were buried for an hour and a half."

"Then why aren't I dead? I remember waking up after the fall and feeling terribly cold. Ninety minutes should have frozen me solid."

"You can thank the layer of ice that encapsulated you. Apparently it insulated you from the really cold ice of the nucleus. Your suit kept pumping out heat and maintained your temperature far above what it could have been. Still, it was a close thing. Your arms and legs were nearly frozen through by the time we got your suit off. I was afraid for a while that we were going to have to pop you back into cold sleep until we reached Earth. Luckily, things hadn't gone quite that far. I was able to regenerate you with the equipment I have onboard."

"What about Kyle? Did he make it out all right?"

"He was pretty well frozen, too. Not as bad as you were, though. His larger mass helped, as did the fact that his coating of ice was thicker than yours. We did have one other casualty."

"Who?"

"Our fearless leader."

Amber blinked in surprise and fought to control her emotions. "Thomas?"

"He came down with second-degree frostbite on his fingers. The damned fool tried to dig you out by hand."

"He did?"

The doctor nodded. "He was first on the scene. We found him manhandling ice blocks larger than himself when we got there. He was also blubbering like a baby."

"You're kidding!"

"I never kid my patients. He loves you very much. Even after we got you back here, he made a complete ass of himself. He pestered me about your condition for hours. I finally had to ban him from sick bay to get any work done."

"Is he all right now?"

Cybil smiled. "Nothing wrong with our leader that seeing you won't cure. But I want to run you through a battery of tests before I let you have visitors. You've been through quite an ordeal."

"When can I get back to work? I imagine I've got a lot of orbital readings piling up."

"Not to worry. Crag coopted Professor Chen to help with the

orbital plot. He's pretty good at it. As for your going back on duty, I'd recommend taking it easy for a week or so. You can work inside the ship, but I won't clear you for surface duty until I've had a chance to observe you for a while."

"But the exploration teams must be shorthanded. We've got to get the survey done before the equipment transports launch. How else are they going to know what to bring?"

An odd look crossed the doctor's face, then she smiled. "That's right, I haven't told you, have I?"

"Told me what?"

"You are going to have to make some adjustments in your thinking. I had to regenerate quite a few cells in your limbs. There was no helping it. The damage from freezing was extensive. Cell regeneration is a painful process at best. I didn't want you in agony while it was going on, so I've kept you sedated. You've been unconscious for six weeks."

Amber frowned. *"Six weeks?"*

Cybil Barnard nodded. "The ships carrying the heavy equipment launched a month ago. They'll be here in another two months. So you see, there's no real hurry about your convalescence."

CHAPTER 26

Tom Thorpe lay in *Admiral Farragut*'s control room and gazed up at the three tiny globes of violet-white light displayed on the viewdome. The lights were the drive flares of the three heavy-equipment carriers. After several months of exploring the comet nucleus alone, the Comet Hastings Expedition was about to receive a massive infusion of help.

It had taken *Admiral Farragut* half a year to make the trip from Earth to Jupiter. The three transports had crossed a similar gulf of space in half that time. The three heavies had departed Earth eighty-three days earlier. After accelerating to more than twice solar-escape velocity, they had coasted outbound. When they had closed to within twenty-five million kilometers, they had begun to decelerate and had halted their flight while still several million kilometers in front of Thunderstrike. Now, having crossed 600 million kilometers of space to reach the comet, they were fleeing before it.

The maneuver was not as paradoxical as it sounded. Like relay runners who saw the baton carrier approaching, the heavy carriers were moving in the same direction as the comet, allowing it to overtake them. They had adjusted their acceleration so that they would match the nucleus's velocity at the precise moment it drew abreast of them.

"How are they doing?" Amber asked as she floated into the control room.

Thorpe smiled at the sight of her and reached out to extend a helping hand. The baby-pink skin of his palms, along with similar patches on her arms, were reminders of how close he had come to losing her.

"They're doing fine," he replied as he levitated her to the acceleration couch. "They'll be here in another four hours."

Amber looked to where the three ships' exhaust flares hovered near the zenith of the viewdome. Except for their brightness, they looked precisely like planetary nebulae.

"Is Professor Barnard still camped out in the telescope room?" Thorpe asked.

"Still at it. I offered to spell him, but he wouldn't hear of it."

"How are things going?"

"Good. He's even humming to himself!"

Thorpe shook his head in wonder. "Once a scientist, always a scientist."

The fleet of cargo carriers had entered the coma two days earlier. As they backed down through the gas and dust, their exhausts roiled the substance of the cloud. Barnard was recording every second of the approach to learn all he could about the gas cloud and its composition. The study had no relevance to the problem of diverting the nucleus from Earth. It was merely something that interested him.

Amber leaned close and nibbled at his ear. "I stopped by to see if you wanted to have lunch. It may be our last chance for quite a while."

Thorpe gestured toward the three points of light on the dome.

"A good idea. Once they get here, we're going to be awfully busy. Of course, we could skip lunch and go to the cabin."

Amber shook her head. The quick motion caused her hair to swirl about her face. "You need to keep up your strength."

"All right," he said. "Lunch it is. Lead the way, my love."

Four hours later Thorpe and Amber helped one another into vacuum suits. The carriers had matched orbits and were preparing to disgorge their cargo. The two of them crowded into the Number Three airlock and cycled out into vacuum. A hundred meters distant a small crowd had gathered on the ice to watch the show.

"Let's go," Thorpe said. They disdained the airlock ladder and jumped free. As they skated across the ice, Thorpe was reminded of their awkward first attempts at moving about the nucleus. The microgravity shuffle had become second nature to them.

"There she is!" someone said five minutes later.

Thorpe turned to the west. Sure enough, a small globular shape had just climbed above the horizon. It grew rapidly larger. His first impression was of a ship that had never been finished. The carrier's hull was a mass of external cargo. As the globe drew closer, Thorpe identified two laser drills, several large gas cylinders, and a boxy portable fusion generator. He also saw a heavy-surface crawler along with hundreds of less identifiable items hidden inside shipping crates or beneath wrappings of reflective film.

Gargantua and her sisters had never been intended to land. As a result, they lacked even the most rudimentary landing gear. And though Thunderstrike's gravity was minuscule, if such an oversize vessel ever tried to ground itself, the hull would crack like an eggshell. Mission planners had long ago solved the problem of how to deliver *Gargantua*'s cargo without landing it on the nucleus. It was the opportunity to see their solution that had drawn so many spectators out onto the ice.

The giant globe floated toward the habitat module. A quick burst of fire from its attitude-control jets brought it to a hover a hundred meters up and one kilometer distant. As the big ship halted, other flashes flickered across its hull. Nothing happened for long seconds. Then cargo began to slough off. Additional bursts from the attitude control jets sent the vessel skidding sideways as it shed its load. The cargo fell with deceptive slowness, taking nearly a minute to impact the crater floor. Ice geysers thrown up by the heavier items were clearly visible to the spectators.

With its external cargo scattered in a long swath across the ice, *Gargantua* continued its low-level flyby. Numerous hatches popped open and thousands of smaller containers were ejected into space. They were, Thorpe knew, mostly supplies—air tanks, packages of food, and spare parts. Having deposited its load, the carrier fired its underjets and lifted back into the black sky.

Ten minutes later *Godzilla* slid over the horizon and repeated the performance. It laid its mountain of supplies next to those of its sister ship, adding to the impression of an interplanetary junkyard. The second freighter then rose majestically into the sky and disappeared. When it had gone, the spectators turned back to the west in time to see *Goliath* top the horizon.

The fleet flagship deposited its load in a line parallel to the two previous deliveries. Once again the external cargo sloughed off on the first pass, with internal cargo dumped on a second, parallel, run. But unlike the others, the ship did not immediately flee back into space. It moved to hover over an uncluttered expanse of ice between the habitat module and supply dump. New hatches popped open, and the sky was suddenly filled with vacuum-suited figures.

Two hundred specialists in all phases of vacuum construction floated down slowly on their suit jets. They were but the vanguard of more to come. When everyone was down, *Goliath* departed. All three ships were to take up parking orbit over the nucleus's south pole, where they would stay until it was time to evacuate men and matériel just before the attempt to split off Ground Zero Crater. As *Goliath* departed, Thorpe glanced at his helmet chronometer. The whole operation had taken less than an hour.

"Mr. Thorpe?" a voice called over the main comm circuit.

"I'm here," Thorpe replied, hitting his visor lamp to show his location. His blink was answered by a light from one of the newcomers. The two of them crossed the expanse of ice between them and embraced in the gesture that substituted for a handshake in a vacsuit.

"I'm Amos Carlton, boss of this bunch of vacuum monkeys."

"Tom Thorpe, in charge of the expedition. Welcome to Thunderstrike."

"Nice place you have here," Carlton said, looking around inside his helmet. About all Thorpe could see of his features was that he was young and blond. "It's going to be a shame to blow it up."

"More of a shame if we don't. Do you and your men need any assistance?"

"You'd just get in the way. With your permission, we'll set up there." He pointed to an open area in front of the supply dump.

"As good a choice as any," Thorpe replied. "We don't exactly have an overpopulation problem."

"Good. We'll be working through the night to get our camp erected. I'd like to get our people together tomorrow morning, if that's all right with you, Thorpe."

"Tomorrow morning it is!"

"I understand this ice ball suffers from temblors."

"Not so many these past couple of months, nor as violent. The interior has just about achieved isostasy. Still, you can expect the ground to shake every couple of days."

"We'll make sure to anchor everything properly then. Anything else I should know immediately?"

"The composition is mostly water and ammonia ice, with the usual impurities. Be careful distilling it. Don't let anyone go outside for a pail of water."

"Oh? Why not?"

"The ice is a clathrate. One of its constituents is cyanide. You get that inside your habitat, and you could find it hard to breathe."

"Thanks. I'll pass the word. We'll need something other than ice to anchor our drills."

"You will find two mountain ranges composed of rocky material. One's only a few kilometers from here."

"I saw it coming in. I'll send my geology team out to look it over. I'd best be getting back to work. I'll see you at our headquarters Quonset at 0800 tomorrow. Come morning, that should be right about where that little hillock is now."

Six expedition members attended the first coordination meeting with the construction battalion: Tom Thorpe, Chen Ling Tsu, Kyle Stormgaard, Leon Albright, and Hilary Dorchester. Thorpe had suggested that Amber come along, but she had been slated for one of the periodic position checks with Earth. There was no longer any doubt that Thunderstrike would hit the Earth on the morning of July 17, 2087. Still, the work of refining the comet's orbit continued. If nothing else, it would give them a precise baseline from which to measure their progress.

As the six left the habitat module they were greeted by the sight of a small city where none had been twelve hours earlier. The buildings were all standard vacuum shelters—pressurized Quonset huts onto whch had been sprayed a fine mist of water. The spraying was still going on, but already it had produced a layer of ice several centimeters thick. The ice made the buildings glisten in the light from the shrunken sun.

Outside the main airlock they found a signpost. In addition to pointing the way to various supply dumps and buildings, one arrow pointed straight up. It read, NEW YORK CITY, 600 MILLION KILOMETERS.

The expedition members cycled through the oversize airlock as a group and found themselves in a large open room with row upon row of lockers. They quickly stripped off their suits and hung them up. Inside the lockers they found lace-up slippers with Velcro soles. The shelters were lined with Velcro carpeting which allowed the illusion of gravity. It seemed strange to walk stiffly along the floor after so many months of arrowing from one point to another.

"Pardon me," Thorpe said to the first construction worker he came upon. "Where is Mr. Carlton's office?"

"Third shelter in, mate. You'll see a headquarters sign just before you get there." The man barely slowed to give directions as he hurried into the suiting room.

They found the headquarters Quonset without difficulty. Inside they discovered Amos Carlton giving orders to half a dozen work gangs simultaneously. As Thorpe had surmised the previous day, Carlton was young and blond. He estimated the foreman's age to be about thirty. Thorpe smiled at the appraising look Hilary Dorchester gave him and at the look Carlton returned in her direction.

Thorpe introduced his companions to Carlton, who ushered them into the next-door conference room. There, a large view window opened up to the outside. It had electric heaters buried in the glass to keep the water spray from freezing over its thick panes. *Admiral Farragut*'s two modules were visible across half a kilometer of open ice. Thorpe could not help thinking that they looked terribly lonely out there.

"Tom Thorpe, may I introduce Walter Vassilovich, my second in command . . ." Carlton went around the conference table, introducing the half-dozen people seated there. Thorpe then did the honors for the expedition contingent. When the introductions were over, Carlton said, "Please be seated, people. We'll have coffee brought in shortly . . ."

"You have coffee!" Hilary exclaimed.

"Why, yes. Couldn't work without it."

"Something went wrong with our freeze-dried stores. We ran out a month ago."

"I'll have some sent over."

"Would you? I'd be most grateful."

"Let's get to the business at hand. Mr. Thorpe, I want to get our drills operating as quickly as possible. We've got the preliminary maps, of course. Is there anything you wish to add to them?"

"Since I'm not sure what you've been told, why don't we start at the beginning? Professor Chen is our expert on asteroid formation. He will go over what we've learned during our time here. Our geologist, Leon Albright, will assist."

Chen Ling Tsu unrolled the large topographic chart which had been his personal project during the past several months. It showed Ground Zero Crater and its surroundings, along with the various fault systems that underlay it. On the chart were twenty-two black crosses. Each carried a cryptic notation alongside.

"This is our master chart of this area. We have mapped both surface features and the fault system down to a depth of twenty kilometers. The nucleus's tectonic activity has helped us in this. The constant shaking gives us a very good picture of what lies below ground."

Chen indicated the chart with an expansive gesture. "What you see here is a snapshot of a cataclysmic event which took place a billion years ago. It very nearly shattered this body. We propose to finish the job. The black outlines show the surface features of the crater and its surrounding crevasse system. The multicolored lines map subterranean features. Each contour line represents a depth variation of five hundred meters. Note that the crater is actually a large, conical plug and that it is not really part of the main asteroid mass. We will eject this plug into space."

"And these black crosses?" Carlton asked.

"Those are the recommended sites for drilling," Chen replied. "The notations indicate depth of bore and angle. We've attempted to pinpoint the weakest points in the fault system, as well as points where a number of faults come together. Drill depths vary between three and seventeen kilometers."

The construction people pored over the chart and asked questions. As Professor Chen answered them, they scribbled notes into their portable notepads. After half an hour Amos Carlton gazed down at the chart and said, "It looks very straightforward. Almost too good to be true, in fact. What haven't you told us?"

Leon Albright cleared his throat. "We do have some concern about the strength of the crust. As you can see, it was totally shattered by the force of the original impact. To spall off a large enough chunk to do any good will require great care in the placement of your charges. Any explosive energy which breaks through the surface will be wasted."

"Perhaps we should drill somewhere else, then."

Professor Chen shook his head. "That would be futile. We need the fault system to channel the steam beneath the crater. We need a large cushion of pressure to eject the crater in one piece. Believe me, Mr. Carlton, we've analyzed this problem for many months now. The points shown are the strongest available which still give us access to the fault system."

Walter Vassilovich gestured at a cluster of crosses. "We'll start on these deep bores to the west. They will take the most time."

"Agreed," Carlton replied.

"How long to drill these twenty-two bores?" Thorpe asked.

Carlton scanned the map, moving his lips as he added up each of the bore depths. "Two months to finish the bores, as long as we don't run into bad drilling conditions, two weeks to evacuate, and a week after that to set the charges and plug the bores. Call it three months to the first shot."

"Can your ships be refueled that quickly?"

Carlton shrugged. "Not my department, I'm afraid. You'll have to get together with the swabbies for that. I can tell you that the distillation and cracking units are being set up."

"We've just about got *Admiral Farragut* refueled," Stormgaard said. "In another week we can use our hydrogen-cracking unit to supplement your output."

"Excellent. Take that up with Captain Palanquin. He's in charge of the fleet. Any other questions? If not, let's get to work. We've got a lot to accomplish in a very short time!"

CHAPTER 27

Tom Thorpe had no difficulty spotting his destination as Jumper Two flew a thousand meters above the rugged terrain of the Badlands north of Ground Zero Crater. Ahead of him, rising into the ebon sky, was an umbrella-shaped plume of ice crystals, emanating from where one of the construction battalion's heavy lasers was drilling a deep shaft. Three other plumes were visible on the horizon. After ten weeks of backbreaking labor, the final four bores were being completed. In another week Thunderstrike would be largely abandoned. A week after that, two-dozen-plus antimatter bombs would simultaneously spill their cargoes to the surrounding ice. They would know then whether their efforts had been wasted.

Thorpe lined up an electronic sighting mark with the base of the nearest plume. A quick press of the thumb switch caused the small vehicle to heel over from a sudden burst of the attitude-control jets. A burp of the main engine altered the jumper's trajectory toward the drill rig.

"Thanks for bringing me along," Amber said from beside him. "I've been cooped up in the ship for too long."

"This was the only way I could think of for us to be together. Besides, it put an end to Hilary Dorchester's harping about my needing an assistant."

"Just try taking her on, and I will scratch her eyes out," Amber warned.

"It's good to be loved."

They rode in silence until the jumper had dropped to within a kilometer of the drill site. The ice plume had grown enormous, and looked like the funnel of a tornado, a twister that seemed to extend up to infinity. Some wit had dubbed the plumes "beanstalks," and drilling crews were often admonished to watch out for descending giants.

"Time to give the crew the bad news," Thorpe said. He keyed for the general comm circuit. "Laser Six, this is Jumper Two. I am two minutes out and descending. Stand by for inspection."

There was an immediate terse acknowledgment, which Thorpe suspected was followed by a sharp string of oaths. Ever since he had taken on the task of Inspector General, his visits had cost a number of workers loss of privileges and pay. Such measures kept the people on their toes but did nothing to endear him to the vacuum monkeys.

The jumper slowed to a hover a hundred meters short of the plume and descended slowly. Thorpe took over manual control and landed the machine. The field was cluttered with equipment and dominated by the drill's power supply. Heavy electrical cables snaked to where a tripod had been erected over a thirty-centimeter bore, the hole from which the "beanstalk" sprouted.

As they approached the hole, they became aware of a deep thrumming sound being conducted through the surface and into the soles of their boots. Then they reached a point where they had a clear view of the laser drill. Its tripod legs were buried in heavy rock anchors, and its head was obscured by the geyser of steam roaring out of the bore. The drill head generated two separate laser beams.

The center beam was ultraviolet and ultrapowerful. It swung continuously through a tiny arc, carving out the bottom of the hole. That inner cutting beam created hard vacuum wherever it moved, and still had enough energy to slice through solid rock at the bottom of the bore.

The second beam surrounded the first and was blue-green. It filled the entire bore with brilliant aquamarine color. The outer beam maintained the steam in a superheated condition. Otherwise, the steam would condense against the hole's super-cold walls and quickly fill the bore with liquid water.

"Hello, Mr. Thorpe, Miss Hastings," Roger Borokin, the drill crew's foreman, greeted them. "I thought I might be seeing you today."

"Why did you think that?" Thorpe asked.

"It was logical. We're one of the last four active drilling sites, and we're about to finish up. This is your last chance to take a crack at us before we shut down."

Thorpe laughed. "Am I that transparent? Actually, the inspection is just an excuse. I wanted Miss Hastings to see a drilling operation up close."

"Excuse or not, we're ready for you. My log's up to date, and all my people know their jobs."

"How far down are you?"

"Seventeen kilometers. We should break into Fault System Twelve any time now. Once we do, we'll lower the remote drill head down the bore and carve out a blast chamber. After that we pack up and head for the ship."

"Arm the cargo module maneuvering jets, Mr. Chief Engineer."

"Maneuvering jets armed, Captain."

"Cargo module systems check."

"All systems are green."

"Did anyone remember to unbolt the anchor cables?"

"Anchor cables released, Captain. I checked them myself. Twice."

"Very well. Final maneuvering check. If anyone has a good reason why we should not launch, now is the time to speak up. No one? A one-minute countdown, Mr. Velduccio."

"Aye, Captain. One minute and counting . . . fifty-nine . . . fifty-eight . . ."

Karin Olafson glanced up at the viewdome, where the cargo module sat poised for launch. It looked much as it had the day they had arrived. Repacking everything had taken three days. Even so, the module massed less than half of what it had on landing.

Among the equipment being left behind were both moon-jumpers. Tom Thorpe was still using Jumper Two for transport. Jumper One lay smashed somewhere in the western Badlands, the victim of a landing accident the previous week. The pilot, Emilio Rodriguez, had suffered a broken arm, while his passenger, Leon Albright, had come through without a scratch. Karin Olafson wondered if either man knew just how lucky he had been.

As she gazed out across the floor of Ground Zero Crater, she felt a momentary sadness. The past months had been some of the most exciting of her life.

"Thirty seconds . . . twenty . . . fifteen . . . ten . . ."

"Arm the automatics."

"Automatic pilot enabled, Captain," came the response from her husband.

". . . five . . . four . . . three . . . two . . . one . . . there she goes!"

Across the ice plain the cargo module came alive as fire erupted from its oversize thrusters. The exhausts sent drifts of ammonia snow scurrying away. The module lifted slowly, then began to accelerate. As it climbed it heeled over and dwindled to the north.

"We're tracking, Captain," came the report from Dieter Schmidt. "The trajectory is nominal."

"Very well, Mr. Schmidt. Prepare us for liftoff."

"Habitat module is ready, Captain."

"Anchors?"

"Disconnected."

Karin nodded. She had checked those anchors herself. Few things would be more disastrous than to have one landing jack still firmly rooted to the nucleus as they tried to lift off. It would be enough to ruin a person's whole day.

"All the passengers aboard?" she asked.

"Twelve warm bodies aboard and tucked in, Captain," Cybil Barnard reported over the intercom. "Tom Thorpe, Amber Hastings, my husband, Chen Ling Tsu, Bradford Goff, and Hilary Dorchester are not aboard."

The captain nodded to herself. She did not like leaving without a full complement, but there was nothing she could do. Thorpe, Hastings, and Barnard were slated to stay aground for another week. They would oversee the setting of the last antimatter charges. The others had continuing duties with the construction battalion.

"Prelaunch check."

"Engineering, ready for launch."

"Communicator, ready for launch."

"All cargo secure. All passengers strapped down."

"Arm the maneuvering jets."

"Maneuvering jets armed."

"Give me an all-hands circuit."

"You have it, Captain."

"Attention, all hands. Prepare for launch. If you have to go, you've missed your chance. Liftoff will be in two minutes. I repeat, liftoff in two minutes."

There was a long pause while she watched the countdown chronometer. "You may start another countdown, Mr. Velduccio. Pipe it through the ship."

"Aye aye, Captain . . . Liftoff in sixty seconds . . . fifty-nine . . . fifty-eight . . ."

"Are you sorry to go, Karin?" her husband asked over their private intercom circuit.

"A little. It's been fun, hasn't it?"

"That it has. I'm sorry to see it end."

"Just think of the fireworks this time next week."

"There is that," Stormgaard agreed.

"Ten seconds to launch, Captain."

"Very well, Mr. Velduccio."

"Five . . . four . . . three . . . two . . . one . . . power!"

A deep growling echoed through the habitat module as the control room began to shudder. Karin Olafson let her gaze sweep across her displays. All readings were nominal. She keyed the circuit that would bring the maneuvering jets to full power. Suddenly, the distant ring wall of Ground Zero Crater tilted as the ground fell away. She had a glimpse of the construction battalion's largely abandoned base camp before the habitat module pitched north. Karin Olafson allowed herself the luxury of a sigh.

She was a space captain again.

A week later Tom Thorpe approached *Admiral Farragut* in Jumper Two. The ship was much as he had first seen her— power section, cargo module, and habitat sphere once again assembled into a functional whole.

"Be it ever so humble . . ." he muttered.

"Agreed," a male voice echoed in his earphones.

The jumper cabin was crowded. Next to Thorpe sat Amber, her suit pressed firmly against his. Beside her, wedged into a bench seat designed for two occupants, was Cragston Barnard. In their final week on the nucleus the three had not been out of their suits for more than a few hours. Earlier that morning they had watched as the last of the deep wells had been filled with water. Within a few hours the water had frozen into a plug more than twelve kilometers thick. The only thing that penetrated the plug was a heavy control cable down which the detonation command would be sent.

They had drilled twenty-eight wells in all, six more than origi-

nally planned. Each explosive device had been carefully located
within a major fault. Unlike fission or fusion bombs, which released their full energy in nanoseconds, antimatter explosives required milliseconds to come up to maximum. The delay would
allow the products of annihilation—pions and gamma rays—to
penetrate deeply into the surrounding ice. The goal was to gener-
ate a cushion of high-pressure steam under the whole of Ground
Zero Crater. To reach that end, a slow energy release was better
than a quick one.

"It will be good to get clean again," Amber said as she gazed
longingly at the ship. "Five days in a vacsuit is an endurance
record I don't ever care to break."

Barnard laughed. "It's a good thing I'm sealed in here by
myself. Even my wife couldn't stand the way I smell."

"There ought to be just enough time to get cleaned up, get
some hot food, and rest a bit before detonation."

"How long now?"

Thorpe glanced at his suit chronometer. "Four hours seventeen
minutes. Just as soon as Thunderstrike turns its Eastern Hemisphere toward Jupiter."

Amber and Barnard watched in silence as Thorpe guided the
jumper toward the freighter. He brought it to a halt a hundred
meters from Number One airlock.

"I don't want to get much closer," he explained. "Hate to
smash anything when we're this close to going home. You'll have
to jump."

"No problem," Barnard replied. The astronomer opened the
hatch and clambered out onto the hull. Thorpe made sure that the
attitude-control jets were disabled. The ship's airlock opened to
reveal a figure silhouetted against the internal lighting.

Barnard jetted across the hundred meters to the ship. He
landed feetfirst on the hull and was helped inside. As soon as he
was in, the airlock door closed for a long minute, then opened
again.

"Your turn, my love."

"I'll see you inside," Amber replied as their gauntleted hands
brushed. Neither could feel the other through the thick gloves,
but somehow that did not matter. Amber followed Barnard's example and floated out through the open hatchway. A minute later
she, too, disappeared through the Number One airlock.

"Well, old steed, I guess this is good-bye," Thorpe said as he punched instructions into the jumper's autopilot. The words were a bit of dialogue from an ancient movie he had once seen. For some reason they struck him as appropriate.

Thorpe moved through the portside hatch and lined up carefully on the ship's habitat module. Pushing off the little flier's hull, he drifted across the gulf of space to land headfirst, catching himself on outstretched arms to absorb the energy. He then grabbed for a handhold and levered his feet around to slide smoothly through the open airlock.

"Welcome home," Dieter Schmidt said.

"Thanks."

Schmidt reached for the airlock controls, but Thorpe stopped him. "Wait a second. I want to see this."

The two of them watched the jumper for another half minute. Suddenly, its engine came to life and it began to move away from *Admiral Farragut.*

"Where did you send it?"

"I just gave it a short ten-meter-per-second burst to get it away from the fleet. Okay, let's go inside."

The outer door closed. Thorpe heard the sudden rush of air as his suit collapsed around him. He unfastened his helmet as soon as the airlock telltales turned green. The inner door opened slowly outward, revealing a helmetless Amber Hastings waiting in the antechamber beyond. Before he could move, she was on him, awkwardly throwing her arms around his neck. They kissed passionately until they were out of breath.

"I've wanted to do that for five long days," Amber whispered. "Welcome home, darling!"

"Welcome home yourself. Care to share a shower?"

Her nose wrinkled. "The sooner, the better."

The small fleet hung motionless in space a thousand kilometers above the nucleus. At that distance Thunderstrike covered thirty degrees of arc, making it appear sixty times the diameter of a full moon as seen from Earth. The vantage point had been carefully chosen. It was far enough removed that the human eye could take in the entire nucleus at a glance, yet close enough that the fleet's instruments would record everything in minute detail. It was also sufficiently distant that the ships should be in no danger from the explosion.

"T minus ten minutes, and counting."

The announcement from the flagship echoed through *Admiral Farragut*'s wardroom, where most of the expedition members had gathered to watch. Amber was wedged in beside Thorpe in a corner, while the others crowded in front of the holoscreen. Captain Olafson, Engineer Stormgaard, and the two Barnards had chosen to watch from the control room. No one, it seemed, wanted to view the detonation by themselves.

"Happy?" Thorpe asked as he momentarily tightened his grip around Amber's waist.

She thought for a moment, then nodded. "You?"

"I'm glad it's almost over. Ten minutes more and we'll be able to plan our lives again."

"What *are* your plans when this is all over, Tom?"

He looked at her for a long moment. "I thought I'd ask you to marry me."

"Are you serious?" she asked, searching his face for some sign that his offer might merely be an example of his warped sense of humor.

He returned her look with a steady gaze. "As serious as can be. If you'll have me."

"You silly goon! Of course I'll have you. I've thought of little else these past six months."

"Well, then. I guess it's settled. We'll have the captain perform the ceremony right after the shot."

"Maybe she won't want to be bothered."

He shrugged. "Then we'll cross over to *Gargantua* and have her captain do it. I'm not particular."

"What about all of your friends and mine?"

"I'd say we've got everyone we need right here." Up until then they had been speaking in quiet whispers. Thorpe raised his voice. "How about it, folks? Care to attend a wedding this afternoon?"

There was a ragged cheer, followed by a flurry of congratulations. Then someone shushed them as another announcement came over the intercom from the flagship.

"T minus five minutes, and counting!"

On the screen, Thunderstrike continued to rotate slowly, oblivious to what was about to occur. The region around Ground Zero Crater was invisible, having passed into night several hours earlier. Detonation was timed to take place the moment the crater was aligned with the nucleus's velocity vector. That way, whatever mass was split off would be hurled back along the comet's orbital path, giving the maximum forward impetus to the rest of the nucleus.

"Nervous?" Amber asked.

"About marrying you? Naw!"

"I was talking about the shot."

"Oh, that! Not nervous so much as excited. It's kind of like waiting for Christmas morning when you're a kid."

"Or getting ready for your first date," someone chimed in.

"Or finals week in school," Amber added.

"I haven't been this nervous since my second wedding," Leon Albright interjected.

"What happened? Did she stand you up?"

"No, more's the pity," the geologist replied. "If I didn't have to pay her alimony every month, I would never have signed on for this crazy expedition."

The joke was met with more laughter than it deserved. Thorpe gazed over to where John Malvan had his arm around Hilary Dorchester.

"Sorry you came along, John?"

"Not me," the Lunarian replied. "I hated auditing. I think I'll see what can be done to mine this little chunk we're about to split off. It ought to be just the right size for moving into Earth orbit, don't you think?"

"You know, it just might!" Thorpe agreed. "I'll have to see if Mr. Smith is still interested in such a project."

"T minus one minute!"

The tension was suddenly a palpable thing in the air. Amber reached out and grasped Thorpe's hand. Throughout the wardroom no one made a sound.

"Ten, nine, eight, seven, six, five, four . . ."

"Here's to luck!" she whispered, giving his hand a quick squeeze.

". . . three . . . two . . . one . . . detonate!"

The night side of Thunderstrike turned suddenly into full day as twenty-eight fountains of eye-searing brightness burst through the asteroid's crust and climbed the ebon sky. On the screen the nucleus was ablaze. Features that had been hidden by darkness stood out in stark relief, their outlines etched by violet-white radiance and sharp-edged shadows.

The multiple geysers of fire roiled skyward, thrusting into space, expanding in the vacuum until they had merged into a single, boiling firestorm of radiance. Far beyond the nucleus the vacuum-thin coma fluoresced as it reflected back the light of the explosion.

There was a long moment of silence in *Admiral Farragut*'s wardroom, followed by pandemonium as everyone tried to speak at once. Thorpe yelled for them to be quiet. It took several seconds before the angry buzzing subsided. Finally, the announcement from the flagship issued from the holoscreen.

"The crust didn't hold! We have multiple crustal ruptures... Surface sensors report a large ground shock but no measurable change in bulk velocity. Radar does not show any significant spalling. There has been no major separation ..."

Beside Thorpe, Amber was gazing in horror at the multiple steam jets boiling furiously to space. It was difficult to see such fury and realize that absolutely nothing had changed. They watched the screen for long minutes in silence.

"How could we have been so wrong?" Amber asked finally. "We knew there was risk with a couple of the wells, but not all of them!"

"You don't know they all ruptured," Thorpe reminded her.

"Enough did. We should have tried spalling off a piece somewhere else. Ground Zero Crater was just too fractured."

He shook his head. "We were all through that. GZC was our best shot."

"What are we going to do now, Tom?"

"Think up a new idea," he said.

"What new idea? We just wasted twenty-eight kilograms of antimatter! We've less than ten kilos left."

Gazing around the wardroom, Thorpe noted expressions of shock. He knew how the others felt. Failure was like being punched hard in the stomach. It made it difficult to think. For the first time he began to wonder if humanity was truly doomed. Until that moment he had ruthlessly banished that thought from his thinking. He disentangled himself from Amber and pushed off.

"Where are you going?" she asked as she wiped large, globular tears from her eyes.

"I think I'll get drunk. Care to join me?"

"That won't solve anything."

"Maybe not, but it will make me feel better." With that, he pushed off for the wardroom hatch. Just before reaching it, he turned and looked at the holoscreen. Thunderstrike's night hemisphere continued to boil with undiminished violence as a geyser of steam roared into the black firmament. Despite the fury, the nucleus continued on its way, undaunted by the worst humanity could do to it.

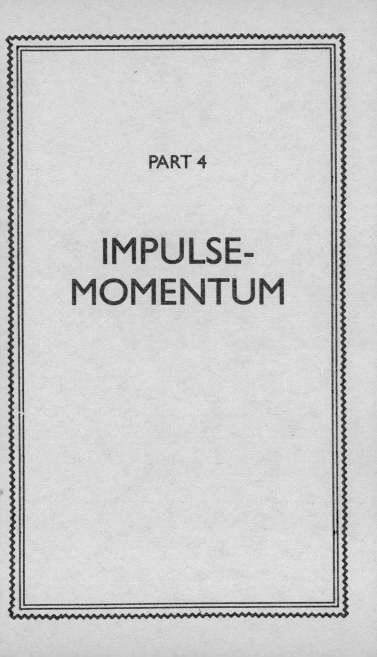

PART 4

IMPULSE-
MOMENTUM

CHAPTER 28

Scarred but undefeated, the planetoid of ice continued its long fall toward the inner Solar system. Humanity's efforts to blast loose a section of its surface had done little more than open up new veins to the sun. The boil-off rate rose minutely, adding to the comet's burgeoning coma and tail. Other than that, the titanic explosions had had remarkably little effect. The planetoid dropped toward the sun, trading energy of position for energy of speed. As it fell, the invisible grasp of Sol reached out to guide its path with mathematical precision. Each day brought it closer to perihelion and the moment when it would swing around the sun and take deadly aim at the Mother of Men.

The week following the abortive attempt to speed Thunderstrike in its orbit was a bad one for all concerned. Tempers ran raw throughout the fleet. There were a dozen fist fights and two suicides. Abuse of alcohol, always a concern in space, was rampant. Hangover cures were the most common remedies dispensed in the four ships' sick bays.

If things were bad in the fleet, they were worse on Earth. For most of the past year the public had not thought much about the comet. Except for a brief flurry of interest at the time the nucleus gained its popular name, Earth's billions had gone about their business confident that the scientists had matters under control. Most had not even bothered to watch the detonations on holovision.

News of the disaster spread quickly. There had been a pause of several hours while the enormity of what had happened sank in. Then, one by one, the riots began.

In New York crowds converged on the old United Nations building, home to Sky Watch and several other multinational agencies. In Toronto they gathered around the North American

Parliament. In The Hague they were drawn to the New Ridder-zaal Tower. Everywhere, they sought out centers of authority for comfort, and when no such was forthcoming, they began to destroy. The disturbances, the first of their kind since the last decade of the twentieth century, caught most police agencies off guard. They raged for four days. At the end of that time a fragile calm descended over the planet. But the center of every major city was adorned with the shells of burned-out buildings.

Even while the riots raged outside, the System Council went into emergency session to decide what to do. They stayed at it for 120 straight hours, adjourning only when fatigue forced a halt. They had organized more than sixty working groups to look into turning the situation around. Unfortunately, no one had any firm idea of how to proceed.

Out at the comet there were those who kept at their duties despite depression and anger. Within hours scientists began to study their recordings to pinpoint what had gone wrong. Their first clue came when they were able to look at the floor of Ground Zero Crater. The ice plain, which had always been ringed with crevasses, was now crisscrossed by them. The new ruptures showed a disturbing congruence with subterranean veins of stony material that underlay much of the crater.

For the first week after the explosion, conditions in and around Ground Zero Crater made landing hazardous. Pockets of superheated steam were trapped below the crust. As the steam cooled it condensed, leaving large, vacuum-filled voids behind. The collapse of such pockets sent powerful shocks radiating through the nucleus. If they were close enough to the surface, giant sinkholes opened up as the crust collapsed beneath the sudden loss of underlying support.

When it was finally judged safe to inspect the crater, Thorpe used his position as head of the Comet Hastings Expedition to get himself assigned to the ground party. He joined Amos Carlton and several specialists in one of *Gargantua*'s auxiliary craft. The party landed next to the largest of the new fissures. Vapor was still steaming off the sides of the crevasse, forming a thick fog which obscured the fissure's floor. Radar soundings put the crevasse depth at nearly eight kilometers.

"Look at that!" Amos Carlton muttered as he gazed at the opposite canyon wall. Down where the layer of fog began, a thick vein of stones could be seen cutting along the length of the crevasse.

"I guess that settles it," Thorpe replied. "The scientists were right. Somehow the rock acted as a stress riser, and the ice plug cracked along the vein when we tried to lift it."

The small party of explorers spent the next six hours obtaining samples of ice and rock for analysis. In that time they safely rode out four major surface shocks and half a dozen minor ones. It was a tired crew that climbed back into their ship as night fell once more over the crater. It was an even more tired Tom Thorpe who cycled through *Admiral Farragut*'s Number One airlock two hours later.

"How did it go?" Amber asked after giving him a welcoming kiss. She and Karin Olafson were the only two people in the airlock antechamber, a circumstance that should have made him suspicious. As it was, Thorpe accepted their presence without thought.

"About as expected," he replied as he stripped off his vacuum suit. "It was definitely the veins of rock that did us in. Also, Carlton thinks that our energy-release formulas were too optimistic. The recordings indicate that the antimatter annihilated much faster than expected. The pressure built up too quickly and cracked the ice plug."

"How could that have happened?" Karin Olafson asked.

"Who knows?" Thorpe replied with a shrug. "Maybe they didn't use the proper temperature in their calculations back on Earth. Or maybe we had a scaling error in our equations. Twenty-eight kilos of antimatter produces fifty-six kilos of pure energy. No one has ever released that much all at once before."

"What now?" Amber asked.

"A good question, my love. Ground Zero Crater is too broken up to try again. And even if it weren't, we don't have enough antimatter to launch a truly big chunk of it. Carlton says we're down to 8.2 kilos. He's checking with Earth to see if they have any better ideas. Personally, I have my doubts."

"Can we in this ship do anything to help?" the captain asked.

"Can't think of anything just now. Maybe when I've slept on it."

His welcoming committee exchanged looks. That something was happening was obvious even through his haze of fatigue.

"What's going on?"

"People have been talking, Tom," Amber said. "They want to go home."

"Home? But we aren't finished out here yet."

"They think we are. As you said, there's not much else we can do. They want to have some time with their families before the end."

"Are you giving up too?" he asked Karin Olafson.

She shrugged. "If I'm going to die, I'd rather do it on Earth. We've been gone for more than a year, and the construction battalion can handle anything that needs to be done out here."

Thorpe was silent for a long moment. To abandon Thunderstrike was to admit defeat. But, damn it, he could not think of any way to retrieve the situation! He sighed. "Let me sleep on it. If I can't think of a good argument against it, I'll talk to Amos Carlton about releasing us."

It was a thoroughly dejected Halver Smith who stood in his office and gazed across the bay toward San Francisco. The black pall that had hovered over the city had largely dissipated. He could see several military jumpers patrolling the business district. They were supporting the troops brought in to quell the rioting.

Not all of the riots had been isolated to the city center. The fact that SierraCorp had mounted the Comet Hastings Expedition somehow made them responsible in the public mind. A mob had tried to force the tunnel leading from the mainland to the corporation's headquarters complex. They had been stopped only when the security chief had ordered the tunnel flooded.

If the illogic of the rioters disturbed Smith, at least he found it understandable. That morning he had seen something that had sickened him. For the past week there had been no news other than Thunderstrike, and one of the morning news programs had featured an interview with several public figures. A buxom holovid star had claimed that the whole thing was a hoax by the big corporations to take control of the economy. Another guest, a world-renowned minister of the gospel, had declared the comet to be God's punishment for a wicked humanity. He warned of dire consequences if any further attempt were made to divert the nucleus.

Mostly, however, Smith was dejected by the news that *Admiral Farragut* had spaced for home. He did not really blame them. Still, it could not help but send the wrong signal. People were looking to their governments and the System Council to save them. The return of *Admiral Farragut* would appear to signal the abandonment of all hope.

Turning from his window, Smith gazed at the large hologram that had hung in his office for the past six months. It showed the comet as it had appeared during *Admiral Farragut*'s approach to the nucleus. The coma was an iridescent backdrop to the crater-pocked nucleus in the foreground. Somehow it did not seem right that such a nondescript astronomical body would be the instrument of Earth's destruction. As he gazed at the picture, he was distracted by the buzz of his desk intercom.

"What is it, Marla?"

"Constance Forbin is on the line, Mr. Smith. She seems agitated."

"I'll take it."

Smith sat down at his desk and soon found himself face to face with the coordinator. "Good morning, Constance, or rather, evening where you are."

"'Morning, Halver. I just got the word that your people have left Thunderstrike."

"That is correct."

"Surely you must know how this looks."

"I know it's awkward."

"Damned awkward."

"Look at it from their point of view. They chased the damned thing down, surveyed every square centimeter of it, probed its interior, and damned near got killed doing it. They've been out there four times longer than anyone else, and they want to come home before the end."

"I'm going to order them back," the coordinator said. "Things are just too sensitive right now."

"They won't go. In fact, they can't. *Admiral Farragut* broke orbit nearly twelve hours ago. That means that they have ended their boost and are now coasting in this direction. They haven't enough reaction mass to turn around. Why not use the situation to our advantage? Announce that the expedition members are being called home for consultations."

"I suppose I'll have to do just that," she replied. "On another subject, how goes antimatter production at Sierra Skies?"

"Good. We've almost got the third accelerator module powered up and online." For the past six months all of the orbiting power stations had been running their antimatter production facilities at full capacity at the expense of broadcast power. Most of them had been adding new antimatter facilities on a crash basis.

"We'll want to take everything we've got stockpiled and get it out to the fleet as quickly as possible. They've got less than ten kilos to work with."

"Then you're going to try the same thing again?" Smith asked.

"I don't know yet. But if the council decides that is our best option, we want to have the antimatter where it can be used. How much can you contribute?"

"Three hundred grams as of yesterday morning. We might have another fifty grams ready by this time next month. What about the other power plants?"

"About the same. I'd say we will be able to ship two additional kilos out to the fleet."

"That isn't very much," Smith said.

"It's all we have. It will have to do."

Tom Thorpe sat in the telescope-control room aboard *Admiral Farragut* and gazed at the screen. There had not been much interest in astronomy lately, and he was taking advantage of the hiatus to review everything in the ship's computer concerning Thunderstrike. Ever since departing the nucleus, Thorpe had been haunted by the thought that they had overlooked something vital. After fourteen hours of study, the feeling was as strong as ever.

He watched as the comet rounded the sun in a computer simulation. The simulation, which had been prepared by the New Mexico study group, showed the comet's course and speed from perihelion to impact on Earth's leading hemisphere. It also attempted to show the effects that would follow such a collision, including atmospheric shock waves, kilometer-high tsunamis, and crustal cracks that would boil the oceans and submerge the planetary land masses in white-hot magma. Thorpe watched the disaster through to the end, then cleared the screen in disgust.

Although the simulation satisfied a certain morbid curiosity, it did nothing to help resolve his problem. What he needed was to step back from the problem and return to basics. He asked the computer to retrieve Halver Smith's doctoral thesis on the economics of asteroid capture. Thorpe remembered one section that dealt with the various methods by which an asteroid's orbit could be modified. Within seconds he found himself face to face with the familiar document:

> ... There are a number of methods by which the needed energy can be imparted to an asteroidal body. Each has its advantages and disadvantages. While some are obviously not suited to the movement of the very large nickel-iron masses which are of most interest to the space miner, all have their place in the grand scheme of things. Each is discussed in greater detail below...

Thorpe let his eyes scan down Smith's list of possible techniques.

> ... Chemical, Fission, Fusion, Ion, or Antimatter Rockets ...

Thorpe continued looking. Rockets had been studied ad nauseam. Except for the last item on the list, they had been found woefully inadequate. The idea of moving Thunderstrike with an antimatter rocket had received very serious scrutiny. It had been dropped only when it became obvious that humanity's stockpile of antimatter was not nearly large enough to do the job. The recent loss of twenty-eight kilograms of the precious fuel had done nothing to make the idea more attractive.

> ... Nuclear pulse ...

Thorpe smiled in spite of himself. In the mid–twentieth century someone had suggested that a spacecraft could be propelled by exploding atom bombs under it. Although serious studies had been conducted at the time, the idea had never gone anywhere— probably due to inability to find anyone willing to fly such a contraption. The idea had been resurrected briefly by the New Mexico study group. As in the case of the antimatter-powered rocket, the nuclear pulse drive required a far larger supply of explosives than the human race possessed. Moreover, there was no time to build the requisite number of bombs before Thunderstrike crashed into Earth.

> ... Smaller Body Impact ...

Halver Smith had recommended the technique of deliberately crashing a small asteroid into a larger one to modify its orbit. The method required that the smaller asteroid orbit near the target, and in such a way that the collision would result in a more favorable orbit. The reason smaller body impact had never been considered for Thunderstrike was that the comet was alone in the firmament. Furthermore, they were trying to accelerate it. To work, they would have to smash a faster rock into Thunderstrike's trailing hemisphere. No such candidate rock existed.

A diagram accompanied the discussion of how the game of cosmic billiards might be used to modify a large asteroid's orbit. Thorpe gazed at it with bleary eyes for long seconds. As he did so, alarm bells began to go off in his brain. He ruthlessly clamped down on his rising sense of excitement as he thought through the ramifications.

Thunderstrike was like an out-of-control sports car approaching an intersection. Approaching that intersection from another direction were a passenger vehicle, Luna, and a very massive truck, Earth. The sportster would barely miss the passenger vehicle and swerve into the path of the oncoming truck. As a result, the truck would broadside the sports car halfway through the intersection.

To date all their efforts had gone into attempts to *accelerate* Thunderstrike. After all, if one's car was about to be rammed from the side, it made no sense to slam on the brakes. Rather, one would jam the accelerator pedal to the floor and pray the car could get out of the way in time.

But what if the sports car slammed on its brakes before reaching the intersection? Would not the two other vehicles sail safely through before the sports car entered? They had never seriously considered slowing Thunderstrike, because at the angle the comet would approach Earth, its arrival would have to be retarded by fifteen minutes. All other things being equal, slowing the comet safely was five times more difficult than speeding it up.

Only, Thorpe wondered, *what if all other things weren't equal?*

Thunderstrike would be crossing the Asteroid Belt seven months hence. What size rock would they have to put in its path to gain those fifteen minutes?

"Let's see," Thorpe muttered to himself as he punched in the numbers, "the comet reaches the Asteroid Belt in two hundred days. If six times ten to the sixteenth tons is to X as two hundred days is to fifteen minutes . . ." A few quick keystrokes told him that the asteroid to do the job would mass three trillion tons. That was ten times the size of *The Rock.* Large, he decided, but not totally out of the question.

His next programming task was more difficult. It involved using computer symbolic logic, something he had not done since college. He momentarily considered getting Amber to help. She was far better at symlog. One look at the chronometer changed his mind. The hour was late, and there would be plenty of time to work the details out in the morning. For the moment he merely wanted to see if the idea were feasible.

He worked steadily for half an hour to formulate his request: "Assuming an energy budget of eight kilograms of antimatter, what bodies of at least three trillion tons mass can be diverted into a collision while Thunderstrike is within the Asteroid Belt?"

NO ASTRONOMICAL BODIES MATCH SELECTION CRITERIA.

He cursed under his breath. The idea felt right. He reformulated his request. Perhaps a combination of rocks could do the job: "What combination of bodies with a total mass of three trillion tons can be diverted to collide with the comet nucleus as it passes through the Asteroid Belt?"

NO ASTRONOMICAL BODIES MATCH SELECTION CRITERIA.

Thorpe frowned. He asked to see the orbital elements of the closest asteroids and was reminded of something he had long known. Despite its reputation, the Asteroid Belt was mostly empty space. The nearest candidates were more than ten million kilometers distant from the comet's line of flight. That was too big a gulf to cross in only seven months.

Thorpe rubbed his burning eyes and decided to try one more time. He stripped his request to its bare minimum: "What objects are sufficiently close to the comet's line of flight that they can be diverted into a collision using no more than eight kilograms of antimatter?"

The computer response was immediate: MP 17634 AND MP 20618.

Thorpe stared at the numbers for long seconds in disbelief. For, despite the fact that they were reference numbers out of the *Catalog of Minor Planets*, he had no need to look them up. He recognized both immediately.

They were Avalon and *The Rock*.

CHAPTER 29

Thorpe stared at the screen for long seconds, not believing the glowing numbers before him. It was too incredible. Out of all the asteroids in the Solar system, the computer had selected the only two whose catalog numbers he knew. Somehow he must have slipped up in his programming. It took a moment to realize that the only way the computer could have learned those numbers from him was to read his mind. Thorpe moved hands made clumsy by fatigue back to the control board and caused the short program he had constructed to be displayed. It did not take long to discover what had happened.

The program had been intended to find candidate asteroids inside the Asteroid Belt. When the computer twice frustrated his quest, he had stripped the question of most of its qualifiers. Then he had inadvertently set the machine to scanning the *Catalog of Minor Planets*. It had checked all known asteroids for their future locations with respect to Thunderstrike. That the only two candidates selected were captive asteroids was not as surprising as he had first thought. On further reflection, it could hardly have been otherwise.

There were approximately 100,000 minor planets in the Solar system. They varied in size from Ceres—twice Thunderstrike's diameter and twenty times its mass—to rocks as small as ten meters. Most lay in a thick belt between Mars and Jupiter. They were the material from which a tenth planet might have formed if not for Jupiter's influence. The belt was a torus some two billion kilometers in circumference and 300 million kilometers thick. It was very sparsely populated.

The sheer size of the belt was what had defeated past attempts at mining the asteroids and had made asteroid capture the only viable solution to the problem. The first step of any capture program was to align the candidate rock's orbital plane with that of Earth, to put it into the ecliptic.

Thunderstrike orbited in the ecliptic. Thus, Thorpe belatedly realized, the very fact that he had been looking to divert the comet from Earth guaranteed that the program would choose asteroids with orbits already in the ecliptic. Avalon and *The Rock* were two such.

Satisfied that fatigue was not causing his mind to play tricks, Thorpe called for a display of Avalon's orbit along with that of Thunderstrike. It took a few seconds for the computer to add the asteroid to the New Mexico study group's simulation. As he watched Thunderstrike sweep toward the sun, he noted that it passed Avalon at a range of one million kilometers. That was practically a direct hit on the scale of the Solar system.

Thorpe keyed for Avalon's vital statistics. He was disappointed. Avalon's mass was slightly more than 1.5 trillion tons, five times *The Rock*'s mass but only half of what he needed to slow Thunderstrike. No, he decided, that was not right either. Three trillion tons was required if the collision were to take place 200 days before the comet reached Earth. Avalon orbited inside Earth's orbit. If Avalon were to be used, the collision would come only eighty days before I-Day. To achieve the same delay would require a mass of eight trillion tons.

The hope that had welled within him was suddenly dashed on the rocks of hard reality. It was beginning to look as if he had been on a fantasy trip.

Out of frustration, Thorpe broke into the comet simulation and modified the program to simulate a collision with Avalon at *I minus eighty days*. Instead of a grazing blow against the Earth's leading hemisphere, he expected to see the comet hit dead center. He watched the golden symbol swing around the sun and head for Earth. As it did so, the comet's vast tail swept across the doomed world. The screen began to blur. After sixteen hours Thorpe's eyes felt like boiled onions. He rubbed them.

When next he looked at the screen, the Earth had moved past

the point of collision and was sailing unmolested on its journey around the sun. Thorpe blinked and looked again. He spent the next several moments staring at the screen, pondering what he had just discovered. He saved the file under his personal security code, then blanked the screen. Adrenaline coursed through his veins as he levered his legs clear of the control board and kicked off. A few minutes later he found himself at the ship's comm center. He was still composing the confidential message to his boss as he entered the deserted compartment.

Once again, it seemed, Halver Smith was to be the guardian of a terrible secret.

If The Hague had been beautiful in winter, it was even more so in late summer. Smith strolled out of his hotel and headed for the New Ridderzaal Tower some two kilometers away. As he passed beneath the sweeping branches of linden and elm, his lungs inhaled the fragrance of flowers. Even so late in the season, the parks and byways of the city were a riot of floral color.

He crossed one of the city's numerous canals and entered a wide park. Once out from under the trees, he was able to see System Council Headquarters bulking large in the distance. When he had been there in January, the black building had merely been the headquarters of one of several supranational agencies. Since then it had become the de facto capital of the human race. In Smith's opinion, if the comet could get people used to cooperating, it might well prove a blessing in disguise.

Smith reached the new security fence that surrounded the tower and showed the guard his identification. He was quickly escorted to the spacious lobby beyond. As in January, he found a guide waiting for him. He followed her to a lift and from there was quickly whisked to the chief coordinator's office.

"Once again the man from California requests an urgent private meeting on a subject he refuses to disclose," Constance Forbin said as she greeted him.

"Sorry to be so melodramatic. I have my reasons."

She laughed humorlessly. "Believe me, after the last time, you are the one man who can get a private audience with me whenever he wants. I take it that the subject is once again the comet."

"It is."

"What now?"

"I'm here to announce a solution to our problem, but one that carries with it other problems."

"Go on."

"Three days ago I got a long personal message from Tom Thorpe. He's come up with a scenario for rendering the comet harmless."

"Interesting, since no one else has."

"When you hear it, you'll understand," Smith assured her. He explained Thorpe's idea for diverting Avalon into Thunderstrike's path, thereby slowing the comet. He then told her why it was a possible solution to the problem of saving Earth.

When he finished, Constance sat back in her chair, stunned. "Of course, you've checked this out."

"Erwin Kanzler did a complete study. I have the results with me. He agrees with Thorpe."

"The price is going to be damned high!"

"Not as high as if we don't stop it."

The chief coordinator regarded Smith over steepled fingers for nearly a minute. Finally, she said, "I must say, Halver, that I find your visits are about all the stimulation I can stand these days."

"Now you know why I insisted on a private meeting."

"We'll have to handle this carefully if we are to avoid a major schism."

"I doubt you *can* avoid one."

"We can delay the inevitable. I'll start gathering up a team of reliable people. If this is going to work, we haven't much time to prepare."

John Malvan sought out Amber Hastings aboard *Admiral Farragut* a week later. The freighter was fifteen days out of Thunderstrike and ten weeks from Earth. Captain Olafson had offered to activate the cold-sleep tanks for anyone who wanted the voyage to pass quickly. There had been no takers. If the human race had less than a year to live, no one wanted to sleep away a quarter of their remaining life span.

"May I speak with you?" he asked after discovering her in the wardroom drinking from a bulb of coffee.

"Sure. Strap yourself down."

"In private."

There was something about the look on his face that made Amber realize that whatever he wanted to discuss was serious.

"Where?"

"Hydroponics ought to be empty this time of day."

As predicted, they found the compartment empty. The chief engineer normally tended the ship's garden, and then only an hour or so each day.

"What's the matter?" Amber asked.

"I've received a coded message from the prime minister."

"Oh?" she asked. So far as she knew, Malvan had not heard from the Republic since the expedition had been coopted for the effort to divert Thunderstrike. "I thought you were out of that business."

"So did I. Apparently we were both wrong. Prime Minister Hobart is concerned about reports he's been receiving from his agents on Earth. About a week ago a number of personnel from the Thunderstrike Project were transferred to Newton Station."

She shrugged. "So what?"

"So, we don't know the reason for the transfers and no one seems to be talking. None of the transferees were Lunarian. There are also rumors that *Gargantua* and *Goliath* have been ordered to space, and that some new classified research is being done on the Sky Watch computers."

"What has all this to do with us?"

"The prime minister thinks the impetus for whatever is going on came from this ship."

"What?"

"That's what his message said. The Republic's intelligence service has been looking into the matter. They discovered that all of these strange happenings began immediately after Halver Smith sought a private audience with Constance Forbin. The two of them then spent most of the night closeted with her close advisors."

Amber blinked. There was something about the way the conversation was going that she did not care for. "Is that supposed to mean something to me?"

"Intelligence checked further. Apparently, we have agents inside SierraCorp Headquarters. They say that Smith received a coded message at home three days before he went to see the coordinator. The message originated on board this ship."

"Thomas?"

Malvan nodded.

"That's impossible. He would have said something to me."

"You say he didn't?"

She shook her head. "Not a word."

"The prime minister wants us to find out what's going on."

Amber lay with her head on Thorpe's chest. The two of them were lightly restrained by an elastic sleeping strap. Despite poets who waxed lyrical on the subject, making love in zero gravity had its inconveniences, not the least of which was the tendency for a couple to drift apart at inopportune moments. Numerous appliances had been invented over the years to solve the problem. The sleeping strap was one of the best.

"What are you thinking about?" Amber asked after a long silence. She shivered as Thorpe's fingers traced a pattern at the base of her spine.

"I've been thinking about getting married. Time we talked to the captain."

"I agree."

After the failure to divert Thunderstrike, neither had mentioned marriage for nearly a week. The mood aboard ship had been too depressing. Later, they had discussed it only in passing. For the past week Amber had said nothing at all, since she had sensed that something was bothering Tom. After her discussion with Malvan, she knew that she had been right.

"What about tomorrow?"

"To speak to the captain?"

"Hell, no! We'll hold the ceremony."

She lifted her head and stared at him. "Are you serious?"

"Why not? We'll tie the knot in the wardroom right after the noon meal."

"We should talk to Captain Olafson first. She may have other plans."

Thorpe laughed. It was a sound she had not heard out of him for far too long. "Somehow I doubt that her calendar is exactly crammed for the next ten weeks."

"Even so, we ought to consult her."

"Fine. We'll talk to her first thing in the morning."

"All right." Amber hesitated, then said, "Thomas?"

"Uh-huh?"

"Are you keeping something from me?"

Nestled as she was in his arms, Amber thought she felt a sudden stiffening of his body.

"What do you mean?"

"John Malvan says that strange things are happening on Earth. He wanted to know if I knew anything."

"What sort of things?"

Amber recounted what Malvan had told her about the new study group being established on Newton Station and the rumors concerning the departure of *Gargantua* and *Goliath* from Thunderstrike. "Malvan thinks you are behind all of this," she finished.

"How the hell can *I* be involved?" Thorpe asked. "I'm still half a billion kilometers from the action."

"He thinks you sent the message that started all of this. We've checked, and there's nothing in the communications log about it, but, of course, that doesn't mean a whole lot."

"Why does he think that?"

She explained about the Lunarian agents at SierraCorp Headquarters.

"I'll have to tell the boss."

"Don't change the subject. Did you send such a message?"

Thorpe sighed and sat up, causing her to brace her feet against the bulkhead to keep from floating away. She grabbed the sleeping strap and rotated herself into a sitting position beside him.

"Did you?" she insisted.

Thorpe nodded slowly. "Guilty as charged, Your Honor."

"What could you possibly have said to get them so excited?"

"I've found a way to stop the comet."

She gasped and clasped her hands over her breasts. "That's wonderful! How can we do it?"

Thorpe told her of his long day and of how he had eventually thought of diverting Avalon into the comet's path to slow it down.

She gazed at him as a teacher does a slightly backward child. It was not the reaction he had expected.

"What's wrong?"

"My poor darling, don't you realize we thought of that? Not Avalon, of course, but we've checked into the possibility of crashing a smaller rock into Thunderstrike quite thoroughly. Nothing large enough is anywhere near the comet's orbital track. How big is this Avalon, anyway?"

Thorpe told her.

Her eyes took on the blankness of one who is deep in concentration, then she shook her head. "It won't work! Not nearly massive enough."

He hesitated for long seconds, unable to meet her gaze. "Actually," he said finally, "my plan involves two collisions. Crashing Avalon into Thunderstrike merely sets up the second hit."

"Don't tell me you've found *two* asteroids to throw into the comet's path!"

"No, not two asteroids."

"Then what?"

"Do you remember how we discovered that Thunderstrike would hit Earth?"

"I'd have more chance of forgetting my first act of love," she replied. "I still blush when I think of what a damned fool I made of myself. First I tell you there isn't a snowball's chance in hell —pun intended—of a collision, then I calculate a strike against Earth's leading hemisphere."

"Not at first," he reminded her. "Your first calculation showed that the nucleus would come close, but miss."

"That's because I wasn't using a complete gravitational model. The one I had didn't include—" Horror crossed Amber's face as her brain outraced her mouth. *"No, there has to be another way!"*

"I wish there were," Thorpe replied, letting the pent-up emotion spill out of him in a rush. "Avalon won't slow Thunderstrike enough for Earth to get out of the comet's way. It *will* allow Luna to interpose itself between the two. If Thunderstrike collides with Avalon, it will smash down in the center of Farside Luna eighty-six days later. Luna will stop it in its tracks—"

"And be destroyed!"

CHAPTER 30

Copernicus Crater bulked large in the view wall of the prime minister's conference room. The scene, taken at an oblique angle from low orbit, showed the crater's terraced walls and the mountainous central peaks in sharp relief. To the south, a thin line marked the route of the Circumlunar Monorail. A cluster of tiny domes was scattered among the central peaks at the end of one of the monorail's spur lines. The domes marked the location of the ice mines that made Copernicus so important to the Republic's economy.

Around the conference table sat a dozen of Luna's most influential men and women. Although many were members of the Nationalist Party, it was by no means a Nationalist assembly. Pierre Robles, John Hobart's predecessor as prime minister, was there to represent the Conservatives, as were the leaders of the two smaller parties. Rounding out the gathering were Niels Grayson from Farside Observatory and Albert Portero from the university.

John Hobart stood at the front of the table and gazed out over the hastily summoned group. It was obvious from his expression that he was far from happy. He lost no time getting to the point.

"We have received some very disturbing news from our agent aboard *Admiral Farragut*. Professor Grayson, if you please."

Niels Grayson stood and walked to the lectern that had been set up at one end of the conference room. Twenty-four hours earlier he had been at Farside Observatory. He had spent twelve of those hours traveling—first an unscheduled rolligon ride to Hadley's Crossroads, then a moonjumper flight to Luna City. He was tired and irritable and more than a little shell-shocked by the news that had awaited him at the end of the journey. Nevertheless, he had had nearly eight hours to study the implications of Malvan's emergency message.

"Those of you with your backs to the view wall should turn around," he warned. Grayson touched a control and the view of Copernicus faded, to be replaced by a familiar diagram of the Solar system. On it, Thunderstrike's elliptical orbit rounded the Sun and ended abruptly at the circle that represented Earth's orbit. A tiny comet symbol followed the ellipse around the sun and then began moving toward the two spheres that represented Earth and its moon. As the comet closed on the double planet, the scale changed to show Earth and Luna in close-up. The comet swept outward toward the two orbs, closing on Earth's orbit from below and behind at a thirty-degree angle. Time and date numbers were displayed in the upper-right corner of the screen.

As his audience watched the diagram, Grayson summed up the impact calculations and the attempts to accelerate the asteroid. "As all of you know, the effort to accelerate the ice asteroid has thus far failed. I won't go into the reasons for that failure, suffice to say that it had to be tried. For the past month the system's scientists and astronomers have searched for a new means of diverting the comet. Our people on Earth recently reported activity which indicated that a new—and secret—attempt was being planned. John Malvan, Luna's representative on the Comet Hastings Expedition, was able to discover the details of this secret plan and has recently reported them to us. It is news which no Lunarian can welcome. Malvan reports that the terrestrials are planning to save Earth by diverting the comet onto a collision with Luna!"

There was a sudden angry buzzing around the room. Most of the participants had been told that the meeting involved a matter vital to the safety of the Republic but had been given no details. One of the Nationalist M.P.'s asked, "How is that possible?"

The angry murmurs died away as Professor Grayson explained. "They plan to position an asteroid named Avalon in Thunderstrike's path on the inbound leg of its orbit. Thunderstrike will collide with Avalon eighty-six days before its arrival in the Earth-Moon system." Grayson used a control to cause a scarlet marker to appear near where the comet's orbital track crossed that of Earth. "If they succeed, the collision will have the opposite effect of the one we've been attempting. It will slow the comet's speed slightly. There will also be a slight change in orbital path, but the change will be too small to be noticed. What *will* be noticed is the timing of the comet's entry into the Earth-Moon system. The nucleus will arrive approximately 150 seconds later than originally planned."

"That hardly sounds significant," Harold Barnes, the banker, said.

"Normally, it wouldn't be. However, it will give the Earth and Moon additional minutes to move across the comet's orbit. In those few minutes, Luna will interpose herself between the comet and Earth. Thunderstrike will crash down in the middle of Farside at 1427 hours, July seventeenth, 2087. Needless to say, such a cataclysm will utterly destroy our small world."

"Are we sure of our facts here?" Pierre Robles asked.

"That we are," Hobart replied. "Ever since Malvan's message, our agents on Earth have been working their sources overtime. All indications are that Constance Forbin has set the Avalon option into motion. The question facing us now is what do we do about it?"

"What *should* we do about it?" one of the Nationalist M.P.'s, who was also an ordained minister, asked. "After all, it would seem a choice between trading Luna and its millions for Earth and its billions."

"No one is suggesting that we sacrifice Earth to avoid Luna's destruction," Hobart snapped. "If we must die to save the home world, then so be it! What worries me is that this new option will foreclose all others. The problem of diverting the comet is a difficult one. Once the terrestrials are given a way out, they will cease seeking better solutions. After all, it isn't their world which will be destroyed any longer."

"Just as we have concentrated on our own affairs these past six months?" the leader of the Radicals asked.

"That is a canard, Juan Aurrelios, and you know it!" Barnes growled. "If Earth is to be destroyed, we must look to our own survival."

Hobart held up a hand. "No, the distinguished member from Tycho Terrace is correct. We've tended to see this crisis in terms of our own survival, not that of the terrestrials. Our task now is to make sure that they don't do the same to us. We must come up with a solution which is *mutually beneficial*. This idea of using Luna for target practice is a bad one, and they must continue seeking a way to accelerate the comet, not slow it down."

"And if there isn't any such?"

"There has to be. We just haven't thought about it enough yet.

What if they suddenly discover an approach after they've diverted Avalon into Thunderstrike? Once the comet is slowed by this collision, there will be no avoiding a disaster. Luna could well be destroyed for no good reason."

"Do we even know that Luna will survive such a cataclysm?"

"Professor Portero has been studying that. Professor?"

Portero, the astrophysicist from the University of Luna, leaned forward. "In truth, citizen, I do not know the answer to that question. At five hundred kilometers, Thunderstrike is very close to the maximum asteroid which Luna can safely withstand without breaking up. Luckily, it is an asteroid of ice rather than one of iron. A metal meteor of that size would split this small globe asunder. It will be very bad in any event, and will throw megatons of debris into orbit. The meteor danger to Earth and all orbital installations will be very high for decades, perhaps centuries."

"Those are both good arguments why humanity should be working to avoid any collision," Hobart replied. "If the nucleus strikes Earth, we here on Luna could be pulverized by the resulting meteor storm. If we are struck, Luna may break up. What will happen to life on Earth if the tides are substantially disrupted? For that matter, what is to stop a large chunk of lunar material from crashing down on Earth anyway, bringing on the very cataclysm that they are trying to avoid?"

There was a murmur of agreement around the table. Hobart scanned the double row of angry faces. "I take it that no one wishes to cooperate in this abomination. Now then, how do we stop them?"

The corridors of *Admiral Farragut* were lit with the soft-blue light with which spaceships simulated night. Thorpe pulled himself hand over hand through the blue gloom. He stopped when he reached the closed hatch leading to the telescope control room. Steadying himself on one of the handholds provided for that purpose, he rapped softly on the hatch, then opened it.

The compartment beyond was dark save for the glow of the big screen. Amber sat in the right-hand observer's seat, her head and shoulders silhouetted against the glow. The telescope was focused on the Earth and Moon, both of which appeared as half-lit spheres. The Earth was dazzling white compared to the softer gray of Luna. The home world was decorated in its characteristic swirls of white cloud and blue ocean.

"May I come in?" he asked softly.

Amber turned to glance at him over her shoulder. "Sure."

He closed the hatch and swam to the left seat, where he strapped down before turning to face her. "Don't you think you're being a bit silly about this?"

"About what?" she asked, her tone flat and her voice lifeless. Her normally immaculate jumpsuit was wrinkled and her hair unkempt. The bags under her eyes gave testimony to the amount of sleep she had had in the past seventy-two hours.

"You can't stay mad at me forever. Time for you to come out of your shell and get on with your life."

"What life, Thomas?"

"Look," he growled, "I'm sorry someone else didn't come up with the damned idea of using the Moon to block Thunderstrike. Unfortunately, I'm the one who stumbled on to it. What would you have had me do, forget about it?"

Anger flashed in her eyes. "You could have told me what you'd found. You could have confided in me, *my love!*"

"How could I?" he asked. "Would you have kept the secret?"

"Why did it have to be a secret?"

"Because they're rioting on Earth, damn it! They're rioting because we failed in our last attempt. What do you think they will do if we get their hopes up again, only to dash them? My God, they would have burned down every city on the planet. No, better to be sure I hadn't made a mistake before announcing the plan."

"You mean before you let the Republic in on your scheme to destroy it, don't you?" she snapped.

He nodded. "There's some truth to that. I'd hoped we could make sure of our facts before the inevitable interplanetary rift. That's impossible now, of course."

"You aren't suggesting that Malvan and I shouldn't have reported what we knew!"

"No, I'm not suggesting that at all. Your government has every right to know. I just hope we haven't stirred things up for no reason. What if my idea turns out not to be practical?"

"It won't," Amber replied. "I've spent the past three days checking your figures. You are absolutely correct. If Thunderstrike can be made to collide with Avalon, its total momentum will be reduced by 2.5 thousandths of a percent. That will delay the nucleus's arrival by 173 seconds, more than enough time for Luna to move across the comet's line of flight. My calculations indicate impact will take place near Korolev Crater, some six hundred kilometers east of Farside Observatory."

"Is that what you've been doing? Checking my math?"

"That and trying to find another solution. In that I've failed miserably, Thomas. Everything I try requires more energy, time, or resources than we have available. It's funny. In discussions with colleagues, I've often spoken of the immutable and unchanging physical laws. I don't think I've ever truly understood what that means until now."

"Then you agree it is necessary to direct Thunderstrike into Luna in order to save Earth?" In the dim light, Thorpe could see that Amber's face had been marked by the fat globular tears that formed in zero gravity.

She looked at him with sad eyes no longer capable of producing tears. "I agree, Thomas. I agree intellectually, professionally, clinically. So why does my every instinct rebel against the idea? Why must my world die to save yours?"

"Listen to what you are saying, my love."

She sighed. "I know. It doesn't come out right. Earth is humanity's home. It must be saved at all costs. The destruction of a little frontier world like Luna is a small price to pay. Those are the facts, Thomas, *only they don't make me feel any better.*"

"I don't feel particularly good about it either. I just don't see that we have any choice. You find me a choice, and I'll by damned take it!"

She leaned over and kissed him lightly on the lips. "My poor dear. You're feeling guilty, aren't you?"

"Wouldn't anyone?"

"I suppose," she replied. "I think we both need some time to think this through. If you don't mind, I'll move back into my own cabin for a while."

"If that is what you truly want."

"It isn't what I want, but it would be better for both of us."

"And our wedding?"

"It hardly seems important just now, does it?"

"It's important to me."

"It wouldn't be fair to marry you when I'm in my current

mood. Give me time to regain my equilibrium. Please?"

"I suppose I don't have much choice in the matter, do I?" He unstrapped from his seat and kicked off for the hatch. He turned to face her. Despite her fatigue and the general gloom in the compartment, she was still the most beautiful woman he had ever seen. "I'll give you some time. All the time until we reach Earth, if you need it. I'll be there when you need me."

"Thank you," she said simply.

Thorpe glanced up at the beautiful blue-white world that was the home of eight billion innocent people. Beyond it was the silver-gray orb on whose surface dwelt ten million other innocents.

"I wish to hell I had never heard of that goddamned comet!" he burst out. He slammed the hatch closed behind him.

It fell to Roland Jennings, Luna's consul-general in San Francisco, to deliver the Republic's response to what was being called the "Avalon Option." Jennings's aide, Austin Branniger, accompanied him to The Hague to meet with Constance Forbin. The two were ushered into the chief coordinator's office near midnight five days after Luna had learned of the plan to divert Thunderstrike into the Moon.

"Consul Jennings. Citizen Branniger," the coordinator said as she greeted the two men. "It's an honor to receive two such distinguished representatives of the Republic, even at such a late hour. Please, be seated."

"We thank you for the courtesy of seeing us, Madame Coordinator. You know why we are here, of course." Despite his confident manner, Jennings was as nervous as a Third Undersecretary for Protocol at his first state reception. He knew the enormous stakes for which he was about to play.

"Your prime minister outlined the discussion in his message."

"Is it true? Are you planning to divert the comet into Farside?"

Constance held out her hands in a broad gesture of helplessness. "What would you have me do, Citizen Consul? Should I lie and tell you that we aren't considering every method possible to save this world?"

"I would have you give me a simple, honest answer."

"Very well. Yes, we are looking into the Avalon Option. We've established a working group aboard Newton Station where they can concentrate on the problem. So far, they can see no flaws in the plan."

"Have you taken any concrete steps to actually proceed with this option?" Austin Branniger asked.

"Not yet."

"What about these rumors that you have dispatched two of the cargo carriers to Avalon?"

"Just rumors for the moment, Citizen Jennings. We won't dispatch ships until we are certain that the option is the only one possible. We will, of course, inform your government if we come to that decision."

"Are we then to die for the sake of Earth?"

"What sort of barbarians do you take us for? We will, of course, evacuate Luna before the comet's arrival. That is one of the things the working group is studying."

"And if we do not wish to evacuate?"

"Does Luna have a better idea for stopping Thunderstrike?"

"Our scientists are working on it," Jennings replied.

"They have been working on it for the past six months," Constance reminded him. "We need an idea now! There's only so much one can do with eight kilos of antimatter, you know."

"Luna is prepared to offer you another four kilograms."

"Oh?" Constance Forbin asked as her eyebrows raised in surprise. "It seems to me that we asked your government just last month to provide antimatter to the common pool. You had none to spare. Are your production facilities so efficient that you can produce four kilos in a single month?"

"You know they aren't, Mrs. Forbin. Your request was turned down because we felt we needed that fuel to survive during the postimpact period."

"And now?"

"Now it seems more prudent to use the antimatter to divert the comet and avoid impact altogether."

"And do you have a scenario in which twelve kilos of antimatter can accomplish that feat?"

"I'm no scientist."

"Nor am I. The one thing I *do* know is that time is running out. If a viable alternative is not found soon, we will have to exercise the Avalon Option."

Roland Jennings regarded the coordinator with hard eyes. "We cannot allow that, Madame Coordinator. That is the message I have been ordered to deliver this night."

"That sounded like a threat, Mr. Consul-General."

"I meant it as a warning, Madame Coordinator. The Republic of Luna will not allow itself to be made a target of this massive asteroid. It is our position that a more equitable solution exists and all that is needed to find it is a proper incentive."

Constance Forbin leaned back in her chair. "And just how do you propose to stop us?"

"We hope to reason with you. If that is insufficient, we are prepared to use force."

"Force?"

"Even as we speak, the Republic is equipping a dozen ships for war operations. Those vessels will put to space at the first sign that you have initiated operations to move Avalon. They will take possession of Avalon, if necessary, and deny your people access. Naturally, we hope matters won't come to that."

"Aren't you forgetting the Peace Force, citizen?"

He shook his head. "The Force has only three ships in Earth orbit at the moment. One of these is undergoing general maintenance and cannot leave. Our own fledgling navy will be strong enough to hold their own against any force you can send against us for as long as it matters. Remember, you must move a massive asteroid into Thunderstrike's path. All that is required of us is to stop you."

"Have you considered that you are sentencing Earth to death?"

"We don't believe that, Madame Coordinator. As I have stated, we are confident that the scientists will come up with another method in time."

"And if they don't?"

"They must. There is no other viable alternative."

"And that is your last word?"

"I have delivered my message, Mrs. Forbin. Let me assure you that on this matter there can be no negotiations."

The coordinator drummed her fingers on her desk. "May I have some time to consult my people, Citizen Jennings?"

"Of course."

"Very well, our ambassador on Luna will give our response to your prime minister no later than 1200 hours, day after tomorrow."

CHAPTER 31

Barbara Martinez was coiffed, perfumed, and dressed in an evening gown that cost more than she made in a year. Her companion was also dressed formally. He sat beside her in the backseat of the chauffeured groundcar and gazed out the window at the streets of Manhattan's Old City.

"I'm not sure I understand all of this, Mr. Smith," Barbara said, finally getting up the courage to speak to the man who had picked her up ten minutes earlier.

He looked at her sharply. "Didn't they brief you before you left the station?"

"No, sir. They piled me into an orbital ferry and told me I'd be briefed when I got here. For the past two hours I've had my head planted in a beautician's helmet."

Smith sighed and leaned back in the plush seat. "It's really quite simple. It has fallen to us to break the news to Carlos Sandoval about the Avalon Option."

"Sandoval?"

"He's chief executive officer of System Resources, S.A. They own Avalon. Elspeth Edwards is hosting a party for him tonight. Constance Forbin thought it would be less conspicuous if I contacted him at a social gathering. You're along to explain the technical details, and also as protective coloration. Haven't we met before?"

"I don't think so."

"Sure we have!" he said, suddenly remembering. "You were coming out of the director's office in New Mexico once when I was there. You had that green-around-the-gills look everyone got when they first learned of Thunderstrike."

"I remember," she said. "You were in the director's anteroom."

"So I was."

"Why this charade, Mr. Smith?"

"Since you're to be my date this evening, doesn't it sound a bit silly for you to call me 'Mr. Smith'? The name is Halver. My friends call me Hal."

"Why this charade . . . Hal?"

"A couple of reasons. Number one, the Lunarians know about Avalon. It couldn't be helped, but it's causing us some significant political problems. If one of Constance Forbin's people contacts Sandoval, the Lunarians might find out and jump to conclusions. In this case, they would be right.

"Secondly, I got the job because Sandoval and I are arch competitors. He's an arrogant bastard, and might just tell anyone else to breathe vacuum when they ask to speak to him. You can be sure that he won't refuse me. As insurance, I have you. Sandoval has quite a reputation as a ladies' man. He'll be inclined to listen to whatever a beautiful señorita tells him. He may not agree, but he'll hear you out."

"Why, thank you for the compliment, Hal!"

"De nada."

It took another ten minutes for them to reach the brownstone where the party was being held. Smith took Barbara's arm and escorted her inside. They entered a lift and were whisked to the topmost floor. The noise of the party pummeled their ears as soon as the lift doors opened. Smith winced visibly as they stepped out into the hall to find their way blocked by an overflow crowd of revelers. They threaded their way through the maze of bodies, being careful not to jostle elbows or spill drinks. After a few near misses they gained the open door of the Manhattan penthouse.

"Why, Halver Smith! I declare, you're the last person on Earth I ever expected to get to one of my parties!"

He smiled and extended a hand. "Hello, Elspeth. Thank you for having me."

"My pleasure," the matron crooned. "And who is this?"

"May I present Miss Barbara Martinez? Barbara, Elspeth Edwards, the most sought-after hostess on two continents."

"Hello, Barbara," Elspeth said as she leaned forward to kiss her guest on the cheek. "How did you manage to get this hermit to bring you here? I've been inviting him to my parties for years."

"Just persuasive, I guess," Barbara replied.

"I should say so. Halver, are you losing weight?"

"A little," he said, grinning. "My doctor has me on a special diet."

"You look good. Do you know our guest of honor?"

"Sandoval?" he asked. "We've never met. I know of him, of course."

"That's right! You two are in the same business, aren't you?"

"Sort of. His company is moving an asteroid into Earth orbit in order to compete with *The Rock*."

"Do I smell a rat? You wouldn't be here to see Carlos, would you?"

"Whatever for?"

"Don't play coy with me. Seems to me that a person who knew you two were here tonight could do well in tomorrow's stock market. That is, if they were given a hint as to which way to jump."

He shrugged. "If I understood the market, I wouldn't spend so much time at my desk."

"What about it, Barbara? Care to take pity on an old woman?"

"If you find out anything, Elspeth, I hope you'll share it with me."

"I can see that I'm getting nowhere. You two go along and have fun. You'll find the bar to your right, the rest rooms straight down the hall. Sandoval is in the drawing room, not that you're interested."

"You're too good to me, Elspeth."

Smith took Barbara's arm and guided her toward the bar. They ordered drinks and watched as the bartender actually mixed their orders by hand, the old-fashioned way. While they waited, Smith turned to gaze at a small clump of people standing nearby. One man in particular was loudly proclaiming what he thought should be done with the comet. There had been few other subjects of cocktail party conversation for weeks.

"As far as I'm concerned," the red-faced man with the vaguely familiar look about him exclaimed, "it's a damned good thing the engineers slipped that decimal point when they tried to blast. The last thing we want to do with this damned meteor is to move it."

"Do you know something we don't?" another man asked. "Or hadn't you heard that it is going to crash into the Earth?"

The red-faced man's answer was a snort. "I've talked to a number of scientists who tell me it's a physical impossibility.

After all, Halley's Comet has never hit the Earth, and look how long it's been coming back!"

Barbara thought to say something but was restrained by Smith's hand on her arm. She relaxed and settled down to listen.

"But why would they lie to us?" one of the women standing near the speaker asked.

"Why, indeed? Who's running this show?"

"The System Council, of course."

"There you have it. Who elected them saviors of the world? The ploy is as old as politics. First you get the people all worked up over something, then at the last minute a white knight rides to the rescue. After that, the knight can do anything he likes."

"All the scientists can't be crooked," the woman insisted.

"I doubt if more than a handful are," the man replied. "That's all that is needed. Do scientists actually look through their telescopes anymore? Hell, no! Their data comes to them prepackaged from some observatory computer. That's where the control is. We've had a number of people testify before my committee on just that point."

With his comment to jog her memory, Barbara finally recognized the speaker. He was one of North America's more prominent legislators, a man with a penchant for keeping his face before the public. Suddenly, she was glad that Smith had stopped her from becoming embroiled in the controversy.

"But, hell," the man continued. "Let's say this whole thing is on the up and up. We still don't want anyone messing around with this damned comet."

"Why not?"

"Because if the scientists are right, that damned hunk of ice is going to crash down in the Indian Ocean come next July. The Indian Ocean is a long way from here. You don't seriously expect an ice cube plowing into the opposite side of the Earth to damage North America, do you? Oh, we might have a few cold winters and overcast skies for a long time, but it ain't like it was made of iron.

"Now, what happens if the scientists try to shove it out of orbit again? They may make it come down somewhere besides India. I still maintain that it isn't going to hit at all, but if it does, wouldn't we rather it be the Indians' problem and not ours?"

The bartender set their drinks on the bar. Smith handed one to Barbara and steered her toward the next room. When they were out of earshot of the debaters, she whispered, "Surely, he can't be serious!"

"I'm afraid he is," Smith replied grimly. "When faced with an unpleasant fact, it is human nature to deny it. Ever since the failure to divert Thunderstrike, you'll find a lot of people who refuse to believe the comet will strike Earth."

She shivered. "How do we convince them of the truth?"

Smith shrugged. "We don't. We save them in spite of themselves. We do that because it's the only way to save ourselves."

Smith led her toward a group of people clustered around a short, heavyset man with a drooping black mustache. The South American looked up as the two of them penetrated his ring of admirers. His eyes moved from Barbara to her companion. She could see the sudden interest as he recognized Smith.

"Well, if it isn't my esteemed competitor!" Sandoval said, holding out his hand. "Your photographs don't do you justice."

"I might say the same about you," Smith replied. "We meet at last. I was beginning to think you were a South American mirage."

"And I wondered if you were the product of a SierraCorp advertising campaign!" Sandoval responded with a deep-throated laugh. "How go your orbital operations?"

"Sierra Skies did herself proud last quarter."

"You know what I mean," the Latin said. "Are your plans to develop *The Rock* on schedule?"

"So so. And your Avalon?"

"We're about to bring our first iron to market. Of course, you already knew that."

"Of course. I get weekly update on the progress of your ore barges."

"I'll bet you do! This ice-mining venture of yours hasn't worked out quite the way you planned, has it?"

"That's something of an understatement. I wanted to bring back some asteroidal ice, but this is ridiculous!"

"Well put." Sandoval chuckled. He turned his attention to Barbara. "Who is this lovely young lady?"

"Pardon me. Barbara Martinez, Carlos Sandoval."

"Buenos noches, señorita."

"Señor Sandoval."

"Barbara works for Sky Watch. She was involved in the attempt to blast a chunk out of Thunderstrike."

"A pity that it did not work."

"Yes, it is," Barbara agreed.

"Do you have any insight into what the next attempt will involve?" the South American asked her.

"Actually," Smith replied, "we do. Are you interested?"

"Of course. SierraCorp has received far too many contracts from the System Council. You sell antimatter to them, you lease ships, you provide technical support services. I would be a poor businessman if I didn't try to garner at least some of that business for my own operation."

"Perhaps we could go somewhere quiet and talk about it."

"Are you serious?" Sandoval asked.

"I am."

"Very well. Elspeth usually keeps the doors to the library closed. I don't think she'd mind our using it."

"Excellent," Smith replied.

"Does Señorita Martinez come with us?"

"She does."

The three of them retired to the library. Smith locked the door to insure their continued privacy.

The South American pulled out an oversize cigar and waved it alight. "All right, tell me what the council plans this time," he said when he had filled the room with blue smoke.

"Barbara."

Barbara outlined the Avalon Option to Sandoval. She told him of the plan to use the asteroid to divert Thunderstrike into Luna, and explained that two cargo carriers were being dispatched immediately to Avalon. Sandoval listened without speaking. When Barbara finished, he puffed once more on the cigar, then scowled.

"Were you the one who thought this up, Smith?"

"One of my people did."

"Very clever of him. You wipe out your only real competition and get credit for saving the Earth at the same time. Whatever you pay him, it isn't enough."

"Is that what you think this is? A business gambit?"

"What else am I to think? You get the System Council to steal my property while yours is untouched."

"Surely, Mr. Sandoval, your balance sheet cannot be more important than Earth's safety!"

The South American turned to Barbara. "Do you truly work for Sky Watch, señorita?"

"Yes."

"Then I will explain, something I would never do for one of Mr. Smith's stooges. I have a responsibility to my investors. We have invested a great deal of money in capturing Avalon. To see it wiped out with no return is a hard thing. In effect, I am being asked to foot the bill for the whole of humanity."

"You'll be compensated, of course!"

"By whom? Not the System Council. They survive through levies on the nations. They'll promise anything now, but what about afterward? It is not difficult to imagine that the various assemblies will find better uses for their funds once the danger has passed. I'll be lucky to get a tenth-piece to the nuevopeso."

"What other choice have you? If you don't cooperate, you could get lynched. Besides, they'll just take it away from you by force."

"I'm not so sure, señorita. For one thing, there is no legal mechanism in place." Sandoval puffed once more on his cigar and gazed thoughtfully out the window at the Manhattan skyline. "However, we here in this room may be able to settle the problem."

"How?" Barbara asked.

"I propose a trade. I will give Avalon to Mr. Smith to do with as he pleases. He, in turn, will give me *The Rock*. That way, I will present my stockholders with an operating iron mine while he becomes humanity's savior."

"Ingenious," Smith replied, "but not practical. My board of directors would never approve. Like you, they would be concerned about repercussions with the investors. However, I don't share your pessimism about humanity's gratitude after we've stopped the comet."

"Then you take the risk, my friend!"

"I will. You cooperate in moving Avalon, and I will get Constance Forbin to agree to reimburse all costs incurred to date, plus a sizable bonus to keep your stockholders happy. I'll even guarantee the deal myself."

"How?"

"If the nations refuse to pay, I'll support your claim in the international courts. If the courts rule against you, I'll cede half *The Rock* to System Resources."

"You are suggesting a merger between our two companies?"

"Not at all. We compete as before. We'll merely mine the same piece of real estate. It will be no different than if you had actually gotten Avalon to parking orbit."

"Are you serious?"

"I am."

There was a long minute of silence. Finally Sandoval held out his hand. "I will set my people to drawing up the necessary paperwork. You may tell Mrs. Forbin that she has an asteroid to do with as she will."

After a few more minutes' discussion, the three of them went back to the party. Carlos Sandoval returned to his circle of admirers while Smith and Barbara circulated. Smith stopped a passing waiter carrying a tray of drinks and asked Barbara if she would like one.

"No, thank you."

"What's the matter? One your limit?"

"I don't like to drink on an empty stomach."

"You mean you haven't eaten?"

She shook her head. "Just a snack on the flight down."

"I apologize for not asking before. What say we get out of here and grab a bite to eat?"

"I don't want to take you away from the party."

"I hate these things. I wouldn't be here tonight except for this business we just concluded."

"In that case, I would very much like to have dinner with you."

"Let me find our hostess to make our excuses. I know a nice little bistro not far from here which serves a pretty good bouillabaisse."

Wilhelm Von Stiller was United Europe's ambassador to the Republic of Luna and the dean of the Luna City diplomatic corps. The post was largely a sinecure, the duties primarily ceremonial. Those few problems that cropped up dealt with trade matters and the use of European ecopatents in Luna industry. Stiller had never expected to have a real diplomatic dilemma to worry about. It was hard to believe that he was striding through the underground tunnels leading to the prime minister's private office with the

Supreme Admiral of the Peace Force at his side. A Peace Force cruiser orbited overhead. In Von Stiller's dispatch case resided a message that could well signal the beginning of humanity's first interplanetary war.

As he strode along in a distance-eating gait impressive for a man of seventy, Von Stiller reminded himself that he had always dreamed of a great diplomatic mission. Now that one was upon him, he longed for the days of visa troubles and receptions for visiting dignitaries. In wishing for a little excitement in his life, Von Stiller had forgotten the classic definition of adventure: Someone else having a hard time far away!

Von Stiller and the admiral reached the doorway where two Luna City police stood guard. They showed their identification and were ushered inside. There they found John Hobart and a close circle of advisors seated around a conference table. Two seats had been left vacant opposite the prime minister.

"Welcome, Mr. Ambassador," the prime minister said as he stood at his place behind the table. He looked haggard, but his voice was strong.

"Citizen Prime Minister," Von Stiller acknowledged with a sharp bow of his head and a click of his heels. "May I introduce Supreme Admiral Sutu Praestowik Suvanavum of the Peace Force?"

"Admiral Suvanavum," the prime minister acknowledged. "We noted your ship's arrival with considerable interest. I hope its presence does not presage bad news."

"We have no wish to provoke Luna, Prime Minister," the Australasian responded in a well-modulated voice. "*Avenger* was merely the quickest way to get me to Luna for this meeting."

Hobart nodded and turned his attention back to Von Stiller. "What do you have for us, Mr. Ambassador?"

"I have been instructed to hand you this," the European responded as he extracted a sealed diplomatic note from his dispatch case. The note had been hand delivered by Admiral Suvanavum an hour earlier. Von Stiller passed the note to the prime minister.

Hobart took the thin sheaf of papers and began to read. It was possible to judge his progress by his complexion. By the end of the first page his ears had begun to turn red. By the second, his entire face had begun to take on the shading of a beet. By the third page, Von Stiller began to worry that Hobart would burst a blood vessel.

"What's the meaning of this nonsense?" the prime minister asked in a raspy voice when he finished.

"My government asked me to transmit that note to you, Citizen Prime Minister. It represents a consensus of all the major nations of the Earth. The nations feel that it is vital to their interests that operations commence immediately to move the asteroid Avalon. Any attempt by Luna to interfere will result in military force being used against you."

"Then you have decided to sacrifice Luna to the comet!"

"No, sir. We merely feel that it is prudent to keep our options open. I have been asked to assure you that should any practical alternative be forthcoming, we will, of course, cease Avalon operations immediately. It is my understanding that Avalon can be diverted from the comet's path at any time up until a week before impact.

"Finally, I have been authorized to begin discussions concerning the evacuation of Luna. This, too, is a precaution. Earth will spare no effort or expense to insure that every Lunarian is removed from harm's way should it be necessary to divert Thunderstrike into Farside."

There was a long silence after Von Stiller finished his speech. It was broken by Alex Sturdevant, Hobart's chief advisor and one of Von Stiller's closest friends on Luna. "I don't think your masters on Earth understand our resolve in this matter, Willy."

"I assure you that they do, Alex. I pray that you understand the depth of our own commitment to this course."

"We have a dozen ships ready to space for Avalon, Admiral," Sturdevant said, turning his attention to Von Stiller's companion. "How many can you muster?"

"We have two warships active within the Earth-Moon system at the moment, Mr. Advisor. We have six others within range of recall. They can be here within the month."

"Kind of spread out, aren't you?" Harold Barnes asked.

"Yes, indeed," Admiral Suvanavum agreed. "The Peace Force has never been a military force in the traditional sense. We are more the policemen on the block."

"One of those two ships is *Avenger*, which is within range of our surface weapons, Admiral. We could take it out in a matter of seconds. That would leave you with a single operational warship in Earth-Moon space."

"That is true."

"How the hell do you expect to beat us at Avalon with a single ship?"

"We do not propose to try," Suvanavum replied matter-of-factly. "If you interfere with the asteroid, my orders are to bombard Luna directly."

"You wouldn't!"

"Yes," Von Stiller replied grimly, "we would. We are talking about the survival of humanity here, gentlemen. The one thing that I can assure you is that Luna will not outlive Earth. If you frustrate our only chance to save our world, then we will take you with us."

"Perhaps we should keep half of our ships here in order to deal with the admiral's paltry force," Hobart responded acidly.

"That will not save you, citizen," Suvanavum replied. "The System Council has asked those nations which still possess nuclear weapons to retarget their long-range delivery systems on Luna. There are more than enough warheads to penetrate your defenses. Let me assure you that Earth has the advantage in any such battle. Taking revenge is the easiest of all military objectives."

"Would you really bomb us?" Hobart asked. In the past several minutes his complexion had gone from red to ashen as the implications of what Earth was threatening began to sink in.

"Only if you force us to," Von Stiller replied. "We have no desire to commit genocide, Prime Minister. Neither do we wish to die. If the only way to stop the comet is by using Luna to block its path, we will do so. We would prefer that no one die. Our offer stands. We will use the Avalon Option only as a last resort and, if necessary, will evacuate every Lunarian for resettlement to Earth."

Von Stiller looked around the table. "The choice is yours, gentlemen. We can cooperate, or we can fight. If you cooperate with us, together we may find a better solution. If we do not, then at least humanity, including Luna's ten million, will be saved. It will be inconvenient for you, but no one need die.

"If you choose to fight, then Earth dies when the comet

strikes, and Luna dies under a rain of warheads. I offer you life or death. The choice is entirely yours."

Like John Hobart, Constance Forbin had not slept well of late. Nor, for that matter, had most of the Earth's chief executives. The strain of getting the nations to agree on a common response to Luna's ultimatum had been very great. Only after several nations had threatened to take matters into their own hands had agreement been reached.

It had been Constance Forbin's suggestion that their demands be delivered on board a Peace Force cruiser. She would have preferred a fleet, but none such existed. Gunboat diplomacy had long been frowned upon as an instrument of statecraft. Still, it had its purposes.

The chief coordinator sat at her desk and tried to concentrate on the work at hand. She reviewed a number of reports while she waited for news from Luna. Halver Smith had reported on his meeting with Carlos Sandoval. That, at least, had gone well. Other reports dealt with the probable aftermath of diverting Thunderstrike into Luna. Earth would still be in grave danger from the ejecta that such a collision would create. Some scientists estimated the quantity of material splashed into lunar orbit and beyond at a full one percent of Luna's total mass! What a cosmic joke it would be, she mused, if they survived the comet only to be killed by a rain of meteors.

Her thoughts were interrupted by the sudden buzzing of her intercom. "Yes?"

"Ambassador Von Stiller is on the phone from Luna City," her secretary said.

"Put him through."

Constance's workscreen cleared to show the grim face of Wilhelm Von Stiller. He gazed outward with the blank stare of someone waiting to be connected. A few seconds later the face came to life.

"Is that you, Coordinator Forbin?"

"I'm here. What's the word, Mr. Ambassador?"

There was another eternity before Von Stiller's mustache twitched upward into a faint smile. "They bought it! The prime minister has given his personal assurance that Luna will not interfere. He asks that a meeting be convened as soon as possible to begin planning the evacuation, should that become necessary."

Constance let out a deep sigh. She had not realized that she had been holding her breath. "Very well, Mr. Ambassador. Tell the prime minister that we'll begin to construct an evacuation fleet immediately. His conference will be convened within ten days. And thank him for me personally. He made the right decision!"

CHAPTER 32

The delta-winged ground-to-orbit ferry slipped through the upper atmosphere at thirty times the speed of sound. As it cut the near vacuum, jets of plasma sheeted away in multiple shock waves from wings and fuselage. The shock waves formed multiple prisms through which the black line of the California coast could be seen sliding slowly over the curved horizon. After sixteen months and nearly two billion kilometers of travel, Tom Thorpe was finally coming home.

Thorpe sat in his seat and gazed out the window at the blue Pacific as the spaceplane fell from the deep black. Tucked into an inside pocket was a message flimsy confirming his appointment as Deputy Director of the newly formed Avalon Working Group. That message, as much as anything, symbolized the recent changes in Thorpe's life. He had left Earth as the leader of a minor expedition to explore a wayward comet. He was returning as Earth's savior.

Thorpe had been lionized in the mass media in the weeks since the Avalon Option had been made public. He had had to submit to almost daily interviews aboard *Admiral Farragut* as the freighter fell toward Earth. At first the interviews had been computer simulations like that in which Amber had inadvertently given Thunderstrike its popular name. Later, when the freighter closed to within two-way communications range, the news people had insisted on talking to him live. Some of their characterizations had been enough to make him blush, and Thorpe did not blush easily.

Despite the acclaim, he was far from happy. For if his discovery that Avalon could be used to stop Thunderstrike had gained him systemwide recognition, it had cost him the one thing he treasured most in life: Amber!

Their relationship had never recovered from Avalon. Amber professed not to blame him, yet it was impossible for her to separate her feelings for him from the pain of Luna's destruction. The frustration of not being able to find an acceptable alternative had not helped. Amber, and nearly every astronomer and astrophysicist in the Solar system, had searched for such an alternative for two months.

The fruitless search had taken its toll on tempers aboard the freighter. Amber had stopped talking to everyone for a while. So, too, had Cragston Barnard and Professor Chen. As simulation after simulation came up negative, the three became more withdrawn and sullen. No matter what approach they tried, it always came down to too few resources or too little time.

Admiral Farragut had reached Earth twelve weeks after departing the nucleus. A few hours from parking orbit, Thorpe had sought Amber out. He found her in her cabin, packing.

"Hello, may I come in?"

"Sure," she said, giving him a wan smile. The frustration of the past several weeks had left its mark on her. Her face was drawn, her eyes sunken and marked with permanent bags. She seemed to have developed an entire set of new worry lines.

"I hear you're going back to Luna."

She nodded. "I got a long message from Niels Grayson yesterday. He wants me back at the observatory. He's offered Crag Barnard a position, too."

"Why go back?"

"They're short of trained people. They'll be tracking the comet through impact with Avalon and then for as long as possible until it disappears behind the sun."

"What then?"

"Niels wants to try and salvage *The Big Eye.* The telescope has four hundred of the most precise optical mirrors ever manufactured. They represent an irreplaceable scientific resource. If we can get them off Luna, we can rebuild the instrument in Earth orbit."

"Is that what you want?"

She shrugged. "Crag and I haven't come up with anything to save Luna these past few weeks. Maybe we can salvage something from this fiasco."

"What about us?" Thorpe asked. "Can we save what we had together?"

The anguish was clear on her face as she looked at him. "Our personal problems don't seem very important just now, do they?"

"They're important to me."

"And to me, Thomas. But I can't very well abandon the observatory, can I? I feel responsible for all of this."

"No one's responsible. This would have happened if you'd never been born."

At that point her self-control cracked. "I know that," she sobbed. "But I can't help the way I feel. I've got to do something. Niels's goal of salvaging *The Big Eye* is important. I want to be part of it."

"All right," he said. "I'll go with you."

"You have your new position to fill. I detest the Avalon Option. Yet my brain says that it may be humanity's only chance. How would you feel if you came with me and something went wrong, something you could have stopped?"

"About the way you feel now, I suppose."

"Worse," she said. "I'll get over the way I feel, in time. You never would."

"All right. We're agreed that stopping the comet comes first. What about afterward?"

"If we're both still alive, we can take up where we left off. You pick the time and place, and I'll be there."

"The observation deck of SierraCorp Headquarters. High noon, one year from today!"

"You've got yourself a date."

"A kiss to seal the bargain?" he asked.

Her answer had been to throw her arms around his neck. He had not begun breathing again for more than a minute.

Even Smith's warning did not prepare Thorpe for the crowd that awaited him at Mohave Spaceport. As the orbital ferry taxied to the ramp, the tall windows of the terminal suddenly filled with a sea of faces. Mixed in among the camera crews were everyday citizens who had come out to witness the excitement. It looked as if everyone within a hundred kilometers had converged on the spaceport.

Thorpe waited his turn to disembark, then trudged across the loading bridge into the building. As he stepped from the embarkation tunnel, he was engulfed in a wall of noise. He had seen old movies of similar scenes in which thousands of flashbulbs had gone off as the celebrity stepped from his plane. He was spared that ordeal, at least. Modern audiovisual equipment operated at ambient-light levels. Still, the noise was impressive, and he felt like a lost little boy for a moment. Then he discovered Halver Smith among the sea of unfamiliar faces.

"Hello, Mr. Smith," he said, extending his hand to his superior after crossing the expanse of open space between them. A security fence kept the crowd back. Smith was one of a few people inside it. "You didn't have to come down to meet me."

"Wouldn't have missed it for the world, Tom. How do you feel?"

"The gravity's hard to take, but otherwise fine."

"The press wants a short statement. Feel up to it?"

"Sure."

"Keep it brief. The office has been taking interview requests for three days. As of two hours ago, they numbered 112!"

Thorpe blinked. "So many?"

"Enjoy it while it lasts. Tomorrow they'll be after someone else."

Thorpe moved to where a lectern had been set up on a makeshift dais. When the crowd noise had dropped to an angry buzzing, he began to speak.

"Ladies and gentlemen, thank you for your warm reception. I appreciate the honor, but I have to say that a great deal of the attention paid me this past month has been unwarranted. When I passed through this spaceport so many months ago, I had no idea I would be going out to meet a comet which would pose a risk to Earth. All of us thought we were engaged in a purely commercial and scientific venture. And while I led the expedition, its success is due to the efforts of a great many people. I would like to take a moment to publicly acknowledge their contributions.

"First of all, without the financial and material support of

Sierra Corporation and the Republic of Luna, there would have been no expedition. Had we not met the comet at Jupiter, it is likely that we would not have learned the danger until too late. Upon arrival at the nucleus, our scientific people and *Admiral Farragut*'s crew worked tirelessly to survey the comet's surface and interior. Without them, humanity would have lost precious months in learning about the comet.

"I would especially like to bring to your attention one individual. She, more than anyone, is responsible for Earth's salvation. I refer, of course, to Amber Elizabeth Hastings. It was she who originally discovered the comet, who made the expedition possible, and who first realized that Thunderstrike was on a collision course with Earth. She is also the woman I hope to marry.

"Now then, I will be happy to answer your questions."

"Mr. Thorpe," a woman with a particularly booming voice shouted. "Is it true that the Lunarian members of your expedition attempted to silence you when you developed the Avalon Option?"

"That's ludicrous," Thorpe replied. "At the time I transmitted my data to Mr. Smith, no other member of the expedition knew anything about it."

"Then you *were* afraid to tell the Lunarians lest they attempt to silence you?"

"I wanted to be sure I had something before I got everyone's hopes up."

"Surely you don't deny that Luna has attempted to block the movement of Avalon into Thunderstrike's path?"

"Look," he said, his level of exasperation growing. "The comet is a problem for the entire human race. First of all, the Avalon Option is still only a contingency. Many thousands of scientists are actively looking for a better solution, one that will cause the comet to miss both Earth *and* Luna. But even if no such option is found, we and the Lunarians are going to have to work closely together for a number of years. Why try to stir up trouble between us?"

"Why years, Mr. Thorpe?" another man yelled. "The comet will strike next July."

"If the Avalon Option is carried out, we will have to evacuate every Lunarian to Earth. Transporting ten million people across 400,000 kilometers of vacuum will not be easy. And once they arrive, we will have to see that they are properly integrated into terrestrial society.

"Then there is the problem of our meteor defenses. There will be considerable postimpact debris floating around the Earth-Moon system, and without a meteor guard to divert the bigger chunks from Earth, all of our efforts will have been wasted. We will need a large, vacuum-qualified labor force to construct the system we need in the short time we have left. The Lunarians will provide much of that force."

"You've been on the surface of the nucleus, Mr. Thorpe," a third reporter said. "Is it really as large as they say?"

"Ground Zero Crater is so large that you can't see the crater rim in any direction when you are in the crater's central region. It's bigger than the Grand Canyon on Earth or Olympus Mons on Mars. It's another world."

"What will you be doing now, Mr. Thorpe?"

Thorpe went on to describe his new position with the Avalon Working Group. Afterward, a reporter wanted to know why they had been unable to blast Ground Zero Crater away from Thunderstrike. Thorpe referred him to the astrogeologists. Finally, Halver Smith stepped up to the lectern and suggested that the conference be ended. There was a general outcry, but Smith held firm. As the crowd slowly began to disperse, a flying wedge of security guards ushered Smith and Thorpe through to the parking garage. Five minutes later they were headed north at 200 kph.

"I didn't realize there was that much hostility toward Luna," Thorpe said as he watched the desert scenery whip past.

Smith told him of the Lunarian ultimatum and the terrestrial response. "They've backed down for the moment, but that hasn't stopped the missile retargeting. Also, the Peace Force is activating several more ships, ostensibly to help with evacuation efforts. Their real purpose is to make sure that Prime Minister Hobart doesn't change his mind."

"What about the evacuation? Is it possible to get that many people off the Moon in the time we have left?"

"Unknown," Smith responded. "The simulations I've seen to date haven't been very encouraging. Still, we humans can move mountains when we're forced into it. This one will just have to be a mountain of humanity."

* * *

Niels and Margaret Grayson were waiting for Amber as the lift delivered her to the main level of Farside Observatory. The rolligon ride from Hadley's Crossroads was as Amber remembered it, except that Varl's younger brother was now driving the big vehicle. If anything, his driving style was even more slapdash than that of his two siblings.

"Welcome back, stranger!" Margaret Grayson said as she rushed forward to embrace Amber.

Niels strode up behind his wife and laid a hand on the shoulder of her vacuum suit. "The prodigal returns. What have you to say for yourself, young lady?"

"It's good to be home, you two!"

"It's good to have you," the elder astronomer replied.

"How's the director?"

"As cranky as ever. He's been grumbling about the time we're devoting to tracking your comet. He says that there are more important things for *The Big Eye* to do before we begin dismantling it."

"What, for instance?"

"Professor Dornier's Cepheid study."

"Hasn't he finished *that* yet?"

"It's beginning to look as though he never will, at the rate he's going."

"Anything else happen while I was gone?"

Grayson shrugged. "A few new faces around here. Your replacement is nowhere near as efficient at checking out the intrasystem sightings, by the way. He seems to think such things are beneath the dignity of a brand-new college graduate."

Amber laughed. "I know how he feels."

"What about Barnard? Did he change his mind?"

"He'll be along in a couple of weeks," Amber said. "He had some business to take care of in Tycho Terrace."

"How is Old Crag?" Grayson asked.

"Changed from when I knew him in school," Amber responded. "He'll be a good addition to the staff when it comes time to salvage *The Big Eye*. He got a lot of vacuum-suit experience out on the comet. We all did."

"Come, Amber. Let's get you out of that suit," Margaret said. "They're throwing a welcome-home party in the lounge, except you aren't supposed to know anything about it. It's a surprise."

"I'll do my best to act it." Amber moved to one of the suiting cubicles and quickly stripped to her skin. She hung the bulky suit in the frame provided for the purpose. The suit was the one she had bought for the expedition, but it no longer looked new. It still bore the dings and scratches picked up during her mishap with the icefall. She quickly sponged herself off, then climbed into a new jumpsuit she had purchased in Luna City. She combed her hair and tied it up with a ribbon. She then returned to where the Graysons were waiting for her.

"My dear, you get more lovely every year."

"Thank you, Margaret. Shall we head out for the party?"

The three of them left the suiting room and walked down the observatory's main corridor. "I hear that it was pretty bad out at the nucleus," Niels said.

"Not especially," Amber replied. "We worked hard, and I got myself buried under an avalanche."

"You gave us quite a scare that time, young lady."

"Not as much as I gave myself."

"I understand that you met a young man," Margaret Grayson said.

Amber nodded. "Tom Thorpe. You hosted a party for him, remember?"

"Indeed I do. Where is he now?"

Amber explained the circumstances of their parting. Margaret Grayson listened sympathetically. When Amber finished, Margaret said, "These things have a way of working out for the best."

"I agree," Grayson said. "This evacuation is going to be hard on everyone. There will be plenty of time when it's over to pick up the pieces of your life."

"Has there been any word yet on what arrangements are being made?"

Grayson shook his head. "Only that the government is negotiating with the System Council. There are reports of additional bulk freighters being modified, and possibly one or two space stations being moved to handle the traffic."

"Can they really evacuate everyone on Luna in only a year's time, Niels?"

"A good question, and one which they'd better answer damned quick. If they can't, there's going to be hell to pay."

CHAPTER 33

Donald Callas stood on Avalon's stark surface and watched the parade of supplies being ferried down from *Gargantua* and *Goliath*. The spherical cargo vessels hung as motionless as two moons above the asteroid while a steady stream of cargo sleds disgorged equipment from their cavernous holds. It had been two hours since the ships had ended their emergency runs from Thunderstrike to Avalon. Their crews were wasting no time in going to work.

For five years Callas and his crew had been slowly raising and circularizing Avalon's orbit. The process had required the expenditure of 200 grams of antimatter each month. In another year it would have brought the big lopsided asteroid to rendezvous with Earth. Now, of course, that would never happen.

It had been a month since Callas had received the message from headquarters that Avalon was to be ceded to the System Council. At first he had resented the decision. His resentment had been fleeting, however, when he realized that it meant that he would be seeing Earth a year ahead of schedule. Furthermore, Sandoval's message had made it clear that everyone's contract would be paid in full.

As Callas watched, a vacsuited figure bounded toward him from where the sleds were landing their cargo. He moved to meet the newcomer.

"Mr. Callas?"

"Yes."

"Name's Vassilovich. Walter Vassilovich. I'm Mr. Carlton's assistant and in charge of this gang of wild men."

"Hello," Callas replied, touching gloves with the newcomer. "How can I and my men assist you?"

"First of all, are we at the right spot? Hate to start excavating and discover that we're drilling in the wrong place."

"We've painted a big white X on the surface where you are to begin excavating."

"Think this big rock will hold together under the stress we're going to put on it?"

"It'll hold. Avalon is nearly pure nickel-iron without significant flaws or faults."

The plan for placing Avalon in Thunderstrike's path called for the expenditure of six kilograms of antimatter in as many months. That was five times the normal rate. The asteroid's existing reaction chamber was too small for the energy that would be released. Any attempt to run it at those levels would result in an explosion. Rather than expand the existing, highly radioactive chamber, a new reaction chamber was to be built. In fact, three such would be constructed. Two of them would be fully functional backups, each instantly available should the first chamber fail.

Callas and his people had spent the past month surveying suitable drilling sites. After the mistake at Ground Zero Crater, no one was taking any chances.

"How soon do you think we can begin to boost?" Vassilovich asked.

Callas shrugged. "From what I've seen of your equipment, the main chamber should be hollowed out in a week to ten days. Then it will take another week to drill the injector shafts, install the focusing rings, and calibrate the control mechanisms. You ought to be ready in three weeks."

"We'd better do better than that," Vassilovich said. "The boss will have my ass for breakfast."

"Perhaps my people can help."

"How?"

"We can overhaul the old thruster towers for you and build the new ones you need. We've certainly had enough practice in both areas."

"Sounds like a good idea. I'll talk to the boss about it."

Getting control of Avalon's rotation had been the first task Callas and his men had faced on the asteroid. With an eight-hour rotation period, the asteroid was too cumbersome to move. To halt the rotation, they had mounted oversize thrusters on sturdy towers. It had taken a year of continuous boost before the asteroid's rotation rate had been bled down to nothing. Even so, the thrusters were occasionally being fired in order to keep Avalon pointed in the proper direction.

To successfully intercept Thunderstrike, however, they would need more than an occasional burst. Avalon would have to be actively steered if they were to place it in the comet's path within seven months. Steering changes would have to be made in a matter of hours instead of weeks. That, in turn, required the existing thruster towers to be overhauled and numerous additional towers to be constructed.

Vassilovich turned to watch as a large mechanism was detached from *Gargantua*'s hull. Off-loading was not as efficient as it had been at Thunderstrike, but they were getting there.

"Here comes the power pack," he said. "If you'll excuse me, I've got to get back to work."

Callas watched the spacesuited figure bound back across the nickel-iron plain that was fast becoming a junkyard. As he watched Vassilovich go, he was overcome with sadness. Three hours ago he had been the undisputed ruler of this tiny world. No longer. The newcomer's manner, though respectful, had made it clear that Callas's status was that of interested bystander. An era in Avalon's history had come to an end. Another was about to begin.

After returning to Earth, Tom Thorpe had planned a few weeks of vacation before taking up his duties aboard Newton Station. Constance Forbin had other plans. He had barely rested from his journey when the coordinator called to invite him to the conference being organized at the Sorbonne to discuss Luna evacuation. The appointment was to be part of a wide-ranging public relations campaign to convince the Lunarians that Earth was serious about keeping its commitments. For his part, Thorpe had personal reasons for wanting the evacuation to succeed. He accepted and, three days later, found himself in Paris. Despite his figurehead status, he quickly immersed himself in the problem of evacuating the entire population of a small world.

Getting the people off Luna was not the only problem. Just getting them to Luna's three major spaceports would require every ground and local-space vehicle on Luna. Most of the outlying settlements would be evacuated by rolligon and moonjumper to the nearest station on the Circumlunar Monorail. From there they would go to Luna City, Tycho Terrace, or Mare Crisium.

Once at the spaceports, they would have to be housed, fed, and provided for until ground-to-orbit craft could transport them to the ships that would take them to Earth.

The latter problem was the reason the conference had been called. Initial simulations had indicated that if every spaceship in existence were used to evacuate Luna, seventy percent of the population would not make it off the globe before the comet struck. Clearly, a new approach was needed.

On average, human beings measure 180 centimeters by sixty centimeters by thirty centimeters. Thus, if people could be stacked like cordwood, each would fit easily inside a box measuring two meters long by one meter square. Two cubic meters per occupant had been approximately the habitable volume of the earliest space capsules. And, as one expert pointed out, some of those had spent weeks in orbit, not the few days required for the trip from the Moon to Earth. Thus, it was theoretically possible to stuff Luna's entire population into a spherical volume measuring a mere 350 meters in diameter!

With that unattainable minimum in mind, the conference formulated its plans. There was no time to construct any new ships. Luckily, eight large cargo carriers had once shuttled between Luna and the space habitats. Three of them were already in service at Thunderstrike and Avalon, but the five remaining were in orbital storage.

At 150 meters diameter, each bulk carrier was large enough to transport up to 300,000 people per trip. With that packing efficiency, the ships would be neither comfortable nor luxurious in their accommodations. Each passenger would be provided with a shallow bunk and the most rudimentary of life-support mechanisms. To increase the load of human cargo, the old chemically-powered engines were to be removed, and the hydrogen and oxygen tanks turned into bunk spaces. Propulsion would be provided by deep-space tugs. The evacuation ships would be minimally habitable, smelly, and no place for claustrophobes. Nevertheless, each would have the capacity to evacuate up to three percent of Luna's population in a single trip. Once in Earth orbit, the ships would be met by fleets of shuttles. Those, too, would be overcrowded, but the flights down to Earth would be mercifully short.

Slowly the design of the evacuation ships took shape as the conference groups met in marathon sessions. As the long days continued, shipyard engineers were briefed on the evolving evacuation plan. They were given rough sketches, which they used to make detailed computer drawings of the needed modifications. By the end of the second week work had already begun on converting the first of the evacuation ships.

With the end of the conference, Thorpe found himself free to continue his interrupted vacation. He was in the midst of packing when he received a call from Halver Smith in California.

"Hello, Thomas. I understand that you are leaving for Newton Station."

"Not quite yet. I'm due to go up at the end of next week. In the meantime, I thought I would tour Europe to unwind."

"Are you dead set on this European vacation?"

"I've made a few plans," Thorpe said, suddenly cautious. There was something in Smith's tone that told him the question had been far from idle. If he had not known the boss better, he would have said that Smith was nervous about something.

"Any chance that I can convince you to vacation here? I'll put you up on my estate."

"I don't want to impose, sir."

"No imposition, Thomas, I assure you."

"Very well."

"Excellent!" Smith replied. "When and where were you scheduled to go up to Newton Station?"

"Sahara Spaceport on the sixteenth."

"I'll have my people reroute you to Mohave and make all your other travel arrangements. Someone will be calling within the hour."

"Thank you, sir."

"You're welcome, Thomas."

Smith switched off, leaving Thorpe to stare at an empty screen. After a few seconds he frowned. Something was definitely going on.

Thorpe lounged, half asleep, beside the pool at Sierra Hills. Overhead a bright sun hung in a powder-blue sky. If he thought about anything at all, it was the difference between the balmy weather and the cold that had seeped through his gloves that awful day when Amber had been trapped under the icefall. He had picked up a new nervous habit from that incident: When he was distracted or worried, he rubbed his fingertips together. The baby-smooth flesh of the skin grafts somehow reassured him. Every day on Earth saw the disparity in color between new skin and old grow less.

"Thomas, are you awake?"

He opened one eye against the glare of the sun to see Halver Smith standing over him. Smith was dressed formally, having just come from headquarters. In the week Thorpe had spent at Sierra Hills, he had seen the boss fewer than ten times. He had heard stories about Smith's work habits, but always thought them inflated. It reminded him that he was playing hooky and needed to get back into harness.

"I'm awake, sir. Just thought I'd soak up some rays while I have the chance. No telling when I'll be on Earth again."

"Vacation been everything I promised?"

"More," Thorpe replied. After most of a decade spent in deep vacuum, the wind, sea, and surf were more than enough to make his vacation complete. When he had arrived, he found all of the facilities of Smith's estate available to him. That included admission to several private clubs in the area, many of which had a surplus of unattached women members. Most were more than interested once they found out he was a guest at Sierra Hills. Despite the rich hunting, however, Thorpe's mind was not on the game. He kept comparing the women he met to a certain blue-eyed blonde on the other side of the Moon. No matter how beautiful or charming, his newfound friends always seemed to lack something in comparison.

"So, you're leaving us tomorrow!"

"Yes, sir. My ship lifts at 1200 hours."

There was a long pause. When Smith spoke again, Thorpe thought he detected the same nervousness he had sensed during their phone conversation in Paris. "I expect you'll be getting acquainted with the other members of the Avalon Working Group within the next few days."

"Yes, sir."

"I was wondering, Thomas, if you will do me a favor."

"Sure," Thorpe replied. "What is it?"

"There is a young woman working with the group. Would you deliver a letter to her from me?"

Thorpe let his eyebrows lift. Ever since Smith's wife had died, he had had a reputation for being a confirmed workaholic. Somehow the thought that he might also have a social life was surprising. "Who is this lady, sir?"

"Her name is Barbara Martinez. She's an analyst on the staff, on loan from Sky Watch." As he spoke, the edges of Smith's mouth turned up in a gentle smile. Thorpe wondered if Smith was aware of that fact. "We met recently when she was assigned to help me break the news to Carlos Sandoval. Afterward, I took her to dinner. She's quite an extraordinary woman."

"And you've only seen her that one time?"

"Actually, we've managed to get together three times now. She came down to Earth on assignment last month, and I stopped over at Newton Station a few weeks ago on my way to Sierra Skies."

"Why not mail the letter? She'll get it before I can get it to her."

Smith laughed. "You don't understand, Thomas. We correspond twice a week and speak on the phone every other day. No, this particular letter is special. I want you to give it to her when you judge the time to be right."

"Right for what?"

"I'm asking her to marry me."

"You're kidding!"

"I know this must sound strange for a man in my position. You have to understand that I'm doing this *because* of my position. Since my wife died I've had any number of women throw themselves at me. It's one of the hazards of being rich and single. Barbara is different. She knows who I am, but that doesn't seem to impress her overly. She laughs at my jokes, tells me when she thinks I'm wrong, and basically treats me like a human being. I've fallen in love with her, and I think she returns the feeling. Only, I'm not sure."

"Then why not call her up this minute and ask her to marry you?"

Smith shook his head. "I don't want her to feel she has to answer quickly. She might accept but then regret it when she's had time to think. Worse, she could say no! This way, she'll have all the time she needs to consider her answer. Will you do it?"

"I'll do it. Where's the letter?"

Smith looked sheepish. "Actually, I haven't written it yet. I'll be up most of the night composing it. You'll have it before you leave in the morning."

The triple habitat rings of Newton Station grew steadily larger as the orbital ferry drew closer to the stationary hub with its multiple docking ports. Thorpe watched the approach with interest. The giant spokes swept by overhead as the ferry ducked under the rotating rings. Beyond the station floated clusters of instruments used by both Sky Watch and the station meteorologists. It was easy to tell the two apart. Sky Watch's instruments pointed out toward the black sky, while the weather people's looked down at Earth.

The ferry pushed its nose in through the docking collar, and a teleoperated transfer tube extended to fasten itself against the port airlock. Thorpe made his way through the lock, towing his kit bag behind.

"Mr. Thorpe!" a voice called to him as he entered the station's hub. He turned to gaze at the wiry man with the prominent bald spot who had hailed him from across the compartment. They were still in the zero-gravity portion of the station. As Thorpe watched, the man kicked off and sailed to where Thorpe clung to a safety line.

"Hello, I'm Terence Zaller, Dr. Fusaka's assistant. He asked me to meet you. He's somewhat busy this morning."

"Oh?"

"God willing, they're going to light off Avalon's engines today. In fact," Zaller added, glancing at his wrist chronometer, "they should be powering up just about now."

"I heard they wouldn't be ready for three more days."

"They're ahead of schedule. Come on. We'll go down to the project offices and watch the show."

Thorpe followed Zaller to a spoke lift, and from there into ever increasing gravity. They got off the lift at Gamma Deck, Habitat Ring Number Two. The gravity at that level was one-third of Earth standard.

The two-dozen members of the Avalon Working Group were in a compartment outfitted as a conference room. As Thorpe arrived, they were gathered around a large screen on which the Avalon asteroid was displayed. The view was from an orbiting spaceship, and showed the lopsided asteroid from a distance of several dozen kilometers. Hovering just above it was one of the large cargo carriers.

The asteroid's surface was pitted with craters from eons spent orbiting just outside the orbit of Venus. A number of tiny man-made shapes had been added to the collection. There were clusters of lights spread over the asteroid's surface. Some were the bright white of work lights, while others were an eye-searing violet color. The latter, Thorpe could see, emanated from several sticklike towers mounted at the ends of the asteroid's major axis. He noted that the asteroid's oversize attitude-control jets were in operation.

"What's going on?" Zaller asked someone. He was promptly shushed by several members of the group. Someone whispered that they had just started testing the propulsion system's antimatter injection channels.

Thorpe took a seat well back from the screen. While he waited he let his eyes scan the room. There were eight women present, but only three the right age to be Barbara Martinez. The assumption that the surname indicated Hispanic ancestry eliminated all the candidates but one. He studied her profile while she raptly watched the screen. He had to admit that the Old Man had an eye for the ladies. She was not as beautiful as Amber, but she came close. Thorpe patted his inside pocket to make sure Smith's letter was still there, then turned back toward the screen.

A violet spark of light appeared on the potato-shaped rock at the point where the asteroid's waist constricted slightly. The spark grew in brightness until the camera's light-compensation circuits were affected. At the same time, a glowing phantom shape seemed to rise from the vicinity of the spark. Slowly, the radiance resolved itself into a fat cone of light as ionized nickel and iron spewed forth.

"We have ten percent power," a voice announced from the screen's speaker. "Stand by for full thrust!"

The spark suddenly exploded on the screen as the camera filtered the sudden burst of light. But where an explosion would have been over as quickly as it had begun, the spark continued unabated for minutes. As it did so, the streamer of ionized material grew until it was a comet tail in miniature. The full plume was an indication that hundreds of tons per hour of asteroidal material were boiling away to space.

"Power is maximum. All indicators are steady in the green. We have a measurable thrust!"

Several more cheers echoed through the compartment. A large Oriental seated in the front row waited for them to die away before commanding, "The furnace is lit and we're under way, people! I want your initial compliance numbers by the end of the watch!"

There was sudden movement from the crowd. They slowly filed out into the corridor and dispersed. The mood was festive. Thorpe watched the woman he had tentatively identified as Barbara Martinez. She left in the company of another woman. Both were laughing and joking.

"Come on," Zaller said. "Let's meet Dr. Fusaka!"

"Thorpe, eh?" Fusaka said after Zaller introduced him. "It's an honor. How the hell did you ever come up with the idea of using Avalon as a billiard ball?"

"To tell the truth, I stumbled across it while fooling around with a computer."

Fusaka laughed. "I've had that happen a couple of times myself. Kind of makes you feel stupid, doesn't it?"

"That it does."

"Did they tell you what it is we do here?"

"You plan Avalon's trajectory and oversee the work."

Fusaka nodded. "We're responsible for making sure that Avalon is in the proper place when Thunderstrike comes roaring through the inner system two hundred days from now. Avalon impact will take place eighty days prior to Luna impact. That means we've no room for mistakes. If we miss, it's all over for Earth."

Thorpe nodded. When it came to Thunderstrike, the laws of orbital mechanics were as immutable as they were inconvenient. If Avalon missed, there would be no second chance.

"By the way," Fusaka said, "I jumped at the chance to get you when they offered your services. We've a good group here, but every one of us is a theoretician. We desperately need someone with practical experience. Otherwise, we're liable to make some stupid mistake and kill everyone. We don't want to be like the biologist who was so interested in the social hierarchy of rattlesnakes that he forgot they were poisonous. With the experience you gained in moving *The Rock*, we hope you can anchor some of our worst flights of fancy."

"I'll try, sir."

"Look over the basic plan and tell me what you think of it."

"Yes, sir."

Fusaka held out his hand once more. "Terence will show you to your cabin and see that you are straightened away. If you will join me for dinner this evening, I'll introduce you to the other members of the team."

The next morning Thorpe was seated in the staff lounge, reviewing the Avalon Project's master plan. Like the ancient PERT charts, the plan included a timeline that detailed every activity that had to take place between launch and impact with Thunderstrike. Events were marked as they occurred, and any deviation from plan was instantly evaluated. Thorpe had been struggling to understand the complex symbology for quite some time when he became aware of someone standing over him.

"Mr. Thorpe?"

"Yes."

"My name is Barbara Martinez. May I sit down, please?"

"Please do," he said. His tentative identification of the previous day had been correct. Barbara was indeed the woman whose profile he had studied.

"Sorry I didn't get to meet you last night. I had a program to run, and the computer was balking."

"I understand."

"You work for Halver Smith, don't you?"

He nodded.

"I thought so. He's spoken of you on occasion."

"Likewise."

"Oh? What did he say about me?"

"Only that you are the most beautiful, intelligent, and charming woman he has ever met."

"Did he really say that?"

Thorpe nodded. "He went on about it at great length."

"When did you see him last?"

"Yesterday morning."

"Is he well?"

"Better than I've ever seen him. Why do you ask?"

"I'm not sure. He seems more stiff and uncomfortable than when I first met him. I was wondering if there is anything wrong."

"He's a busy man with a lot on his mind."

Barbara shook her head. "I get the impression that it's me. I've been wondering if he's tiring of my company."

"And you think he's trying to find a polite way to dump you?"

"The thought has crossed my mind."

Thorpe grinned and reached into his pocket. "Well, you can uncross it. Mr. Smith asked me to give you this when I thought the time was right. It's right."

She touched the depolarizer spot on the envelope and fumbled with the letter. As she scanned it, her eyes began to grow larger. Finally, she looked up. "Do you know what this is?"

"In general terms." He went on to explain Smith's desire not to put any pressure on her. She got up before he had finished his explanation. "Where are you going?"

"To find a screen," she said breathlessly. "I have a phone call to make!"

CHAPTER 34

It was three days after sunset when Amber Hastings came on duty in the telescope control room. *The Big Eye* was now manned continuously whenever the comet or Avalon was in the sky. And since the observatory staff was currently at half strength, even Amber's newfound celebrity had failed to keep her name off the duty roster.

As she sat at the operator's station she gazed at the light-amplified image of the great telescope on the main viewscreen. The mirror bowl was tilted on its side with the cherry-picker booms stretched out parallel to the crater floor. Each of the 400 ultrasensitive hexagonal mirrors was aimed toward the eastern sky where comet and asteroid were slowly closing the black gulf between them. The telescope optics were divided into two sections. One collection of mirrors tracked Avalon at full power, while the other performed a wide-angle scan of the comet. It was the latter view to which Amber switched after a few seconds. The ghostly image of the comet that materialized on the screen was nothing like what she had observed during the long stern chase from Jupiter. The seven months since her return to Luna had transformed Thunderstrike beyond all former recognition. What had been a pale cloud of gas and dust had blossomed into a full-fledged comet!

By the time Thunderstrike had reached the Asteroid Belt in January, it had developed the characteristic fan-shaped coma caused by increased buffeting from the solar wind. By March a streamer of gas fifty million kilometers in length had been ripped from the coma. On April first Thunderstrike made its first appearance in the night sky of Earth. It was far from spectacular, merely a faint smudge that was apparent only to those with superior vision or optical aids. Even so, its appearance convinced billions of skeptics that the scientists' warnings were real. And the patch of light in the sky set off a new wave of worldwide panic.

After April there were no longer any public pronouncements that the System Council was spending too much money preparing for the comet. Suddenly, everyone was interested in how the evacuation and meteor-guard system were progressing. Anyone who doubted the seriousness of the situation had only to step outside any clear night for a reminder of what the next year would bring.

As Amber scanned the body of the comet, her attention was drawn to the once-each-second pulse of red light from within the far-flung gas cloud. The beacon was a powerful laser that always pointed at Earth and Luna. The pulsations were controlled by an atomic clock. Each pulse had a coded time mark embedded in it, as well. By monitoring pulse arrival times, the observatory was able to continuously monitor the exact distance between the nucleus and Luna. With that data, they computed the comet's orbit to an accuracy of plus or minus a single meter. So far Thunderstrike was following precisely the orbit Amber had predicted for it more than a year earlier.

Walter Vassilovich stood on the black iron plain of Avalon and watched as the ungainly shape of a heavy-beam constructor shivered, then rose on the flames from four small boosters. The big machine pitched over and arrowed toward where *Gargantua* hung in the black sky. The constructor was the last piece of equipment to be returned to the ship, and followed the last boatload of workers by an hour. Their departure had left Vassilovich and his pilot Avalon's only inhabitants. In another few minutes they, too, would abandon the nickel-iron asteroid for the last time.

As Vassilovich gazed across the body of the asteroid, he found it hard to believe that five days later, the small world would be swatted from the sky. Yet the scientists were predicting that the flash would, for a few minutes, rival the Sun. It was difficult to imagine the violence of such a collision, and even more difficult to remember that Thunderstrike would hardly be staggered by it.

Forty days after Avalon's destruction, Thunderstrike would reach perihelion. Forty-two days after that, it would finish the long climb to the Earth-Luna couplet. Because of the work of Walter Vassilovich and hundreds like him, Thunderstrike would arrive at its appointment with the Earth-Moon system three minutes late. On those three minutes hung the fate of worlds. They would allow Luna to interpose itself between the comet nucleus and Earth. On its way to destroy the Mother of Men, Thunderstrike would encounter a mass a thousand times greater than itself. Just as Avalon had done before it, Thunderstrike would vanish in a cataclysmic flash of light and heat.

Vassilovich did not bother to watch as the beam constructor reached the hovering cargo carrier. He turned to face in the opposite direction. There, silhouetted against the black of space, was the comet, now only twenty million kilometers distant. Viewed head on, it took on the appearance of a misshapen cloud. The comet's tail was a great translucent sheet through which the diamond points of individual stars could be seen. It swept upward from the asteroid's horizon to the zenith. At the very peak of the sky lay a solid-looking ball of milk-white cloud.

The coma was as large as half-a-dozen terrestrial harvest moons. Somewhere in that ball, Walter knew, lurked a 500-kilometer-wide asteroid. Thunderstrike would remain hidden behind the coma's veil until the very moment of impact. Even then it would arrive much faster than a rifle bullet, and far too quickly for human vision. But the instruments would record its approach. They would also record the ensuing cataclysm.

"Ready to go up, Mr. Vassilovich," his pilot reported over his helmet comm circuit.

"Thanks, Pierce. Stand by while I make the final checks."

Vassilovich moved across the nickel-iron plain and entered the

pressurized Quonset he and his men had so painstakingly constructed. The hut was one of three. Though it still contained
breathable air, he did not bother to unseal his helmet. Rather, he
gazed one last time at the machines that would report the destruction of the tiny world on which he stood.

All over Avalon cameras and radar antennas were pointed
skyward to observe the nucleus's approach. Other instruments
were buried deep within Avalon's nickel-iron heart. While they
lasted, they would record the first few milliseconds of Avalon's
breakup. Nor were Avalon's instruments the only ones that would
observe the event. *Godzilla*'s crew had spent the last six months
instrumenting Thunderstrike. It was hoped that at least some of
the inertial sensors planted on the side of the nucleus opposite the
point of impact would survive the collision. If they did, humanity
would have its first direct measure of whether or not they had
succeeded in altering Thunderstrike's course.

Vassilovich made one last careful circuit of the control room,
insuring that everything was in its place, switched on, and operating. He checked the triply redundant power packs and instrumentation cables. He observed that all telltales were showing
green and that no fault indication had appeared on the health-
monitoring equipment. Finally, he keyed for a continuity check
between his instrumentation control center and the two others.
When everything checked out properly, he turned to go. As he
entered the airlock, he reached out to switch off the overhead
lights. The door was nearly closed when he began to chuckle at
his action. They were about to destroy this miniature world, and
he was still trying to save a few millicredits worth of electricity.

Old habits died hard.

Halver Smith stretched out on the foredeck of *Sierra Seas* and
lay his head in his bride's lap. He steadied a pair of wide-angle
electronic binoculars and scanned the sky. It was an hour before
dawn, and overhead, the stars were cold points of blue-white
radiance. There was the barest hint of color low on the eastern
horizon to presage the coming Sun.

"There it is," he said, using one hand to point to a spot in the
sky low in the southeast.

Barbara Martinez Smith turned from the large holoscreen she
had been fiddling with. She followed his pointing finger to the
milk-white splotch of light in the sky.

"I see it," she said. "It's awfully dim. How are we going to spot it later with no landmarks to guide on?"

"We'll use the stars," Smith replied. "See those two bright ones to the right? The comet lies on the imaginary line connecting them, two star distances to the left of the reddish one."

"Got it," she said before returning to her adjustment of the entertainment screen. They had carried the monitor up on deck in order to split their attention between the sky and the live broadcast from space. Aft on Smith's yacht, an antenna pointed upward toward Commstat Two. Despite having been checked out earlier in the week, the receiver had malfunctioned periodically ever since they had left San Francisco the night before. It had kept losing lock on the communications station while the yacht rolled in the gentle swell. Smith had almost given up fixing it when Barbara got the screen to work. She had been fiddling with it for the past twenty minutes. She currently had it tuned to the program that was being broadcast live from Newton Station.

"Look!" she said, laughing. "There's Tom Thorpe!"

Smith turned his attention from the sky to the screen. On it, Thorpe was seated next to a well-known holo reporter. "Turn up the sound. Let's hear what he has to say."

Thorpe's voice emanated from the screen's speaker. ". . . That's right, Brad. We will be able to tell how we did almost immediately after the collision. We've got inertial sensors on the back side of Thunderstrike. They will give us a precise reading of the change in the nucleus's velocity vector. Once we have that, it will be a relatively easy task to project the impact point on Luna."

"I understand that the project scientists are concerned about the survival of those sensors," the broadcaster with the mellifluous voice said.

Thorpe nodded. "When Avalon hits, the shock will be horrific! You've seen Ground Zero Crater, of course. The impact which made that crater wasn't as great as the one we're about to induce. There's a chance that the shock wave will dislodge our instrumentation. That's the reason why we're using so many redundant systems, and why we've taken so many precautions to protect them."

"But what if those precautions don't work? What if all your sensors are destroyed?"

"Then we'll be forced to fall back on visual and radar methods to determine Thunderstrike's new orbit. That would take a few days longer, but would still work . . ."

Barbara reached out and ran her hand through her husband's thinning hair. "There, except for the grace of God, go I!"

"What?"

"I was slated to be public spokesman for the Avalon Project," she explained. "That was before you rescued me. They only allowed me to play hooky after poor Tom offered to take my place."

"Remind me to give him a raise," Smith said with a chuckle. "After four months of marriage, I think this is the first full week we've had together."

The wedding of Halver Smith and Barbara Martinez had taken place in an office of the Newton Station commander. The entire wedding party had consisted of the bride, groom, Tom Thorpe as best man, and one of Barbara's coworkers as maid-of-honor. It had hardly been what one would expect from the nuptials of one of the ten wealthiest men in the system. The honeymoon had lasted two days, both of which were spent in the most expensive suite in the station's hotel section. After that, Barbara had gone back to work with the Avalon Project, and Smith had returned to his duties on Earth. They had seen each other only occasionally since.

"How long?" she asked after watching Thorpe answer several more questions.

Smith glanced at his wrist chronometer. "Twelve minutes."

Despite her light jacket, she snuggled close for warmth in the predawn chill off the coast. As she watched the screen, she wondered if this was what it had been like to wait out the first Moon landing.

"Five minutes," Smith said sometime later. The interview from Newton Station had been replaced by a view of the comet nucleus from the cargo carrier pacing it. The screen split, and an image of Avalon appeared next to that of Thunderstrike. The camera ships, he knew, were monitoring from a range of ten thousand kilometers. Any closer and they would be in danger from flying debris. To obtain their pictures they were using high magnification, causing the images to jitter slightly.

"I wonder if we were successful?" Barbara mused.

"We'll know in a few minutes," Smith replied.

Because the collision was taking place 200 million kilometers from Earth, it had already happened. Only the speed-of-light delay, which at that distance was eleven minutes, kept them from knowing how Avalon and Thunderstrike had fared. It was a strange feeling to know that Earth's fate had been sealed, yet to be unaware of the outcome.

"One minute," Smith said finally.

Both he and Barbara retrieved their binoculars, found their guide stars, and traced the imaginary line in the sky. They lifted the instruments to their eyes and quickly found the comet. Built into the binoculars were light-amplification circuits that made the hazy patch of light seem brighter than it truly was. One of the reasons for taking *Sierra Seas* a hundred kilometers offshore was to avoid the sky glow from the coastal strip cities. At sea the skies retained their pristine blackness.

The comet was a ball of light in the sky with a long feathery tail. Barbara tried to keep the coma centered in her field of view. At first she had difficulty compensating for the rocking of the boat, but she soon fell into the rhythm. Smith divided his time between stealing glances at his chronometer and the screen, and also viewing the comet directly.

"Fifteen seconds," he said.

Barbara held her breath for what seemed like forever. Then, just as she was beginning to wonder if they had missed, the comet's coma exploded in a flash of light. The binoculars' brightness controls dimmed the image. She dropped them and stared upward in awe. Her husband did the same. A new star had appeared in the sky. It grew in brightness for long seconds until it rivaled Sirius. Then it began to fade.

"My God!" Smith muttered. "I had no idea of the power!"

Low in the southeast, Avalon's funeral pyre continued to burn, a beacon of hope for all the frightened people of the Earth.

PART 5

CATACLYSM
AND HOPE

CHAPTER 35

The planetoid of ice had been staggered by humanity's blow. Staggered, but not destroyed. For days afterward Thunderstrike spewed a column of superheated steam skyward from a gaping wound in its side. Robot probes sent into the geyser relayed pictures of an inferno bathed in a red-orange glow. The new crater was more than 200 kilometers across. It had obliterated the Little Alps Mountains and had become the most prominent feature in the Western Hemisphere. Ground Zero Crater had nearly been knocked loose by the impact. The plug of ice that humanity had failed to dislodge was now surrounded by an escarpment more than ten kilometers high.

Of Avalon, there was no sign. The billions of pieces that had composed the nickel-iron asteroid were lodged deep in Thunderstrike's frozen heart. There they gave up their white heat to the surrounding ice, turning parts of Thunderstrike's interior into a subterranean sea. As the ice turned to liquid water, it contracted, leaving great pockets of vacuum behind. Despite the minuscule gravity, the ice that overlay those giant voids collapsed, producing surface crevasses and causing fierce temblors to ripple across the plains of steaming ice.

As the wound in the planetoid's side cooled, the steam jet lost much of its vigor. At the edges of the impact crater new ice formed a thin skin over the subterranean ocean. Eventually the concentric rings grew together at the center, completing the formation of the new crater's floor and sealing the underground sea against the vacuum of space.

Tom Thorpe took a private flier from Mohave Spaceport direct to SierraCorp Headquarters. It had been a week since the successful conclusion of the Avalon Option, and most members of the working group were still evaluating the data. As violent as the collision had been, Thunderstrike had not broken up, as a vocal minority of scientists had contended it would. If anything, the nucleus had come through the collision in remarkably good shape.

As assistant director of the Avalon Working Group, Thorpe was responsible for coordinating the scientists' efforts. He had been doing that when he received an urgent message from Halver Smith ordering him to report to headquarters by the fastest available transportation. There was no other explanation.

The flier pilot treated Thorpe to a panoramic view of the Golden Gate as he made his approach to headquarters at a thousand meters altitude. Barbara Smith was waiting for him on the windswept landing stage as he deplaned.

"Tom, welcome home!"

"Thanks, it's good to be home."

"I saw your broadcast last week."

"How bad was I?"

"I thought you handled yourself very professionally," she answered. "What was it like, talking to five billion people?"

"Strange, and a little frightening."

"I can imagine."

"How goes married life?"

"Great! I only wish I had taken it up earlier, say right after my wedding."

"What's happened? Why the hurry to get me back here?"

"I'll let Hal explain that," Barbara replied. "Come on, he's waiting in his office."

They took the lift down to Smith's private office. When they arrived, Smith boomed out, "Come in, Thomas!" in his hardiest voice. Despite his manner, Thorpe noted the pain behind his eyes as they shook hands. Barbara moved to the office bar and poured each of them a drink. She came back with a silver tray on which three glasses of dark liquid were balanced.

Thorpe took one of the glasses and thanked her. The liquid turned out to be Kentucky bourbon of remarkably high quality.

"How is Amber?" Smith asked.

"She's fine," Thorpe replied. "I got a letter from her the day before yesterday. She's helping with postcollision analysis. They're on round-the-clock operations there. As soon as the nucleus disappears behind the sun, they'll begin tearing down *The Big Eye* and packing it for salvage. They've arranged to have the mirrors picked up by one of the government's chartered freighters."

"When is that to happen?"

"I don't know. They've slipped the date twice now. I'm getting anxious about how long it's taking."

"I understand that you've been helping with the postcollision observations yourself."

"Only coordinating the efforts of others. Frankly, I've been too busy to really study the data, except to note that Thunderstrike will definitely collide with Luna next July seventeenth. Director Fusaka has been looking over the big picture, while I stay busy putting film in the camera."

"Have you talked lately with Fusaka?"

"Not in the last three days. He went down to The Hague to some big conference the System Council is sponsoring. Why? Is something wrong?"

Smith grimaced. "Constance Forbin called yesterday. Apparently, Avalon didn't hit Thunderstrike as square as we hoped it would. Don't get me wrong! It was damned good shooting, all things considered. But the comet is going to come down near Hertsprung Crater rather than Korolev. The point of impact has been moved a few hundred kilometers to the east."

"Just so it hits!"

"Agreed," Barbara said from beside him. "However, the System Council is concerned that an off-center strike may cause a lot more debris to be sprayed in Earth's direction than would a central strike at Korolev Crater. They've asked Halver to assist them in correcting Thunderstrike's path."

"How?" Thorpe asked.

Smith gazed at him with a somber expression. "They want to crash *The Rock* into the nucleus, just as we did Avalon."

"That's silly! *The Rock* is too light, and we wouldn't be able to intercept Thunderstrike far enough from Luna to do any good. I doubt we could intercept Thunderstrike more than one day out."

"One and a half, maybe two days," Smith corrected. "The System Council will provide us with humanity's last reserves of antimatter, so energy won't be a problem. If we can keep *The Rock* together under the strain, we can intercept five million kilometers sunward from here."

Thorpe suddenly understood the look in his superior's eyes. Moving *The Rock* into Earth orbit had been the crowning achievement of Smith's adult life. Now they wanted him to destroy everything he had worked for to gain Luna a few more precious seconds in which to cross the comet's line of flight.

"Are you going to do it?"

"Have I any choice?" Smith responded. "I was the fellow who told Carlos Sandoval he would have to sacrifice Avalon, remember? Can I do any less?"

"This is different. The comet was going to destroy Earth. Now we're merely arguing about a few hundred kilometers' difference in where it will land on Luna."

"What good is an iron mine in the sky if all your customers are dead? They will be, you know, if the meteor-guard system is overwhelmed by debris splashed up from Thunderstrike's impact with Luna."

"But SierraCorp will be bankrupt without *The Rock*!"

"There's always compensation from the nations," Barbara said. "Constance Forbin will give us the same guarantee she gave Sandoval."

"Which we all know isn't worth the magnetic characters it's encoded in."

"Even if the nations renege, we'll at least come out of this alive," Smith said. "Anytime you can say that, you're ahead of the game."

Thorpe shrugged. "It's your money. Still, I'm glad I won't have to watch it."

"I was hoping you would do more than merely watch, Thomas. I want you to take command. We've fewer than seventy-five days left, and we need to rendezvous with the comet as far from Earth as possible."

Thorpe chewed his lower lip and slowly rubbed his fingertips together. "I'm sorry, but I can't."

"Why not?"

"I'll go out to *The Rock* as your personal representative, but Eric Lundgren will have to command the operation. I'll be leaving as soon as the comet reaches perihelion."

"What happens after perihelion?"

"That is when I plan to go to Luna to get Amber out. I'll put her aboard an evacuation ship even if I have to knock her out to do it!"

* * *

The sky above *The Rock* was the eternal black of space, but a dim purple glow peeked above the horizon aft. The glow came from ionized particles that escaped the converter nozzle's magnetic field and flooded across the Acorn's Cap. The glow was brighter than Thorpe had ever seen it in the old days, an indication of the quantity of antimatter they were pouring through the conversion chamber. The asteroid had been thrusting at a full one ten-thousandth of a gee for a month, recklessly spilling precious antimatter and its own incandescent substance to space. This was one journey where brute force counted for far more than finesse.

After escaping Earth, they had sent *The Rock* directly across the chord of the planet's orbit in an attempt to head Thunderstrike off. Impact would come in thirty-nine days, a mere seventy-one hours before Thunderstrike crashed down in the middle of Farside.

Thorpe gazed across the doomed landscape and shook his head ruefully. He thought of all the people who had given their lives for this bit of solar flotsam. Happy-go-lucky Perry Allen had been killed without warning; and Lars Borlon had died after days in agony from a crushed rib cage. There had been those who were only somewhat luckier: Walt Sewell had been invalided back to Earth with a disease that still baffled the doctors. Garrett Timcox had been exiled to space by a heart that would never again stand up to full gravity. Those men and hundreds like them had sweated to turn *The Rock* into a cornucopia of metals, an inexhaustible iron mine in the sky. But that era was over. In a few short weeks *The Rock* would follow Avalon into incandescent oblivion.

Thorpe shivered inside his vacuum suit and chided himself for falling into such a frame of mind. In truth, he reminded himself, all the work and sacrifice had given the human race their one chance to survive the greatest natural disaster in history. Had it not been for the sacrifices of Perry Allen and all the others, Earth would not have a future. Looked at from that perspective, the whole struggle to capture *The Rock* seemed almost preordained.

"What are you thinking about?" a voice asked in his earphones.

Thorpe turned to Nina Pavolev, who was watching him from inside her own helmet. He smiled. "Sorry, I was just thinking of everything that's happened since I first came to this overgrown hunk of iron in the sky."

Her own nod was silhouetted against the backdrop of the Sun blazing down on the nickel-iron plain. "I know the feeling. I'm going to miss this place, too. It's been my home longer than anyplace else I've ever lived."

"Mine, too. I only wish there were another way for it to end."

"Look there," Nina said, pointing with her gauntleted hand to the southeast. He turned to follow her gesture. A steady pinpoint of light had suddenly appeared low in the sky.

"Right on time," Thorpe muttered.

The ship was one of a half dozen that were shuttling between Earth and *The Rock*. Mostly they transported antimatter toroids and other essential supplies. That particular ship was the one in which Thorpe planned to begin his journey to Luna. If he made all of his connections and his luck held, he would ground at Luna City Spaceport a full thirty days before the end, in plenty of time to coax his reluctant fiancée off her doomed home world.

"I'll be sorry to see you go," Nina said from beside him as she stared at the ship's flare.

"It's something I have to do."

"I know it is." The tone of her voice made him turn in her direction. The two of them stepped forward and embraced, not an easy maneuver in a vacuum suit. "Be careful, Tom, and come back safe."

"I will."

With that, the two of them turned and headed back for the airlock that would admit them into *The Rock*'s underground living spaces. Thorpe had some last-minute packing to do.

CHAPTER 36

The evacuation ship *Preserver* was a big, spacious barn of a vessel with a smell best described as indescribable. Since it was on the outbound leg of its Earth-Luna shuttle run, there were fewer than 500 people on board. For *Preserver* that was a skeleton crew.

Captain Jesus Garcia-Gomez was a big cheerful man who did nothing to hide his opinion of Thorpe's request to be transported to Luna. The captain, who had made five evacuation runs so far, thought anyone going in the opposite direction was insane. He had, in fact, refused Thorpe permission to board his ship until Halver Smith had personally interceded with the evacuation authorities. Even with all clearances in hand, Thorpe had only been allowed to leave Columbus Station after a stern warning that his departure from Luna would be on a "space available" basis.

Captain Garcia-Gomez had met his special guest at the airlock and treated Thorpe to a quick tour of the ship. They started in one of the big bunk rooms that until recently had been one of *Preserver*'s liquid-oxygen tanks. It reminded Thorpe of photos he had seen of troop ships during the first and second world wars. Wide shelves were stacked ten high from deck to overhead. Individual bunks were marked off by red-lined boundaries. When the bunks were filled, Thorpe realized, heads would be bumping into feet and almost everyone's elbows would overlap the boundaries.

"It must get pretty noisy in here when you're fully loaded," Thorpe commented to the captain.

"Noisy, hot, smelly, and messy," Garcia-Gomez confirmed. "Worst of all is the chain-reaction vomiting. No matter what precautions they take on the ground, every bunk room seems to have at least one idiot who hasn't taken their antinausea medicine. No sooner have we got them strapped down than they lose their dinners, causing practically everyone else in the bay to follow suit. That, in case you haven't already identified it, is the source of most of the smell. The bulkheads are practically saturated with the contents of people's stomachs."

Thorpe had identified the smell, but had been doing his best to keep his mind off the subject.

"If you have any extra credits, you might want to try your luck in the crew's pool," the captain went on.

"What sort of pool?"

"Each crew member tries to guess how many babies will be delivered during each trip. If you're interested, the stats from all of our previous runs are posted in the wardroom."

"I take it there are a lot of them."

"More than anyone expected or made provisions for," the cap-

tain confirmed. "I don't know what it is about a space voyage
that sends women into labor. But with a ship's population of
300,000, you can count on two things: some of the old ones are
going to die, and an awful lot of babies are going to pick that
particular time to be born. We always arrive with more than we
started out with."

The ship left Earth two hours after Thorpe's arrival on board.
Because it lacked engines of its own, it was accelerated into
escape orbit by a deep space tug. Three days later a similar tug
met them as they fell behind Luna. It locked on and retroboosted
until *Preserver* was in a high parking orbit. As one of the crewmen remarked, the tugs were engaged in a long-range game of
catch, with the evacuation ships playing the part of the rubber
ball.

The tug had no sooner released itself from *Preserver*'s rein-
forced thrust frame than the first of the ground-to-orbit ferries
swarmed around them. A dozen at a time latched onto the big
ship's multiple airlocks. They immediately began to pour their
cargo of humanity into the converted bulk carrier.

"Well, Mr. Thorpe," Captain Garcia-Gomez said as he shook
Thorpe's hand at one of the airlocks, "I still think you're crazy.
Still, if I should happen to be in orbit when you're ready to come
back, make sure you get aboard one of *Preserver*'s shuttles. I'll
find room for you even if I have to share my own bunk."

"Thank you, Captain. I appreciate the offer. Who knows, I
may have to take you up on it!"

With that, Thorpe gathered up his kit bag and vacuum suit. As
he turned and kicked off toward the airlock through which a mass
of humanity was pouring into the ship, he felt like a salmon
swimming upstream to spawn.

Luna City Spaceport was much as he remembered it. The big
mass driver still stretched across the lunar plain straight as an
arrow, and the underground departure concourses were still arrayed like the spokes of a wheel around the surface dome of the
main transit hall. What was different was the number of people
crammed into the spaceport's confines.

Everywhere he looked, evacuees waited their turn to board the
ships. For the first time Thorpe began to understand the logistics
of moving ten million people off-planet. Crying babies, lost children, and grim-faced parents returned his stare as he elbowed his

way toward the lower levels and ground transportation.

The tube cars were nearly empty in the direction he was headed. With twelve hours to kill before his chartered moon-jumper was to take him to Hadley's Crossroads, he had booked a room in the same hotel as on his previous visit. It was not until he reached the Grand Concourse that he realized just how far the evacuation had gone. What had been the bustling commercial and cultural center of Luna City was nearly deserted. Fashionable shops were closed, their display windows still full of merchandise. The few cafés that remained open were gathering places for the very old. He could feel their eyes on him as he strode downramp toward his hotel. He asked the harried desk clerk about them as he checked in.

"They aren't going."

"You mean they aren't being evacuated?"

"Nope."

"Why not?"

The clerk shrugged. "Lots of reasons, I guess. Some just refuse to leave. Others are too old. They can't take Earth gravity."

"They won't have to," Thorpe replied. "Anyone who can't withstand Earth gravity will be housed on the space stations until other arrangements can be made."

"Maybe they don't like these other arrangements," the clerk replied. He handed Thorpe a keycard. "Third level down, second room on the right. You'll have to carry your own bags, I'm afraid."

"No problem."

That night Thorpe had dined at Luigi's, even asking for the same table he and Amber had occupied the night they had been there. The wall scenics were the same, but somehow the forest clearing did not sparkle as it had. The few waiters were obviously not professionals. Thorpe suspected that they were merely warm bodies awaiting evacuation. And the food, when it came, was the bland fare put out by an autokitchen. The waiter apologized half-heartedly and explained that the chef had been evacuated the week before.

Later, as Thorpe walked back to his hotel, he saw that the old people seemed to have disappeared. In their place were scattered gangs of youths. Something in their manner told him that they, too, had no plans for departing Luna.

For the first time he began to seriously wonder how complete the evacuation would be. The first simulations at the Sorbonne had been atrocious. By the end of the conference the computers had been telling them that it was possible to evacuate Luna in the time available—barely. But computers were programmed by human beings, and as he watched a trio of youths swagger past him, Thorpe wondered just how many contingencies the programmers had considered.

He braved the crowd at the spaceport the next morning, fighting his way to a suiting stall where he climbed into his vacuum suit. He then walked with his helmet under one arm to the local departure lounge. He found his pilot already there.

"You Thorpe?" the short, grizzled man asked.

"Yes."

"I'm Gianelli. Got your gear? Good, let's get out of here before someone gets it in their head that I've got transportation off this rock. Could start a riot."

"Have there been many riots?"

"Depends on how you define many," was the curt answer.

They loaded aboard the jumper, which was similar to the ones Thorpe had flown during the expedition to explore Thunderstrike. The pilot blasted away from Oceanus Procellarum as soon as they were both strapped down.

"Can you make orbit?" Thorpe asked as he gazed out of the cabin bubble at the landscape drifting by below.

"If I could, do you think I'd still be here?" Gianelli asked. "I'm not scheduled to go up for another two weeks, because they need jumpers to chauffeur the bureaucrats around. Damned Republic hardly pays me for my time. That's one reason why I jumped at this charter. What kind of a damn fool are you, anyway?"

"I've been wondering the same thing myself for the last twelve hours," Thorpe responded. "It looks as though things are getting out of hand in Luna City." He told Gianelli about the gangs of youths he had seen.

"Yeah," the pilot confirmed. "Mostly they're kids who have missed their assigned slots for one reason or another. Some stayed behind to loot, while others had arguments with their parents and ran away. The government has a policy that anyone who misses their slot goes to the back of the line. Those who still want to go are slated for the last ships."

"Why does the city allow them to roam the concourse that way?"

"The city ain't got much choice. All the police are down at the spaceport keeping order among the evacuees. They run occasional sweeps up and down the concourse, but with its spiral structure, it's easy for the gangs to see them coming."

They did not speak much after that. Gianelli was busy with navigation and Thorpe was deep in thought. They grounded at Hadley's Crossroads without incident. Thorpe quickly learned that the rolligon had been requisitioned by the government to assist in the evacuation.

"How are the observatory personnel going to get out?" he asked the functionary he found assisting with the monorail schedule.

"Damned if I know, mister! Word is that they've made their own arrangements. I know there's a lot of them still out there. They're trying to take that damned telescope of theirs with them. A waste of good lift capacity if you ask me."

"How can I get to the observatory?"

"You've got a moonjumper," the functionary pointed out. "Why not use it?"

"I thought flights to the observatory were prohibited."

"They've relaxed those restrictions quite a bit since the emergency began. I know for a fact that ships have been landing and taking off out there for the past month."

"Thanks," Thorpe said. He tracked down his pilot, who was attempting to arrange a return charter with the few families waiting at the crossroads for evacuation by monorail. Thorpe offered Gianelli the same price for the 120-kilometer hop to the observatory that he had paid on the trip from Luna City.

When they reached Mendeleev Crater, Thorpe directed the pilot to put him down a full kilometer from the big telescope. No sense, he thought, in ruining all of the work the astronomers had put into salvaging it. He clambered down one of the jumper's four landing legs and began trudging in the direction of the observatory. He had barely gone 200 meters when a brisk wind whipped the lunar dust around him. He turned to see the jumper climbing swiftly into the black sky on a fountain of white flame. It heeled over and disappeared to the west.

As Thorpe approached the telescope, he noticed numerous figures swarming over its girders. One of them detached itself from the work crew and bounded to meet him. Whoever it was had obviously seen the ship take off and had only been waiting for Thorpe to come to them.

"Who the hell are you?" a male voice asked over the general comm circuit. The voice belonged to Cragston Barnard.

"Hello, Crag. It's Tom Thorpe. Is Amber Hastings here?"

"Thomas!" Amber's voice squealed over the same circuit. He turned to see another figure jump from the upper portion of the telescope support frame and drift slowly downward in the lunar gravity. As soon as she hit, Amber bounded forward in space-devouring leaps.

She arrived with enough velocity that she nearly bowled him over. She threw her arms around him and pressed her helmet against his. Both of them leaned forward to get as close to one another as possible. The kiss, separated as it was by two layers of indestructible plastic, was one of the least satisfying Thorpe had ever participated in. Still, it was better than nothing. When she finally released him, she asked what he was doing there.

"You were supposed to leave by the time the comet was thirty days out. Why are you still here?"

"I can't leave yet, Thomas. We're still packing up the telescope."

"I'm here to take you out."

"Take *me* out?" she exclaimed with a touch of anger in her voice. "How do you propose to get yourself out?"

Niels Grayson gazed at Thorpe across a table in the observatory lounge. Amber sat beside Thorpe, her head resting on his shoulder.

"Order is beginning to break down," Grayson said as he watched Thorpe devour a steak. "Too many officials have abandoned their posts and gone on the ships. Only essential services are manned, and then only to the minimum levels."

Thorpe told them about the gatherings of old people and the roving gangs he had seen in Luna City.

"It's worse in Tycho Terrace," Amber replied. "There they've lost total control of the city. The police and all evacuees have crowded into the spaceport. The monorail hasn't been running since gangs attacked it outside the city."

"I can believe it. Transport seems to be at a premium. I

thought I was stranded when I couldn't get a rolligon at Hadley's Crossroads."

"The Republic has pressed everything that moves into service," Grayson said. "They even took the two crawlers we use for transporting heavy equipment. They just came in here, slapped down a requisition order, and took both of them!"

"That wasn't all," Amber said. "They moved Farside Station around to Nearside. Now our long-range communications are by low satellite. We're out of touch most of the time."

Thorpe nodded. "I tried to call you before I left. They said communications wouldn't be restored until late today." After another moment he asked, "So how are you people going to get out?"

"We've chartered a ship. It's a small freighter currently being used to lift cargo to orbit that won't survive launch on the mass driver. It's scheduled to arrive here two weeks before the comet hits. The freighter will take out the mirrors, the more important sensors, and ourselves. I just hope we're ready in time."

"How many of you are there?"

"Fourteen," Amber said. "Niels, his wife, me, Crag and Cybil Barnard, Professor Dornier, and various technicians and junior staffers. Everyone else has left. Oh, Thomas, I nearly forgot. Niels has been appointed Director of the Observatory!"

"Congratulations."

"For what?" the astronomer asked. "I'm presiding over the disassembly of the place."

"You're salvaging the finest telescope ever built," Amber said. "If you succeed, you will have done more for astronomy than Director Meinz ever did."

"Besides," Thorpe continued, "the position will look good on your résumé."

Grayson snorted in derision. "What good is an astronomer trapped beneath that soup Earth calls air? Even if we save the essentials of *The Big Eye*, do you have any idea of how long it will be before we can have it reassembled and in operation?"

"It will take a few years, I imagine."

"Decades."

"It sounds as though you folks are a little busy here," Thorpe said. "Could you use another set of hands?"

"That we could."

"Will there be room for me when the freighter shows up?"

"We'll make room."

Thorpe grinned and held out his hand. "In that case, you've hired yourself another day laborer. I'm strong as an ox and almost as smart, and I don't eat hardly anything."

"I wonder about that last part," Grayson said, eyeing the empty plate in front of Thorpe.

Before *The Big Eye*'s mirrors could be packed into shipping containers, they had to be thoroughly cleaned. After years in the open lunar environment, they had developed a fine patina of dust. The mirrors were not kept cleaner because the tiny percentage of light loss from the dust was insignificant compared to the possibility of damaging a mirror during cleaning. Since there was no telling how long they would be in storage, however, that risk had to be taken in order to protect their delicate surface coatings.

The astronomers had set up a special cleaning facility inside the observatory complex. Once dismounted, the mirrors were transferred through the airlock and down to the facility. There, technicians in the bunny suits so familiar to clean rooms carefully vacuumed the mirrors front and back. They then repeated the process using an electrostatic device to collect dust particles. Finally, they sprayed the entire mirror with a plastic film to which any remaining dust particles would adhere. Once the film dried, it was stripped away, leaving a pristine mirror without dirt or blemish. Finally, they maneuvered the clean mirror into an airtight shipping container, secured it, and then injected a helium atmosphere.

It took approximately two hours to clean and pack each mirror, and only two could be worked simultaneously. Before Thorpe's arrival, the observatory staff had managed to process 200 of the five-meter-wide hexagons. With his help, and working round the clock, they finished the rest in only nine days. They spent another day piling the mirrors near the makeshift landing site where the freighter would ground.

It was a tired group of staffers that gathered in the lounge for a final party the night before the freighter was due. Because of the occasion, dress was formal and all remaining supplies of gourmet food were served. One of the young staffers managed to open Director Meinz's wine locker. Inside they found several magnums of Earth champagne.

The evening began with a round of toasts and quickly devolved into graveyard humor. After dinner, however, the jokes gave way to a feeling of camaraderie. It was the sort of feeling that comes with the end of a long political campaign, or a graduation party. Everyone was suffused with a feeling of accomplishment, of a job well done despite difficulties.

"Where's Grayson?" Thorpe asked as he nursed his third glass of champagne. Beside him Amber snuggled close. Their long separation had taught them both a lesson. Neither had strayed far from the other's company during the past ten days.

Professor Barnard heard the question and laughed. "You know Niels. He has to worry about everything, or else he doesn't think he's doing his job. Last I saw he was headed for the communications center. The comsat's due to be above our horizon about now. He's checking the ship's arrival time."

"How long do you think it will take to load the mirrors?"

Barnard shrugged. "Depends on whether they'll have any power equipment. We have our two small handcarts, of course, but if we have to hoist them into the holds by hand, it will take us most of the day. Too bad the sun isn't up. We'd at least be able to see what we're doing."

Thorpe nodded. It had been near local sunset when he had arrived at the observatory. The sun was due to rise again in three days' time. By then they would be gone, of course.

He opened his mouth to say something to Amber and realized that the background buzz of conversation had disappeared. The lounge was tomb silent for the first time that night. He swiveled his head to see what was going on. All eyes were on the entrance where Niels Grayson had just appeared. The director's expression told everyone that something was wrong.

"Niels, what is it?" Margaret Grayson asked as she rushed to her husband's side.

Grayson ignored his wife. He walked stiff-legged to the table where they had placed the liquor. He picked up one of the smaller bottles and upended it, drinking three large gulps before putting it down again. After seconds that seemed an eternity, he turned to face them.

"It's the ship," Grayson croaked out. "It's not coming."

There was a sudden clamor as everyone tried to speak at once. When order was finally restored, Grayson continued. "They sat down at Tranquility Monument to load up with relics. Apparently, a crowd had gathered, stormed the ship and damaged it. Luna City says it won't be lifting again."

"They'll just have to send another," Allison Nalley, one of the young staff assistants, said.

Grayson shook his head. "None available. Luna City recommends that we trek overland to Hadley's Crossroads as quickly as we can get there. The trains are still operating, but sporadically. They say it will take at least three days to get from Hadley's to the spaceport even under the best of circumstances."

"What about the mirrors?" another staffer asked.

"We'll have to leave them. Maybe once we're in Luna City we can arrange to have them picked up. It's certain we can't do anything about them while we're still in this wilderness."

"You mean all of our work has been for nothing?" Jamie Bryant, one of the technicians, demanded.

"I mean that order is breaking down," Grayson replied. "They've declared martial law in Luna City. The controller there doesn't know how long they will be able to keep the spaceport open. They'll try to hold a ship for us, but they can't make any promises after essential personnel abandon their posts."

CHAPTER 37

A hike of 120 kilometers on Earth was little more than two days' healthy exercise. On Luna, in vacuum suits, it was an expedition. After quick consultation in the staff lounge, Thorpe and the others spread out through the facility to prepare for the coming ordeal. Their first act was to collect and fill every air bottle they could find. After that, they gathered food, water, vacuum tents, first-aid kits, and electrical power packs, which they loaded onto two handcarts that normally transported delicate equipment around the observatory. When the handcarts proved too small, Niels Grayson assigned three staffers to fashion several Indian-style travois from pieces of tubing. The remaining equipment was divided up and each staffer assigned to pull a suitable load.

It was nearing midnight when all fifteen of them gathered in the surface Quonset. Everyone was in his or her personal vacuum suit sans helmet. Because Thorpe's suit contained an inertial mapper, he had been placed in charge. His first official act was to inspect everyone else's suit.

Thorpe's own was a heavy-duty industrial model much favored by vacuum monkeys. Likewise, Amber wore the deluxe suit she had purchased for the Comet Hastings Expedition. However, most of the others were typical urban-dweller models— good for a few hours in vacuum, but with underpowered coolers and simplified environmental controls. They also lacked the oversize water reservoirs, food tubes, and sophisticated waste-disposal capabilities of the professional models. Even a few hours of moderate exercise in sunlight could render their interiors unbearable.

When he finished his inspection, Thorpe turned to Grayson. "How the hell did your people come to buy this junk?" he asked.

The director shrugged. "We don't go for many afternoon strolls on Luna."

"Can any of your suits communicate with the satellite?"

"Sorry, no. The satellite is an old one they resurrected from storage. It uses the low-frequency communications bands. All of our suit radios are too modern for that."

"How low a frequency?" Thorpe asked, suddenly suspicious.

Grayson told him.

"Damn! I'm not on that frequency either. What about you, Amber?"

"Sorry."

"Barnard?"

"Me neither."

"Just fine!" Thorpe growled sarcastically. "We've got a communication satellite going over a couple of times a day, and we won't be able to talk to it! That means we'll be deaf and dumb the whole time we're out there."

"What about the observatory radio?" Amber suggested.

Grayson shook his head. "It's a system we cobbled together ourselves. The whole thing is strewn out across three equipment racks and has a tracking antenna up top. Even if we could get the radio put back together, we'd never be able to aim the beam."

"Then we don't communicate," Thorpe said. "No sense wasting any more time worrying about it. Let's gather everyone together for a final briefing."

Everyone gathered around at Thorpe's order. He gazed at them with a scowl on his face. "Look, people. It's three days before dawn, and we lack both transport and communications. That means that we're going to have to walk all the way to the crossroads before the sun comes up. Those suits most of you are wearing would be down-checked during their first inspection on *The Rock*. On the other hand, they're the best we have, so they'll have to do.

"Those are the parameters of the problem. It will do no good to wish they were different. In order to make it before dawn, we're going to have to average forty kilometers a day. That means we don't stop unless I say we stop. You are going to have to keep the pace I set. If you can't, the rest of us will have to carry you. Frankly, I don't think we've the strength for it. Any questions? If not, let's get to it."

Everyone clamped their helmets in place and performed a pressure-integrity check. Thorpe used the opportunity to listen on the general comm circuit. It was a trick he had learned while on *The Rock*. What he heard gave him reason to hope. There was considerable black humor but no grumbling . . . not yet! When everyone signaled that they were ready, he ordered the Quonset hut's air spilled to vacuum.

They began their hike in single file, with each staffer dragging his or her assigned portion of the supplies. Navigation proved to be childishly simple. Thorpe merely followed the multitude of tracks left by the rolligon over the years, taking care to keep in the center of the wide, impromptu highway. It took four hours and two brief rest stops to reach the top of Twelve Klick Rise. It was there that Thorpe called their first long halt. He still had not heard any complaints, but for the past twenty minutes he had been listening to a chorus of increasingly ragged breathing over the open comm circuit.

Several members of the party lay down as soon as he gave the order. Thorpe gathered two of the younger men together and set about inflating one of the tents. Once the half transparent, half translucent hemisphere was taut, he directed his charges to enter two at a time. There was just enough room inside to remove helmets, purge overloaded waste-disposal tanks, and refill water reservoirs and food supplies. Three people needed new battery packs, giving Thorpe reason to worry about their stock of batteries.

After topping the rise, they found themselves on fairly level ground. The march turned into a routine. Thorpe was followed by Amber, the two Graysons, Professor Dornier, the two Barnards, and then the younger technicians and staffers. By assigning the younger people to the rear of the procession, he hoped to keep others from straggling. His efforts were only partially successful. By the time they had been hiking eight hours, they were strung out for nearly 300 meters. Ahead lay the base of the Mendeleev ring wall. They would begin climbing it in another quarter hour.

"How far have we come?" Amber asked over a private comm circuit she shared with Thorpe.

He checked his mapper. "About thirty kilometers."

"We've got to stop. Niels is ready to collapse."

"All right," he said, not unhappy to have someone suggest it. Between the cumbersome suit and the weight of the supplies he was dragging, any advantage Luna's low gravity might have given his Earth-bred muscles was totally negated. In addition, his suit had been chafing at him for several hours. He would walk funny for days after the ordeal was over, he knew.

"We'll make camp, get some sleep, and tackle the climb when we've rested. We're ten klicks behind schedule, but we can't have the people dropping of exhaustion."

Camp consisted of four vacuum tents into which the weary travelers crawled. They got out of their suits one at a time, opened up cold rations and wolfed them down. There was considerable shuffling of suits and bodies before everyone got comfortable. Thorpe set his helmet alarm to go off in four hours, closed his eyes, and was instantly asleep.

The buzzing woke him on schedule. After a fight with his conscience, he sat up and stretched. That proved to be a mistake, as every muscle in his body protested. Amber came awake beside him, and the two of them gazed into each other's eyes for long moments. Near them, Niels Grayson and his wife slept in each other's arms.

"Maybe we should let them sleep," Amber whispered to him as Thorpe glanced at the supine figures.

"Wish we could," he responded. "We don't have the time.

Better they wear themselves out than be fried when the sun comes up."

"You're the voice of reason, my love." She held out her hand to him. "Are you sorry you came to get me?"

"Not so far. I've been happier these past few days than any time since we parted. If we miss those ships at Luna City, though, I'll have to consider revising my opinion."

"Do you think we will? Miss them, I mean."

He shrugged. "No way to tell. If we do, we'll just have to find some other way off this barren lump of dirt."

"Careful what you say about my home world, sir!" she said with mock severity.

"Pardon me," he chuckled. "This *beautiful* barren lump of dirt."

"Better."

Thorpe clambered into his suit, no small feat in the crowded tent. He then sent out the radio call that would set helmet alarms to buzzing in every tent. Waking everyone took fifteen minutes. Breakfast was a single nutrition bar hurriedly gulped with a few sips of tepid water. After that it took nearly an hour to strike the camp and prepare for the second day's march.

If the first day had been bad, the second was even worse. Whatever refreshment four hours of sleep had given them was quickly eliminated by the climb up the crater's ring wall. Eventually they reached the top and descended the other side, to find themselves on the crater-pocked plain that characterized the vast majority of the Farside highlands. After leaving the ring wall behind, they threaded their way along ridges between craters. The rolligon trail had been preselected for easy traveling, and they made good time. Despite their best efforts, however, the rest stops came more quickly and took longer than they had the day before. Sixteen hours after they started out, the older members of their party were staggering from exhaustion, and the younger were making ever more frequent missteps.

Amber asked the ritual question. "How far have we come?"

Thorpe glanced at the glowing symbols inside his helmet. In the past forty-eight hours he had learned to hate them. They changed ever more slowly as the hours dragged on, until a single kilometer seemed like five, and five kilometers was a distance that did not bear thinking about.

"We passed the halfway point in our trek about an hour ago," Thorpe said. "We're fifty-eight kilometers from Hadley's."

"We're not going to make it, are we?"

"Not at this pace. Not before sunrise."

"What do you want to do? Keep on?"

"We can't," he said. "If we keep at it another hour, they're going to start dropping in their tracks. About the only thing I can think of is to make camp and get at least six hours sleep. Four hours last night wasn't enough."

"God, Thomas, I could sleep a week!"

"I wish we had the time. But if you haven't noticed, we're starting to run low on breathing air. It's all this inflating and deflating the tents."

"Maybe we should set up the tents and then send a small party for help," she suggested. "They could travel faster."

"In normal times I would agree with you. But then, in normal times, we'd merely camp out at the observatory until they sent a rolligon for us. What if the advance team gets to Hadley's to discover they can't come back to get the people left behind?"

While they had been discussing their options, they came upon a flat area large enough to inflate the tents. It was as if automatons were setting up camp. There was no longer any of the chatter that had echoed on the main circuit early in their trek. Everyone did their job with a minimum of conversation.

That night as people shucked their suits, wolfed down protein bars, and then fell into a fatigue-drugged sleep, Thorpe considered ways that he might speed up the pace. No brilliant ideas came to him, and he found himself looking at the sky. Overhead, the stars were bright sparks distorted by the transparent plastic of the tent wall. He was still watching them when he drifted into a dreamless sleep.

By the end of the third day they were still twenty kilometers from Hadley's, and the air situation was becoming critical. They camped on a rise from which they could see the lights of the surface installations across a wide depression that had once been a crater but subsequently had been obliterated by other meteor falls. Having their destination in sight allowed Thorpe to talk to the Republic representative he had met during his brief stopover two weeks earlier. He aimed a communications beam at the settlement as soon as he entered the vacuum tent.

"I have a group of fifteen from Farside Observatory," he reported after making contact. "We're worn out. We need help getting in. Can you assist us?"

The hissing of the stars filled his earphones for several seconds. The answer when it came was expected. "Sorry, no. We have no transport here. You will have to make your own way in."

Thorpe explained the conditions of his party's vacuum suits and what would happen when the sun finally rose in a few hours. The representative had no suggestion. Worse, he told Thorpe that the next train was scheduled to arrive in less than eight hours and that he did not know when there would be another.

"Damn," Thorpe muttered after signing off. He had been using one of the channels that the rest of the party could not receive.

"What's the matter?" Amber asked. She was half in, half out of her suit, preparing to bed down for the night.

In a whisper, Thorpe told her what he had learned.

"What are we going to do?" she asked.

"What *can* we do?" he asked. "We're too worn out to go on, but we're going to have to anyway. We'll rest here for an hour, get everyone fed, then suit up and strike out for the crossroads. We'll abandon all but one tent and most of the supplies. We either make it within the next eight hours, or else we might as well forget it. We'll take the carts and travois with us. If anyone collapses from exhaustion or heat prostration, we'll drag them along. Come on, let's get the bad word out."

He called for everyone who was out of their suits inside the other tents to put their helmets on. He then explained what they would have to do to make the train in time. To his surprise, there was no argument. In his and Amber's tent the Graysons quietly began slipping back into their suits. Elsewhere he could see dark shadows of bodies, silhouetted against the artificial lights, doing the same.

They headed down the near slope of the depression an hour later. Two hours after that, sunrise caught them as they reached the broad floor. Thorpe felt the sudden heat and heard his cooling system switch to high within seconds. He could only imagine the effect on those whose suits lacked his cooling capacity.

Despite what must have been agony, they managed to continue onward for two more hours before they had their first casualty.

Dr. Dornier, the oldest of the astronomers, muttered something unintelligible in German before falling forward to land on his faceplate in the brown-gray dust. No one said a word. Two of the younger staffers hurried to where he had collapsed and put him on top of one of the travois. He did not quite fit, and his boots hung over the end, to drag in the dust. That did not seem to bother the man pulling him.

They started out again after Cybil Barnard hurriedly gazed through Dornier's faceplate and diagnosed heat prostration. By the time they had closed the distance to ten kilometers, they had suffered three more collapses. Three others reported their helmet reservoirs empty of water. Not only did those reservoirs provide drinking water, they humidified the air in the suit. The reports had come from rasping, husky voices damaged by breathing the superdry air. The situation was getting desperate.

At five kilometers they had the monorail towers in sight. The party reached the point where everyone still erect was pulling one casualty. One young astronomer was pulling two. Amber, Thorpe noticed, was also becoming unsteady on her feet. Even her more efficient suit could not totally stave off the effects of three days of sustained effort.

"We've got to stop," he told her.

"We can't. We're almost there."

He shook his head. "At the rate we're going, we'll never make it. We'll put the tent up and use our last reserve air to inflate it. These people have to get into the shade, or else they'll be boiled alive!"

"All right," Amber said. "We'll put up the tent and get the worst cases in the shade. You go ahead and see if you can get someone to help. If nothing else, you can bring back some of Vern's rental suits. They're old and dirty, but they've got better environmental units on them than these."

Thorpe grinned inside his helmet. "I should have thought of that myself. I must be getting tired."

"We're all tired," Amber replied. "Who do you want to take with you?"

"No one. If they faint, they'll just slow me down. I can make better time by myself."

"At least take a cart and one of the oxygen bottles in case you run low."

"I can move twice as fast without them. See you."

He wished he could have given her a kiss, but settled for a gentle hug instead. Then he turned and bounded off in the direction of the monorail tower. He moved in distance-eating jumps, mindful of the danger of falling but afraid that if he slowed down, he would be too late.

Once, in high school, he had entered a marathon. He had thought the experience would kill him. His efforts now put him in mind of that earlier experience. As he bounded across the lunar wasteland, his muscles began to ache from fatigue poisons, and his breathing came in deep-throated gasps. His heartbeat pounded in his temples with the sound of thunder. The air that the suit blew on the back of his neck no longer seemed cool. As he jogged along, the temperature inside his suit began to rise. It made him wish for the freezing cold of Thunderstrike's ice plains.

At one kilometer he saw a glint of light out of the corner of his eye. He turned to watch as a twelve-car monorail train rushed silently down the opposite slope of the depression. The string of beer cans slowed and pulled into the station. He did not wait to see any more. He redoubled his efforts, bounding in giant leaps across the rocky landscape. His head grew lighter with each passing minute, and he realized he could not keep the effort up for very much longer.

Finally, Thorpe reached the top of a small mogul and found himself a hundred meters from the train strung out along its single wispy rail. He could see the flexible pressure tube attached to the train's forward airlock and a number of vacuum-suited figures milling about outside.

He shouted once, then felt his legs give way beneath his weight. He did not feel the impact as he hit the ground. Rather, his next conscious moment was of someone leaning over him and peering in through his faceplate.

"Mr. Thorpe, isn't it?" Vern Hadley, the small settlement's owner asked.

Thorpe nodded.

"Where are the others?"

"Five klicks out. They had to take shelter from the heat. I came in to get them better suits."

Hadley's answer was unexpected. He laughed.

Thorpe's head refused to stop buzzing. "What's so funny?"

"Sorry," the gruff, outland entrepreneur responded. "I should have told you. This train has orders from Luna City to wait for your party. They've also brought a small tractor/trailer rig. We were going to come out to find you."

CHAPTER 38

NEWS ITEM:

UNIVERSAL FAX, LUNA CITY, REPUBLIC OF LUNA—07 JULY 2087

(FOR DISTRIBUTION TO AUSL, CHN, NORAM, SOAM, UNEUR, XTERR)

THE EVACUATION OF LUNA ENTERED ITS TWENTIETH WEEK TODAY. THE EFFORT, WHICH HAS ALREADY SEEN THE RE-SETTLEMENT OF SOME 9.7 MILLION PEOPLE, WAS ORIGINALLY SCHEDULED FOR COMPLETION NO LATER THAN JULY FIRST. SOURCES IN THE LUNA PARLIAMENT ATTRIBUTED THE DELAY TO AN EARLY SHORTAGE OF FERRY CRAFT AND SOME INITIAL CONFUSION BEFORE THE EVACUATION PROCEDURES WERE REFINED. MECHANICAL BREAKDOWNS AND SOME INCIDENTS OF VIOLENCE WERE ALSO CITED AS CONTRIBUTING FACTORS. DESPITE PAST PROBLEMS, THE GOVERNMENT CONTINUES TO ESTIMATE THAT THE LAST EVACUEE WILL BE ON HIS WAY TO EARTH AT LEAST NINETY-SIX HOURS BEFORE THE COMET'S ARRIVAL.

OFFICIAL ESTIMATES PLACE THE NUMBER OF PERSONS STILL ON LUNA AT APPROXIMATELY 300,000. THIS INCLUDES PER-SONS WHO EARLIER REFUSED EVACUATION BUT WHO ARE STILL EXPECTED TO CHANGE THEIR MINDS. WHEN ASKED IF THERE WERE SUFFICIENT FERRY CRAFT TO EVACUATE 60,000 PEOPLE EACH DAY, THE SPOKESMAN FOR THE REPUBLIC OF LUNA ASSURED THIS REPORTER THAT "THERE ARE MORE

THAN ENOUGH SHIPS, EVEN IF OUR CURRENT ESTIMATES OF
UTILIZATION RATES ARE OPTIMISTIC."

ON ANOTHER NOTE, PRIME MINISTER HOBART'S REPRESENTA-
TIVE WAS ASKED ABOUT CONTINUED HEAVY CENSORSHIP OF
NEWS ACCOUNTS AND ALL CHANNELS OF COMMUNICATION
BETWEEN EARTH AND LUNA. HE STATED THAT SUCH CON-
TROLS WERE NECESSARY, "OTHERWISE, RUMORS WOULD GET
OUT OF HAND AND IMPEDE THE EVACUATION. REMEMBER,"
THE SPOKESMAN WENT ON TO SAY, "THAT WE STILL HAVE
PEOPLE COMING INTO LUNA CITY FROM THE HINTERLANDS.
SINCE THEY ARE NOT HERE TO SEE THE SITUATION FOR
THEMSELVES, WE DON'T WANT THEM FRIGHTENED BY SOME
REPORTER'S OVERBLOWN RHETORIC." WHEN ASKED TO CON-
FIRM THAT THIS WAS THE REASON FOR THE CENSORSHIP, THE
PRIME MINISTER REFUSED COMMENT.

END

The trip to Luna City took three days in the cramped confines
of the monorail. By the time they approached the capital, there
were over 300 people stuffed into the twelve cars. Tom Thorpe
and Amber Hastings had been relegated to the floor in the third
car in the string. They both sat most of the time with their backs
pressed against the knees of other passengers. The car was hot,
cramped, and stank of too many unwashed bodies. It reminded
Thorpe of *Admiral Farragut*'s storm cellar during the times they
had orbited through Jupiter's radiation belts. Despite the car's
shortcomings, it was infinitely more comfortable than wandering
the wilds of Farside in a vacuum suit.

The train pulled into Luna City Station well past midnight. As
the tired travelers disembarked, carrying their suits over one
shoulder, they found a cordon of police to direct them. Each held
a riot gun. The guns convinced Thorpe that the reports of civil
unrest had been accurate. Like the fabled London bobbies, Luna
City's police force had never needed firearms to keep order. That
they needed them now spoke volumes.

Thorpe and Amber moved along the underground platform to
where Niels Grayson and the other astronomers were gathering in
a clump. The party had been split up at Hadley's Crossroads, and
the members had not seen one another for the full three days.

"Well, what do we do now?" Amber asked her superior.

"I understand we have to register," Grayson replied. "Let's pile our suits here, then go up to the next level and find out where we do that."

The next level up was a sea of humanity even more dense than the one Thorpe had observed on his arrival. The crowd was different in composition, however. Instead of the large number of families that had been there before, there were more singles, many of whom were obviously from the lower strata of Luna society.

The process of evacuation, the observatory group soon learned, took place in two parts. The first involved registering with the spaceport authorities. At one time citizens had been assigned priorities based on a range of factors. Now priority was on a strict first-come, first-served basis. Once a person registered, he or she was assigned the next available berth on a ground-to-orbit ferry and given a boarding pass to the embarkation concourse where the ships were being loaded. If anyone lost his pass or otherwise missed his ship, he went to the end of the line.

The tension was palpable in the long registration lines. As each moved forward at a differing speed, those in the slower queues gazed covetously at their neighbors. It was a situation designed to rub people's psyches raw. It took nearly three hours for the group from Farside Observatory to make their way to the front of the line. Niels Grayson handed over his own and his wife's identity cards and, after a few seconds, was given a white slip on which a date, time, and ship's name were printed. Amber was next in line behind the Graysons. She, too, obtained a pass without difficulty. Then it was Thorpe's turn.

"Card, please," the tired functionary behind the desk said as he held out his hand without looking up.

"I don't have one," Thorpe said. "I'm a tourist."

That brought an angry look. "Step out of line."

"But I need a pass."

"Step out of line. Non-Lunarians are being processed in Concourse B, one flight up."

"What about me?" Amber asked. "We're engaged and want to be on the same ship."

"Concourse B, one flight up," the functionary repeated.

The two of them elbowed their way to the exit. The Graysons and Barnards were there, waiting for the rest of their people to make it through the lines. Amber told them what had happened.

"I plan to go up to the surface dome and look over the evacuation after we're finished here," Niels Grayson told Thorpe. "We'll wait for you there."

Thorpe shook his head. "Don't miss your flight on my account."

"No danger of that," Grayson replied, showing him the pass. The date on it was four days from then, and only seventy-two hours before the comet was due to strike.

"But that's a whole day past when the evacuation is due to end!" he protested.

"Apparently they've rescheduled the end of the evacuation," Barnard drawled.

"What about you, Amber?"

"Same date, different ship."

"Come on, let's see what we can do about me," Thorpe said.

The two of them pushed through the crowd to the ramp leading to the next level. That area was not as busy as below, but it was still crowded. From their bearing, Thorpe took most of the people in the crowd to be government officials. Apparently, Concourse B was the evacuation point for essential personnel and V.I.P.'s.

"Hello," he said twenty minutes later when he had worked his way to the front of the inevitable line. "I'm a non-Lunarian. They said that I should come here."

"When did you arrive?" another tired functionary asked. She was a young woman who would have been pretty if not for the dark bags under her eyes.

Thorpe told her. Her reaction made clear her opinion of people who chose this particular moment in history to tour Luna. She asked a few more questions, then punched his name into her computer. Her scowl grew even deeper.

"It says here that you are to have an A-one priority. Here—" She handed him a green card. "Take this to Embarkation. We should have you on a ship within the hour."

"This young lady is traveling with me. What about her?"

"Name?"

Amber told the woman her name.

After a few seconds the woman looked up. "Sorry, you have no priority. You'll have to wait your turn."

Thorpe shook his head. "I've come a long way to find this woman, and I will not lose her again."

"I'm sorry, sir, but we have no time for individual requests. Please take your priority pass and move out of line."

"Go ahead, Tom," Amber said. "We'll meet as we'd planned on Earth."

"No! I refuse to go without you." He handed the woman the green pass. "Could you please issue me a pass for the same ship Amber is assigned to?"

"Let me see your pass, citizen," the woman said, holding out her hand. There was something in her voice that caused Thorpe a twinge of uneasiness. For just an instant he thought he detected the inner smirk of a bureaucrat about to get even with a truculent client. Amber handed over her document. When the woman handed Thorpe's green card back to him, it bore the same notations as Amber's pass. He could feel the woman's eyes on the back of his neck all the way to the rear of the concourse.

Amber led him up to the transit hall. Around the dome were a series of large viewports overlooking various sections of the spaceport. They found Grayson and the other refugees from Far-side Observatory clustered around one such port, watching the ships as they landed and took off. Thorpe gazed at the dozens of ground-to-orbit ferries scattered across the surface of Oceanus Procellarum. It was an impressive sight.

Because there were far more spacecraft landing than Luna City Spaceport had been designed to handle, most of the ships had been forced to set down in temporary landing areas. To expedite their loading, reaction mass was pumped out to them through insulated hoses that crisscrossed the lunar plain. People, too, were delivered via pipeline. From the embarkation concourse, dozens of transparent loading tubes snaked their way across the flat mare toward the ships. Each was filled with lines of people waiting patiently for their turn to go aboard. It seemed impossible that so many could crowd into a single small vessel. When the boarding tube was empty, it would be pulled back and the loaded craft would stagger into the sky on a tail of fire. A minute later another would land to take its place, and the process would begin once again.

"An efficient operation," Thorpe said as he watched the closest ground-to-orbit ferry take off.

Niels Grayson turned from the viewport and asked how things had gone. Amber told him.

"That was very gallant of you, Thomas," Grayson said, "but not very wise."

Thorpe shrugged. "Wise or not, it's done. What do we do now?"

"We thought we would go into the city. The police still patrol the sectors near the spaceport, so they are relatively safe."

"Let's go retrieve our suits," Amber said, "then find accommodations where we can wash up. I have a week's stink to get off of me!"

They found a small hotel on the third level, fourth residential ring. Although deserted, all of the hotel's services were still operating. They assigned themselves rooms in a single wing and, despite the police patrols, decided to take extra precautions. As in all dwellings on Luna, the hotel had a number of emergency pressure doors designed to seal in the event of a blowout. Two of the observatory's technicians rewired the doors at each end of the long hall. They closed one immediately and installed a switch that would close the other on command.

After a sponge bath and a shave, Thorpe felt like a new man. As he came out of the bathroom he saw that Amber had the entertainment screen switched to a news program. For the past six months Luna's news services had been government-controlled and heavily censored. Their primary function was to control the spread of rumors and to aid in the evacuation, and as such, they lacked much of the excitement of preevacuation times. Even so, they were the primary source of information for those awaiting evacuation.

"What have you learned?" he asked, still drying his hair.

"I know why they were scheduling everyone out four days from now."

"Why?"

"That's the last day of the evacuation. All five ships are currently in orbit. They will stay there until forty-eight hours before the end. After that, the tugs will send them to Earth."

"Are they going to have enough room to take everyone on board?"

"They say that it will be crowded, but that everyone will be evacuated if they follow instructions exactly."

Thorpe nodded. There had been a group at the Sorbonne whose primary task had been to consider the final days and hours of the evacuation. In many ways, bringing the giant enterprise to a close was very like disengaging an army under enemy fire. If the exercise was not done properly, disaster would result.

Once they all were clean, a scrounging party went out to find food. Rations on the train had been skimpy, although not as bad as on the trek from the observatory. The hotel's autokitchen was still operating, and everyone soon had a full stomach for the first time in a week. Then one of the junior staffers discovered several bottles of Lunarian vodka in a small bar, and nightcaps were poured all around.

When Thorpe awoke late the following afternoon, he discovered that Amber was already up. She showed him a note Niels Grayson had hung on their door, informing them that he would be calling a strategy session that evening. What it was he wished to strategize about, he did not say.

Thorpe and Amber arrived at the meeting early. They had bathed again and scrounged up a snack from the leftovers of the previous night's feast. They found approximately half of their party already there.

"What is it, Niels?" Amber asked after seating herself on the couch.

"We've got three days before we are to be evacuated. We can spend those days in this hotel eating and drinking ourselves into a stupor, or else we spend the time trying to salvage the mirrors we left at the observatory."

"How can we possibly salvage the mirrors now, Niels?" Dr. Dornier asked. The elder astronomer still showed the strain of the cross-country trek. "They are on the opposite side of Luna, and we have no ship."

"I don't know *how* we're going to do it, Feliz. All I know is that we ought to try. I am open to suggestions."

"What about a jumper?" Thorpe asked. "Maybe we can add enough tankage to make orbit."

"The Republic has already done that. Many of the evacuation craft are converted hoppers. Any moonjumper which has not been converted is too small for our purposes. I'm afraid that we need a real ship."

"Perhaps we can repair the freighter at the Tranquility Monument," Cragston Barnard suggested.

Amber shook her head. "It's too far. There would be too much chance of missing our evacuation ships."

"Repair some other ship then!" Margaret Grayson said. "Surely there are some hulks on Luna which fifteen technically trained people can make minimally ready for space in the next three days."

"Do you have any idea of how much needs to be done to a ship to make it spaceworthy? We would never finish in time."

"No," Grayson said, holding up his hand. "The idea has merit. We shouldn't reject it without looking into it. Where would we find such a ship?"

"There's a salvage yard on the other side of the spaceport," Amber said. "I've seen it dozens of times when flying in and out of Luna City."

"How does one get there?"

"A good question. I'm not sure the tunnels run that far."

"Then I suggest that you and Thomas don your suits and check it out. Meanwhile, my wife and I will go to the authorities and try to talk them out of a ship. Perhaps I can be more persuasive than I was that last night at the observatory."

"Even if we find a ship, how can we save the mirrors?" Feliz Dornier asked. "The authorities will never allow them to be taken aboard one of the evacuation ships."

"One step at a time," Grayson responded.

MAY YOU LIVE IN INTERESTING TIMES!

Halver Smith stared at the luminescent letters and contemplated their significance. He had coded his work station to prominently display the ancient Chinese curse whenever it was activated, as a reminder that the events that made the times interesting to historians usually terrified those who lived through them. The times were especially "interesting" for Smith.

Narrowly averting the Earth's destruction should have been enough excitement for one life. And though Thunderstrike was finally on a collision course with Luna, the problems resulting from the wayward planetoid were far from over. A full-scale effort was under way to protect Earth from the debris thrown up by the comet's impact on Luna Farside. Refining the comet's orbit with *The Rock* was an attempt to minimize the quantity of ejecta. Still, no amount of orbit shaping would completely eliminate the problem. For that reason, Earth was also building an in-depth defense against meteors.

The meteor-guard system was to be composed of two dozen orbiting search radars, each with the power to track millions of targets simultaneously. Those pieces of debris discovered to be a danger to Earth would be targeted by antimatter-propelled missiles tipped with nuclear warheads. The resulting explosions would hopefully push the debris into a safer orbit.

Several thousand industrial facilities were feverishly rushing to complete the orbiting necklace of radars and missile carriers. Because of its expertise in orbital construction, Sierra Corporation was one of the prime contractors. In addition to working on the meteor-guard system, Halver Smith's people were also manufacturing as much antimatter as Sierra Skies' accelerators could produce. Half of the powerstat's output of antimatter was going to power the interceptor missiles. The other half was being used to fuel the exodus from Luna.

Nor was the meteor-guard system Halver Smith's only worry. He also had to concern himself with the financial health of his corporation.

The stock market had reacted swiftly to the news that Sierra-Corp was about to direct *The Rock* into a collision with Thunderstrike. Within a handful of days the price of the corporation's stock had plummeted seventy-five percent. Since he had no hope of stopping the downturn, Smith had resolved to take advantage of it. For the past three months Smith had been liquidating his assets to raise cash with which to buy back his own stock. He was gambling that the nations would make good on their promise to pay for *The Rock*. If they passed the necessary legislation quickly enough, the corporation's coffers and Smith's own personal wealth would be vastly enhanced. If not, he and his brainchild would face the bankruptcy courts together.

Smith's reverie was interrupted by his desk intercom. "Your wife is here, sir."

"Send her in!"

Barbara swept through the door almost simultaneously with his words. He rose, crossed the thick carpet, and kissed her with an ardor that some would have found unseemly in a man of his years.

"Good morning," he said when he finally released her.

"'Morning, yourself."

"Something the matter?" he asked, noting the crease marks in her forehead.

"The evacuation is running behind schedule."

With Avalon's successful intercept of Thunderstrike, the working group aboard Newton Station had been disbanded. Barbara had chosen to join the working group that served as advisors to the Luna evacuation.

"How far behind?"

"Too far. They aren't going to make it. There will still be people left on the ground when the comet hits."

"Are you sure?"

"I've run the figures through the computer a dozen times. The pace of the evacuation is slowing precipitously. The flight crews are exhausting themselves, and their fatigue shows up in the daily figures. The totals are down ten percent in the past ten days alone."

"How many will be left behind?"

"At least fifty thousand. It could be two to three times that many if they lose control of the crowd."

Smith nodded. As soon as those on the ground realized that there was a good chance they would not be leaving, the riots would begin. The onset of widespread rioting would effectively end the evacuation. Without an orderly boarding process, no flight crew would dare land at Luna City for fear of being overrun by panic-stricken crowds.

"I'm glad Tom Thorpe and Amber Hastings got away in time."

"Oh?" Barbara asked. "Have you heard from them?"

"No, but it shouldn't be long now. Their special ship should have the whole observatory off the Moon by now. I've got a car and driver standing by to pick them up once they arrive at the spaceport."

"We need to pick up the pace," Barbara said, returning to the subject of the evacuation. "That means we'll have to find more ships somewhere."

"If only we could," her husband said. "Unfortunately, there aren't any ships to be had. We're using everything else for *The Rock* or the meteor-guard system. It's heartless to say so, but we will just have to rescue as many as we can. After all, we've saved ten million of them."

"You're right, of course," Barbara said. "It could have been a lot worse."

From her tone it was obvious that her brain might agree but her heart never would.

CHAPTER 39

"Look at all of these old hulks!"

The salvage lot stretched in front of Thorpe and Amber for nearly a quarter kilometer. From their vantage point it was possible to view a hundred ships that ranged from two-seat moon-jumpers to a large ground-to-orbit bulk freighter. Despite differences in size, the hulks all resembled one another. Each was a jumble of geometric shapes ending in the cruciform landing gear characteristic of vessels designed to operate from the Moon's airless surface. Unlike a similar collection on Earth, the vessels' hulls sparkled vacuum bright in the rays of a late afternoon sun.

As Amber had commented in the hotel, Luna City's system of pressurized tunnels did not extend to the old salvage yard. To get there, they had been forced to exit through a surface lock and approach overland. En route they had passed close to the complex that served as the breech end of the Luna City mass driver.

The giant electromagnetic cannon sat idle, with dozens of cargo pods scattered around as if dropped there by some careless giant child. At the time of Thorpe's arrival on Luna, the mass driver had been working overtime. With a shortage of orbit-capable ships, the Republic had been loading everything that could withstand the stress of launch into pods and launching them into space. The cargo had been sent into solar orbit, there to remain until someone collected them. It would take years to retrieve everything. But nothing was ever lost in space, and the mass driver was the only way to save many of Luna's priceless treasures.

"Maybe we should have launched *The Big Eye*'s mirrors into storage orbits," Amber said, eyeing the mass driver as they trudged past the quiet complex.

"Could they withstand the acceleration without cracking?"

"You would have to fill the crates with foam, of course, but I think you could do it."

"Keep it in mind," Thorpe said. "If we can find a way to transport the mirrors from Farside, we might try it."

They had trudged on until they reached their destination.

"Let's look at that big one over there," Amber said, pointing toward a large splay-footed sphere with four exhaust nozzles clustered around its base. It appeared more or less intact, and sported no obvious external holes or missing pieces of equipment.

They bounded over to the big ship and climbed the access ladder leading up its side. Fifteen minutes later they came out again, sorely disappointed. The freighter was older than it looked. Its engines had been fission-powered, and the reactor had long before been removed for burial. The hull had been systematically stripped of everything of value, leaving an empty shell behind.

The ship's open upper airlock had offered a panoramic view of the spaceport and the dozens of ferries that were taking on passengers. If one stood far enough inside the ship to remain in shadow, it was also possible to see the milk-white patch of sky glow that was the approaching comet. As they stood together and gazed up at the sky, Thorpe spent a few minutes searching for the star that was *The Rock*. He knew that it was too small to be seen with the naked eye, but that did not stop him from searching.

They tried again. The next ship was not as thoroughly stripped as the first had been, but it was also beyond repair. Over the next six hours they explored a total of thirty ships, hoping each time that the next would be the one they needed. They even considered the possibility of cannibalizing several ships in order to repair one. After six hours of frustration Thorpe called a halt to the search.

"Let's head back," he said over the suit comm channel. "Maybe Niels had better luck today."

*   *   *

"How did it go?" Thorpe asked Niels Grayson as soon as he and Amber returned to the hotel in Luna City.

"Not good," Grayson replied. "We went straight up to the top official still on Luna. In case you're interested, that is your old friend John Malvan! He listened politely, then turned us down. There just aren't any ships to be had. What about you and Amber?"

Thorpe told him what they had found at the salvage yard. Grayson listened quietly, then nodded. "I was afraid of that. I'd heard something half a year ago about the Republic salvaging a lot of old ships. Apparently, they swept the cupboard clean."

"What do we do now?" Amber asked.

"I have no idea," Grayson replied.

"There's one more possibility," Thorpe said. "I can call Halver Smith on Earth and see if SierraCorp can spare a ship."

"An excellent idea, Thomas."

"Maybe not so excellent."

"Why is that?"

"Because Mr. Smith can't afford to be philanthropic. He's taken a beating in the stock market over losing *The Rock*. Ships cost money, and he'll have to demand some kind of payment to defray the cost."

There was a long pause finally broken by Margaret Grayson. "Will the university pay, Niels?"

Her husband shook his head. "For all practical purposes, the University of Luna no longer exists, my dear. A promissory note from them is worth about as much as a communist ruble."

"What about salvage?" Cybil Barnard asked.

"There's an idea."

"What salvage?" Thorpe asked.

"*The Big Eye*'s mirrors are literally priceless," Amber explained. "They are four hundred of the most optically perfect surfaces ever produced. If they can be saved, the astronomical community will pay handsomely for their return."

"You mean SierraCorp could hold them for ransom?"

"Why not? It will take decades to replace them. Paying for their return might not be any cheaper than building new mirrors, but it will most certainly get *The Big Eye* back into operation earlier."

"Can we get the Astronomical Union to sign a contract to that effect?"

"They're probably too busy at the moment to worry about it."

"What about you, Niels? You could sign a contract as director of Farside Observatory."

"I told you, Thomas, we no longer have the means to pay."

"Not necessary. It would establish SierraCorp's right to the mirrors. Salvage law is tricky. The fact that Luna is being evacuated under an agreement with the System Council will also cloud the issue."

"If a signed contract will get us a ship," Grayson replied, "I'll be more than happy to provide you with one."

"Excellent," Thorpe said. "Then I'll put in a call to Mr. Smith. It would probably be better if you put the proposition to him, Niels. What time is it in California? Noon? I hope he hasn't gone to lunch."

Like most telephone systems, that of Luna City had been designed to operate unattended. Thus, even though most of the Luna population had already been evacuated, phone calls could still be placed throughout the city. That was the case anywhere on Nearside. The loss of Farside Station had limited communications to the far hemisphere, but even that was possible while the communications satellite was above the receiving party's local horizon. When it came to placing a call from Luna to Earth, however, one ran into special difficulties. Censorship had been imposed on all forms of communication, including telephone calls.

Thorpe punched for off-planet service and was rewarded by the appearance of an efficient-looking young woman on the screen.

"Earth long-distance operator. How may I help you?"

"I would like to place a call to San Francisco, please." He gave her Halver Smith's private office number.

"You understand that this call will be computer monitored for compliance with emergency regulations, citizen?"

"I do."

"Very well. Stand by. There will be a five-second monitoring delay when your party speaks. Please remember that when you are waiting for his responses."

The method the censors used to monitor screen calls was the same as that invented for radio talk shows a century earlier. Rather than take a chance on an obscenity going out over the airwaves, the stations had delayed transmitting their signals for seven seconds. That gave programmers the opportunity to cut off any offending words before they were broadcast. In the current situation, computers listened to the conversations and broke the connection if certain taboo subjects were broached. Since the monitors were attempting to keep unauthorized information from flowing in one direction—from Earth to Luna—only the portion that originated on Earth was delayed.

There was a long pause before Halver Smith's features appeared on the screen. "Thomas, is that you?"

"Yes, sir."

"Where the hell are you?"

"Luna City. I have Director Grayson of Farside Observatory here with me," Thorpe said, taking advantage of the long delay. "He has a business proposition for you."

Niels Grayson took Thorpe's place in front of the phone pickup and explained their idea to Smith. He stressed the value of *The Big Eye*'s mirrors and the amount of money that the astronomical community would pay to get them back. Smith listened quietly, but his expression told Thorpe that he had something else on his mind. When Grayson finished his pitch, Smith stared blankly out of the screen for eight long seconds. Then he slowly shook his head.

"I'm sorry, Director Grayson, but there are no spare ships to be had. We are supporting operations on *The Rock*, as well as helping finalize the meteor-guard system. If I had even one more ship, I'd have a dozen other uses for her. I thought you people had arranged to have a ship take the mirror components out for you."

Grayson recounted what had happened to their freighter and told Smith of some of their adventures since.

"And you are all in Luna City?" Smith asked, his brow furrowed in a worried look.

"Yes," Grayson replied. "We've got priorities to ship out on the fourteenth. We were hoping to save the mirrors before then."

"Is Thomas still there?" Smith asked after the requisite delay.

Thorpe returned to the pickup's field of view. "Here, sir."

"Barbara was asking about you the other day. She has a new job, you know. She works for one of the big travel agencies here in the city."

"Travel agency, Mr. Smith?"

"That's right. They specialize in all kinds of tours—round the world, orbital vacations, that sort of thing. She says that the comet has really messed up her scheduling. She was telling me the other day about one tour group whose reservations had gotten screwed up. It was so bad that she suggested that they make their own alternate arrangements."

Thorpe frowned, not sure what he was supposed to say. "And did they?" he asked, finally.

"I don't know," came the slow response. "I hope so. Otherwise, their vacations were ruined. Sorry I can't help you with the ship, Tom."

"It was just a thought. Thanks, anyway. Good-bye, Mr. Smith."

"'Bye, Tom. Good luck. Give me a call when you get back to Earth."

"We will," Thorpe said as he cut the connection.

"What was that all about?" Grayson asked. His irritation was evident in his tone.

Thorpe chewed on his lower lip for a moment before answering. "I think we were just told that we won't be evacuated in time."

"*What?*"

"Barbara Smith doesn't work for a travel agent. She's been an evacuation facilitator ever since the destruction of Avalon. I think Mr. Smith was trying to tell us that they aren't going to get everyone off before the comet hits."

"Then he would have said so," Margaret Grayson said.

Thorpe shook his head. "Not with the computer listening. Speculating on the evacuation timetable is prohibited, remember? That's what set off the riots at Tycho. He told us as directly as he could that we'll have to find our own way off Luna. If we wait our turn, we'll still be here next Thursday when the comet arrives."

"But, Tom, there must be a couple of hundred thousand people left in Luna City!" Amber said.

He nodded.

"Are you telling me that all those people are going to die?"

"Everyone who doesn't get evacuated in time will."

"We have to tell someone!"

"Why?" he asked. His mind had been working furiously ever since he had cut the connection to Halver Smith. He did not like the conclusion it was drawing, but that did not change the situation. "If we spread the word, what will happen? There will be riots, and the evacuation will come to a screeching halt. Tens of thousands who would have otherwise been saved will be trapped here."

"We must go back to the government officials and confront them with this information," Grayson said. "They have to put us on ships. Between us we have more than a century of hard-won astronomical knowledge."

"What makes our lives any more valuable than anyone else's?" Thorpe asked. "I know John Malvan. He won't buy it, even though he knows some of us personally. He won't play favorites. He can't! If word got out, it would start the disturbances as fast as if they announced that some people aren't going to be saved."

"What else can we do, Thomas?"

"Precisely what Mr. Smith suggested. Save ourselves."

"But what if Smith is wrong?" Margaret Grayson asked. "Wouldn't we be giving up our places aboard the evacuation ships for nothing?"

"There is no need to give up our slots. If everything is going well the day we're scheduled to leave, then we present our passes to the guards and load up. If we find our departures postponed, then we'll have our alternate to fall back on."

"All of this assumes that we can find an alternate arrangement," Barnard said.

"That is a problem," Thorpe agreed. "Anyone have any ideas?"

There was a long pause. Grayson broke it. "We're back to the idea of repairing that freighter at the Tranquility Monument. It must be in better shape than the ships in the salvage yard."

Thorpe frowned. It was 1300 kilometers from Luna City to the Tranquility Monument. They would undoubtedly be able to find a small moonjumper that could take them there, but any mishap could easily strand them. With no details as to the extent of the freighter's damage, it was hard to fault the idea. Still, it was a horribly risky thing to do. On the other hand, what choice did they have?

"I suppose it's worth a try. Where can we lay our hands on a moonjumper?"

CHAPTER 40

Professor Barnard knew of a landing field on the southeast side of Luna City where corporate moonjumpers were based. Such vehicles were popular with the mining companies, whose business took them wherever ice was to be found. Jumpers were often the only means of access to wilderness mines.

It was decided that the initial scouting party would consist of five people: Barnard, Thorpe, Amber, Jamie Bryant, and Allison Nalley. The advance team planned to acquire a jumper that they would then fly to the monument to inspect the wrecked freighter. If it were repairable, they would phone the hotel with a list of needed spare parts and supplies. The remainder of their party would try to obtain whatever was needed and then fly out to join the advance party at the monument.

There had been reports all week of individuals and couples being set upon by roving gangs, so each member of the scouting party was armed with a long knife from the hotel kitchen. In addition, Thorpe and Jamie Bryant carried heavy metal bars they could use for clubs. Their route would take them well beyond the fuzzy boundaries of the secure enclave. Thorpe did not expect any trouble, but he was not taking any chances. To make sure that they had their hands free, he had everyone lash their vacuum suits to their backs.

Their path through the city was to be straight down the north radial tunnel, across the Grand Concourse, and out the southeast spoke. When they reached the center of the city they found the great cavern deserted. The spiral gallery was still lit by the artificial sun, which glowed a mere hundred meters above their heads as they cautiously crossed one of the spider bridges. Gazing down, Thorpe could see the outermost edge of the spiral terrace all the way to the cavern floor. Nowhere, however, did he see any sign of other people. It was as if they were the last human beings on Luna.

The thought intrigued him. Neil Armstrong had been the first man on the Moon. Someone else would have to be the last. Thorpe wondered who that would be. If Halver Smith's suspicions were correct, the honor would go to upward of 100,000 souls. Would two of those be Thomas Thorpe and Amber Hastings? If they were, would anyone remember their names as long as they had remembered Neil Armstrong's?

He shook off the morbid thought and concentrated on the business at hand. Twice as they rode the slidewalk southeast they caught glimpses of others. The first time was when they came upon three scruffy men lounging in a side corridor. The trio watched them slide past without moving or speaking. A few minutes later the scouting party caught sight of a man and a woman hurrying away. Each encounter ratcheted up Thorpe's feeling of unease. Luna City had become a tomb, and it was too easy to let his imagination get the better of him.

They reached the landing field ten minutes after leaving the Grand Concourse. Thorpe put Bryant and Allison Nalley on watch while the rest of them suited up. He then waited with Barnard in the corridor while the two technicians slipped into their suits. The whole operation took fifteen minutes, and nothing untoward happened to interrupt it. Once encased in their suits, they searched out a surface lock and cycled through into the vacuum beyond.

The landing field reminded Thorpe of the salvage yard, except that the ships lined up neatly in multiple rows were new. All were jumpers—there were no true spacecraft in the lot—and they ranged in size from single-passenger models to buses seating up to eight. The dearth of larger machines was a further indication of the thoroughness with which the Luna government had converted the more capable jumpers into orbital craft.

A quick check of the nearest jumpers found each with full reaction tanks and sufficient antimatter charges for several flights. They chose one of the larger machines, and Bryant went to work bypassing the security locks on the instrument panel. Thorpe watched him as he worked; as power came on in the flight cabin, the young technician looked up and grinned.

"I learned to do this during my misspent youth," he explained.

"Remind me to write a note of appreciation to your parole officer."

"Ready to go," Bryant said, slipping into the pilot's seat. "Let's get them aboard."

Thorpe ordered everyone into the jumper. He and Amber took the third pair of web seats and strapped themselves down. Gazing out through the jumper's bubble in the direction of the surface lock, Thorpe was surprised to see three heads silhouetted against the light streaming through the lock window. Whoever they were, they seemed content to watch with their noses pressed against the armor glass. Their presence sent a shiver down Thorpe's spine.

The jumper lifted and heeled sharply over toward the east. As in all ballistic point-to-point travel, the engines fired for a few dozen seconds before shutting down. After that, they rose slowly under the influence of Luna's gravity. It took twenty minutes to reach the apex of their flight, after which they started down. The jumper fell to within half a kilometer of the Sea of Tranquility before its engines flared once again.

They grounded one hundred meters distant from the damaged freighter, which was itself located close to the southern edge of the monument's geodesic framework. After a series of hurried suit-integrity checks, they disembarked and moved alongside the ship that was intended to have been their savior.

The freighter was the *Neaptide*, Thorpe noted as he climbed the external accommodation ladder. He stepped into the emergency airlock halfway up the big sphere's side and waited for Amber and Barnard to join him before keying the lock to cycle. The main lock circuits proved to be inoperative, and he switched to the emergency override circuits. The damage to the airlock controls did not bother him. In fact, they would accept a great deal of internal damage so long as the engines were operable. All Thorpe really cared about was whether the ship could be lifted and contained sufficient fuel to make orbit. Landing it again was not his problem.

The airlock filled with pressure, and the inner door swung open to reveal a shambles. There was evidence of a battle royal having taken place everywhere. As soon as Thorpe removed his helmet, he could smell burned insulation and other less identifiable odors in the stale atmosphere. They moved up a ladder to the control room. The damage there was extensive. Every control seemed to have been smashed. Shards of glass lay underfoot on the steel deck and crunched as they walked on it. Here and there the deck and bulkheads still sported dark stains which Thorpe suspected were blood.

"What a mess," Amber said from beside him.

"Nothing to save in here," he said, surveying the destruction. "No wonder they declared her a complete write-off. When the mob didn't seize control in time, they must have taken out their frustrations in here."

"Does this mean we can't use her?"

He shrugged. "We could fly her from the engine room if that's intact. Remember, we only have to achieve orbit."

"Let's look at the engines, then."

The ship's engines were four decks down a long ladder that ran the entire length of the ship. As they slid down, Thorpe let his eyes scan those corridors they passed. Once again they found evidence of a frantic fight for control of the ship, a fight that everyone had lost. However, the damage in the passageways was not nearly as extensive as in the control room.

The engine room was spotless. Its brightwork was so shiny that it looked as if it had been wiped down that morning. The ship's engineer must have heard the commotion, Thorpe realized, and sealed himself in before the mob's arrival.

Thorpe jumped the last three meters to the deck and immediately moved to the engine-control panel. It was the work of a few minutes to bring the instruments online. However, it only took a second for him to realize that all their efforts had been in vain.

"Shit!"

"What's the matter?"

"The containment field is switched off. We haven't got any antimatter on board. Not even the tiniest microgram."

"Perhaps we can get some more."

"Where?" he asked. "Besides, if they shut down the containment toroid, you can bet they drained the reaction mass as well."

He quickly keyed for the displays that showed the ship's fuel state, and was not surprised when the reaction-mass reading came up zero. The tanks were as dry as the lunar plain outside. Some other ship had undoubtedly long since used *Neaptide*'s fuel and reaction mass in the evacuation.

"That does it. Let's get back to Luna City."

"Perhaps we can get more reaction mass, Thomas."

"Sure," he said. "And when we do, we'll need a tanker to get it here. Of course, if we had a tanker, we could use that to make orbit and forget this hulk."

It was a dejected group that climbed into the moonjumper and headed back west toward Luna City. Their ground track was the same as it had been coming out, even though their destination was different. After seeing the faces in the airlock window, Thorpe had recommended not going back to the landing field. Rather, they would set down near the salvage yard and return to the hotel through safe territory.

As the jumper followed its low ballistic trajectory back toward Luna City, Thorpe gazed out across one of the largest mares on Luna. It was hard to believe that the changeless terrain out there would very soon be smashed beyond recognition. Once again he was struck by a morbid thought. If they were unable to escape in time, it might be worth blasting off in a moonjumper just before Thunderstrike smashed into Farside. That way they would be able to view a few seconds of the Moon's destruction before it reached up to envelop them. He roughly put the thought out of his mind. Such thoughts bred defeatism, and it was far too early for that.

They reached the top of their trajectory and started down again. As Copernicus Crater came into sight, Thorpe's eyes searched out the straight line that was the Luna City mass driver. Something stirred deep within his brain at the sight. The thought never had a chance to form. At that moment, Amber let out a whoop that startled everyone in the jumper cabin.

"What's the matter?" Thorpe asked, mistaking the yell for one of fright.

"That's it!" Amber said, pointing excitedly out the bubble.

"That's what?"

"The mass driver! That's how we'll do it. We'll load ourselves into a cargo pod and shoot ourselves into space!"

Thorpe thought about it for a second. It would be risky and take a lot of work, but it ought to be possible. Cargo pods had never been designed as manned vehicles. At the least, a supply of oxygen and a radio would be needed, along with some method to protect the passengers against the brutal acceleration of launch. Still, they had eighty-four hours before Thunderstrike was due to arrive. With luck, it would be enough.

"The mass driver? Impossible!"

Feliz Dornier stared at Amber in horror. They were once again gathered in the Graysons' suite at the hotel. Amber had just explained her idea to them, and though Dornier's reaction had been the most vocal, he was not alone in his assessment.

"Why impossible, Doctor?" Amber asked.

"The mass driver accelerates its loads at thirty gravities! No human can survive that!"

"Thirty gravities peak, Dr. Dornier," Thorpe said. He had studied the mass driver's operation while looking into the economics of ice mining. "It can be turned down, you know."

"Turned down how far and still make escape velocity?"

Thorpe shrugged. "Perhaps as low as ten gees."

"That would still kill us."

"No, it wouldn't," Amber said. "Fighter pilots used to routinely take nine gees."

"Perhaps I am being selfish, but it would most certainly kill *me*, young lady. I'm not a young man any longer."

"There would be a risk," Amber agreed. "But there are acceleration drugs that we could use. If you are properly cushioned and drugged, there's a good chance that you would survive launch."

"Survive to do what? Drift in space until our air runs out?"

"That is a problem," Thorpe said. "We'll have to make sure that we have enough breathing gas on board to survive until rescue. We will also need a radio to differentiate our capsule from the debris that Thunderstrike's impact will throw up. We don't want the meteor-guard system to shoot us down."

"It beats being in Luna City when the comet arrives, don't you think?" Amber asked.

"She has you there, Feliz," Niels Grayson said.

Barnard nodded, as did several others.

"There is one problem," Dornier said, undeterred.

"What is that?"

"The mass driver is a secure facility. How are you going to get access to it?"

"Simple," Amber replied. "We tell John Malvan that we know his dirty little secret and we want to save ourselves."

"No, we don't," Thorpe said. "If it becomes known that we are converting cargo pods into escape pods, we'll be mobbed."

"Do we have the moral right to keep this to ourselves?" Margaret Grayson asked.

"Look," Thorpe growled, hating himself for it even as he said it, "not everyone is going to get off Luna. There are too many of us left to be evacuated. Those are facts. I wish we could take everyone along, but we can't. Therefore, we keep our escape route a secret long enough to allow us to use it."

"What if someone else comes up with the same idea?"

"Then we welcome them, show them where to find their own cargo pods, and help them all we can without retarding our own efforts."

"I agree," Niels Grayson said. "As distasteful as the facts are, we must still face them. That still leaves us with the problem of what we tell the authorities."

"The mirrors!" Amber said, snapping her fingers. "We'll tell Malvan we want the mass driver to launch the mirrors." She hurriedly explained the plan that she and Thorpe had discussed on their first visit to the salvage yard.

"He won't believe us," Barnard said. "The mirrors are at Farside Observatory. We're due to be evacuated in less than twelve hours."

"Not any longer," Grayson told him. "They announced that everyone should delay their arrival at the spaceport by twenty-four hours. They blamed 'technical delays' for the problem and assured us that there was still time to get away."

"When was this?"

"About two hours ago. I haven't had the chance to tell you."

"There's the answer," Amber continued. "We can tell them that we are using the extra time to fetch as many mirrors from Farside as we can. Remember, if the evacuation is lagging behind schedule, he won't care what we do. His only concern will be to keep the lid on as long as possible. If he can get us off his back by handing us the keys to the mass driver, he'll probably do it."

Grayson mulled the plan over for a long minute, then nodded. "It just might work."

"I know it will work," Amber insisted, still running on adrenaline. "Once we have access to the mass driver, we can begin converting a cargo pod in full view of God and everyone. They'll just think we're crazy."

"Two pods," Thorpe said. "There are fifteen of us. We'll need air tanks, radios, food, acceleration webbing, and God knows what else. We won't all fit into a single pod."

Amber sidled up to him and put her arm around him. Now that there was hope again after so many disappointments, she felt like celebrating. "All right. Make it two. Just as long as we go out in the same pod."

As Amber had predicted, the scam went off without problem. When Niels Grayson arrived at the head of his delegation of concerned astronomers, John Malvan greeted his shipmates like old friends. If he was disturbed by the fact that a cruel universe had sentenced them to death, he did not show it. Having spent the last several hours soothing thousands of angry evacuees, any remorse on Malvan's part could easily have been hidden by his harried expression. He was only too happy to provide the astronomers with the access code to the mass-driver control room.

What Thorpe saw at the spaceport convinced him that Halver Smith was right. As they passed through the cavern where they had registered for evacuation, they found it empty. By that time everyone still on Luna had received his or her evacuation priority. Those without priorities were people who, for reasons of their own, had decided to die with their world. What impressed Thorpe was the absence of police. Save for a squad at the entrance to the embarkation concourse, they were gone. Their sudden disappearance told him that essential personnel were being taken up to the ships in preparation to calling a halt. Whatever the deadline to get all ships out of orbit, it was approaching quickly.

They returned to the hotel and packed their bags. The corridor leading to the mass driver was a large one designed for cargo. It was barred by a large pressure door. Grayson keyed in the combination he had obtained from Malvan. The emergency door swung back to reveal a vast cavern beyond. The small band of refugees walked inside.

The cavern was a quarter kilometer long and half that wide. It reminded Thorpe of pictures he had seen of airplane factories. There was a long unsupported space a hundred meters tall. Hugging the overhead was a large traveling crane used to move heavy cargoes from one section to another. Around them they found empty pods stacked neatly in rows. At the opposite end of the cavern was a long conveyer ramp that disappeared upward. This was where filled pods were transferred to the mass driver. Once on the surface, the pods were loaded into the breech and accelerated into space on a massive magnetic field.

Thorpe, Amber, and Barnard walked to a personnel lift at one side of the cavern. They took the lift upward to the mass driver's control room, which was just below the surface. It reminded Amber of *The Big Eye*'s control room. Here, too, outside cameras allowed the operators to survey the entire line of the giant machine they controlled. Amber switched the view from one tower/accelerator ring combination to another. Everything seemed intact and operational. Next she powered up the control board using one of Grayson's combinations. A large screen came to life with a computer display showing the orbit a pod launched with the current settings would pursue.

"Can you run this?" Thorpe asked her.

She nodded. "After some study. That board over there is for power control. See, it shows an outline of the capacitor bank. This one controls the strength, duration, and timing of the pulses. Once I get the hang of it, I can reprogram for a minimum-acceleration launch."

"Good. We want a departure orbit which will swing us around Earth in order to maximize our chance of being picked up."

"I'll see what I can do," she said.

Thorpe left Amber poring over the controls and descended back into the cavern below. Programming the mass driver to orbit two pods in quick succession was the easy part. Now they had escape vehicles to prepare, vehicles that would keep them alive long enough for them to be rescued.

CHAPTER 41

The cargo pods were seven meters long and three meters in diameter. They were constructed of low-carbon steel rather than the special alloys that had been developed for space vehicles. In order for the mass driver to accelerate them, the pod hulls had to be made from a magnetic material. And though they looked like railroad tank cars bereft of wheels, the pods were actually sophisticated space vehicles in their own right. Each was equipped with a thruster system that was used for midcourse corrections and to keep the cylinder from tumbling in flight.

Pods came in three basic types. One was well-insulated and equipped with a refrigeration system able to keep cryogenic liquids cold for long periods. Another maintained Earth-normal pressures and temperature to keep seeds, pharmaceuticals, and other perishables from going bad. The third, and most common, was merely a gas-tight barrel into which all manner of bulk materials were loaded. The pods they found in the service cavern were all of the third, and simplest, type.

Thorpe climbed into one of the cylinders and was surprised at the interior room. He wondered briefly if all fifteen of them could be squeezed into a single container. He began mentally to block out the volumes they would need for breathing gas, water tanks, food, medicine, tools, waste disposal, and communications equipment. As he put each necessity into place, the volume available for people shrunk precipitously.

The largest space requirement by far was for the liquid oxygen they would boil off for breathing gas. The simple transport pods lacked both the heavy insulation and the refrigeration equipment of the cryogenic storage modules. As a result, they could expect to lose most of their oxygen to solar heating and boil off. He estimated that devoting half the pod to oxygen storage would give them a two-week supply. With everyone in a single pod, those two weeks would be cut to one. That alone, Thorpe decided, was reason enough to go with two pods.

In addition to oxygen storage, the passengers would need to be protected against launch acceleration. Thorpe considered salvaging acceleration couches from the nearby scrap yard but quickly discarded the idea. Not only would there be too much surface activity—thereby calling unwanted attention to themselves—the couches would take up too much room. A better approach would be to rig several nets across the cylinder and use them as acceleration cushions. Once in space, the nets could be stowed to increase the usable volume.

Thorpe reviewed his ideas with Neils Grayson, who had accompanied him inside the cylinder. Grayson reminded him that they would need portholes cut in the sides. With Thunderstrike's arrival imminent, neither man relished missing the excitement by sealing himself into a windowless steel can.

Following their discussion, the two adjourned to one of the offices that dotted the cavern's periphery. There they found a computer drafting station. During his tenure on *The Rock*, Thorpe had become fairly proficient at producing sketches of projects he had planned. Within two hours he had a full set of conversion blueprints for each of their makeshift spacecraft.

While he and Grayson planned, the other members of their party explored the cavern. The mass-driver complex proved to be a cornucopia of things a castaway might find useful. In addition to large stocks of lunar ice awaiting export, they discovered two giant flasks filled with liquid oxygen and liquid hydrogen. A storeroom yielded dozens of large rolls of heavy electrical cable, which they could use to weave their nets. From another storeroom came a stock of radio transmitters and electrical-generating equipment. Those would be turned into radio beacons to allow their rescuers to find the pods in the vastness of space.

After listening to the cavern's inventory, Thorpe organized the refugee astronomers into working parties. Four hours later the first interior partition was welded into place in one of the pods. Thorpe watched while several staffers manhandled a large piece of steel into the first pod. It took him a moment to realize that Niels Grayson was standing beside him.

"Hello, Niels. I didn't hear you come up."

"I'm not surprised. You look like you're about to drop."

"I'm all right."

"How long since you slept?"

"Thirty hours, I guess."

"More like forty, I would say. Why don't you curl up some-where? They can do without you for a few hours. Besides, you'll want to be chipper for the big show tomorrow."

Thorpe blinked in confusion. "What happens tomorrow?"

"You ought to remember. You're the one who set things in motion."

"Oh, yeah? *The Rock* intercepts Thunderstrike, doesn't it?"

"That it does."

"I must be more tired than I thought. I think I'll take you up on your suggestion. What about Amber? She's been awake as long as I have."

"No, she hasn't. She fell asleep while trying to decipher this damned complex's operating manual. I had her go into that little anteroom just off the manager's office."

"I guess I'll find a hole to crawl into as well. Wake me just before the crunch, or if anything bad happens."

"Will do."

Thorpe walked to an office he had noticed earlier. It had a table where he could stretch out and a door that could be closed. The latter requirement was the most important. His crew of ama-teur ship fitters was making more noise than he would have thought possible.

Thorpe came awake as a rough hand shook his shoulder.

"Time to wake up, Mr. Thorpe. The director wants you up in the control room. You'll have to hurry."

Thorpe opened his eyes. Jamie Bryant was looking down at him. He groaned and then struggled to a sitting position with his legs hanging over the edge of the table.

"How long have I been asleep?"

"Six hours. It's nearly 1000."

"How are the modifications coming?"

"Pretty well. We have the center bulkhead welded into both pods. We're installing a second bulkhead one meter in front of the first. We should be ready to pressure test the oxygen tanks in another hour or so."

"Two bulkheads?" Thorpe asked, still trying to clear his head. "Who ordered that?"

"It was Dr. Dornier's suggestion. He pointed out that we would be up to our armpits in liquid oxygen if a single bulkhead were to give way during launch. We plan to fill the space between the two with water. The water will freeze once we load the oxygen. The combination of steel and ice should make a strong barrier."

"What about expansion when the ice freezes?"

"We've taken care of that. We've glued Styrofoam blocks to the inside of the forward bulkhead. The ice will compress it as it freezes. Also, it will help insulate the tank."

Thorpe nodded. "Tell Dr. Dornier he had a good idea. It would be a shame to finish this trip as an icicle."

Thorpe got to his feet, stretched, and moved stiffly toward the door. He felt worse than before he had gone to sleep. If there was one consolation, it was Luna's gravity, which made a hard table as soft as any bed on Earth.

Niels Grayson and Amber were both in the mass driver's control room when he stepped from the lift.

"Morning, my love," he said, reaching to gather Amber in for a kiss.

She resisted his advance. "Not too close. My breath isn't anything to brag about this morning."

"Whose is?" he asked, kissing her anyway.

"Look at this, Thomas," Grayson said, gesturing toward a screen that had been tuned to a news broadcast.

The screen showed the familiar white fog of the comet's coma. Thorpe had imagined what the comet would look like as it approached Earth. He had had visions of a gossamer arch stretching from horizon to horizon. He could not have been more wrong. The comet was a lumpy ball of diffuse light that covered a patch of sky ten times the diameter of a full moon. Earth had entered the comet's tail three weeks earlier, and there were few less flattering vantage points from which to view a comet than by staring straight up its ass.

Perihelion passage had seen the coma grow perceptibly thicker. Thunderstrike's ice plains must have boiled furiously during the close approach. In the process the nucleus had added millions of tons of water vapor, gas, and dust to the surrounding cloud. Hidden somewhere in that cloud, Thorpe knew, were two solid masses, each of which was fast closing with the other. In a matter of seconds there would only be the one.

He listened in silence to a garrulous announcer explain for the twentieth time what was about to happen. Then an official-sounding voice announced that the time was one minute to impact. Thorpe waited without breathing as the voice continued to mark off the final seconds. Suddenly the screen went blank as an overpowering brilliance blossomed at the center of the coma. The light slowly dimmed as it expanded from a dimensionless spark. Then the rapidly expanding flood of radiance suffused the whole coma, making it glow like an old-fashioned fluorescent lamp. Slowly, minute by minute, the glow faded, dimming finally to something approaching its former brightness. In its heart a tiny fire continued to burn with furious abandon.

"Well, I guess that's that," Thorpe said, hoping that neither Grayson nor Amber would notice the quaver in his voice. "How are you coming with the launch programming, Amber?"

"I should have it shortly," Amber replied. "According to the manual, we'll have to go out at a minimum of ten gees if we hope to achieve Luna escape velocity."

"Then ten gees it is."

"How goes it on the floor?"

"Bryant reports that we're on schedule. I guess I'd better get down there to check things out. See you for lunch?"

"Sure," she said.

He glanced at the screen and gestured at the still-glowing point of light in the coma's center. "I guess that means Thunder-strike is definitely on its way. One thing's for sure. We don't want to be here when it arrives."

Eight hours later they were testing the habitat secion of the converted pods for pressure integrity. The test consisted of sealing one of their people into the pod and then slowly bringing up the pressure to three standard atmospheres. The shut-ins then listened for leaks—using their eardrums to sense minute changes in pressure rather than actually hearing them.

"No leaks, Mr. Thorpe," Jamie Bryant reported after half an hour.

"No leaks at all?"

"No, sir. We sprayed soap solution around the portholes and all the new fittings. No fizzes."

"Very well. Tell your caulkers that they did a good job. Now, let's depressurize, power up the overhead crane, and get that first pod to the loading docks. I want the oxygen tank chilled for one hour before you actually put liquid in it. We've come too far to thermal shock our welds."

"One hour chilldown before filling. Yes, sir!" The technician who had become Thorpe's de facto assistant moved off to issue the orders.

"How long before we can launch?" Niels Grayson asked.

"Give us another couple of hours after we top off the oxygen tanks," Thorpe said. "The longer we let them cold soak, the more gas volume we can store."

"I'll have the people start gathering up their things. We'll want them stowed through the launch."

"Damned right!" Thorpe said. "At ten gees, anything loose will bounce around like a shot. We'll need everything doubly tied down before we can—"

Thorpe never had a chance to finish his sentence. At that moment Margaret Grayson appeared from inside the makeshift kitchen they had set up in one of the offices along the cavern periphery. The cavern's acoustics were not the best, and it took a moment for Thorpe to realize what it was that she was yelling. When he finally did, it was like being punched in the stomach.

There was a riot at the spaceport!

The small cubicle was not large enough for everyone. Nevertheless, nine bodies squeezed inside. Margaret was watching the news on a small screen in the corner. The local station had been broadcasting commentary concerning *The Rock*'s collision with the comet nucleus. They had interrupted to report a disturbance at the Luna City Spaceport. As Thorpe and the others arrived, the scene shifted to a reporter who was crouching behind a pillar. The reporter's voice was a hushed whisper as he explained what was going on.

"The firing began two minutes ago, Mary Ann. Eyewitnesses say that several youths attempted to force the checkpoint at the departure concourse. Who fired the first shots is unknown. All we do know is that there is a gun battle going on up the ramp and around the corner from here. I can hear occasional small popping noises, punctuated by loud bangs. These latter are from police shotguns, I believe. There was complete panic among the citizens waiting to be evacuated, although that seems to have been brought under control. You can see the indecision on the people's faces. Many want to flee, but they are also afraid of missing their ships. The firing has died down a bit now. Perhaps it is about over. Wait a second! I can see people running down the ramp now. My God, they've got guns and they're coming this way——!"

The screen and every other light in the cavern went dark. Thorpe looked around as cries of alarm erupted from his team. But in a few seconds the emergency lights began to come on.

"Everyone keep calm. Power will be restored momentarily." Even as he said it, he knew it was not true. On Luna, electrical power was as essential to life as oxygen. The Luna City power grid had been built quadruply redundant to prevent even momentary outages. It required a failure more major than he cared to think about to plunge the mass-driver complex into night.

Amber's voice echoed through the darkened cavern. "Tom! Come here, I need you."

Thorpe fought his way out of the press of bodies and found her standing on a catwalk that ringed the cavern's upper walls. As soon as she saw him, she turned and stepped through the door that led to the main control room. He hurried to a ladder and climbed to the catwalk. A few seconds later he joined Amber in the darkened control room.

"The power's off all over the city," she said without preamble.

"Are you sure?"

"As soon as the lights failed, I called several public screens. Everything shows emergency lighting."

"The power plant?"

"It has to be."

"I wonder what happened."

She shrugged. "Either the government cut the power to stop the riot, or else someone has done something to damage the power plant."

"If it had been the government, the lights would have been back on by now."

"Agreed," she said. "That means that it must be the rioters. They probably coordinated the attack at the spaceport with one on the power plant. Maybe they thought they could blackmail the authorities into letting them board a ship."

"Switch on the outside cameras. Let's see what's going on at the spaceport."

Amber keyed for an external view on a screen that was powered off the emergency circuits. At first everything seemed normal. As they watched, flame erupted from the tail of one of the

ferries on the opposite side of the wide plain. The ship rose
slowly into the black sky, heeled over, and disappeared from the
picture. A moment later a second ship followed it. Then more
and more ships lifted and disappeared into the black sky, until
there was no longer any doubt.

The authorities were abandoning their posts. The evacuation
was over.

"Well, I'll be damned!" Thorpe growled as he realized what
was happening.

"I never thought they'd do it," Amber said, uncomprehend-
ing. "I suppose I knew it would happen, but *I never thought they
would do it!*"

The two looked at each other for long seconds. So far they
were alone in the control room. Only they were aware of what
was happening.

"Who's going to tell them?" Amber asked, inclining her head
to indicate the cavern where the rest of their party was waiting.

"I will. I think we'd better launch as soon as we can get
loaded."

Amber put the back of her hand to her mouth and stared at
him wide-eyed. "Oh, no!"

"What's the matter?"

"We *can't* launch! There are warning signs all over about
being careful not to leave the capacitor bank fully charged for
long periods. Apparently that can damage them. I planned to
charge them just before launch."

"We're out of power? We don't have any at all?"

"Not enough to achieve orbit," Amber said. "If we try to
launch with what's left in the capacitors, we'll drill a hole in
some ring wall on the way out!"

Thorpe gathered everyone together in the service cavern. They
took the news of their abandonment well. Whether that was because they had expected it or because their exertions over the past
week had worn them down, he was not sure. Nor was their reaction to the news concerning their lack of power what he had
anticipated. Rather than blame Amber for not charging the capacitors sooner, most took that latest hurdle in stride.

"Maybe the power plant can be brought back online," Allison
Nalley said.

"Unlikely," Thorpe replied, explaining his and Amber's theory about what had happened. "It was probably a bomb. In any event, the power generators are on the other side of the city. We don't want to alert anyone to what we're planning."

"We've got lights," Jamie Bryant pointed out. "What sort of emergency system does the mass driver have?"

Thorpe frowned. The thought that there might be a source other than city power to charge the capacitors had not occurred to him. "What about it, Amber?"

"I saw a reference to emergency power in the operating procedures," she mused. "I didn't read it, though."

"It's easy enough to find out," Thorpe replied. He directed the younger staffers to move the first of the pods to where it could be loaded with liquid oxygen while he, Amber, Grayson, and Dornier adjourned to the control room. They clambered up the ladder to the catwalk, and from there headed back through the gloomy corridors to the control room. Amber sat in front of the big control screen and keyed for the instructions. A long list of options flashed on the screen. Near the bottom was a section on emergency-power procedures. She keyed for it and was soon reading instructions on what to do in the event city power was lost.

"This doesn't say anything about launching during a power outage," she said after scanning the first several screens of data. "Mostly it talks about keeping the cryogenic storage tanks and other essential equipment operating."

"All that equipment takes a certain amount of power," Dornier said as he read over Amber's shoulder. "Perhaps we can divert that to the capacitors and accumulate sufficient charge for a launch."

Grayson gestured impatiently at the screen. "Put up the power-system schematic."

It took a few minutes for Amber to search out the system's electrical schematics and find the one she wanted. Soon, however, she had the mass driver's power circuits displayed as a series of multicolored, glowing lines. Normal circuits were displayed in green, mass-driver control circuitry in yellow, and emergency-power components in red.

As Thorpe had suspected, the lights and other low power devices were all fed from the city's emergency power system. They did not interconnect with the complex's machinery at all. Mass-driver essential equipment was powered by a small fusion generator located two levels below the control room. The generator had never been intended to provide power for a launch. Still, the complex's essential equipment drew enough power that the generator had to be fairly large to supply it. In time, it would also charge the capacitors.

Dr. Dornier immediately set out to calculate how long it would take. When he finished, he looked up at the others and said, "I make it six hours to full charge, possibly as little as four hours to accumulate enough energy for a launch. That last is a bare minimum, and I wouldn't trust it too far."

"Then we're back in business," Thorpe said. "We'll begin charging the capacitors immediately and load the first pod while we're waiting."

"You realize, of course," Grayson said, "that the first launch will alert everyone that the mass driver is still operating. How long do you think it will take them to figure out that this is their last chance to get off Luna?"

"Maybe they'll think it's a late cargo launch."

"So what? They'll still see it as their last chance. This place will be mobbed within minutes. What chance of getting the second pod off then?"

"Have you a better suggestion?"

"I've already made it. Everyone should go in the first pod."

"Damn it, Niels, we've been all through that. We aren't carrying enough oxygen. We'd be asphyxiated within a week."

"You don't know that," Grayson responded. "The boil-off rates are nothing more than a guess. The oxygen may last twice as long as we think."

"Or half as long."

"We may be overlooking something here," Dornier said. "Do we even have time for a second launch before Thunderstrike gets here?"

Grayson turned to him. "You said that it would take six hours to accumulate each charge, twelve hours total. That leaves a good ten hours to spare before the comet arrives."

Dornier nodded. "Before it *arrives*. But how long before that must we launch to insure that we can be clear of the explosion? Maybe we don't have time for the second pod to get far enough away to be safe."

Grayson turned to Amber. "It's your discovery. Will we be able to get to a safe distance if we launch ten hours before impact?"

She shrugged. "Define 'safe distance' where sixty million billion tons of ice are concerned. Hell, we could be sitting in the deepest cave on Earth and still not be safe. If ten hours is all we have, then it will have to do."

"Look," Thorpe said, tiring of what was threatening to become an academic discussion, "we're wasting time. Sticking with two pods isn't something I prefer doing, it's something that is necessary! We'll need some time to cross-connect the wiring. I propose that we shoot our first pod no later than eight hours from now, our second as soon after as we can manage."

"And how do you propose keeping the mob from beating down the door while the capacitors are charging?" Dornier asked.

"We've got eight hours to figure something out. In the meantime, let's get those capacitors charging so we can get the hell out of here!"

CHAPTER 42

Harold Barnes was more frightened than he had ever been in his entire life. Six months earlier it had seemed so simple when he had given up his evacuation priority to stay in Luna City until the very end. The decision had been an easy one. By staying behind, Barnes hoped to become a very rich man.

The idea had first come to him shortly after Prime Minister Hobart had capitulated to the terrestrials' demand that Luna allow the Avalon Option to proceed. Barnes's position as one of the prime minister's unofficial advisors had afforded him an early look at the problems of evacuating Luna. Evacuating the Moon involved far more than merely transporting its people to Earth. There was also the matter of dealing with the disruption to their lives. Luna's people had worked for generations to turn their airless world into a home for their children. In the process they had accumulated considerable wealth. And while wealth is often measured as patterns of ones and zeros in a bank computer, there was still plenty in the form of possessions that were too bulky to load on the ships.

The personal-possessions allotment for each refugee was five kilograms of mass or half a cubic meter of volume, whichever was less. These were sufficient for the clothes on a person's back and a few family mementos. Most Lunarians had been forced to abandon prized possessions and, under the agreement with Earth, were entitled to be compensated for the loss. One of the first acts of the Republic following the public announcement of the Avalon Option had been to establish a system for authorizing compensation for property losses.

The first step in the process was for an individual seeking compensation to file a claim with his local branch of the Bank of Luna. For most items the claim was granted without further effort. For certain high-value properties, such as works of art, gold, and other precious substances, an appraisal was required. The petitioner was then required to deliver the item in question to a central clearinghouse where teams of appraisers established the item's fair market value.

Once an item was appraised, the owner was credited with its value in his evacuation account on Earth. He then surrendered the item to the bank to prevent a second claim being made. That precaution was primarily necessary for the gold bullion and other items that were not individually identifiable. Even though it was not necessary, paintings, sculptures, and other works of art were handled in the same way.

A month before the comet was due to arrive, Harold Barnes had put his plan into motion. He used his influence to obtain launch rights for six cargo pods, which he loaded with the gleanings from the bank's storerooms. Only the most valuable items were loaded into the cargo pods. Along with the works of art and rare collections, he piled several tons of precious metals into the pods. Barnes had then watched each of the pods leap across the gaps in the accelerator towers to disappear into the black sky.

And only he knew the parameters of their orbits!

It had then been a matter of waiting his turn for evacuation. He had originally been assigned to go out a week before the comet's arrival, but had then been notified that there would be a two-day delay. Two days had turned into four. Then had come the nerve-wracking ordeal of standing in line for more than a day while he waited his turn to board.

He had finally had the debarkation lock in sight when an organized group of armed men had tried to crash through Security. Like thousands of others, Barnes had cowered on the floor, shivering, as the bullets flew overhead. He had expected the security forces to make short work of their attackers, but they had not. At the moment the lights had failed, the attackers had rushed the security barrier, only to discover that the defenders had fled. Their whoops of triumph had turned into screams of frustration when the ground-to-orbit craft had begun to lift off one after another. And inside the terminal, Harold Barnes had found himself abandoned within fifty meters of his goal.

Afterward, Barnes had gravitated toward the transit hall. That, at least, had windows to let in sunlight. He was not the only one. More than a thousand people packed the dome shoulder to shoulder as they milled about in confusion. Barnes found a bare spot near one of the observation windows and collapsed into it. He was slowly beginning to realize that valuable as they were, those six cylinders full of riches were not worth his life.

"Hey, citizen! How about moving your legs so someone else can sit down?"

Barnes looked up listlessly at the young punk who stood over him. There seemed to be more of them than ever. Just a few months ago no such dreg would have dared talk to him, let alone with such insolence. Now they swaggered about as though they owned the Moon! Barnes thought of complaining, but decided not to make a point of it. Around them hundreds of others sat hugging knees and rocking in quiet desperation. Some people sobbed, others cursed, but mostly they sat in silence. It had been hours since they had lost all hope of rescue, and now there was nothing to do but wait for the end.

"Hey!" someone yelled. "What's that?"

Barnes glanced toward the view window. For an instant he saw nothing. Then he noticed a cylinder traversing the mass-driver towers. He snapped his head around to look through the window to his left. He was just in time to see the cylinder leap the gap between two towers and disappear into the distance. It had still been accelerating as it went. Of that, Barnes was sure!

There was a sudden buzz in the observation dome as those who had seen it told their neighbors who had not. The buzz quickly grew to a roar as the same idea occurred to nearly a thousand people simultaneously. Like so many of the others,

Harold Barnes found himself on his feet, screaming at the top of his lungs. Whether the scream was in rage or relief, even he could not have said. His lips were turned upward in a snarl that belonged more to a wolf than a man!

"They're off!" Amber said, watching the dwindling pod on the screen inside the mass driver's control room. The displays showed a near-perfect launch. The pod's velocity as it exited the last of the launch towers had been 3.2 kilometers per second, comfortably above escape velocity. Its orbit showed it sweeping around low behind Earth before climbing up toward the Moon once more. The pod would never complete that orbital track. When they passed behind Earth, the pod's occupants would use their limited supply of maneuvering fuel to slow down and go into a highly elliptical orbit around Earth. After that they would wait for either rescue or the end of their oxygen supply.

"How much power did we use?" Thorpe asked from beside her.

"Eighty-five percent of full charge," she reported. "That means we can be back to full power in five hours."

"Push it all you can. I'm going down to check our defenses."

Up until then they had relied for security on the fact that no one knew that they were inside the mass-driver complex. Thorpe was sure that lack of knowledge had been changed by their first launch. Hundreds must have seen the pod accelerate past the transit hall. Soon thousands would know. And for people whose last hope of escape had just vanished, the reminder that there was still a way off Luna would be a revelation from on high. Thorpe had no doubt that they would soon have visitors. The only question was, when?

The access route that had appeared the most difficult to defend had turned out to be the easiest. The main corridor from Luna City was one of the city's major thoroughfares. As wide as a two-lane highway on Earth, with a vertical dimension of four meters, the corridor was the main route through which ice cargoes and other bulk materials were shipped to the mass driver.

All corridors on Luna were interrupted every few hundred meters by emergency pressure doors, designed to limit the damage in case of a blowout. As they had at the hotel, the observatory's technicians had quickly fooled two adjacent sets of doors into closing. The stretch they sealed off was one with a branch corridor leading to a surface airlock. After closing and welding the doors to their frames, a vacuum-suited technician then disconnected the safety devices that kept the airlock's doors from being opened simultaneously. He then opened the inner door, wedged it open with an iron bar, and punched to have the outer door cycle. The resulting hurricane of escaping air smashed the outer door and nearly swept the technician out with it.

In normal times the sudden decompression of an entire section of main corridor would have set alarms to sounding all over the city. Perhaps it still did. There was no one to answer the alarms. The double barrier with vacuum in between would slow down any intruders. Whether it would slow them enough to allow the astronomers to make their getaway was a question no one could answer.

Before closing the emergency pressure doors, Thorpe had had the corridor cameras rewired to show the city side of the barrier. Fifteen minutes after Pod One was launched, Amber notified him via hand radio that people were milling about on the opposite side.

"What are they doing?" he asked.

"Nothing. They look confused."

"Good, let's hope they stay that way!"

As he continued his tour of inspection, he tried not to visualize the scene on the other side of the barrier. If he could have seen the crowds of desperate people pounding their fists against the barrier, it would have been too easy to wonder what right he had to deny them their only possibility of escape. What he was doing was necessary, but it did not make Thorpe like himself any better.

The next stop on his tour was a maintenance corridor just under the breech end of the mass driver. There, too, they had rigged the airlock—they had latched the inner airlock door open after mounting a camera outside to cover that approach. With the inner door open, the outer door, held shut by several thousand kilos of force, could not be forced. One of the technicians was watching the monitor that showed him the surface. He was wearing his vacuum suit, with his helmet hanging from its carrying strap in front of his chest.

"Any movement?"

"Not yet, Mr. Thorpe."

"Keep an eye out. It won't be long. Once they discover the

inner door is open, they may try to break the safety port. Make sure the decompression doesn't catch you on the wrong side of the emergency door. We won't have time to rescue you."

"Understood," the technician, a young Lunarian named Albert Segovia, replied.

"Tom!"

"Yes, Amber."

"I see men in vacuum suits outside our front door. They have something with them. I think it's a portable airlock. They're going to depressurize the section in front of our barrier and see if they can't penetrate it."

"Smart," he replied. "Keep me informed as to their progress. How's the charging going?"

"On schedule, maybe a little ahead. I've turned off everything I can and am using what little city power we're getting to help."

"Good thinking. I'll be in the cavern if you need me."

Thorpe glanced at his wrist chronometer. It had been twenty-five minutes since they had launched Pod One—they had more than four hours to go!

The second pod was illuminated by two lone work lights, both of which operated from battery. All other power was being diverted to the capacitors. They had loaded the liquid oxygen hours earlier, and the rear end of the capsule glistened with a thick layer of frost as the humidity from the air condensed and then froze on the cold surface. Jamie Bryant periodically wrapped a cable around the hull and scraped the frost away. Thorpe was afraid that if they let it get too thick, it would clip one of the launching rings on takeoff and cause the pod to tumble.

"How are things going?" he asked Bryant.

"We're all set to send it up into the breech. When should we load up?"

"Not for a while yet. There's not much the seven of us can do against that mob if they get in, but there's nothing we can do if we are sealed inside of this thing. Are you listening to the radio?"

Bryant nodded.

"Listen for my order to don suits, then do it as quickly as you can. Where are Niels and Margaret?"

Bryant hooked his thumb toward the pod. "Securing the cargo inside. We didn't weld nearly enough padeyes to the hull as we should have. They're having trouble finding places to tie things down."

"I'm sure there are a hundred things we could have done better," Thorpe replied. "We did all we had time for."

"Uh, Thomas . . ."

"Yes?"

"I've been wondering. What happens if that mob gets in here?"

"They will tear us limb from limb, then fight over who is to get the pod, and probably destroy it in the process."

"And if they realize they can't get in? What will they do?"

"If it were me out there, and I was really frustrated, I think I'd try to damage the mass driver and stop the launch. Misery loves company, you know."

"What a happy thought!"

Thorpe gave him a quick smile of reassurance. "Let's hope they don't think of it."

Three hours later it was obvious that they would not have to think of it. The crowd in the main corridor had gone efficiently to work on erecting their portable airlock, and had managed to pump down the section of corridor in front of the barrier. The whole operation had taken a little more than ninety minutes. As one group worked, more and more had disappeared back up the corridor. Presumably they had gone to get their suits, because a like number of vacuum-suited individuals showed up several minutes later.

If Thorpe had been working to break through the barrier, he would have closed another pressure door upstream of the break, then vented the corridor to space. That would have eliminated the need to set up the bulky emergency airlock. Of course, it would also have trapped everyone on the city side of the newly closed pressure door, leaving access only to those vacsuited individuals who took part in the breakthrough. The crowd, Thorpe suspected, had not been willing to do it the fast way.

The penetration effort hit a roadblock when they discovered that the pressure door would not open even when the differential had been removed. That slowed them another fifteen minutes while they conferred on the opposite side of the emergency airlock. The airlock was made of a translucent material that allowed shapes to be discerned but hid the details from Thorpe's cameras. The gloom of the emergency lighting did not help matters, either.

The reason for the delay became obvious when the corridor

camera suddenly failed, and a few seconds later, a distant *whump!* was heard through the cavern walls. The first barrier door had been blown with explosives.

"It won't be long now, people. Into your suits! Quickly!"

Thorpe had already taken the precaution of putting his own on. It limited his mobility, but would save his life if the crowd in the corridor managed to vent the complex to space. The service cavern was of a size where compartmentalization was not feasible. If the pressure doors in the corridors were breached, the entire volume would undergo explosive decompression.

He hurried to the control room. "How long until we have enough power to launch?"

"We still need ninety minutes to full charge," Amber said. She, too, had her suit on and was carrying her helmet.

"We aren't going to have the time for a full charge. What's the earliest we could launch, assuming nothing goes wrong?"

"Twenty-five minutes," she reported. "That will barely get us over the curb."

"The curb" was Luna's escape velocity. A ship that launched with just above Luna's 2.38-kilometers-per-second escape velocity was said to have "coasted over the curb." It would nearly halt in space before crossing over into Earth's gravity field, and then begin its long fall toward the larger planet.

"All right," he said. "Set the controls for launch in thirty minutes, then get to the pod."

"We ought to have more margin," she warned.

"We don't have the time. Now do as I say, damn it!"

"Yes, Thomas. I'll be on my way in five minutes."

Thorpe next checked with Segovia. "Anything?"

"I'm not sure. I think I saw a shadow cross my field of view a few minutes ago."

"Where?" Thorpe asked.

"Right there!" he said, pointing to the lower edge of the screen. The Sun was behind the camera, and if someone had crossed behind it, their long shadow might well have intruded into the field of view.

Thorpe was thinking about what to do when the screen went blank.

"We're sure now!" he said. "Get to the pod. I'll look this over."

As Segovia raced down the corridor, Thorpe edged forward,

stepping over the raised coaming of the emergency pressure door just inside the airlock. He cautiously peeked around the airlock coaming until he could see the small ten-centimeter window set in the outer door. Beyond it was the bright sunlight of the lunar plain. Suddenly, there was a shadow across the window, as if someone were standing in front of it. Then the shadow went away to reveal a toroidal object with wires extending from it plastered to the outside of the glass.

Thorpe lunged backward, tripping over the pressure-door coaming just as the glass pane exploded inward and a hurricane of air rushed past him. The hurricane lasted for just an instant as the pressure door fired its explosive charge and slammed out of its recess in the wall to cover the corridor. As it did so, it missed Thorpe's boot by one centimeter. He gazed at it for a second and shivered. Pressure doors were designed to close regardless of what they found in their way. Had his leg been in the door, it would have been amputated.

He got to his feet and stepped forward to look at the door. The invaders were left with two choices. They could unlatch the inner door, close it, and pressurize the space between, which would allow them to open the emergency door. Or else they could blast it open with explosives, venting the mass-driver complex to vacuum.

"Helmets on, people!" he ordered into his radio. "Acknowledge."

He waited until he received the weirdly echoing responses that were the result of transmitting inside a cave, then put his own helmet on.

Five minutes later he was back at the pod. All six of his people were already there.

"Let's get on board. I'll stay outside to operate the winch."

When a pod was ready for launch, an automatic loading system sent it upward through an airlock and into the breech mechanism of the big electromagnetic cannon. Since the mechanism was automatic, anyone who initiated the sequence had less than thirty seconds to cross the cavern, clamber aboard, and seal the hatch behind him before they were positioned in the launcher. Without his vacuum suit, it would have been easy. With it, there was a chance that he would not be able to make it.

"Ready, Tom," Amber reported to him. She was leaning out of the pod, watching him. He moved to the nearest computer terminal and punched the control that started the sequence. Next, he bounded back toward the pod as the automatic hoist reached down to grab hold of it with long, flexible arms.

He made it with five seconds to spare, diving headfirst through the pod hatch just as it was upended and carried toward the roof access tunnel. Inside he lay on the acceleration net they had woven from electrical cable. He helped Amber secure the makeshift hatch from the inside and then lay down on the net to catch his breath.

They heard the explosion just as the pod was entering the equipment lock that would transfer them to the surface.

Thorpe turned his head to look at Amber lying beside him. "Well, one group or the other has managed to punch through. How many minutes to launch?"

"Six," she replied.

"How difficult will it be for them to cancel our launch?"

"They can't," she said, shaking her head inside the helmet. "I put everything on priority. They'd need the password to get in and stop us."

"And what is the password?"

"Sesquicentennial," she said with a laugh.

"That ought to do it. Can they smash the equipment in the control room and stop us?"

"Only if they get at the computer one level down. That door is armored."

"They've got explosives."

"I hope they won't think of it until too late."

Once through the airlock, the rest of the loading sequence took thirty seconds. They found themselves resting in a cradle that aligned the pod with a long series of coils. The structure was not solid, however, and Niels Grayson reported that he could see sunlit ground beyond the braces of the breech accelerator.

They waited in silence for two minutes. Suddenly, Niels reported that he could see figures moving outside.

"Oh, my God, Thomas! They're climbing up through the structure. They can see the pod."

"Keep calm. How long now, Amber?"

"Two minutes twelve seconds," she reported through clenched teeth.

"Tell me when they arrive," Thorpe said. His brain was racing, trying to think of what he could do. Finally, he was struck with an idea. "Quick, everyone, switch to Channel Seven. When they get close enough to see you through the port, Niels, signal that your radio is out."

There was a series of clicks as each of them changed to one of the special-purpose channels that were hardly ever used for communications.

"They're here," Grayson reported a moment later. There were pounding noises on the side of the pod. Then one of the vacsuited figures leaned close to look in the darkened port. "They see me."

"Signal that your radio is out."

"I am. He seems agitated. I'm signaling that I don't understand . . . Now he's telling me to come out with hand signals . . . I'm sending back that I don't understand . . . Wait, he's disappeared."

"How long?"

"Ninety seconds."

"Is there anything out there that will tell them we're about to launch?"

"I don't think so."

"He's back," Grayson reported. "He just stuck something to the port. It looks like a doughnut, with thick wires extending outward. He's signaling me to come out again, pointing at the object and making hand gestures. I can't quite make it out."

"I can," Thorpe said. "He's telling us to come out or else he'll blow us up. Start unstrapping, then move up one net. Can he see anyone else?"

"No." The portholes were just in front of the pod's midpoint, near the rear bulkhead. Grayson had claimed the window seat by right of seniority. Thorpe heard him rather than saw him as he moved slowly off the net and clambered forward as though he were heading for the hatch.

"How long?" Thorpe asked.

"Thirty seconds."

"Make sure you are secure," he warned Grayson. "Now only one worry to go."

"What's that?"

"Will they have time to set that thing off when we begin to move, and if not, will the magnetic field induce enough current in the lead wires to set it off?"

There was nothing to say to that. Amber began counting off the seconds until launch. The pod suddenly echoed with a loud banging noise as those outside increased their demands that they come out. Amber reached five and Thorpe held his breath.

He was about to comment that her chronometer must be slow when a fist smashed into his entire body. That was the last he remembered for a long time.

CHAPTER 43

Thorpe woke to the feel of a wet cloth on his forehead. He lay there for a moment, luxuriating in the sensation. He opened his eyes to see Amber's face hanging over him. Concerned blue eyes searched his features.

"How long have I been out?"

"About two hours," she said. "We've been worried about you."

He took a deep breath. The movement caused a grating sensation inside his chest. He also noticed for the first time that his neck muscles were stiff, as was his right knee. "How are the others?"

"Niels has two broken ribs. Apparently, he was still strapping himself down when the electromagnets kicked in. We got him out of his suit and taped up. Jamie sprained his shoulder. Margaret tore some ligaments. Albert and I have a few sore muscles and bruises where the nets cut into us. Allison is fine. All in all, not a bad launch."

"Did we make escape velocity?" he asked. It had suddenly occurred to him that the minor casualties might be an indication that the launch had been too soft and they had failed to achieve orbit.

"I think so," Amber replied as she folded the cloth and pressed the clean side to his forehead. "We seem to be rising more slowly than we were, but we're still rising. I think we'll make it over the curb. Care to see?"

"Indeed I do!"

Thorpe sat up and unhooked the crude restraining strap that had secured him to the net. As he did so, he noticed a few more aches and pains, but they were minor compared to the sudden throbbing that started in his head and threatened to spread down his neck. He wondered if the launch could have torn his brain from its anchor points, leaving it to rattle around inside his skull.

Amber noticed his sudden grimace. "Hurt?"

He tried to nod, but thought better of it. "It's like an anvil going off in my skull."

"Hardly surprising," she said. She handed him two white pills and a drinking bulb. "You've got a nasty bruise on the side of your head. The padding in your helmet must be thin there."

He swallowed the pills with a quick gulp of tepid water. After a few minutes he moved gingerly, pulling himself to where the acceleration net had been unhooked from one of its anchor points. The three other nets had likewise been unhooked, yielding a clear passage to the cluttered rear bulkhead. He noted that the air in the compartment was very dry. Each breath irritated his nasal passages. The rear bulkhead was covered with a thin layer of frost, giving visual evidence of where all the humidity had gone.

Margaret Grayson was huddled next to her husband on the net directly below the one he and Amber shared. One level down, Jamie Bryant, Albert Segovia, and Allison Nalley nodded to him as he floated past their perch. The arrangement was not as it had been during the launch, a further indication of how long he had been unconscious.

The interior lights were on, transforming the viewport into a dull mirror. As he gazed at his own reflection, he noted that his hair was plastered down into a dark mass on the right side. He moved his gauntleted hand up to touch the spot, and was rewarded with a quick flash of pain. He realized that he had been lucky not to have split his skull open. To do that much damage, his helmet must have hit the bulkhead sometime during the launch.

"Mind if I turn off the lights?" he asked. When no one objected, he reached for the switch that had been one of the last items installed in the compartment.

The canister was steady in space, he noted, held there by occasional bursts from its attitude-control jets. He could see some vapor emanating from the tail. Whether that was from the jets or from oxygen tank boil off, he could not tell. The canister's attitude was such that Luna was visible through two of the four viewports. Immediately after launch, they had been moving back along the Moon's orbital track with a velocity of some 9000 kilometers per hour. As the canister climbed, it had been slowed by gravity—Luna's last attempt to claim six more victims for the coming cataclysm. After several minutes spent staring at the Moon, Thorpe thought he could detect a slow dwindling of its diameter. They were still rising, and far enough from Luna that it appeared that they would indeed escape its influence.

Having assured himself that they would not fall back, Thorpe let the other features of the scene seep into his consciousness. The sight, he realized, was decidedly odd. Space was no longer its normal midnight-black. It had taken on a faint milk-white radiance, making Luna appear to be a dull pearl set against pale ivory. He puzzled over the effect for a moment before realizing that they were looking at Thunderstrike's coma from the inside. At more than a million kilometers in radius, the coma preceded the comet nucleus by several hours. Apparently, its leading edge had swept past them while Thorpe had been unconscious.

Thorpe turned and squinted in the direction of Sol, which was ninety degrees from Luna in the sky. He was surprised to see that the Sun had a faint ring around it. Normally in vacuum, it had the appearance of an incandescent light bulb. With the majority of the comet's coma between it and Luna, the Sun had begun to take on the appearance it had during a hazy day on Earth. Gazing toward the Sun did not help his headache. He looked away quickly, trying to find Earth. It must be out of sight above them, he decided. He then turned back toward Luna. The Moon was definitely smaller than it had been when he first looked at it. Since their path took them back along Luna's orbit, each hour they climbed gave them a better view of the small doomed world. Their vantage point showed them fully one-quarter of Farside, with Mare Crisium and Mare Smythii directly beneath them. Copernicus Crater and Luna City were almost out of sight behind the western limb of the Moon.

Thorpe turned around in the cramped quarters and quickly let his gaze scan the other three viewports. He then pulled himself to the one through which Niels Grayson had pantomimed at the poor bastard who had been unlucky enough to be inside the mass driver breech when they had launched. Thorpe did not know what effect the sudden surging magnetic field would have had on the interloper, but suspected that it had not been good.

The small, yellow explosive charge of the type miners used for seismic testing was still attached to the viewport. Of the detonator wires, however, there was no sign. Apparently they had snagged on something as the canister rocketed out of the breech. Thorpe gazed at how close they had all come to death, and took the opportunity to do something he had not had time for previously. He was quietly sick as reaction overtook him.

The next ten hours were quiet ones inside the crowded compartment. Niels Grayson found it progressively more difficult to breathe, causing his wife to give him a sedative to let him sleep. She stayed by his side, stroking his furrowed brow.

"It will be a shame if he misses Thunderstrike's arrival," Amber told her.

The astronomer's wife looked up and smiled. "He would never forgive me. Besides, we'll have to wake him to get him back into his suit before the big event."

Periodically, either Amber or Thorpe would move to the viewport and judge their progress. The canister was rising very slowly now, its momentum nearly spent by the long climb out of Luna's gravity well. Even so, they appeared to be safe. The Moon was no longer a nearby world that had to be seen in separate pieces. It had shrunk to a sphere small enough to be seen in a single glance. The haze that enshrouded the universe had grown thicker. Amber was keeping a journal of her observations for a paper she planned to write.

Between observations the two lovers huddled together on the forward acceleration net and whispered to one another. Mostly they talked about what they would do after they were rescued. Neither made note of the fact that their continuous radio calls had yet to be answered. Also absent from their conversation was the very real possibility that they would not survive the coming hours.

So far as they knew, they were the last people to escape the Moon. Their tardy departure, coupled with their relatively slow velocity, made it nearly certain that they would be the closest space observers to the coming explosion. All previous estimates of the destruction Thunderstrike would cause seemed woefully inadequate. Thorpe remembered that there were still scientists who maintained that the force of the blow would shatter the Moon, causing it to break up into millions of pieces. If they were right, Earth was about to become a ringed world like Saturn. Whatever the damage, it would not take much to end the seven lives in their tiny lifeboat. One large chunk of debris thrown off at the wrong angle would leave no trace.

As the time grew short, they began their preparations to monitor the nucleus's arrival. As promised, Margaret Grayson roused her husband and helped him into his suit. Niels tried not to wince during the process, and the others pretended not to notice when he failed. When they were all suited up and on internal air, they stowed the two lower nets to give themselves more room to move about. They split into groups of three and four and gathered around the two viewports where Luna was visible. Amber, Thorpe, Jamie Bryant, and Allison Nalley clustered around one port, while a groggy Niels Grayson, his wife, and Albert Segovia took the other.

Thorpe gazed into space some thirty degrees off the line between Luna and Sol. Since it had only been three days since *The Rock* had crashed into the nucleus, he hoped to see some sign of its approach. The nucleus was surrounded by a much denser gas cloud, and the point where *The Rock* had impacted was almost certainly still incandescent. But he saw nothing. He turned back to Amber.

"How long until impact?"

She glanced at her suit chronometer. "Three minutes."

"Check your polarizers," he ordered.

Each of them chinned the helmet control that caused their faceplates to darken. From inside the dark bubble Thorpe could barely make out the Moon's outline. He chinned again to relieve the darkness, then watched as each of the others' helmets cleared one by one.

"Amber, please instruct us in proper procedure."

She nodded inside her helmet. "We go to dark one minute prior to impact. At fifteen seconds, squint until you can barely see your helmet instruments. In any event, do not look directly at the Moon. And for God's sake, if your eyes start to ache, close them fully until the flash has passed. Pain is your body's way of sending you a message."

"Everyone got that?"

They each acknowledged on the common circuit. Before he

knew it, Amber announced that the time to impact was down to a single minute. Thorpe waited until the other helmets had turned glossy black before once again chinning his polarizer. At fifteen seconds he squinted as instructed.

Amber's voice continued the countdown. As she reached zero the interior of his helmet turned violet despite the polarizer. He had planned to watch the whole thing, but the daggers stabbing deeply into his retinas caused him to wince. It was worse than the time he had been caught by sunrise on the monorail. He turned away and screwed his eyelids tightly shut. It helped a little. After a dozen seconds the glow began to fade. After a minute he was able to open his eyes and turn back to gaze at the Moon. The glow was still uncomfortably bright, but tolerable. For the first time he caught sight of Luna.

He gasped.

A fireball was trying to dig its way into Luna's heart. The outer edge of the expanding zone of destruction was defined by a spherical shock wave. The shock wave was a transparent bubble that was already several times Luna's diameter. Below it, another shell of destruction glowed incandescent and had shaded down from violet to blue-white — it consisted, Thorpe knew from reading the scientific projections of the impact, of millions of tons of lunar crust and cometary ice and iron that had been vaporized by the impact. The glowing gas was racing outward from ground zero. Soon it would cool and start to condense into molten rock and iron. It would be from the shell that billions of micrometeoroids would form. They would provide Earth with spectacular meteor showers for several centuries to come.

Behind the incandescent gas shell was a layer of solid material from the periphery of the impact crater. It had been thrown outward in the crown-shaped splash that was characteristic of impact craters. That third layer was the dangerous one. Some of its individual pieces were the size of small mountains, and all were speeding away at greater than lunar-escape velocity. Finally, at the center of the expanding cloud of debris, was a vast inferno of violet-white heat still too bright to look at directly.

As Thorpe slowly reduced the degree of polarization in his faceplate, other details began to appear. A moving line of dust was working its way across the Farside highlands near the Moon's eastern limb. As he watched, other dust lines appeared at both poles and began marching toward the equator. Even though he could not see it, he knew that such a line was also marching westward and that all would converge at a point diametrically opposite from where the comet nucleus had struck.

The line of dust was caused by the moving ground shock. As it moved through Luna's interior at the speed of sound, the surface wave produced a moving moonquake. As the quake passed, it tossed grains of dust and even small boulders high into the sky. Behind the dust, vast chasms of red appeared as the ancient surface split open under the stress. For the first time in four billion years, molten lava flowed again on Luna.

The marching wave fronts converged at the end of ten minutes, leaving the lunar surface a raw, red scar. All across Nearside the mares were once again seas of liquid rock. Thorpe's gaze was drawn to where the Tranquility Monument had been. It had become an unbroken red-orange glow. No longer were the bootprints of two intrepid astronauts embedded forever in the soft gray soil. In just a few minutes, Thunderstrike had wiped clean any sign that humanity had ever visited its nearest neighbor in space.

Luna's normally sharp features suddenly began to soften, as if seen through haze. Thorpe blinked, thinking his own tears were clouding his vision. It took a few moments to realize that the effect had nothing to do with his eyes. It was very real and entirely external.

"What's happening?" he yelled into his radio. Up until that moment, no one had said a word. Each had watched the cataclysm wrapped in their own cocoon of thoughts.

"It's the water vapor from Thunderstrike," Amber replied, her voice as excited as his own. "The Moon is being engulfed in a vast cloud of steam. It should begin to rain there any minute!"

As though to underscore her words, the canister was buffeted as though by high winds. The viewport suddenly dulled as it was coated with a thin film of frost. Moments later the interior clattered as their craft's hull was scoured by unseen particles. Several tiny pits appeared in the transparent surface of the viewport.

Amber pointed to the haze on the port's exterior. "Ice! We've entered the debris cloud! It won't be long until the next phase."

"Next phase?" Jamie Bryant asked, turning from the port to look at Amber. Thorpe did the same. For the first time he noticed that she was very pale behind her faceplate. The spectacle of

Luna's destruction had excited her. That had been evident just a few seconds earlier. But that excitement had turned to fear.

"What's the matter?"

"We've been overtaken by the outermost debris layer," she explained. "It's mostly microscopic ice particles, so there's not much to worry about. Pretty soon, though, we'll be engulfed by the large stuff. This light snowstorm is about to turn into a blizzard of rocks. If we survive that, we may get through this alive."

Thorpe frowned. "When will we know?"

"Eight hours."

"So if we're alive in eight hours, we're liable to stay that way?"

"Correct."

"Then I guess we wait and trust our luck," Thorpe said. He reached out and took her hand. "Scared?"

"You're damned right I am!"

"Me, too. Whatever happens, we'll meet it together."

CHAPTER 44

Thorpe gazed at Luna and shook his head in wonder at the difference a mere hundred hours could make. No longer was the Moon the gray-brown rock that had decorated Earth's sky since the beginning of time. The Man in the Moon was gone, his unchanging stare never to be seen again. The familiar landmarks were no more. The renowned craters were filled with magma and shrouded in mystery. For Thunderstrike had not so much destroyed Luna as transformed it. The changes had started only a few hours after the nucleus's impact. None aboard the makeshift lifeboat had seen the transformation begin, however. They had been too busy coping with Amber's blizzard of rocks.

The clatter of particles hitting the sides of their escape pod had marked the arrival of the debris cloud, the sound they made reminding Thorpe of hailstones falling on a metal roof. The microscopic debris had rebounded from their hull for four long hours without respite. Sometimes the sound became a machine-gun staccato, other times it softened to a few clangs per minute. The two viewports facing Luna were almost immediately sandblasted into uselessness, their surfaces so pitted that it was impossible to see out.

And the micrometeoroids were not the only components of the storm. Three hours after the first clattering noises, the refugees were surprised by a bang that rattled their teeth inside their suits. Thorpe looked up and was startled to see a centimeter-wide hole not a meter in front of his nose. Across the pod a nearly identical hole marked where something had exited the ship. The black of space was visible through both holes, and a brisk wind was blowing in their direction. Thorpe had patched the entrance hole with shaking hands while Jamie Bryant took care of the gap where the meteor had exited. After that, everyone lay down on the acceleration nets to ride the storm out. With each new sound, however, Thorpe could not help wishing for a deep foxhole to crawl into.

Eventually the clattering noises subsided, and Amber announced that the worst was over. It was another three hours, however, before the pod's slight rotation brought the two undamaged ports into line with Luna. Their first sight of the Moon in more than twelve hours brought home the extent of what had happened.

"What the hell?" Thorpe asked as he gazed down on a snow-white world of cloud centered where Luna had been. The clouds were like a comet's coma, only far thicker. Luna had become a miniature Venus, growing appreciably in the process. Thorpe estimated the cloud layer to be more than a thousand kilometers thick. That was ten times the depth of Earth's own atmosphere.

"My God!" Amber exclaimed. "I had no idea there would be so much steam."

"You mean that's water vapor?"

"What else? Thunderstrike massed sixty million billion tons, and most of it was ice. That ice was vaporized by the impact."

"All of it vaporized?"

"Every last gram. Most of the steam must have been driven down into the interior, or else we'd see a much thicker atmosphere."

"Any chance of there being liquid water under that blanket?" Margaret Grayson asked.

Amber shook her head. "Not yet. The Moon's still too hot. Give it a few months. The rains will begin in earnest then. Once started, they will go on for years."

Thorpe frowned. "Are you saying that Luna is liable to develop oceans?"

"Fairly sizable ones, I should think. Thunderstrike contained one-twentieth as much water as Earth's oceans. It dumped its load onto a world with only one-thirteenth Earth's surface area."

The idea that Luna would come out of this with an ocean was one Thorpe had to think about. It was just too alien an idea.

All of them had thought about it for three days. They rested, ate, talked, watched Luna, and took turns calling for help on the radio. They had long since gone "over the curb," and were falling toward Earth. Despite the closing range, the blue-white planet seemed oblivious to their pleas.

"The antenna must be gone," Thorpe told Bryant after inspecting the radio for the twelfth time. A loopback test proved that the transmitter was putting out a signal. Either everyone on Earth was ignoring them, or else that signal was not being broadcast to space.

"How can we check it?"

"I'll have to go around back to take a look. Let's get everyone into their suits so we can depressurize."

As soon as the cabin's oxygen had been vented to space, Thorpe opened the hatch and clambered out onto the flat forward face of the pod. The dust had thoroughly scoured everything, totally erasing the marks they had painted during the modification process. He slowly made his way aft, grabbing the occasional handhold like a mountain climber going up a sheer rock face. He reached the guidance pack and was careful to give the business ends of the attitude-control jets a wide berth.

"Here it is," he relayed back through the electrical cable they had rigged for him to stay in contact. "The antenna must have been carried away during launch. No wonder it's been so quiet."

"What can we use to fix it?" Amber's voice asked in his earphones.

"Unravel one of the acceleration nets. We'll use the wire as an antenna."

A few minutes later Amber's helmet appeared around the forward edge of the pod. She passed him the stiff cable, and he quickly attached it to the stub of the damaged antenna. He tugged gently on his repair job to make sure that it would hold.

"Send something," he ordered. He was rewarded by Albert Segovia's voice calling any ship within range on the emergency circuit. The signal was loud and strong.

Ten minutes later Amber helped him inside. They had barely repressurized and removed their helmets when Segovia yelled that he had made contact. Thorpe immediately swarmed to the back bulkhead where the radio was located. The cold air caused a streamer of exhalation fog to trail him.

"We are seven survivors from Luna, falling toward Earth in a mass-driver cargo pod," he said after a demand to identify himself. "Who is this?"

"This is Meteor Guard Station Number Sixteen," a voice with a British accent responded. "Are you in difficulty?"

"You're damned right we're in difficulty. We need help!"

"Understood," the voice answered. "Give me your position and your orbit."

Amber read off several figures. They were her projections of their orbit. She warned the meteor-guard operator that the numbers were very rough and recommended that he attempt to triangulate on their radio signal.

"Give me a continuous count."

She began counting slowly. A few minutes later he told her to stop. "All right, we have you triangulated from three meteor-guard stations. We'll be listening for you next hour and every hour thereafter. Once we've plotted your orbit, we will see what can be done to get a ship to you. I warn you, however, that it may take some time. We are a trifle busy just now."

They were aware of just how busy the meteor-guard system was. Several times in the past four days large tumbling objects had appeared near them, then veered off to disappear into the black. In space there was no way to judge distance. The mere fact that they could see the pieces of debris told everyone that they were big enough to be very dangerous.

Over the next forty-eight hours space was illuminated by a series of flashes as nuclear warheads rose from the meteor-guard stations to explode against bits of dangerous space junk. Despite the stations' efforts, they had not always succeeded in deflecting their targets.

With the radio repaired, they listened to news accounts. They quickly learned that the casualties on Luna had been enormous. The official toll of those left behind stood at 26,000. More cruel, perhaps, was the evacuation ship that had been holed while in Earth orbit. It had been offloading during the disaster, and there was, as yet, no official estimate of casualties. Finally, there were the meteors that had fallen near Brisbane, Kansas City, and Le Havre. The destruction had been especially bad at Le Havre. Relief workers were still digging through the remains of the city.

"So many!" Amber said as they listened to the growing list of casualties two days after establishing contact with the meteor-guard station. The two of them were sitting cross-legged on the acceleration net on the level of the viewports. They were out of their vacuum suits for the first time in days. Two hours earlier a meteor-guard communicator had announced that a ship was on its way. It would arrive within forty hours. Amber rested her head on Thorpe's shoulder. For the first time since they had left Far-side Observatory, she felt safe and secure.

"It would have been a lot worse if Earth had been the target," he reminded her. "We were lucky."

"I agree, but not for the reason you think."

"Oh?" he asked as he nuzzled her hair. It was matted, un-kempt, and very dirty. He did not mind at all. "Care to enlighten me, my love?"

"If you like," she said, swiveling around to face him. "Niels and I have been doing some calculations. We think Luna may acquire a real atmosphere."

"The Moon's too small. The gas molecules leak off into space. That's why its original atmosphere dissipated billions of years ago."

"True enough," she said. "This atmosphere, too, will eventu-ally leak away. The question is how long the process will take. With all that water that was driven deep, we estimate that Luna will be able to keep its new mantle for anywhere from a hundred thousand to one million years."

He whistled. "Too bad it's all superheated steam."

"That won't last long. As soon as the cloud cools, most of it will condense into rain. Ultraviolet light will begin to disassoci-ate the water molecules, releasing free oxygen and hydrogen. The hydrogen will rise to the top and be swept away by the solar wind. Eventually the Moon ought to have a climate approximating Earth's tropics—at least, in temperature. The atmospheric pressure is liable to be higher than Earth's."

"Are you telling me that Luna's about to develop an *oxygen* atmosphere?" Thorpe asked, dubious.

"A rudimentary one," she replied. "Photodisassociation tends to be self-limiting, you know. It only goes on until the ozone layer forms. And, of course, there are all those virgin rocks to oxidize. They'll eat up a lot of the free oxygen as soon as it is produced. No, if the Moon is to develop a real atmosphere, we'll have to help it along."

"*We?*"

"Of course. I'm going back. I hope you'll go with me."

"I haven't thought much about it."

"You should. It will rain most of this decade. By the end of that time, the weather ought to settle down sufficiently for the first colonies to be planted. They'll be very different from the old ones. We'll have to learn all over the lessons of living on the Moon."

"You're serious! You want to go back?"

She nodded.

"Why?"

"It's my home," she said simply. Her blue eyes searched his.

"But we just risked everything to escape the place!"

"Going back will be even more difficult. It will take generations to produce a breatheable atmosphere. Someday our children or grandchildren will play in green fields beneath a blue sky filled with fluffy white clouds. Only they won't have to fight Earth's gravity, and they will be able to fly under their own power. The combination of thick atmosphere and low gravity may make Luna perfect for flying."

"It might be fun at that," he admitted. The idea had been a shock, but the more he considered it, the more it intrigued him. Perhaps one day he would find himself sailing the Sea of Tranquility, or braving the high, slow waves on the Ocean of Storms. He grinned. "In fact—"

Amber lifted her face to his and silenced him with a kiss. "Enough deep thinking for one day, my love. We've got plenty of time for that later. Please, hold me!"

He slipped an arm around her waist and lifted her effortlessly into his lap. They sat and gazed out the viewport at the cloud-covered world that would one day be as hospitable as Mother

Earth. On that day, Thorpe knew, the human race would finally be safe. Never again would a single wayward asteroid, comet, or meteor threaten humanity's extinction. As he looked at the tiny world that was even then rising from the ashes of its own destruction, he knew that there was Homo sapiens' second permanent home in the universe.

Second but far from last!

About the Author

Michael McCollum was born in Phoenix, Arizona, in 1946, and is a graduate of Arizona State University, where he majored in aerospace propulsion and minored in nuclear engineering. He has been employed as an aerospace engineer since graduation, and has worked on nearly every military and civilian aircraft in production today. At various times in his career, Mr. McCollum has also worked on the precursor to the Space Shuttle Main Engine, a nuclear valve to replace the one that failed at Three Mile Island, and a variety of guided missiles.

He began writing in 1974 and has been a regular contributor to *Analog Science Fiction*. He has also appeared in *Isaac Asimov's* and *Amazing*. *Thunder Strike!* is his sixth novel for Del Rey.

He is married to a lovely lady by the name of Catherine, and is the father of three children: Robert, Michael, and Elizabeth.